Madame Matisse

www.penguin.co.uk

Also by Sophie Haydock

The Flames

Madame Matisse

Sophie Haydock

doubleday

TRANSWORLD PUBLISHERS
Penguin Random House, One Embassy Gardens,
8 Viaduct Gardens, London sw11 7bw
www.penguin.co.uk

Transworld is part of the Penguin Random House group of companies
whose addresses can be found at global.penguinrandomhouse.com

First published in Great Britain in 2025 by Doubleday
an imprint of Transworld Publishers

A CIP catalogue record for this book
is available from the British Library.

ISBNS 9780857527592 (hb)
9780857527608 (tpb)

Typeset in 12/16pt Minion Pro by Jouve (UK), Milton Keynes
Printed and bound in Great Britain by Clays Ltd, Elcograf S.p.A.

The authorized representative in the EEA is Penguin Random House Ireland,
Morrison Chambers, 32 Nassau Street, Dublin D02 YH68.

Penguin Random House is committed to a sustainable future for our
business, our readers and our planet. This book is made from
Forest Stewardship Council® certified paper.

For Rosa

Ultimatum

Nice, 1939

Madame Matisse enters Lydia's room, the prongs of the fork sharp in her pocket. Everything is tidy, in its place, the spines of the books aligned just so, three pears positioned along the windowsill at the most satisfying distance apart; all much as it was the last time she entered to look around. This woman has lived alongside Madame Matisse and her husband in Nice for the best part of a decade, but what, really, does Amélie know about the mysterious Lydia Delectorskaya?

Ever since that young woman joined their household back in the spring of 1932, Amélie has been relentless in her support of her. What was it that set Lydia apart from all the other girls? If Amélie's memory serves her, there was a compliment about her hand-embroidered shawl, the eagerness with which the young woman jumped to accept the challenging role when another failed to impress, and then the way she turned up clutching fresh flowers. No one had done that before.

When Lydia first arrived – a strange twenty-two-year-old for-eigner, down on her luck – she'd been just another in a long line of girls, hired to be helpful around the house, to support Amélie as her health deteriorated. Unobtrusive, efficient, sweet Lydia solved every problem without fuss or flapping – and what a pleasure it had been to find a helper who didn't talk back or take liberties. That was rare. Then, as time went on, Amélie had been impressed with the Siberian's resourcefulness, her initiative, her willingness to blend into their lives. Lydia had attended to Amélie, making her periods of confinement more bearable.

Henri had barely noticed her those first years. He didn't want anyone interfering in his studio, and certainly didn't aspire to draw the girl. She wasn't his type. Amélie had assumed Lydia wouldn't be interested in a man old enough to be her father – and that her husband wouldn't form a bond with a woman a decade younger than his own daughter, Marguerite.

The Matisses had treated all their girls well over the years – paying wages higher than was necessary, bending the rules to make sure they had some stability. They'd been kind. But now, Amélie can see it clearly: this woman has preyed on her good nature, taken advantage of Amélie's persistent ill health to infiltrate the fabric of their home, to make herself indispensable. Now Amélie sees her husband only at mealtimes, when they eat opposite each other in silence. He spends all his time with Lydia, getting up to who knows what . . .

She has had enough.

Amélie shuffles around the room, her cane knocking insistently on the floorboards.

The air is damp, which seems out of character for a resort such as Nice, famous for its blazing summers. Where sunbathers sizzle on the beachfront or loll in the sensuous sea. It has been a long time since Amélie indulged in any such pleasures herself. Her chronic illness, a bad back and pains in her stomach, alongside slumps of inertia and hopelessness, which have plagued her since the birth of her children, mean she must spend long swathes of time in bed.

Amélie stops and listens carefully for footsteps. Her hearing isn't quite what it used to be, but her eyesight is as sharp as anything. When she's certain nobody's around, she props her stick against the wardrobe, stiffly kneels on the floor then pulls a briefcase out from under Lydia's bed and places it on the eiderdown. Initials are embossed in the leather: ND. She wonders about the previous owner. A lover, perhaps, a man from Lydia's past?

Briefly, Amélie experiences guilt for encroaching on her employee's privacy in this way. Everyone has secrets, things they'd rather keep hidden; the worst sides of themselves, which never see the light. But Amélie shakes off the feeling. She needs to do this, needs to know once and for all what kind of woman she's dealing with.

Amélie fiddles with the clasps on the briefcase – with a little luck, Lydia might have left it unlocked. But alas, no. Lydia guards her privacy with a ferocious intensity. In all the time Amélie has known her, the woman has rarely let slip even the smallest anecdote about her life outside these walls, or the time before she became an assistant to the Matisse household. Amélie has often wondered what it must have been like for the girl to grow up in Siberia, and how and why she ended up in France, alone.

The first question Amélie wants answered, definitively, is what claim Lydia thinks she has to her husband. The two of them have grown very close and are fools to think she hasn't noticed. Only an astute observer would recognize it, but the woman is ruthless, always on the hunt to extract whatever she can, from anyone she can, while Amélie has been pushed further and further to the sidelines until she has become a stranger in her own home. At every turn, it's the trace of Lydia she confronts, Amélie's own truths erased. Outwardly, Lydia claims it's all about Henri, his needs, his precious schedule. He must have no diversions or distractions – which seem to include his wife. But inwardly, Amélie knows, it's a battle for control. Well, this is a fight she's not prepared to lose.

Everyone around her seems to have forgotten one crucial fact: Amélie is *formidable*. She may be sixty-seven years old, with a head of fading hair, hips thick and slow, but she's not just some silly woman who'll be pushed into the footnotes of another man's story. It's true that she may have lost something over the years, but at her core, she has a constitution of fire, at her most competent and dynamic when the house is burning down around her. Ultimately, Amélie has survived it all, and together she and Henri have achieved the impossible, against all the odds.

Amélie tried broaching the subject with Henri last month, but he persuaded his wife that Lydia was essential to his art. At the time, she let it go, but she won't do the same again. Marguerite, his own daughter, told Amélie to look for evidence, something to support her concerns. Marguerite has never liked Lydia and is equally suspicious of her father's reliance on another. Do what it takes, she said. Amélie is not proud of it, but she has been searching Lydia's room for weeks, trying to unearth anything that might make Henri take her – and her suspicions – seriously. She hasn't found anything, except that damn locked briefcase under the bed. What is that woman hiding? Letters from Henri, promising her the world? Drawings that he has given her, or that have perhaps been taken without permission?

Or something altogether more worrying?

So, this time, while Lydia is out running errands for Henri, Amélie has come prepared. She takes the utensil from her housecoat to prise open the lock. She eases the tips of the fork into the clasp. She tenses her wrist. So close . . .

There's an intake of breath, and at first Amélie thinks it's her own, before the hairs rise on the back of her neck. She turns to see Lydia, standing at the threshold of the room.

'Don't you dare,' Lydia warns, her eyes burning on the case.

But even though Amélie has been caught in the act, she won't back down.

'If my husband is writing to you, giving you gifts, I have a right to know.'

Lydia sucks in a breath. 'Don't insult me,' she replies.

'It wouldn't be the first time he's broken my trust,' Amélie adds, 'so forgive me if I refuse to close my eyes to my suspicions this time.'

'Your suspicions are unfounded with me.'

'Why not open the case and put my fears to rest?'

Lydia shakes her head.

'Then I will form my own conclusions, if you don't mind.'

Amélie jiggles the fork in the lock, just to try her luck before she is forced to leave, and this time there's a click, like a heartbeat. She seizes the moment. Without taking her eyes off the younger woman, she flips the catch, and eagerly opens the case. Lydia leaps across the room and tries to seize it, but Amélie holds on, her fingers tight around the handle, battling to get even the briefest glimpse of what's inside. There appear to be reams of papers, official-looking documents, in French and another language. She can't quite get a satisfying look and yanks the case determinedly again, making the papers shift and slide.

Beneath, there's a glint of metal. 'Good Lord,' Amélie gasps. 'Is that a gun?'

If there's a gun in this house, that changes everything.

PART ONE

AMÉLIE

1

Paris, 1897

O f all the people she could have been seated next to at the wedding feast, this unkempt young man, all red hair and rough beard, is the last person she'd have hoped for. Amélie approaches her seat at the head table, which is strewn with crystal decanters, fine china and flowers in full bloom, and averts her eyes before he can strike up a conversation. Light bounces off the polished silver and cut glass and gemstones worn by the long-necked, high-haired women seated around the grand hall. The effect is dizzying and Amélie takes her place with determination, although inwardly she groans.

As maid of honour, she could have been consulted about the arrangements. The bride, her dear friend Juliette, now Madame Fontaine, the new daughter-in-law of the mayor of Bohain-en-Vermandois, knows she has her prejudices, her *tastes*. Amélie and Juliette bonded as friends at the Parisian boarding school their parents believed would bestow upon them a fine education. Could Juliette not have seated Amélie on the other side of the table, next to the groom's brother? He looks approachable, without seeming too maniacal. At twenty-five years old, contrary to societal expectations and pressure from friends her age, Amélie isn't desperate for marriage, just for some stimulating conversation for an evening. Although, if anyone were to catch her attention and dare hold it, she wouldn't be opposed to more.

Ultimately, she wants to be made better by another person's knowledge of her.

Amélie hadn't failed to notice the red-headed young man during the ceremony, standing next to the groom, attempting to straighten his cravat as the bride walked down the aisle. He has the air of a prankster, of energy unearthed. In his badly fitting brown suit he resembles a clerk, one who likes to spark the wrath of his superiors. Amélie – the product of an expensive liberal education, daughter of socialist parents who nonetheless rub shoulders with the Parisian elite – has her own disdain for authority, but she isn't keen on confrontation for confrontation's sake. In her opinion, that marks a person out as a fool. If you're going to burn the house down, better to light the match before anyone expects it of you.

Yes, Juliette should have seen to it that Amélie was placed next to an engaging, interesting young man, not this wild specimen, who keeps catching the arm of the waiter to ensnare another bottle of wine. There are already two, as yet unopened, concealed beneath the table between her chair and his. Her feet knock against them as she adjusts her position. Amélie carefully unfolds her serviette and places it on her lap.

'Henri Matisse,' the man repeats once she's comfortable, holding out a hand. There's no way to avoid him. She'll have to swallow her standards and engage in conversation.

'Mademoiselle Parayre,' she says, with a small smile that does not attempt to conceal that she deigns to give him her attention. 'Amélie.'

'Amélie, are you a woman who likes her glass to be filled to the brim?' he asks directly, addressing her informally, without invitation, forfeiting all manner of respectable convention, as he brings the neck of the wine bottle to the edge of the crystal. He looks her in the eye. 'Or one who prefers just a small splash?' He tips no more than a thimble's worth of the ruby liquid into the glass. 'So that she can give the illusion of restraint, and better enjoy the satisfaction of being refilled time and time again?'

He smiles again. She searches his features for something lecherous, or uncouth, to confirm her initial judgement of him, but his expression is warm and wide, his pale skin freckled from exposure to the sun, even though it's a damp day in mid-October. His eyes are a deep blue, and kind, flickering with a mischief that is not unappealing.

How she hates to be in the wrong.

'I'm a woman who prefers to pour her own,' Amélie says decisively, taking the bottle from him, and adding more than a splash, less than a full measure.

She places it back on the table between them.

'I see,' he says, appraising the line as she takes a sip. He finishes his in one motion, the soft inside of his lips already stained with tannins.

Amélie smiles, despite herself. The meal will last a couple of hours, at most. She can endure. She always does. A waiter places a platter of oysters in the middle of the table, the flesh glistening. 'How do you know the groom?' she asks.

Henri reaches for one and swallows it with a flourish before he answers.

'Ferdinand and I grew up together in Bohain; we went to the same lycée. From the moment we could walk, we schooled ourselves in evasion. His father – that man over there' – he points to a round man with a heavy moustache, his jacket adorned with gleaming medallions – 'has been the mayor for a long time. We were always terrified of him and quickly learned where to go and where not to go. We took our beatings, more than once. And it seems Ferdinand learned the intended lesson . . . Just look at him now.' The groom, a handsome man beside his blooming bride, is surrounded by the great and good of Paris, money pressed into his pockets, connections forged. 'Whereas I clearly did not.' Henri smirks and swallows another oyster, while she helps herself to her first. It's salty and smooth.

'I'm a failure at every turn,' he continues. 'As a son, I'm my father's greatest disappointment, for I refused to take over the family business. I never had the makings of a seed merchant. My hands are too delicate.' He shows her. They are elegant and would be soft to touch. 'As a man,' he adds, 'I flung away a promising career as a lawyer. And as a father . . .' He sips his wine, shakes his head. 'But I shouldn't be telling you all this. A beautiful woman whom I have the great fortune of being seated next to for an evening of unbridled celebration doesn't want to hear the misfortunes of a resoundingly unexceptional man.'

He stops a passing waiter and intercepts another bottle for his stash beneath the table. 'Oh, don't look so concerned – I won't drink all of these at once,' he says, as he notices her narrowed eyes. 'They'll be smuggled out, to share with my friends. Our cupboards are bare.'

He brushes his hands together and she notices that he does not wear a ring.

'So, what occupies you now, Monsieur Matisse, if not the law?'

'I'm an artist,' he sighs. 'And not a particularly good one, if the opinions of my teachers and the Salon are to be believed.'

She almost laughs. Amélie has always avoided artists; it's another of her golden rules, along with men with beards. Too much trouble, not enough reward. Too much . . . ego.

And all that insecurity. A woman should not be expected constantly to bolster a man's confidence, to reassure him as he strives for a greatness that may always be out of reach. Artists, she knows, are forced to search their soul at every turn. She cannot abide such indulgence. She's about to say as much, when there's a hush of conversation around them as waiters bring in the next course: sizzling plates stacked with tender duck breast, leafy vegetables, wedges of potato dauphinoise.

There's a clatter of cutlery before the volume rises again.

She lifts her knife and fork.

'An artist?' she says, politely, trying not to raise her eyebrows. 'My family entertained a great number of artists during my childhood in Beauzelle, in the south. My father used to be the editor of an activist newspaper. Now he works for the wealthiest couple in France. As you can imagine, we've always had an eclectic mix at our table.'

'Well, count yourself lucky. My childhood was all seeds and sawdust. Until the age of twenty, I'd not even heard the word *artist*, let alone met one or understood it was possible to be such a thing. It was Mother who first pressed a box of paints into my hands. I was in hospital recovering from appendicitis, bored out of my mind. She thought it would help me pass the time. As soon as I took up that brush . . .' He pauses, looks at her out of the side of his eye. 'Instantly, I felt that art was worth dying for, that I would throw everything I had into pursuit of it. My instincts were correct, as here I am, approaching thirty, with nothing left to show for it at all.' He raises his glass in mirth, but there are clearly strong feelings beneath his words.

'You can't be that bad,' she says.

'Take a look for yourself! I gifted Ferdinand a still life I made in Belle-Île. It's very conventional. Apples.' He rolls his eyes. 'Tell me, who wants to look upon apples all day?'

'Ferdinand, I hope.'

He looks at her and laughs.

'He's not as uncultured as that,' he continues. 'Ferdinand has an eye, an appreciation for such things. I even gave him that very first painting I made using my mother's paintbox. Maybe it will make him rich one day, owning original work by the great Matisse, that unappreciated fool.' He spreads his arms. 'I'll paint my next one for you, how about that?'

'You must promise the subject matter will be more exciting than apples,' she says.

He feigns a wounded heart, before miraculously reviving to pluck another bottle from the tray of a passing waiter.

'I could paint you,' he says, expanding as he tests the limits of his boldness. 'You have beautiful shoulders.' He delicately traces the exposed curve of one with the tip of his knife. The moment feels molten with danger. Then Henri abruptly changes tack, setting down his cutlery and wiping his mouth. 'Or how about these flowers?' He reaches over and takes a stem of white baby's breath – as delicate and luminous as a constellation – from the bouquet in the middle of the table, which earns him a disapproving glance from Juliette's mother. Henri doesn't notice. He holds the long stem between his teeth, smiling like a circus clown.

'You're a silly man,' Amélie concedes, rubbing her skin. She takes the gypsophila from his mouth and returns it to its vessel. 'You must strive to be taken seriously one day.'

'What are your favourite flowers, mademoiselle?' he asks, pouring himself more wine. He goes to top up her glass, but stops himself, placing the bottle on the table in front of her, his hand gesturing an invitation that she help herself. 'Roses? Lilies?' he continues, looking at her shrewdly. 'No, you're not that kind of woman. Already that much is clear.'

'Violets,' she replies. 'I've loved them ever since I was a girl.'

'As a boy, I'd roam the fields around Bohain. I used to part the long grass looking for them. I'd collect as many as I could and bring them home for my mother. She'd put them in a jar, and there they'd stay on the table until the petals wilted.'

'Beautiful things don't last for long – that's why we must

appreciate them while we can,' she says, looking around the party. 'This second, like all the others that have come before it, will be swept away like so many petals and consigned to history.'

'Well, I feel that I might want to press this particular moment between the pages of a weighty tome, and look at it from time to time,' he says, his eyes searching hers once more.

Amélie feels a tingle of connection, a sense that Henri is urging intimacy between them. She can't deny the attraction is there, at the edges, pushing to get in. She enjoys the challenge of him. It's rare to find a man who is earnest without being contemptible, who seems to notice every detail about her, without being cloying. Who treats her as an intellectual equal, not a prize to be won and flaunted. It's unnerving.

She regains her earlier thought process. 'Even if you press flowers, they lose something of their essence,' she replies, her words emerging slowly. 'They might crumble, or fade. Their scent departs. The joy is in the knowledge that their beauty will be fleeting.'

He begins to formulate an answer, but the sound of a knife against cut glass makes everyone fall silent.

'Well, here I go,' he says. 'Wish me luck.' Henri takes a breath, looks at her with wide eyes, then reaches into his pocket and pulls out sheets of paper covered in ink, long illegible lines that she would struggle to decipher. 'Now they expect me to shine,' he says and winks before slipping on thin-rimmed spectacles, and standing to address those gathered.

Henri gently teases the groom, toasts the bride, and thanks both sets of parents, his eyes lingering on Amélie as he makes a second toast to the bridesmaids. He runs a hand through his hair, his shirt slightly untucked, his teeth stained with wine, but the exuberance of him, this bold glint of devilry that is visible to all, has charmed most of the wedding party.

While Henri speaks to Ferdinand, the groom's mother – resplendent in grey silk, jewels hanging from her earlobes – sweeps over to Amélie with an alarming sense of purpose.

'Mademoiselle, if I may? You're clearly a well-brought-up young woman,' she says, addressing Amélie respectfully, her accent polished, her eyes crinkling with the cruel kindness so particular to the upper classes. 'So please, with respect and eternal patience, heed my word of warning.' Her irises are green, clear like the emeralds on her fingers. 'We've known Henri Matisse since he was a child. He comes from a good, hard-working family who have always wanted the best for him, and strived to help him succeed in life. But alas, in recent years, he has become the fool, gone off the rails and squandered his potential. I wouldn't want to see him drag a good woman down with him.' She pauses. When Amélie's response doesn't come, she continues: 'Young Matisse is a careless man. I'm sure you've gleaned as much already. But it's worse than that, I'm afraid. He has a child, out of wedlock.' Amélie bristles, less at the revelation than at the indecency of this woman, spilling such privacies at this moment. 'We heard recently that the child's mother,' she continues with a frown, 'a young woman who we know modelled for his artworks – of no standing or material reserves whatsoever – has seen it in her own interest to leave him. That's how bad it must have become! Can you imagine? His poor parents!' The woman elongates the words to show the depth of her distress. 'To be burdened with a son such as that . . .'

Amélie's back stiffens in defiance. She hates this kind of goading concern, a thinly disguised mask for malicious gossip. 'I appreciate your concern for my reputation, Madame Fontaine, but I must kindly insist that I make up my own mind,' she replies, her words light but direct. Amélie realizes she feels more affinity with Henri Matisse than with anyone else in the grand hall. He's unconventional. That's what she's used to. Perhaps it's all those conversations she overheard at the table, growing up – her mind filled with the eclectic words of anarchists who'd lost hope, writers and poets permanently down on their luck, failed farmers and forlorn trade unionists – but she has always rooted for the underdog. She watches the mother of the groom sail back to her chair, no doubt convinced she has done her duty.

When Henri returns, Amélie is ready to top up his glass. He drinks from it gladly. After a few moments of comfortable silence, she stands and offers him her hand.

'Would you care to dance, Monsieur Matisse?'

Henri turns his full attention to her, his eyes flickering with more of that boyishness that has been on show all evening, a smile tugging at the corners of his lips.

There's something in her own recklessness that makes her feel strong.

'The pleasure would be all mine,' he replies.

He takes her hand. His is warm, pulsing. Amélie thinks of a paintbrush between his fingertips, of the canvas on which he conducts the paint. The way he changes the energy in the room. She knows instinctively that this man is a long way from being a serious prospect – all that drinking and unruliness. But she cannot deny that she's intrigued and feels something akin to desire. She's happy to throw off her own rules for once. She is her own surprise.

Together, they walk to the dance floor – the groom's mother's eyes widening in astonishment – as the band starts up a lively number.

But she cares not. For this moment and those to come, Amélie will enjoy the dance.

2

Paris, 1897

Amélie's dark hair is rolled up around her head in her signature style. She has inherited the delicate features and narrow bones of her ancestors, and she likes to add width, and a touch of gravitas, where she can. She was brought up in the heat of Beauzelle, in south-west France, close to the border with Spain. One would be forgiven for thinking there was more Spanish blood than French flowing through her veins. Those who came before her must have crossed the Pyrenees, carrying hope on their shoulders along with their food. As a result, she has very little in common with those dour northern types – their pale faces and red hair, rough hands and stern, stoical dispositions – who have grown up in a colder climate. Amélie and Berthe, her younger sister – by three and a half years – have been raised with the sun. Berthe decided at the age of ten that she wanted to become a teacher. No other romantic cause could sway her. She now works as a schoolmistress. They're both dark-haired and full of passion, like all the women who preceded them. They do things their own way, without reserve. Berthe likes to say they're from a family of 'plucky people'. Amélie feels this to be infinitely true.

Henri, at the end of the wedding reception, had asked to see her again.

She'd been able to think of several reasons to refuse him, and perhaps it was the wine, or the words of the groom's mother, but she found she wasn't inclined to deploy any of them. So here she is now, waiting in a café opposite the Grand Guignol in the Pigalle district of Paris, a seedy part of the capital, but one that pulses with life, bright lights and painted ladies. Amélie has never been fazed by the kinds of things that set other women's teeth a-chatter.

The theatre is open for the Saturday matinée. Already people are milling about in line for tickets, laughing, gossiping, pulling their coats closely around their bodies as they wait for the doors to open and the performance to begin.

Amélie is early, so cannot fault Henri for arriving after her, for he is not yet late. He'd suggested this café, one where the waiters are discreet and the coffee is strong enough to fuel penniless art students long into the afternoon. She reads a page of a novel to fill the time.

When she sees him, he's a version of the man she remembers, but already, even after a week, he has taken on new proportions in her mind, and she has to adjust her mental image of him to match this real-life man; this figure who is hurrying along, weaving through the theatre crowd, his eyes intent on her, carrying something behind his back.

'You'll never believe it,' he says, reaching her table. He hasn't even said hello.

From behind his back, he gently produces a flurry of purple, held between his thumb and index finger. 'I walked from the Louvre, and look, look!' He holds the pinch of petals in front of her nose. She inhales and receives the most delicate scent: fresh and woody. 'I found them growing from a crack in the paving stones on my way here,' he continues. 'Violets! Can you believe it? After our conversation at the wedding, it must be a sign!'

There are flashes of green in his brown eyes, she notices.

Amélie takes the flowers. 'Oh, but you should have left them to grow,' she says.

His shoulders lose some of their surety at the implication he has done something wrong. 'Would you ever have believed me if you hadn't seen the proof for yourself?'

'Perhaps not,' she admits. 'It isn't the typical season for them, but I suppose a seed can grow at any time, given the right conditions. Wild flowers in particular.'

'Now that we have them, what should we do with them?' he asks. He places the stems in a glass of water, and the hearts float like buoys.

She retrieves them and blows them dry on the tablecloth. They're shades of purple, with streaks of yellow. The petals are tiny and delicate, and Amélie feels as if they could dissolve on her tongue like sugar. She knows instinctively that she doesn't want them to be damaged or torn, so places them inside the pages of her novel, arranging the stems and petals to give the most pleasing effect. Henri watches her as she presses them with her fingertips.

'Their colour will fade, and their scent will depart if you press them,' he says.

'Their beauty is certainly fleeting,' she replies, recalling her words from the wedding. 'But we must try to hold on to whatever brings us joy.' It's only now, faced with something she doesn't want to lose, that she realizes the paradox of the sentiment. 'Perhaps I'll frame them,' she adds, and considers how they might look behind a sheet of glass. An artist like Henri could capture them in pigment, painting their likeness so they might be remembered.

Henri orders coffee and pays the waiter when he delivers the cups to the table. 'I must apologize for my behaviour at the wedding,' he says, sighing at his confession. 'I'm not usually so rambunctious. I was nervous before the speech and drank too much as a consequence. There was something wild and unleashed about me that night. But typically, I'm a restrained, serious man,' he says. 'I go to bed early, I wake early, to get the best of the day. I drink very little. Truly,' he adds when he sees her glance of amusement.

Already, he seems more controlled and serious than he'd been at the wedding.

'Drinking to excess is certainly a costly habit for a man,' she replies. 'And you don't seem able to afford it,' she adds, noticing the details of him that money does better to hide.

She's aware that the artist is keen to reform her image of him.

But she must make up her own mind: which version is the real Henri Matisse?

'It's true I don't have much. But I'm single-minded,' he says. 'Which you may decide is a good thing, or, like my friends and family, believe to be quite the burden. They regret that my focus is on art rather than the world of business or law. They believe I could be comfortable financially. They think in choosing art I've sacrificed my sanity, which is true beyond all doubt – but I didn't feel I ever had a choice.'

'What use is sanity, if it leads you not into temptation?' she asks.

Amélie adds a sugar cube, stirs, then sips her coffee.

The theatre crowd has vanished, she notices. Now the street is dotted with maids and housewives, bread positioned in the crook of an arm, groceries in a basket, children in prams.

Henri looks at her curiously. 'And what motivates you, Mademoiselle Parayre?'

'One day, I want to open my own hat shop, as a way to stand on my own two feet.'

He's choosing to present himself as steady and stable. She wants to highlight her initiative and drive. She can be an asset, an ally. Why are men so often threatened by that?

'My mother, you know, made hats,' he replies. 'I was obsessed with her box of textiles and colour charts when I was a boy.

When she let me, I'd help her by taking a sharp pair of scissors and cutting out the shapes she needed. It certainly was more fun than the back-breaking work in the seed store. I was bed-bound for most of my formative years, so there was no carrying hefty sacks for me, much to my father's disappointment. I was lucky that my younger brother, Auguste, obliged.' He pauses, sips. 'You must have talent,' Henri continues. 'I'd like to see your designs one day. Perhaps I could be a model for you, although I'm not sure I'd attract the clientele you'd be hoping for.'

She raises her eyebrows to show her amusement.

'My dear aunt already has a shop of her own, and it's very successful,' she says. 'I work there most days, designing and making hats, and modelling them from time to time.'

'You could hand out my calling card with every purchase. "Your chance to be painted by France's most esteemed artist, the inimitable Matisse."' He indulges the fantasy. 'You would tell those women with their fancy hats to seize the opportunity before it's too late, before he's batting away commissions and has too much money to count!' He leans back in his chair, as if this vision of his future has exhausted him. 'You're quite the combination, mademoiselle. A man with potential would be wise to snap you up,' he adds.

He looks at her carefully, and she's not naive to the implication of his words.

'And how old is your daughter?' she says, changing the subject to put distance between them. The remnants of his coffee spill. He dabs the splashes from his shirt.

'Ah, little Marguerite, my daisy . . .' he says, looking ambushed, forgetting that he'd mentioned her existence at the wedding reception. 'My daughter is three years old. She's a beautiful child, if a little sickly, but in that respect you could say she takes after her father.'

'And her mother?'

With the tip of his shoe, Henri nudges a pigeon that is fossicking under the table.

Amélie doesn't see why she shouldn't ask simple, straightforward questions. Her father, when he worked as a journalist, encouraged her to ask difficult ones in the most direct manner. If people squirm, you'll know you've hit a nerve, he'd say. That's where the truth lies. She can still recall the glint in his eyes as he spoke these words to her. Armand Parayre, a man of dazzling intelligence and strong morals, thrives on bringing truths to the surface.

'Marguerite's mother left me,' Henri says, and Amélie is relieved to know that he has spoken honestly, and that he has said the difficult thing, the one that does not paint him in the most flattering light. She nods, but leaves the avenue of conversation open, waiting for him to fill the gap – another trick she learned from her father.

'We had a difficult relationship,' he continues, taking a deep breath. 'It was never a smooth union. In the end, much to my disappointment, Camille was unable to tolerate the precariousness of life at the side of an artist. Well, certainly not one as determined as I am to do things the wrong way – to create art that will challenge, not just appease those who select the most conventional pieces for the Salon.' He shakes his head with a dash of resentment. 'My attempts to bring a new way of seeing into the world were simply intolerable to her,' he continues. 'During our trip to Belle-Île over the summer, I'd paint every day, and she came to the conclusion that she'd rather be alone.' He pauses, and Amélie is sure he's back there, in his mind, that place of rocky cliffs, plunging seas and high winds, the woman he loved pulling away, packing her bags in tears. 'I certainly tested her limits,' he says. 'I'm sad Camille left, that in her desperation she took our daughter with her. I'm nearly twenty-eight and it feels as if my life is in tatters. But, while I'm being candid, I'll also say I was relieved, just a little. I need a woman by my side who'll believe in my art as much as I do. Someone who's prepared to sacrifice everything for it – all of life's comforts, all of its certainties.'

'Sacrifice?' Amélie asks suspiciously, jumping on the word. 'Must any woman you encounter be willing to diminish herself?'

'There's no weakness, in my eyes, in committing one's life to the pursuit of something bigger than oneself. Only the strongest can devote themselves and survive.'

'Women do that all the time, but it's rarely recognized as anything resembling glory.'

'Art is bigger than scrubbing floors and darning socks,' he says, his tone teasing, seeing if he can get a rise out of her, falling back on such worn stereotypes.

'You misunderstand what it is to be a woman,' Amélie replies. 'The power, the pain.' She pauses to see if he's taking her seriously. 'I'm not a wife, nor a mother, but I can see that everything we know and need is built upon the work of women, the suffering they endure so that others might succeed. Yet our society barely acknowledges it.'

'Very true, of course. It's clear that we men are lacking and that we fool ourselves into thinking we can make up for our shortcomings by chasing higher pursuits,' he admits. 'And still, we try.'

'But you're saying a woman must align herself with some grand project in order to leave her mark? She must inspire? And yet she must also give birth, nurse and nurture – the greatest act of creation. With no expectation of thanks, recognition or remuneration?'

'If I were to meet a woman prepared to do both, it would be a miracle.'

It's Amélie's turn to feel uncomfortable. When she looks up, she realizes she's not mistaken – Henri, in his unusual and provocative way, is asking something of her.

She has never been a slave to the steady progression of things, and yet, neither does she consider herself to be a woman in a hurry to marry. But suddenly the thought is upon her, and she can't articulate it: for all her adult life she has been looking for something to pin her colours to, something that radicalizes, that beats a drum with ferocious urgency; that challenges the world to be different, more authentic. Artists, she understands, have more freedom than most. They can exist outside society's parameters, for better or worse. Maybe that is a space that could also accommodate Amélie, her own ambition and drive? She has enough resources – financial and intellectual – not to let this man sink her, and maybe, just maybe, she can become a catalyst for pushing him to greater daring.

Has Amélie found her calling in Henri, this strange, pale man, born to the hard cold earth of the north, so in need of light? She can tell he needs someone to believe in him and in what he is trying to do. 'And if such a miracle were to occur, what could a penniless artist promise in return?' she asks.

'I can't promise a thing,' he admits. 'If you want stability, a steady hand, or a certain future, there are other men far more suitable than me. But I get the impression you aren't like other women. You won't be limited by the conventional path.'

'Well, when you make such an attractive offer, how could one refuse?'

She cannot say why it makes sense, the two of them together, but just as she knows that she will press the violets, frame them and hang them on the wall, against all her initial judgements she knows that this is the man she's prepared to commit her energies to. He will be made more because of her – he will stretch, like a growing bud, to meet his potential, with her by his side. And she will be made more substantial by his presence at hers.

After a few moments, Henri touches her fingers, a smile passing between them. 'What do you say, Amélie Parayre? Do you find you could tolerate me?'

She examines his face in profile, his lashes, the red gold of his beard, the nose that is large but well balanced. 'Perhaps I could,' she says. 'But I'd have to visit your studio first, to see exactly what it is I'm getting myself into. What if I don't like your work? I have to admit, I don't have a great deal of knowledge when it comes to art.'

'I'll let you be the judge. I have no expectations. Either way, I want to hear your thoughts. I have a feeling I'm going to value your opinion.'

Amélie is intrigued to see Henri's work, to get more insight into how he operates.

Once again, she finds herself ready to be surprised.

3

Paris, 1898

Their wedding takes place on 10 January, a matter of weeks after their first meeting. '"Why hurry headlong to thy fate, poor fool?"' Amélie has whispered to herself, more than once, as she contemplated the union. But once her mind is made up, she isn't known for her patience. Besides, waiting is the preserve of the feckless and unforceful, her father likes to say.

Amélie is braced against the cold of this new year – when even the city pigeons seem to shudder against concrete skies – and she yearns for the heat of the future. The arrangements have been made quickly, her family rallying into action. Her sister, Berthe – who found Henri utterly contrary to the men Amélie had been close to in the past and, for this reason, liked him instantly – took it upon herself to source a suitable dress, one that wouldn't do her sister a disservice on her wedding day. Her parents agreed to cover all expenses, whatever the cost. Yet, at the news of their engagement, Amélie had detected an edge of discord from her mother and father, who, when faced with the prospect of their daughter marrying a man with neither money nor discernible prospects, and with an illegitimate daughter to boot, had to confront their liberal values head-on. Amélie is sure discussions took place behind closed doors, debates over theory versus reality, on the politics of permissiveness – but, as former revolutionaries, they'd be hypocrites if they complained now.

Amélie's mother, Catherine, with the cool efficiency of her breeding, delicately broached the subject with as much tact as she could muster. Did her daughter need any kind of 'help', she'd asked one day as she wrote in her ledger, her back turned to Amélie, the question hanging in the air between them. Might she want to visit an aunt in the south for a matter of months, until certain things were resolved? Amélie had to laugh. No, she was not in trouble, certainly not that kind. She had simply met her match.

Ultimately, the Parayres have been conditioned to admire artists and poets; they understand that they lead a more noble kind of life, cut off from the things that typically offer comfort or reprieve. They are confident their social standing will protect their daughter from scandal and the worst degradations of poverty. So whatever discussions took place were swiftly resolved, and, outwardly at least, her parents are pleased about the engagement, and keen to make the union a lively affair. Things must be done properly. Her parents have invited friends from Paris – politicians, journalists and educational reformers – as well as neighbours and colleagues from Beauzelle, where the girls spent their childhood.

The guests of honour include her parents' employers – the Humberts, Thérèse and Frédéric – who have been present in Amélie's life since she was born, and who have always been exceedingly generous. Amélie's mother first met Thérèse Aurignac when they were children – long before Thérèse acquired the riches and status that now surround her. Theirs was an unlikely friendship: Thérèse's father was a thoroughly disreputable man, who gambled and sank into debt, telling tall stories about a lost inheritance. Catherine's own father was the town bailiff, tasked with chasing missed payments. He was frequently at Monsieur Aurignac's door, his daughter in tow. Despite their differences, the girls became firm friends and have watched each other's fortunes fluctuate over the years. Since their childhood, the tables have turned, with Catherine now employed to run the Humbert household, and Amélie's father, after he left journalism, working as their chauffeur.

Thérèse's husband, Frédéric, is a tolerant man – shy, sensitive, respected. Rake-thin and awkward, his background and personality are directly at odds with those of his wife, which seems to balance them out. He tries to make up for his lack of charisma by laughing gently after every sentence – the more mundane the statement, the more forcefully he expels his amusement. By contrast, Thérèse is grand, loud and riotously funny, revelling in the finer things in life. Indeed, it was Amélie's parents who brought Frédéric and Thérèse together, seating them next to one another at a dinner party at their home.

And now Frédéric has offered to stand as a witness to Amélie's marriage, and there could be no greater honour or endorsement of her and Henri as a couple in the eyes of the Parisian elite. Frédéric's father, Gustave, was an old friend of Amélie's father. A political heavyweight, Gustave had helped frame the Constitution of the Third Republic before becoming a senator. Gustave also owned the activist Republican newspaper *L'Avenir de Seineet-Marne*, of which her father used to be the editor. Over the years, Gustave rose to become France's Minister of Justice, a position he held until his passing just a few years ago.

Now one of the most powerful couples in France, the Humberts have pulled a few gilded strings to see to it that their local church – the spectacular Église Saint-Honoré-d'Eylau in the 16th arrondissement – will host Amélie and Henri's wedding.

Inside, the structure of the bleached exposed beams, stretching from the ground to the grand ceiling, made Amélie feel as if she were inside the belly of a whale the first time she saw it. But the stained glass was the most arresting sight – floral panels of oranges, reds, turquoise and blues, like swimming through molten colour.

It's true that the most fashionable weddings of Paris take place here. Henri and his family must certainly view it as a step too far to have secured such a venue. Amélie can imagine their dismay on receiving the missive from their wayward son; they must have thought he was joking – marriage, to a woman they had never heard him speak of, so soon after his relationship with Camille ended. There's suspicion, she can sense it, combined with relief that their son is finally marrying so well. His parents and brother have made the journey from Bohain – and, in his words, two of his 'most presentable relatives', Henri's uncles, will also stand as witnesses. His daughter, pretty Marguerite, will be their flower girl. That will certainly ruffle the great and the good.

Amélie's mother comes in to help set her hair, curling and twisting, teasing with irons. She usually finds all this intolerable, but today Amélie relents. The young woman observes her reflection. She believes she's bordering on a kind of beauty, with her smooth skin and dark hair. She knows she's not an unappealing woman, with her youth and fine complexion, but she has never put a premium on her looks, as some do, especially in Paris.

She'll have competition in this marriage, she knows that much. Henri has made it clear that art, for him, is more than a passing fad. She saw the evidence in his living quarters, that cramped space that was taken over by paint and canvas, hardly room for a man to stretch out to sleep. She'd been impressed and surprised that day by Henri's bold interpretation of the world around him. And she'd been seduced, seeing it through his eyes, wanting to step into his scenes and live more authentically as a result.

She'll not fight it, this urge in him to pursue his artistic vision. She's deeply impressed by his talent, by his rhetoric. There's a steel core to Henri. If anyone can succeed in this punishing arena, it's him. Henri is introducing her to a new world, one she feels she comes alive in – he has walked her around the Louvre and other galleries, talked to her of the great artists, their strengths, their failings, and his own vision, why he's not content to replicate the certainties of the past. Already, he has a reputation as a loose cannon, a man whose work must be shunned. She knows this unsettles him, the reluctance of others to collaborate with his earnest vision. But she admires his antagonism and wants to be part of it.

In one early letter, Henri made his intentions clear: *Mademoiselle, I love you dearly*, he wrote, *but I shall always love painting more.* She'd been tickled by his candour, his need to spell things out in this way, as if his passion for art were an entanglement with another woman. Amélie would not hope to change him, as Camille had. Amélie believes she has the capacity to surprise Henri – not to compete with his passion, but to charge it with her own energy and enthusiasm.

Over the last few weeks, her fiancé has barely mentioned Camille, the mother of his child, and Amélie has been surprised at the efficacy with which he has excised her from his heart and mind. Amélie, on the other hand, thinks of her often. She hasn't articulated it to anyone, but she feels this great, spine-stiffening opposition to Camille Joblaud, that woman who couldn't appreciate what she had and left those who loved her to pick up the pieces. Amélie is aware that there's a painting – one that her fiancé told her caused quite the scandal at the Salon just before she met him – of Camille standing at the dinner table, wearing a pinafore, dressed like a maid, tending to the flowers in the centre of the lavish setting.

It had been turned to the wall in his studio. Was he ashamed of it? she'd asked. Henri told Amélie that he'd intended to paint a family gathering, and it hadn't escaped her notice that the seats at the table were empty; Camille on her feet, her eyes downcast, her face pinched, ready to depart a scene that promised so much satisfaction.

Camille is not Amélie's rival. She'd already left. There's no need for Amélie to assert anything. But Amélie measures herself and her new relationship against this invisible woman, feels a desire to prove that she's of a different cut, that she has the initiative and resources to navigate Henri's painful path; that, as his social equal, she can make a better job of this role than that other woman ever could.

Marguerite, Amélie has been pleased to discover, is a sweet, silent child – harbouring a tender nature born of shyness rather than a lack of wit. At their first meeting, the dark-haired girl clung to Amélie's legs, refusing to reply to gentle questions, all the while ignoring her father's suggestions to run off and play. Amélie had felt nervous around the child, unsure of whether to embrace her, but instinct had taken over and she'd swaddled her in a hug.

After the wedding, Amélie and Henri have made plans to spend a long honeymoon travelling south, sailing from Marseille, the journey culminating in Corsica – an island where she spent many happy weeks during her childhood. There, she believes, the heat will breathe new life into Henri, seduce him with possibilities unknown before. The light might inspire a new direction in his art, too. They'll visit Toulouse and Beauzelle, and Henri will see the life she knew as a child – the streets where she grew up, the landscape that formed her before she moved to boarding school in Paris. She remembers the desire to escape the parameters of those school walls, how she felt disconnected from the preoccupations of other girls her age. But first, Henri has proposed London, to visit galleries, to see the work of a painter he admires. It's imperative they take in his bold approach in the flesh.

Amélie's mother loops a loose tendril into the pile of hair at the nape of her neck, and pins it in place. Her deep-set eyes, so like Amélie's own, look back at her in the mirror. Amélie has certainly inherited that decisive mouth. Henri, after meeting Catherine in

December, announced that Amélie was clearly descended from a family of Spanish queens.

'*Ma chérie?* You are sure about this?' her mother asks gently.

Amélie has a hollow knot in her stomach; she cannot tell if it's nerves or excitement. She's about to answer, to brush away her mother's uncertainty, when there's a knock at the door and Thérèse appears, her hat at a jaunty angle, her dark eyes sparkling with mischievous energy. Thérèse produces a silk drawstring pouch, the size of a lemon, the contents of which jangle melodically as she moves it from one hand to the other.

'My darling,' Thérèse says, coming closer and putting her hand to the material at Amélie's waist, pressing it to test the quality. 'Don't you look divine?' She pulls her fingers away, satisfied, and smiles once more. 'These are for you and your soon-to-be husband, to see you through any rough patches – of which I'm sure there will be many, as there should be in any successful marriage.' She looks to her good friend Catherine for confirmation. 'But I admire him. And I admire you,' she says, raising her chin. 'You're a brave woman, and that should be celebrated in our day and age.'

'Women get married all the time, Madame Thérèse,' Amélie replies.

But the elegant older woman continues as if she hadn't spoken. 'I hear what you're saying with this union,' she adds in a dramatic whisper. '"I will not be contained. I will not be curtailed."' Thérèse ploughs her fist into the air vigorously. 'Not for you the restrictions of a bourgeois partnership. So these' – she passes the pouch – 'will come in handy. They'll shield you from the worst ravages of poverty, at least until that man makes a name for himself.'

Amélie takes the offering, blushing, though she is about to protest, when Catherine places her palm on her daughter's upper arm. 'That's too kind of you, Thérèse, but really, there's no need,' her mother says.

'Nonsense,' she replies. 'I need to feel that I'm doing my best for our little Amélie, and this is simply the way I know how. So please, Amélie, open it.'

Amélie looks to her mother, who offers a small nod. She undoes the string and pours the contents into her palm. A huge emerald is the first object to tip out, set in a gold band. It is magnificent and Amélie's heart flutters, despite herself.

'I couldn't. It's too much, much too much,' she says.

'I know you've admired this one since you were a child. I have acres of jewels, and not enough fingers to enjoy them all.' Thérèse dances her hands around, revealing diamonds and sapphires. 'Someone young and beautiful may as well make the most of the finest ones. What's the point of wealth and precious things, if they can't inspire joy in others?'

This gift is designed to impress – to pass on the message to anyone who glances at it that Amélie and Henri are a couple who can take on the world, that they have status and money, even if the truth is quite the opposite. Alongside the ring there are smaller gemstones, some sparkling and others uncut, that could be made into finer jewellery, or sold for a solid price.

This kind of excess is Thérèse's trademark. There's no need for such extravagance. Most friends of the family have proffered modest – by comparison – gifts of cash that are more than generous. But Thérèse always desires to be the most extravagant, the most lavish.

All this wild generosity, Amélie knows, is founded upon the fabled Humbert inheritance. For many years, there has been disagreement over the will of an obscure relative, of which Thérèse is the beneficiary. When the matter is settled, she'll get her hands on one of the greatest fortunes France has ever known. It's refreshing to see a commanding woman, playing in the same court as the men. But Amélie has things of her own to prove – marriage hasn't taken away her own aspirations; indeed, it has augmented them. 'I couldn't, Madame Thérèse,' she repeats. 'Really, it's too much, and you're too kind.'

'Just wear the ring today, see how it feels. You won't want to take it off,' Thérèse replies confidently. Catherine Parayre helps slip the ring on to her daughter's finger, pushing it on with a little pressure, alerting her not to protest any more than is polite.

Amélie looks at it uneasily.

'If you say no, the jewels will only end up being thrown out with the slops,' Thérèse warns. 'So please, do me a kindness, and accept with a little grace, there's a good girl.'

There's no more time to think about it. Her sister is knocking at the door, bright-eyed.

'Madame Matisse?' she teases. It's the first time Amélie has heard her future name spoken aloud and, she admits, there's a ring to it. 'Your carriage awaits.'

Their guests will be waiting at the church. As will Henri. Amélie mustn't be late. Well, no more than is fashionable for a young woman in Paris on her wedding day.

4

London and Corsica, 1898

Lesson is not what Amélie Matisse expected. It's a squat city; the buildings look as if they've been battered with a rolling pin, and its people seem characterized by a perpetual failure to rise. The whole setting is a sleeting grey – the weather, the colours, the temperament. Even the Matisses' accommodation, the Hôtel de Paris in Leicester Square, positioned as it is near the rear entrance to the National Gallery, is French in name but British in spirit, with scratchy bedsheets, tepid baths and coffee as weak and greasy as dishwater.

On the journey to England from France, the newly-weds had braced themselves against the biting winter wind as their steamer crossed the Channel, the sea churning against the prow, the cawing seagulls battling the fierce gusts. Henri had cleaned the salty spray from his glasses, kissed Amélie's cheek and embraced his wife tightly, trying to shield her from the whipping wind. And she'd marvelled at how her life had been transformed, in a matter of months, from one state to another – ice on a pilgrimage to steam.

Amélie had a new name, new family, responsibilities and a future that, at the start of October, would have seemed outlandish.

By the end of the year she might even be a mother and a fresh shift would take place, translating anew the woman she'd been.

As she'd removed her leather gloves on the ship, replacing them with thicker wool-lined ones, the Humbert emerald had glittered on her finger, singular against the grey of the sea, and Amélie thought again of Madame Thérèse's petulant persistence that she keep it, that she enjoy it – and, if the times called for it, that it be pawned to make ends meet. There was something peculiar about it all, but Amélie had conceded defeat, fuelled by her mother's not-so-subtle insistence. Henri, who had never seen anything so excessive, so raw with ruddy wealth, had shrugged and simply said, 'Who are we to disobey the Madame's wishes?'

⤵

They've been in London now for three days, and Amélie has been a wife for more than a week; so far, it has been a not unpleasant role to occupy. She and Henri basked in the mirrored joy of their wedding day, everyone wishing them well and pressing money into their pockets. Indeed, they accumulated enough that they can afford to take the next twelve months away from Paris, freed from any obligation to earn a living. He'll miss Marguerite terribly, of course, but he'll make regular visits to Paris to spend time with his daughter – as much as his former partner, Camille, will allow. In the meantime, they both know an opportunity when they see one: Henri can concentrate on his art, until the collectors and gallerists start approaching *him*, which, he tells her, is what happened with the Impressionists. He tries to be confident that public opinion will catch up with his vision before too long.

On their first night together, Henri did not make assumptions about Amélie's level of knowledge of the act to follow. As a young woman from a good family, and one in possession of an expensive education, it was of course deemed appropriate that she knew little, that her desires were muted, that she might even feign a certain unwillingness. But the urgency with which Henri undressed her, the hunger he had for her physically, charged Amélie with new levels of passion and she found herself quickly addicted, willingly complicit. Henri is a hefty man, with large bones and muscles inherited from generations of honest labour. Whatever clandestine experiences Amélie had had with her intellectually minded peers in the past seemed meagre and objectionably earnest by comparison.

In the daytime, Amélie and Henri wrap themselves in respectability and visit museums. She's eager to become an informed connoisseur of the art world. Her husband's works – still lifes and landscapes – are considered infantile by his tutors, influenced as his style is by the Impressionists, who shook the art world with their emphasis on prioritizing 'feeling' over traditional rules of composition and perspective. The Impressionists, Henri informs her, are no longer considered quite as controversial as they once were, but the Salon and the public are still sceptical about anyone who engages with their principles.

She and Henri visit the National Gallery to see the work of the artist J. M. W. Turner.

'Turner,' Henri says, angling himself in front of a large frame, 'was a master of denial. This is a man who, at times in his career, locked himself in a cellar, and only had the shutter flung open to let in the light *once a week* so that he could fully appreciate the impact of it. That way, he could better absorb and understand the intensity, its incandescence, the way it dazzled his senses.'

'To live in darkness, for the sake of art . . .' Amélie wonders out loud.

She stands close to the canvas in the dimly lit gallery. She sees the brushstrokes and, like her husband, looks intimately at the surface. She admires the way the thick paint – burnt sienna and greys against pastel pinks – seems to have been pushed on with a burning rage.

Before she met Henri, Amélie had little idea about art, and had evaded the opportunity to really see it. But she's learning to understand the passion, the purpose. She knows what she likes, what she doesn't – and isn't afraid, even in front of Henri and his serious artist friends, to state her opinion. Even if it raises a few eyebrows.

Henri asks: 'Does it move you?' It was the same question he'd asked in his studio the second time they met, when she'd been so overwhelmed by his art that she couldn't find the words. Now, Amélie is learning to wait a moment, to look at the work from a new angle, then look away, and back, as if she's really pondering the question. Then she'll choose a part of her body, interior or exterior, and eulogize about the emotion she feels there: a tenderness in her fingertips, a gnawing in the depth of her, a frisson of sparks in her chest.

Henri looks at her through narrowed eyes, and the muscles tighten around his mouth, causing his red beard to twitch. Her eyes, too, crinkle with amusement. Look at me, she thinks, playing the artist's wife. And he takes her arm and exhales, wry and gentle.

⤺

The boat journey from the southern shores of France, across to the island of Corsica, is a very different affair to the one they took towards the cliffs of England. The sea shimmers with an interior light, the sun's bright coruscations sending shockwaves of blue and turquoise through the waters. Here, the sea birds don't battle the winds, but soar on the breeze. The couple stand close, shoulders loosening with every nautical mile as the boat pulls towards the port on the island's south-western coast. The Matisses plan to stay for three months.

This is a great gift for Henri, the brightest opportunity of his life to date. This breathing space, away from the stuffy École des Beaux-Arts – the school to which he plans to return after their honeymoon – promises to unlock something in him, to allow greater leaps of creativity than would have been possible if he were slaving for an income.

They've secured rooms in the Villa de la Rocca on the outskirts of Ajaccio, a pretty coastal town surrounded by mountains – the birthplace of Napoleon Bonaparte. Already, Henri is taken by the vibrancy of the colours, the play of sunlight and shade. It reminds Amélie of a line by her favourite poet, Victor Hugo: 'To contemplate is to look at shadows.'

The hotel has expansive, seductive views of the ocean. Her husband throws open the shutters each morning and seems to swallow the sunlight in greedy gulps, absorbing it the way soil soaks up rain after a long spell of aridity, painting from the first ray until the last.

Already his art is taking a new angle, one Amélie has not seen before. Henri tells her that he feels the unique landscape is shifting his style, and she can see it – his work is becoming bolder, wilder. His colours are vibrant, less natural, unhooked from what in the past might have been used to portray the shade of a tree or sea spume.

'It's not enough to place colours, however beautiful, one beside the other,' he tells her. 'Colours must also react to one another.' Amélie loves watching him paint. She is delighted, feeling the contours of her own part of this great transformative shift.

⌒

Over the months, as summer approaches, the heat of Ajaccio intensifies. Neither of them is prepared for the way it overcomes a person, stultifying the senses, making sleep the only reasonable response. They endure sheetless nights, the overhead fan shunting sticky air around the small room. Henri sleeps naked and dreams of the north, where the cold grips him by the throat, but wakes shaking with relief that he's no longer there. Amélie has a permanent slick of moisture between her breasts, and her ankles are swollen. Still, she and Henri sleep close, their bodies leaning into one another, their pulses finding a joint rhythm.

Henri has not asked Amélie to be his model, but he does expect it of her, assumes it without a second thought. He watches her throughout the day. He selects his pencil or paintbrush and creates an artwork of her sitting on the rocks, her dark hair tied at the nape of her neck, daubing on the pinks of her kimono. He sketches her on the balcony, the breeze lifting her skirt, bougainvillaea in the background. Henri imbues his canvases with bolder lines, fiercer colours, more extreme versions of what he sees before him. She wonders how this new style will be greeted in Paris. With derision, as his last works have been, or with some kind of wisdom, seeing beyond seemingly simple strokes to the possibilities beneath?

He laughs at the suggestion that any critic will show understanding or appreciation.

The fat emerald on her finger sparkles with renewed crudeness beneath the Corsican sun. To pass the time, Amélie reads, crochets; she manages her husband's correspondence, runs errands, orders new supplies to be sent from Paris. Henri has plenty of friends who are willing to act as a conduit and make the journey south, bearing gifts.

Her plans to open her own boutique, selling hats, are on hold. But here, Amélie has time to work on her designs. She shows them to Henri when he returns in the afternoon. He never makes her feel as if she's wasting his time. He looks them over with interest, shares his observations. Why shouldn't she be taken seriously? Her talent has no less potential than his.

As she sits and reads, pausing after a poignant paragraph, she lifts her head to watch the waves batter a low, flat rock and feels a twinge in her left side. She finds her fingers on her abdomen, pushing beneath her underwear to loosen it. The sensation feels like flickerings of moths beneath the surface of her skin. And the thought lands on her, without surprise.

Later, she'll tell people that she hadn't expected it to happen so quickly, falling pregnant so soon after they married. But the emotion she feels is satisfaction. It has come to her so easily, just as meeting her husband and marriage, so far, have been effortless. She takes them all in her stride, these big slices of life. She'll have her first baby before the end of the year. This development, of course, changes everything. They have money, but it won't last for ever. They must adhere to a budget if they're to make the most of the time left to them. Already, they have extended their stay in Ajaccio from three months to five. Afterwards, they'll spend time with her parents in Beauzelle, for as long as is reasonable.

Amélie feels only a little apprehension at the thought of becoming a mother. She can't dwell on what could go wrong or might become complicated, or come up with reasons why a child will disrupt her life. She'll cope admirably, as she always has. Her own mother was not defined by her ability to rear children. Her father has always encouraged her to take the rough with the smooth. She does not intend to be one of these women who fall apart, who aren't able to manage or organize their affairs. She will not be Camille. A child will not stop her, nor slow her down. For it is imperative that she and Henri leave their mark on the world.

5

Paris, 1899

More than a year after they left, Henri and Amélie return from the south, with its light and limitless potential, to Paris in the wiry days of spring. Their baby, Jean, was born in Amélie's home town. Her parents came from Paris to help in those first weeks. It gave her a chance to recuperate after the birth, which tested the limits of her endurance. She's recovering, but still doesn't feel strong again.

The city, after they've spent so long away, offers new richness, and the chiselled skies do nothing to dampen their enthusiasm to see friends and family, to talk of their experiences, and to re-engage with the cultural and intellectual life of the capital. Amélie persuades her parents to book tickets to the theatre, while Henri acquaints himself with the galleries. The works he sees there still haven't caught up with the breadth of his own artistic ambitions.

Henri is expansive, buoyed, during this initial phase. Amélie knows this gregariousness will wear off soon enough, and he'll want to shut himself away, where no one can disturb him. He says that for the sake of his art, he'd be happy to live as a monk, having no interaction with the outside world at all. She reminds him he has two hungry children and a wife who needs him, without whom he'd hardly have any promise at all. At that, he tries to suppress his surprise, before laughing good-naturedly and admitting that she's quite right.

Her husband loves the renewed chance to spend time with Marguerite, who has grown in height, if not confidence, since they last saw her. He delights in introducing his daughter to the baby, her little brother, Jean. It seems the girl is baffled and hurt that she must share her father when she sees so little of him already. Amélie, having not seen the girl for many months, is shocked by her appearance. Marguerite is tall, but scraggly, as skinny as a pole, and, on closer inspection, her gums seem inflamed, and her nails are ridged and brittle. She'll see to it that Marguerite receives nutritious food, grooming and care when they're together.

Henri spends his afternoons looking for an apartment that might accommodate them within their meagre budget. He has been seduced by the constant presence of the sea in Ajaccio and now wants to live with a view of the Seine. He finds one at the Quai Saint-Michel – a small space with tall ceilings and plenty of light, up on the fifth floor, with views of Notre-Dame, standing proud like a bride. He can't wait to paint the scene through the window. But the Seine is not the sea. It's thick with the city's rubbish, human and industrial. Bodies of bloated animals float to the surface. The river attracts riddled birds and rats. Desperate people live under its bridges, burning scavenged lumps of coal. The area feels dangerous and alive, pulsing with the energy of a snake. Anybody with sense and money does well to avoid it.

Once they are settled, Amélie intends to be resourceful. She's not the first woman to have her own ambitions paused while she accommodates a man's more expansive drive, but this interval of pursuing her husband's artistic aspirations has only made her more determined. Yes, she has enjoyed the twelve months with Henri, their precious time away from Paris as newly-weds, the ways in which he took to the land of her birth, and absorbed the heat and vibrant colours of the south. And the ways in which they got to know each other, gently at first, unfurling, before more of their true selves emerged; their preferences and foibles and flashes of ego leading to their first married arguments, passionate matches in which ideas were debated, interior worlds shifted, and untold fears and secrets were sifted to the surface. Amélie takes pride in the fact that Henri has had the chance to flourish thanks to their partnership. But now she's ready to show what she's capable of, and the value she can bring to their marriage. She has the skills, the temperament – they just need a little more money.

Henri's father still sends his son a modest allowance, but there's nothing to spare. What they have seems not to go as far as it did in the south, where the sun allowed freedom without demanding payment. In Paris, if she wants to meet a friend, it's the coffee shop or some other space that demands coins from her purse like a hungry bird; she must pay, or shut herself away all day, shivering against the biting early spring. But she and Henri are used to economizing. She recalls reading by candlelight during her pregnancy, and the weak camomile tea she sipped that had to be reheated time and time again, as it was the only thing that eased her morning sickness. She didn't buy new clothes for the pregnancy, just let out seams and refashioned swathes of material she found at the local market.

Madame Thérèse has offered to fund her hat shop, to help Amélie find a location and introduce her to those who'll pay to be seen wearing fresh designs from the wife of an artist – even one who's making a name for himself as a 'dissenter of sanity and reason'.

Well, it must be possible to change the received wisdom, Amélie considers. Can Henri's reputation as a madman, a fool, someone who doesn't do things in the expected ways, be reframed? He's an iconoclast, a freethinker. That's how the world should view him. Her husband has unrivalled talent; his vision is extraordinary. But how can she let the world know as much? She resolves to do whatever it takes to change the narrative for good.

⟿

Months later, Amélie is trying to settle Jean when she hears her husband drop his keys on the other side of the door to their apartment. She looks up from the baby, who's crabby, refusing to sleep. She hears him try again and, once more, the keys jangle in the lock, then slip and fall. She opens the door to save him the indignity of having to try for a third time.

'I can only presume there was wine after your studies today?' she asks pointedly, taking the keys from his hand. Since their extended honeymoon, Henri has returned to the École des Beaux-Arts. 'Is that why you're late and can't fathom how to enter your own home?' she adds. It's then that she notices he's blinking back frustration. 'Are you hurt? What happened?' Amélie takes Henri's shoulder and leads him to a seat. He starts to speak, then shakes his head, the words inaudible. She has never seen him like this before.

'Is it your mother? Not Marguerite?' she asks, the ground shifting beneath her.

'No. No,' he manages. 'It's nothing like that.'

'Well, tell me, before I suffer a bout of nerves to match your own.'

'There was an incident . . . at des Beaux-Arts.' He pulls at his hands and looks at her, his eyes hardening as he places himself in the centre of a memory.

While they were in the south, Henri received the news that his admired tutor, Gustave Moreau, had sadly passed away. This was grief enough for him, but to add insult to injury, he has been replaced by a new art professor, Monsieur Fernand Cormon, who quite profoundly cannot tolerate her husband. The feeling is mutual.

'Did someone fall ill?' she asks, willing it to be Monsieur Cormon.

'Would you believe I was mocked? And insulted. But it's worse than that.'

Amélie straightens her spine. 'You were mocked?'

'I was mocked,' he says gravely.

'And what's new about that?' she asks, not unkindly. Her husband often complains that his classmates don't take him seriously, and she has to remind him daily that the opinions of his jealous peers are hardly to be trusted.

He clenches his jaw. 'This time the cruelty came directly from Cormon.'

'Your tutor has resorted to mocking you? To your face?'

The baby is still fighting his fatigue, and Amélie tries to jiggle him to sleep.

Henri rubs a closed fist against his open palm. 'I was finishing up a painting,' he begins. 'A fine one from Corsica, with which I was more than happy. Yes, it was bolder than the other artists' work, but I hardly imagined it would offend anyone. Until Monsieur Cormon showed up. He looked at it, then, in front of everyone, he demanded to know my age. Through gritted teeth, I admitted I'll soon be thirty. Of course, the rest of the men in that room are closer to twenty. I must seem like a dinosaur to them.'

'Nobody is judging you based on your age, Henri. You're making progress at your own pace.'

Henri gives a bitter laugh. 'Then Cormon spoke over me, as if I weren't there,' her husband continues. 'He addressed his next question to his assistant, a weaselly student in charge of running the studio. He had the nerve to ask *him* if I knew what I was doing. The fellow had the decency to look embarrassed, and replied quite graciously that I was indeed of sound mind, and that, yes, it seems I do know what I'm doing. I can only presume the chap thought he was helping. But at that, Cormon snapped his fingers. "Then he'll have to go." ' Henri rubs his balled fist on the table, the mounds of his cheeks turning a deeper shade of red. 'They were all staring at me, smirking. You can't imagine how I felt at that moment. I knew they were all fools, and cruel, but I never imagined it could become so personal. I'd no choice but to leave at once; the paint wasn't even dry on the canvas.' He shudders afresh. 'They stepped back as I passed, as if they were afraid of catching something, as if I were morally contagious. I can never set foot in that place again.'

The faculty at the École des Beaux-Arts have long been uneasy with the style in which her husband paints, all the more so since he returned from the south, but this kind of treatment leaves no space for discussion. People with vision – her parents or the Humberts – have taught her you need to break with the past in radical ways in order to embrace what the future might offer. The world is always being smashed and remade – Amélie knows that intimately.

'Your talent doesn't hinge on his approval,' Amélie says. But she can see it's no use: her husband feels diminished, degraded by the memory of the exchange. Her father often says that radical people are more lachrymose and prone to depression than most. It's the nature of striving for greatness that leaves them feeling drained. And she can see it clearly in her husband. She is reminded of the words of the philosopher Denis Diderot: 'Only passions, great passions, can elevate the soul to great things.'

'Some days I might agree with you,' Henri says. 'But I'm not sure today is one of them.' He rubs a thumb against his forehead. 'Perhaps it's time I admit it. That my fate is to be a copyist, working for peanuts at the Louvre, only fit to recreate the artworks of the past.'

She never wants Henri to feel he must beg for approval from anyone. 'Listen to me,' she instructs. 'We've not come this far to be deterred by the opinions of those who are wedded to the past. You've shown great courage. You mustn't regret it.'

48

Amélie sees his relief. Perhaps he'd been nervous to bring this news to her. But he doesn't know her fully; he doesn't understand that she intends to defy everyone's expectations.

～

Generosity breeds generosity, and bad luck breeds like bacteria. To make matters worse, Henri's work has been rejected for the grand 1900 Exposition Universelle, the World Fair held to celebrate the achievements of the past century and accelerate confidently into the next.

The irony has not been lost on either of them.

His work is 'not up to the expected standards', according to the selection jury.

Her husband has received the news stoically, and withdrawn, asking not to be disturbed.

Amélie gently bats away visitors and manages their home with her usual efficiency. She can afford him a few days to recover, before she'll encourage him to pull himself together. While dealing with his correspondence, she's unsettled to find a letter from his former lover, Camille, the mother of his daughter. She has written to ask for more money.

Marguerite cries for you, Camille writes. Amélie's eyes dart over the words, the neat cursive that conveys so much anguish. *I can't keep doing this; how can I – a woman on her own, with no resources – be expected to make a living and care for a child at the same time?*

Perhaps she should have considered that before, Amélie thinks, folding the letter. Perhaps, when Camille left Henri, she didn't imagine that she'd be put aside quite so effectively – nor that a competent woman would step in so quickly. Perhaps she'd imagined her departure would inflict a crisis of confidence upon Henri, that he'd feel compelled to return to law, and to her, full of promises for a more stable future.

Amélie may question the woman's actions, but she doesn't harbour resentment towards Marguerite, who's a sad, strange little girl. She hates to think of her pining for her father, worried she won't see him again. But as a mother, she has her own issues to grapple with. Jean is less than a year old, and already, unexpectedly, there's another baby on the way. Amélie hasn't found the right moment to tell her husband. The pressure of a third child could unravel him entirely. As a woman, Amélie feels grasped in the nettled fist of her gender, held hostage by biology. She wouldn't have chosen for a new pregnancy to happen so fast, when their finances are strangled. But such things cannot be denied. Sometimes, the best way to cope is to throw yourself head first into chaos, and worry about it later.

On the other side of Camille's note, there's a hurried request for Henri to meet her the following day at the Jardin du Luxembourg, in their 'usual spot'. That woman is still adept at making demands, at expecting Henri to be there at the drop of a hat, but Henri hasn't left his bed in days and won't be going anywhere. Perhaps this is the moment for Amélie to set in motion another plan she has been considering for some time.

6

Paris, 1899

At the Jardin du Luxembourg the next day, Amélie spots Camille straight away. She has dark-blonde hair and a slender frame, and is hurrying along, pulling Marguerite by the hand, practically dragging the reluctant child, whose laces are trailing. But even if she hadn't been with the girl, Amélie would have known Camille instantly, as Henri has captured her likeness in earlier portraits. Today, her eyes seem almost bruised from fatigue, and her temper is frayed. The woman lifts her head and stops short when she realizes that she's being observed.

'Amélie!' Marguerite breaks free of her mother's hand and runs to her, wrapping her arms around her legs. Amélie puts a hand to the girl's damp hair, and notices it's matted at the scalp. She'd run a comb through it, if the action wouldn't be seen as a declaration of war. But she can't resist bending down to tie the laces of Marguerite's left shoe.

The light drizzle of the autumnal morning is turning heavier, and the two women take shelter under the foliage of a wide-brimmed tree.

'You must be Madame Matisse,' Camille says, raising her eyebrows and looking Amélie up and down. Her eyes rest briefly on the emerald on her finger.

'Mademoiselle Joblaud. I recognize you from your portrait,' Amélie says.

'I can't say I've seen yours,' Camille replies. Her lips turn down in dissatisfaction at having to face her former lover's new wife, but her eyes betray her intrigue at the nature of their meeting. 'Marguerite was expecting to see her father.'

'I'm here on his behalf,' Amélie says.

Camille blinks. 'I hope you are accompanied by the money he promised me.'

Amélie must proceed cautiously. 'I have come with good intentions,' she begins. 'So I hope you'll interpret what I'm about to say in the best possible light.' She watches the woman closely. Camille is experienced; she doesn't flinch. 'We want to make you an offer.'

'If Henri thinks he can worm his way out of sending me money because he has another family, he'll never see Marguerite again,' Camille snaps.

The daughter whimpers by her mother's side.

'This isn't about that money,' Amélie says.

Camille scoffs. 'It's *all* about money, every damn thing. Your actions, mine, Henri's. Everything we cannot do is fuelled by it.'

'I do admit, there's not a huge amount to go around,' Amélie replies.

Camille smirks, her eyes darting again to the emerald.

'Why else would you be here? To rub my face in it?'

'I wanted to give you this.'

Amélie reaches into her pocket and passes over a brown envelope.

Camille counts the cash quickly, her eyes distrustful.

'I want to make your life a little easier,' Amélie says, as delicately as she can. The grass is soggy beneath her feet, and rivulets of rain are running down the trunk of the tree. There isn't much time before they'll be forced to go their separate ways. 'There can be more where that came from.' Amélie has already sold some wedding gemstones to achieve the sum.

Camille pushes the envelope back at her. 'Make my life easier! I'm not falling for that.'

'Henri and I want to take Marguerite,' Amélie says decisively, just as she rehearsed. 'I promise I'll look after her as if she were my own.'

The idea had begun to blossom in Amélie when she first met the child, and it only grew as she came to understand more about Camille's position. As a woman, Amélie knows exactly what she's offering Camille – her freedom, her independence, a chance for a different future – but what she's asking of her as a mother, too, comes at the greatest possible price.

The question is, will the mother be able to put her needs aside and do what is best for the child? That little girl is so clearly unhappy and untended.

Before approaching her husband on the topic, Amélie had thought carefully about how she and Henri would cope. Marguerite would slip right into the fabric of their family and find her place soon enough. Amélie would read to her, brush her hair before bed, buy her pretty dresses, put ribbons in her hair. In return, Amélie could imagine the girl helping out with the babies. It was Marguerite's chance to be part of a family, not dangling loose by the side of a woman unable to fathom a break. So Amélie had discussed it with Henri, after reading Camille's note. Her husband had asked what he'd done to deserve such a wife.

'My daughter, here with us,' he said. 'Nothing would bring me more happiness.'

Now the child's large black eyes stare up at her, fearful and hopeful at the same time.

Camille sucks in a sharp breath, puts a hand on the tree trunk, sways at the statement.

'You want to take my daughter away from me?'

'You've said it yourself: you can hardly cope.'

Camille squeezes her eyes together, as if tortured with pain.

'It's my poverty I want to be free of, my days of desperation, the way I'm not taken seriously as a woman, not given the same opportunities, nor a fair chance. That's the noose around my neck, not my daughter. She's my pride and joy,' she says, her eyes on the girl. 'I don't want to be freed from her. I want to give her everything.'

'If you want to give her everything, give her a family.'

Camille shakes her head, her lips tight. 'Never.'

Amélie starts to speak, then changes her mind. She looks pointedly at the girl. Camille bends to whisper in her ear. The girl runs to another tree, dark eyes looking out into the rain.

With the child out of earshot, Amélie continues. 'Marguerite's left alone all day and night while you work. She hardly speaks, poor child. With us, she'd be taken care of. There's always help on hand, family to call on. She can be alongside me when I open my boutique. She shouldn't suffer because you have no choice but to labour in bars late into the night.'

'She'd be an unpaid maid for your little brat!' Camille counters.

'Marguerite will get the love and attention she needs to thrive.'

Amélie knows that to Camille it must feel as if she's sticking the knife in, but she is genuinely trying to help. Progress is painful, her father says, and the way to negotiate is to state the benefits to all parties as calmly and clearly as possible.

'You're determined to strip me of everything, to steal it away,' Camille says quietly.

'You didn't want it when you had it,' Amélie replies.

At this, Camille bows her head. 'You don't know me. You might have seen my portrait, but it was all an act. Henri always misses the most important things in his art. Don't mistake the woman in his portraits for the one before you now.'

Amélie straightens her back. She should disagree, defend her husband, but something prevents her. 'You can go wherever you like, leave Paris.'

'So that's what it boils down to? I'm bribed to step out of the picture.'

'Henri is a good man; he'll make sure you get what you deserve. He'll be fair.'

'Fair is for fools. I won't do it,' Camille says.

'We only want what's best, for everyone.'

Camille hasn't the energy to laugh. It's as if light has been drained out of her.

Instead, she picks up a leaf that's fallen from the tree and tears a nail through it, like scissors shredding paper. 'Who do you think you are? You haven't the faintest idea what's best for a woman like me. Now, if you don't mind, I have a job to get to.'

7

A t home, Amélie dries herself, and dusts herself off mentally. The interaction with Camille has left her nerves on edge and filled her with a vague sense of guilt. She knows she's trying to do what's best for the little girl – acting with pure intentions, as her father would describe it – but she cannot shake the look of anguish on Camille's face as she weighed up the impossibilities of her current reality and the future. Amélie can't help but shudder. She's not surprised that Camille rejected the offer outright. She'd have done the same. Camille is a spirited woman, caught in difficult circumstances that don't reflect well on society in general.

But Amélie cannot dismantle the world they live in. She has done her best and made a fair offer. Now they'll just have to wait to see if Camille changes her mind.

She knocks gently on Henri's door, then steps inside. The room – the shutters closed to the Parisian landscape – swirls with disappointment, the air musty and dank. Her husband is deep in an afternoon nap. On the floor, she notices a letter that bears the Exposition stamp. She picks it up. Perhaps they've reconsidered, written to let him know that they've changed their mind, that Henri's artwork will be displayed at the esteemed exhibition after all. She sits quietly on the wicker chair next to the bed to read it. But even before she has scanned the first line, Henri's hand darts from beneath the eiderdown and snatches the typed sheet.

'That isn't what you think it is,' he says, sitting up, looking wild and crumpled. 'My art will be at the Exposition,' he adds, 'but not in the capacity it should be. I'll be working as a labourer. I've been offered the venerated role of painting the laurels that will line the great hall. I'm sorry I didn't tell you sooner that I'd applied. My pride prevented me.'

'Oh, Henri. How much are they even paying you?' she asks.

'Next to nothing. One measly franc an hour for ten-hour shifts.'

'My love, it's beneath you,' she says. She wants to be supportive, but the figure is insulting.

'What choice do I have? I'm not stupid enough to believe I'm indispensable to the progress of art. I need to earn my bread. No one else is offering to pay me anything at all. I'm nearly thirty, with two children. I'm persistently mocked. Painting as a labourer is all I'm good for.'

Amélie feels sympathy, and also a little impatience, at her husband's despondency. She knows he doubts himself. In recent months, he has contacted his most stable and least artistically minded friends – those with careers in law, teaching and accountancy – asking about junior positions. To do so feels like admitting failure, and she's suddenly worried for him: worried that his burning flame of ambition will be extinguished, and the man she chose to marry, gone with it. Of course she doesn't want to see her children starve, but Henri must fulfil his potential. What else is there in life, if not the drive for greatness?

'I won't let you pawn your wedding gifts,' he says, sensing her mood.

'We can't eat them. What do jewels matter? Besides,' she adds carefully, 'I've been waiting for the right time to tell you. There's been an unexpected development. Another baby on the way.' She turns away from him – busies herself opening the shutters and the windows, letting fresh air sweep the room – unable to witness this final blow.

'Well, that settles it. I'm taking the damn job,' he says, taking aim and, with one determined flick of his wrist, tossing the tattered letter out into the street below.

‍

Every morning, at the earliest light, Henri leaves for the Grand Palais, which is being erected to house part of the greatest show Paris has ever seen. The Exposition Universelle is billed as the artistic event of the new century. Millions of people are expected to attend, and the names of the selected artists are on the lips of practically every person in the country.

When Henri returns eleven hours later, he tells Amélie how sawdust flies in the air, how joists for the adjoining pavilions are being hoisted into place, how the vast hall is a sea of men in overalls carrying various tools – sharp-toothed saws, heavy-headed hammers, paintbrushes. Henri is one of a line of men – thinner and less muscle-bound than the physical labourers – stationed away from the main activity, working in silence, painting decorative laurels that will garland the space in mile-long stretches.

He tells her that as he bends to the paint on the floor, he can see his reflection in the polished leather boots of their supervisor, Monsieur Le Louët, who comes round at intervals, inspecting the work, searching for imperfections or evidence of haste.

Henri describes his boss as a sour man, who exerts power through punishment of the smallest misdemeanour. The swine won't be seen for an hour, then turns up with a scowl as soon as the men start a conversation. He carries a cane and is not afraid to use it, cracking down on the curve of a spine, or the hunch of a shoulder. Amélie knows that Henri will struggle to bite his tongue against the indignity of it all, the way in which grown men are disciplined like wayward children, while earning a pittance. Even worse, she intuits that he's well and truly losing the belief that he's destined for greater things. There he must be, day in and day out, surrounded by other men whose names he'll hardly get to know.

But he has not lost his passion for art entirely. One morning, on his way to the Exposition hall from their home on the Left Bank, Henri was passing a nook of shops. Too early for the doors to be open, he peered through the window, and saw a framed painting that took his breath away. Henri tells Amélie that it was by an artist called Cézanne, who also trained under Moreau when his former tutor was a younger man. Cézanne, too, had studied law before art, so Henri feels a kinship.

It's not the subject matter that makes the painting interesting, it's the use of colour, he says. 'But it costs a fortune – hundreds and hundreds of francs,' Henri grumbles. He cannot indulge in works of art. He can hardly afford to create them, let alone buy one.

⌒

Amélie reaches into her coat pocket to fetch the key to the apartment building, trying not to upend her basket of cheap cuts and baguettes in the process. The street in front of their building is always busy, and often heavily littered, attracting rats, so she always aims to get through the front door and up the stairs as quickly as possible. Her neighbour, Anette, is listening for Jean while he sleeps. Amélie promised she wouldn't be long while she fetched supplies for the evening meal. She's closing the door behind her when there's a forceful push. Amélie kicks at the frame, to stop whatever is trying to work its way inside.

'My damn fingers!'

She's shocked to recognize her husband's voice.

She opens the door a crack. Henri barrels through sideways, clutching his hand. 'You fear the rapist of the Seine, at ...' He glances at his wrist. 'Two o'clock in the afternoon?'

This aggressive tone is not like him. Amélie catches her breath enough to offer an audible tut, then lifts the heavy basket to pass it to him, but he strides straight up the stairs without a second glance, still muttering about his injury.

'Good job I don't need my fingers for anything of importance,' he says loudly.

Amélie follows, her heels loud on the polished steps. 'If you turn up in the middle of the day, you can at least be expected to help.' She stops. 'Why *are* you home so early?'

He glances back down the stairs at her, showing a mix of disgust and disappointment.

'There was an incident,' he forces himself to say.

She places the basket at her feet, gripping the bannister. 'Not another one.'

'A little support wouldn't go amiss,' he snaps. His words echo in the stairwell.

'What has got into you! You never raise your voice.'

'I'm taking the train tomorrow to see my father. I've made up my mind,' he replies. 'I need a new job. One that doesn't involve holding a brush.'

'Henri, really?' she says, losing her patience. She'd hoped his disappointments had hardened him, made him more resilient, but at every setback he seems to crumple faster. She climbs the remaining stairs to their apartment and opens the door, dropping the basket at the threshold.

'Don't you want to hear what happened?' he demands, following her inside.

She already has Jean in her arms; his face is wet with tears.

'I quit my job at the Exposition hall,' Henri announces. 'I'm incapable of conformity, he continues, and it's clear he's mimicking his superior.

'I'm your wife – that's hardly news to me.'

'I used the wrong shade of green for the laurel.'

'And you have sacrificed our meagre income for that?'

'I'm the wrong man for the job.' Once again, the words are a projection of his boss.

'The other men seem to be able to get on with it,' she says mildly.

'Gunter kicked me in the ribs.'

Amélie looks at him dispassionately. Jean's cries become increasingly desperate. It's just months until she has another of these charges to drive her to distraction, she realizes.

'That does seem rather excessive,' she concedes.

He looks at her triumphantly. 'So you are on my side?'

She almost laughs. 'I didn't say that.'

'But you can understand why I couldn't stay there a moment longer?'

'Your pride wouldn't allow it?'

He seizes the moment and sidles up. 'You'd have been proud of me,' he says. 'I placed my paintbrush down with the greatest reverence, then I stood up and dusted off my knees. I made eye contact with all the men in the room, those cowards who did nothing to stand up for me. And with my head high, I walked out. Calm and collected. I wasn't going to let that visionless bastard Gunter see that he'd riled me. I still have my pride, if nothing else.'

Amélie is quietly impressed. Maybe her husband has more nerve than she has come to believe. 'Fine,' she sighs. 'You have my full, unfettered support.'

He loosens his shoulders. 'Of course, I won't be paid for the work I've done.'

Amélie can't help but roll her eyes. She can feel a fierce headache brewing. 'Just promise me that you don't intend to take over your father's seed shop,' she warns.

'The seed shop – now there's a good idea. Why haven't I considered that before?'

She looks at her husband with a frown, wondering when life became so complicated.

He moves in to kiss her cheek.

'Sarcasm, Monsieur Matisse, is a shallow expression of wit,' she says, batting him off. 'Now make yourself useful, at least.' She passes him the baby, who instantly stops crying, the little traitor.

She retrieves the basket and takes it to the kitchen. Amélie is worried for their future. They're hardly able to make things work in the present – and at every stage, their situation takes a tighter turn. Amélie watches her husband cradling Jean. She feels a wave of tenderness, and a small dash of pity. She doesn't want to doubt her husband, his talent or potential, but, in this moment, she feels it would take a miracle to turn their fortunes around.

What she does know is that one has to fight one's instincts at times like this.

She has to be bold – for greatness can't be won by playing it safe.

8

Paris, 1899

T he emerald from Madame Thérèse, given as a wedding gift
almost two years earlier, is a gaudy thing, but Amélie has
grown to love it. She feels a tingle of decadence wearing it, as if she
were a woman with secrets that nobody could fathom. Neverthe-
less, Amélie had it valued by a pawnbroker when she and Henri
first returned to Paris; she knew it could fetch a hefty price.
Madame Thérèse hadn't been exaggerating – it could cover the
Matisses' living expenses for a long time. She has been saving it for
a rainy day, and now, that day is upon them.

Amélie takes it to the same pawnbroker the following morning.
It's a cold winter, in the run-up to the end of the year. The shop is in
a salubrious part of the capital, it's clean and orderly, and the broker
is a smartly dressed man; he examines the gem again with a loupe
hanging from a chain around his neck. Even so, she isn't prepared to
trust him completely, no matter how respectable the environment.

Amélie looks at the rows of brooches, charms, crucifixes and
signet rings. All these objects have personal value, and yet were
handed over in desperation. Has the money received by the sellers
made any difference, she wonders, and if so, for how long?

The broker pinches his lips before offering less for it than he did

originally. 'The demand for fine gemstones has declined considerably, even at this time of year,' he says.

Amélie holds firm. She won't take less than she needs. She points
out the quality of the setting and the stone. She isn't going to be
fobbed off with talk of internal flaws and cloudiness when there is
nothing of the sort. She doesn't want to part with the ring, but she
knows now isn't the time for sentimentality. And she doesn't have
to be without it for long. That's the point of pawning an item – it
can be redeemed once funds are available. With a little luck – a
keen investor seeing her husband's potential, or the boutique finally
being ready and turning a profit – she'll return before the end of
the pledge to repay the sum and no one will be any the wiser.

After a standoff, the broker relents. He cannot honour the original quote, but he can see she has more knowledge than the
average housewife who walks through his doors, so he offers an
amount that comes close: five hundred francs. It's still a huge sum.
She agrees, determined to place the ring back on her finger in the
coming year. Before he counts out the cash, the broker fills out a
contract explaining the rate of interest and giving her a billet
which will allow her to return and reclaim it. She tucks it away in
her purse with satisfaction.

～

An hour later, Amélie enters a shop with an envelope of cash. She
takes a breath.

'I'm here for the painting by Monsieur Cézanne,' she says to an
elderly man who is reading the daily journal, the pages spread out
neatly across the counter.

The owner raises his eyebrows in surprise. He takes a moment
to get to his feet before heading to the window. He returns carrying a small artwork. He smiles proudly at it. 'An unusual piece, but
not unappealing to the appreciative eye.'

It's the first time she has seen it: the painting her husband has hardly stopped talking about. She's surprised and a little embarrassed to be faced with three naked figures, each in a different position around a bathing spot, the trees forming a natural arch above them.

It's not exactly what she imagined it might be.

What is it about this artwork that has captured Henri's enthusiasm so fully?

Amélie looks more closely. It's a fine work, she supposes, of muted blues and greens. She certainly appreciates the quality of the brushstrokes. Her eyes are pulled to the three bodies, looking divine in their nudity, stripped of artifice.

Amélie shifts her view. 'It's a gift for my husband,' she ventures. Five hundred francs suddenly feels like an awful lot of money to hand over.

The gentleman affects a bow.

'You have exquisite taste. And your husband is a very lucky man,' he adds.

Amélie thinks of Camille and what that amount would mean to a woman like her. She thinks of Marguerite, and how the child's scraped knees poke out beneath threadbare fabric. This money could make a world of difference to a great number of people. Or it could be an investment in one man whose vision, she believes, could potentially lead to a shift in perception for a whole generation. Amélie knows this is ambitious thinking. But all she can do is to throw her full weight into believing in Henri, and let that inspire him.

'He has suffered a streak of rather bad luck recently,' Amélie admits. 'But with the help of this artwork, I hope to see his luck reversed.'

꙳

At home, Henri is roughly cutting cheese, and has opened one of the jars of pickles that her mother preserves and sends in batches each year. He looks up as she enters their home, offers a warm greeting. In her satchel is the small painting, wrapped carefully. Amélie places the bag down, propping it against the wall as she removes her shoes.

'Don't make any unnecessary noise,' he says. 'Jean has only just succumbed to sleep.'

The smell of pickling juice is overwhelming at this stage in her second pregnancy and she goes to open the window, edging around the frame of her husband's easel. Her bare fingers flutter at the latch, and she experiences a shock that the emerald is no longer there.

Amélie keeps her back turned to her husband, as she knows she won't be able to keep the look of nervous excitement off her face. If he were to make eye contact, he'd know something was amiss, which would ruin the surprise. She wants to reveal the painting properly, with the appropriate degree of gravitas. She busies herself tidying the area by the window to calm her eager anticipation and give Henri time to finish lunch.

She picks up Jean's stiff dungarees, which have dried on the sill, and three pairs of brown socks, freshly washed, which she should darn as the toes are wearing thin. She takes them to their bedroom. When she comes out, Henri is holding the wrapped painting in one hand, a gherkin in the other, the juices running down his wrist. She watches as he pops the last bite in his mouth, wiping a hand on his trousers, before unfolding the first layer of paper.

'What's this?' he asks, raising his eyes to her.

She freezes. He sees the look and turns his attention back to the package, removing another layer. Before she has a chance to say anything, he's holding the artwork in his hands, stupefaction rippling across his face.

'Don't be angry,' she says, stepping towards him.

Henri sucks in a breath. 'But how did you get it?' he asks, turning it over. 'Did you steal it? You didn't forfeit our unborn child to pay for it, did you?' The lilt of his voice suggests he's teasing her, but she can hear the nervousness as his mind races to puzzle the pieces together. 'It would have cost a fortune,' he says slowly, examining the three bathers closely, then holding it at a distance. 'A fortune,' he repeats, looking at Amélie.

It takes a moment, but his eyes drop to her fingers, bare except for her wedding ring.

'Do you know what this means to me?' he breathes.

'I have an inkling,' she replies. She feels a little bashful before him.

'I can't believe I'm holding a work by Cézanne.'

'Well, it belongs to you now,' she adds simply.

Henri passes the painting to his wife, recognizing the state of his hands, rushing to the sink. As the tap runs, she cleans the frame with the hem of her skirt and holds the painting to the light. It looks better here, in their home, than it did in the dusty shop. Amélie can't take her eyes from the substantial thighs and wide bare bottom of the figure on the left. She wonders about the women who modelled for this painting – and just how she might feel about another woman looking at a similar depiction of her own flesh.

To Amélie's knowledge, Henri has never painted a nude before, and she wonders if this will inspire him. The idea tickles her, along with the realization that she may have unwittingly implicated herself as his future model. He'd have to find a way to make her unrecognizable, so that any viewer would be unaware of her identity. She has no intention of displaying her nakedness to gallery-goers in Paris and beyond.

Henri returns and she passes him the painting.

'My exceptional wife, thank you. From the bottom of my heart,' he says, kissing her.

'It's nothing less than you deserve,' Amélie says. 'Let it propel you. What you see in that artwork must become a talisman for your future as an artist. Don't fail me now.' She smiles. 'Or them,' she adds, eyes on the nudes.

Henri has been working on a self-portrait recently – him at his easel with his shirtsleeves rolled up. It's an oil painting that disquiets Amélie, for its use of sombre colours, and his dead eyes depicted by daubs of black paint. It hints at his disappointments, his turmoil.

She wonders if he'll soon sell some of his work, so that she can get the emerald back.

At his wife's words, his eyes crinkle and the tenderness of his kisses develops intensity. He places the painting reverently on the sideboard, then takes her hand.

9

Paris, 1900

In the summer, the Matisses travel to Vosves – a rural hamlet an hour south of Paris, near the banks of the Seine and the forest of Fontainebleau – to spend a week with Amélie's family, who are in charge of the palatial eighteenth-century Humbert residence, Château des Vives-Eaux. It's a beautiful four-storey castle, with more rooms than Amélie can count. Her mother and father spend most of the summer here, a perk of their employment. As a child, she explored the flower gardens, ancient woods, rivers and hidden waterfalls. Berthe once got locked in the orangery – which had nothing to do with her older sister – until her parents picked the lock.

Thérèse and Frédéric are usually in attendance for days at a time, arriving with little announcement, bearing crates of wine, with an entourage of servants and brusque orders.

The weather today is wet but warm, a fertile heat that promises thunderstorms. The air is thick with the scent of damp grass, cut in a hurry, and the smell transports Amélie to childhood. The family sit in the manicured garden to eat, red petals falling in clusters like blood-spill. Later in the week, Berthe – who's working hard as a junior schoolmistress, specializing in history and

French – will visit for three days. She has written to say she's excited to see her sister and meet her latest nephew. Not long ago, Amélie gave birth to her second child – another boy, Pierre. The birth was long and painful, and she lost a great deal of blood, so she's grateful for every moment's help from her family.

Henri, too, has executed a coup by convincing Camille to let them have Marguerite over the summer – supposedly to give her a break while she makes ends meet. In reality, he's concerned, as his daughter has been increasingly unwell. Henri believes that time in their care will restore her enough to get her through another winter. She's taller than the last time Amélie saw her, the roundness of her face sharpening as she grows. Amélie tries to encourage the girl out of her silences, striking up conversations that might engage a soon-to-be six-year-old, buying trinkets and toys to keep her entertained. But Marguerite still can't hold a pencil properly, Amélie notices, when she lays out sheets of Henri's drawing paper to practise her cursive. Has she even received the most rudimentary lessons at school, she asks her husband? He says yes quite categorically, but she can tell he's not so sure. And that cough of hers never diminishes, despite Amélie's efforts. It's as if the child has a bag of nails rattling in her chest.

'What time will the Humberts arrive?' Amélie asks her mother, noticing the quickening choreography of the staff. She must get Jean's clothes laundered, rather than let him roam in dungarees that are muddy at the knees from his constant tripping.

She almost misses it, but her mother and father exchange a low-lidded glance.

Amélie is instantly alert. 'Papa?' She knows her father can't tell a lie.

Her mother moves uncomfortably in her chair, adjusts her straw hat.

'They'll be arriving this afternoon and I expect they'll be staying for the rest of the summer,' her mother says. 'Madame Thérèse has been unwell, I'm told, and they need to be out of the city, to avoid further stress.'

Catherine deliberately sets her mouth to make clear the conversation is over.

'Unwell in what capacity?' Amélie pushes. She watches Henri lead Jean down to the Great Lake, which is filled with curiosities such as open-mouthed carp and water beetles. She cradles Pierre and enjoys the peacefulness of a sleeping baby.

Her mother rolls her eyes in frustration, but it's their fault that Amélie has learned to question everything. They can't start complaining now.

'I might have known her for forty years, but she only confides in me when it suits her.'

'If it was anything serious, she'd have told you, surely?' Amélie says.

'She needs rest. And here, away from the city, is the best place for her to do that.'

Amélie senses that there's more going on than she's being told. She glances at Marguerite, who is lying on her tummy on the grass, her feet kicking the air as she draws. She's wearing new socks topped with frilly lace. It never appears as if the child is listening, lost in a world of her own, but there's also a feeling that she doesn't miss a single utterance.

'Thérèse Humbert is under no obligation to tell me, or you, anything,' her mother continues. 'Despite appearances, Thérèse is a private, guarded woman. I know it seems she shares secrets haphazardly, her own included. But she plays her cards close to her chest.'

Amélie isn't surprised at her mother's revelations. She has thought as much about Thérèse over the years, but everyone always seems so enamoured with the couple, and they occupy positions of such power that people gravitate towards them without question.

'Father, you must have your suspicions about what's going on?' Amélie probes.

'Don't ask me,' Armand replies. 'Noticing the truth is above my salary.' She looks at him in disbelief. Her father holds his tongue for three solid seconds before he breaks. 'I do suspect there's something serious afoot,' he can't resist adding.

Her mother shoots him a scolding glance.

Amélie sits forward, and the baby grumbles. 'What have you heard?'

'Nothing that would stand up in a court of law.'

'It'd be a scandal if they were to separate,' Amélie replies, jumping to conclusions.

'Oh, it's nothing like that,' Catherine snaps, brushing pollen off her pale-lilac summer dress. 'If anything, I believe the matter is of a financial nature,' she says, relinquishing some of her defences.

'But they're the wealthiest people in France!' Amélie scoffs.

'They certainly like to give that impression,' Armand replies.

Amélie looks between her parents. 'Maman,' she says. 'Surely those rumours are born of jealousy? People cannot stand the wealthy, the way they flaunt their money and forget their privilege. Thérèse and Frédéric are unconventional, but they always manage to charm the right people. You've said it before: they're untouchable.'

'You might be right,' her mother says, taking the baby from her. 'But all I'm saying is that things aren't always as they seem. And it would serve us all well never to forget that.'

At that moment, little Marguerite catches Amélie's attention. The child's eyes dart to the chateau, seconds before the crunch of gravel is heard. Moments later, Thérèse and Frédéric appear, a harried retinue of staff following obediently. Catherine and Armand jump up, her mother brushing down her skirts, her father shuffling into motion.

Henri returns from the lake with Jean. Their son is smiling but soaked from the waist down. 'He took a tumble,' her husband says, apologetically.

Children so often drag a person away from the company of adults and intelligent conversation, which frustrates her as a mother, but in this moment Amélie is relieved to have an excuse to get out of the way for a short while. She scoops up her eldest son.

'I'll say hello, then change Jean into dry clothes,' she says as the Humberts approach. The couple appear tired, stretched. Amélie wonders if, over the coming days, there'll be further hints of scandal. But knowing Thérèse, their stay will be perfectly composed.

After greeting them, she walks towards the house, Marguerite chasing after her, wanting to help with her brother. Amélie watches as her husband reaches out to shake hands with Frédéric. So often, Henri isn't comfortable with those who've reached the upper echelons of wealth and society. He's 'a merchant's son, from the rough north', he likes to tease, affecting the thick accent of those who live near the Belgian border. And yet, here he is, on this summer's day, enjoying the trappings of chateau life, being handed a glass of champagne by a waiter carrying a silver tray – from a vintage bottle, no doubt, selected from the Humberts' extensive cellar – with their elaborate eight-course supper still several hours away.

Amélie laughs at the foolishness of her thinking. Her husband will be hating every second, desperate to get back to his cramped studio, and to his great punishing mistress – art.

⤳

Days later, when they arrive back in Paris, Amélie congratulates herself on successfully reaching the front door of their apartment building. It has been one of those days. Jean woke up crotchety, his gums bright red, Marguerite was sick on the train all over her clean dress, and Pierre can't seem to keep his milk down. To top it off, Henri was insufferably hungry, because he drank too much last night and missed breakfast in favour of sleeping another hour. Her parents exchanged wry glances when he failed to appear. She suspects it's because her father also drank too much but was forced from his bed to the table for appearances' sake. Now Amélie realizes she has left Jean's treasured wooden toy horse back at the chateau. He won't settle until it's in his hands again. It's another thing for the growing list in her mind.

Once inside the building, Amélie sees that fresh correspondence has been delivered. There's a letter for her husband, and what could be demands for payment, as well as a large package tied in string, with Amélie's name written across it in a shaky hand.

Amélie's curiosity grabs her, and she stops in the middle of the stairwell.

'You go on up,' she says to Henri, passing him Jean's hand and baby Pierre. She shoos Marguerite after her father; the little girl's eyes stare back down the stairs unnervingly.

Amélie waits until she can't hear their footsteps any more, before tearing open the brown paper, pulling the string away in the process. She lowers herself to sit on the step.

She stares at the contents for a few seconds, trying to make sense of what she sees.

On the top of the bundle, there's a photograph of Camille, wearing a silk shirt, pearls. She's looking into the distance, a hint of a smile on her lips. Amélie turns the photo over.

Written in neat cursive are the month and year, followed by the words: *My darling Marguerite, with all my love. I pray you never forget me. Forever yours, your mother.*

Amélie puts the photograph to one side, an uneasy knot forming in her stomach. She shakes out the largest of the items and a wide knitted blanket unfurls, in burgundy. Amélie brings it to her nose; it carries the faint scent of hawthorn – the flower that symbolizes love, protection and new beginnings. Wrapped inside is a letter to Amélie. She opens it.

I relinquish my rights as Marguerite's mother. I'm no longer in Paris, and do not intend to return. You have your wish: my daughter. You'll be a better mother to her than the world has allowed me to be. I do not expect to see her again. Nothing could cause me greater grief. There will never be a day when I don't think of her. Take good care of my little flower.

Amélie's eyes linger on the woman in the photograph. She's sorry it has come to this, even if it is the best outcome for Marguerite. Camille has sacrificed herself and behaved with great dignity.

Mustering her courage, Amélie takes the stairs, giving herself a few moments to regain her composure before she enters the same space as her family, her wonderful little family, whom she'll never take for granted – and never abandon, come what may.

10

A year later, Marguerite has become central to Matisse family life. She dotes on her father, sitting in his studio silently as he works. She has an intuitive calm. Henri hardly notices she's there. Every day, Amélie, too, bonds further with Marguerite as if she were her own. The child comes to sleep between them when she cries out in the night after an unsettling dream, the small boys in crates on either side of the bed. The girl is transfixed by her baby brothers, treating them gently, helping to feed and soothe the youngest, gently batting away any attempts at rough play from Jean. Marguerite is thriving and has grasped her alphabet and grammar. She's coddled and chided, as any daughter would be. The girl never mentions her mother, and Amélie senses it's out of fear that if she shows any sentiment in that regard, Camille might be conjured back, and she'll be taken away from her father.

⤺

In summer, Henri and Amélie travel to Bohain for a wedding. Auguste, her husband's younger brother, is getting married to the daughter of a grain merchant from Saint-Quentin. Henri is honoured to stand as best man, even if the dynamics within the family are complicated. Their parents have recently made the decision to retire, and Auguste has offered, in the absence of any display of willingness on the part of the elder son, to take over the Matisse seed store. Henri can't help but feel relief as well as shame that his younger brother is taking on the responsibility, a task that should rightfully have fallen on his own shoulders.

It will be the first time he and Amélie have attended a wedding together, aside from their own, and the one they met at nearly four years ago. Amélie tells Henri that he must not harass the waiters this time in a bid to hoard an excessive stash of wine. They'll only be away for one night and, bearing in mind Marguerite's travel sickness, they decide to leave the children at home. Anette, a kindly woman in her sixties who has much experience and an excess of patience, will look after Marguerite, Pierre and Jean.

Anette is one of those women Amélie envies, who never seems to tire of children and has limitless energy for their noisy games, unrelenting questions and sticky fingers. Amélie supposes Anette never hears a buzzing in her ears, experiences frayed nerves, or has to lie down in a darkened room when it all gets too much. Not that there's much noise from Marguerite, who's as contained as a church mouse. Jean and Pierre, however, are finding their lungs. Pierre, at one year old, is a bad sleeper, like his father, and vocal when he's hungry. Jean is subdued with a tummy bug right now. Anette assures her she'll keep an eye on him, make sure he regains his appetite before his maman returns.

The morning after the wedding, Henri spends time with his father at the seed shop. His father, Émile, wants to show him the cash register that he bought to help with transactions, even though he's about to retire. It should help Auguste, who's not the best with arithmetic, he confides. It's a large, imposing contraption and Amélie suspects Monsieur Matisse just wants to show it off.

She spends the time with Henri's mother, Anna. They visit the tearooms, where Amélie receives the gossip and is quietly thrilled to have earned these confidences.

As the plates are being cleared, Henri rushes in. His mother halts her sentence, her latest anecdote half formed. She stands when she notices the urgency on his face. 'What is it?'

'It's Marguerite,' Henri says, out of breath. 'Anette sent word. She has fallen ill.'

'That can't be possible,' Amélie says, trying to take in his words. The girl seemed fine when they left yesterday. Ever since Camille relinquished her daughter, the couple have taken great care of her, worrying over the white marks on her fingernails, the cloudiness coating her tongue. Amélie believed the sickliness that plagued her could be reversed.

'Anette sounded worried half to death.'

Henri's mother holds her hand to her mouth, all her jollity evaporated.

'We must get back to her right away,' Amélie says.

'We'll get you on the very next train,' Anna replies, reverting to her practical nature.

⟲

Under normal circumstances, on a train journey, Henri would enjoy taking in the views of the passing countryside, but today he's like a cocked pistol. At every station, he paces the compartment, cursing the delay. Amélie tries to reassure him that his daughter will be fine, but the child is such a fragile thing that her words don't carry conviction. She can't shake the knowledge that children who grow up in the poorest areas of Paris, as Marguerite did under Camille's care, often perish. Disease, infection, pollution and paltry meals all play a part. They're doing their best by Marguerite, but still, she is as thin as a rake.

When they arrive back at the apartment by the Seine, Henri dashes up the stairs. Anette is there, pressing a cold compress to the girl's forehead. She tells the couple that Jean and Pierre are being looked after by her sister next door. Marguerite looks worse than Amélie could have imagined. Anette has wrapped her in blankets and shawls, including the burgundy one sent by Camille, but it's clear that Marguerite can't get enough air, so Amélie strips them off.

'She's burning up,' she says to Henri, who's kneeling by his daughter's side.

'She has a frightful temperature,' the older woman says. 'The fever started in the night, and the child was so weak by morning that I sent word very first thing. I've done everything I can,' she adds, rubbing her knuckles against her palm as she speaks.

'My darling girl,' Henri says.

Marguerite turns her head at the sound of her father's voice and tries to speak.

'Can't get her words out. Poor soldier,' Anette worries. 'She's had a spoonful of medicine every few hours.' There's a bottle at the bedside. 'It hasn't broken the fever.'

'We must send for a doctor, straight away,' Amélie instructs. She moves to the door.

'I'll go,' Henri says. He kisses Marguerite's head. There's electric fear in his eyes.

Amélie makes the child comfortable, cleaning her frail body with a cool cloth and ointment, brushing her dark hair out and plaiting it neatly. She reads a story, but Marguerite doesn't stir. The only sign of life is her chest rising and falling like a baby bird's, and a rattle that seems to get more menacing with every breath.

It takes a long time, and when her husband and the doctor

return, the child's skin has taken on the faintest tinge of blue. Amélie and Anette sit in silence on either side of the bed.

'This is Marguerite Matisse?' the doctor asks as he enters. Amélie nods. The doctor places his bag down and immediately takes the girl's wrist, counting the pulse. Anette is massaging the girl's feet, an old wives' remedy to ward off illness.

Marguerite's chest is taut, her neck swollen, the glands on her throat protruding.

'How long has she been exhibiting signs of respiratory distress?' the doctor asks.

'She was fine when we left yesterday,' Henri replies.

'It began as a sniffle,' Anette adds. 'The medicine seemed to help at first.'

'Does she normally have breathing problems?'

'She has a cough,' Amélie says. 'But she's never struggled to catch her breath.'

The doctor opens his satchel and takes out a stethoscope. He places the gleaming circular disk on Marguerite's body, listening more carefully.

'My professional opinion is that your daughter is suffering from an acute case of diphtheria or possibly croup,' he decides, a downward turn to his mouth. He repositions the instrument as he speaks. 'Such an infection can take hold of the lungs quickly and affect the airways, causing inflammation. The priority now is making sure she can breathe.'

In response, Marguerite tries to take a deep breath, but it seems to shudder up from her chest and she trembles with the effort. The doctor sits back on his heels, shaking his head as he listens to her sounds. The tiniest amount of air escapes her lips.

'Is she in pain, doctor?' Henri asks.

Marguerite's eyes roll back. She was weak before but now her whole body goes slack.

'What's happening?' Henri demands, as the doctor attends to the patient with urgency.

'She can't breathe,' the doctor replies. He fumbles in his satchel. In doing so, he knocks over the medicine bottle, and it breaks.

'Do something! You must be able to do something.' Henri braces.

Everyone around her is losing their mind, and Amélie must keep her own.

'Can we not breathe for her?' she asks, uncertain as to the viability of such a thing. The doctor considers it. He pinches the child's nose and places his mouth to hers, breathing deeply, to mimic her own breath. Marguerite's chest rises slightly, but she's unconscious. Amélie watches him, the position of his mouth and hands.

'Let me do that,' she offers.

The doctor relinquishes his spot to Amélie, and searches in his bag once again.

'It's too late for the oral administration of drugs,' he says. 'I could inject her with an anti-inflammatory, but it could take several minutes to work and we don't have that time.'

Henri holds a hand to his mouth, his eyes fixed on his daughter.

Amélie blows into the girl's mouth, but the air she's pushing into her is met with total resistance. The child's airway is utterly closed.

'I can't fail her; I promised Camille she'd thrive,' her husband laments.

'Please do something!' Amélie will not accept the girl's death. Not on her watch. After everything she went through with Camille, convincing the woman this path was for the best, Amélie would never be able to forgive herself if the child perished under her care.

Each of them looks at the other desperately.

'You have to do something, doctor,' Amélie pleads.

The doctor straightens himself, and in his hand she notices the gleam of a scalpel.

'Monsieur Matisse, do you give permission for me to go ahead with an emergency tracheotomy?' Henri seems unable to understand the implications. The doctor explains. 'I need to cut your daughter's throat to open up the airway. Do I have your permission?'

There's not much time; Marguerite is getting weaker by the second.

Henri closes his eyes.

'Is it safe?' he asks, desperately.

'It's a gamble,' the doctor admits. 'I can't promise it's not without risk.'

Henri looks to his wife. She has never seen him so terrified, and it rips her heart. If they go ahead with this and it fails – one wrong move of the scalpel, one degree of miscalculation – Marguerite will die. But if they are not brave enough to try, she will certainly die anyway. She looks at her husband and offers him the smallest nod, to say, Yes, we must go ahead. It's impossible not to try.

'Whatever it takes, doctor,' Henri says. 'You have our permission.'

The doctor looks around. 'We need a firm surface if we're going to get this right.' Through the open door, into the next room, he spots the dining table. 'Clear it,' he instructs.

Henri picks up Marguerite, the girl's limbs limp, and whisks her to the table, which Anette has cleared. A jar of flowers tips over, the water spilling, as the doctor settles his patient. Marguerite's lips are turning blue. Henri paces. For a man who prides himself on his vision, his radical view of the world, at this moment he cannot look. The doctor instructs Amélie to hold Marguerite's arms. The edge of the scalpel reflects the cruel afternoon light.

It feels barbaric to hold a child down, but this is their only chance to save her.

'I need you to help keep her still as well,' the doctor tells Henri. Henri falls into place. He grips his daughter, his knuckles white.

Then the doctor positions the scalpel in the centre of Marguerite's throat. He hesitates for a moment, drawing his finger along the delicate machinery of her neck, until he has identified a tender spot, where the cartilage will be at its most pliable.

Amélie is so close that she can hear the words of prayer the doctor mutters.

He draws a breath, then pushes the sharp metal through the skin of the child's neck.

Marguerite's flesh quivers and blood bursts forth, air bubbling to the surface. Amelie intuitively decides that the girl will have to wear a ribbon, to hide the scar, in the future.

The doctor's hand shakes as he cleans the three-inch opening he has made, pushing in a small tube to facilitate airflow. Instinctively, the child pulls herself from their grip. Henri finds the strength to hold on, so the doctor can finish. Amélie tries to calm her with a hand to her forehead, whispering, until the girl slips once more into silence. Henri weeps. His daughter, dissected on the kitchen table, with crumbs from breakfast pressed into her elbows.

11

Paris, 1902

Amélie tries to shake off the nerves she is feeling ahead of her lunch today with Madame Thérèse. She hasn't seen the woman since that summer two years ago – when the champagne flowed and any cracks were papered over – but Thérèse sent word yesterday that she was keen to see Amélie urgently. Amélie was surprised by the summons, but pleased to accept. She's been trying to pin Thérèse down for months to finalize the opening date for the boutique. They have found a fashionable location and plan to open in a matter of weeks.

Today they're meeting at the Café de Flore. Amélie arrives early and mentions the Humbert name, for Thérèse has made the reservation. Is that a flicker of displeasure in the waiter's eye? Regardless, Amélie is shown to a pristine table out front, a prime position. Thérèse still clearly has influence; nothing has changed in that regard.

Amélie has brought her proposed guestlist – friends and family – and hopes Thérèse will be willing to invite all the most influential people she knows in Paris. It's unusual for her to be late, and Amélie has already finished one *café au lait* before she spots the woman's distinctive form crossing the road, her hand raised to stop the traffic.

Thérèse approaches the café and sits. She doesn't address Amélie. Flustered, she is rude to a waiter while ordering a strong espresso. She rubs a hand across the back of her neck.

'My dear, I'm mortified to have kept you waiting. I beg your forgiveness.'

'It's quite all right, Madame Thérèse,' Amélie replies, trying to defuse the tension.

Amélie wants to get down to business quickly. With Thérèse's help, she found the perfect location in the 9th arrondissement – between Montmartre and the city's department stores – and she and Henri spent three days painting the walls, inside and out, to get it ready. Amélie just needs to pull in some of Thérèse's glittering contacts to guarantee its success.

Thérèse offends her by not even glancing at the list. 'The ring,' she says. 'I'm terribly sorry to have to be so forthright, but I do need it back.' She says it with such a disarming smile, such easy charm, that Amélie misses her meaning the first time. 'Oh, my darling girl, I can see I've upset you. It was a gift, I know, I know.' Madame Thérèse's eyes settle on a spot above Amélie's head. 'I'm terribly sorry to inconvenience you. You know me – I wouldn't ask for it if the circumstances weren't exceptional. But needless to say, something quite unexpected has come up. I'm in the unfortunate position of needing to call in all my favours at once. I came to you as we have such a bond, do we not, such an understanding, that I knew you wouldn't mind. You never really liked it anyway,' she adds.

The woman checks her watch as she speaks. Amélie knows it's engraved with Thérèse's motto: *Je veux, j'aurai.* Whatever I want, I will have.

'Oh, Thérèse,' she replies, her cheeks reddening. 'I'm so sorry . . . I had no idea . . .'

'It's fine, dear child, no need to worry about me. Just hand it over.'

'It's more complicated than that. You see, Henri and I, we needed . . .'

'You've pawned it already?' Thérèse sighs. 'Which broker did you use? We can collect it. It's worth far more than they'll have given you.'

Amélie shifts in her seat while Thérèse knocks back the strong coffee, careless of its capacity to scald. She thinks of the pawn ticket she has carried with her for so long. She has already had to extend the pledge by paying some of the interest, and knows the recall number by heart. She and Henri have been saving to get the ring back before its absence is noticed. He has earned a couple of commissions, galvanized by the *Three Bathers* by Cézanne – a few more and they'll finally be able to pay off the full amount. But Madame Thérèse is already gesturing for the bill. She takes Amélie by the arm and before she realizes what's happening, they're marching down the street. With a tug of her heart, Amélie knows that any progress with the opening of her boutique just isn't on the cards.

The two women arrive together to collect the emerald, Amélie retrieving the frayed slip and pushing it across the counter. The money from this ring enabled her to give her husband the painting he'd admired for so long – a painting that has become a symbol of daring, their shared vision, the promise of their potential to turn adversity and chaos into success. Perhaps it was stupid to use the money for such a thing, but it seems to have worked.

Amélie stands beside Thérèse in the pawn shop as the clerk, not one she's seen before, looks at the number, checks it again, runs a finger down the ledger. He stops at the name MATISSE, and slides his finger across the columns.

He looks up in surprise, his eyes darting from Madame Thérèse to Amélie.

'This ticket, mesdames' – he licks his lips – 'is expired.'

Madame Thérèse stiffens beside her while Amélie cringes.

'But I renewed the pledge. The owner, your boss, he said . . .'

'He'd have made it clear,' the clerk says, his voice rising, 'that we'd only hold on to it for a certain amount of time, even if you did renew the pledge, after which we'd presume you had defaulted on the debt and the item would be put on display, for the purposes of sale.'

'I thought we had until the end of next month. I . . .'

The clerk is about to reply, but Madame Thérèse interrupts.

'Just find it, so we can resolve the matter,' she snaps.

'I'm very sorry, but the ring in question – I remember it well, it was so striking – was bought by an elderly gentleman for his lady friend just yesterday.' His forehead creases into an elaborate apology. 'I hope this won't be too much of an inconvenience.'

Madame Thérèse slams a small fist on to the counter.

'You have failed to understand,' she says, slipping a high-denomination banknote from the sleeve of her dress and pushing it across the counter. 'I will be back here in three hours and I expect to see that ring in your hand. Or the consequences will be dire.'

⌒

Amélie is not expecting to find her mother in tears when they meet one another on the steps of the Louvre later that day. She has been battling whether to confide in her about the encounter with Madame Thérèse, the way the woman belittled and berated the clerk when he insisted that it would not be possible to retrieve the ring – they had no way of tracing it, no record of who had bought it. Thérèse made such a scene that it reminded Amélie of the tantrums Jean and Pierre throw after not having slept or eaten enough. She was shocked that a grown woman could lose control in such a dramatic way.

But now is not a good time to bring it up. Her mother clearly has concerns of her own.

The Louvre, once a royal palace, now an art museum, bears down on them from all sides. It exudes a sense of grandeur that never goes out of style, and Amélie feels the weight of history on her shoulders. The gallery houses masterpieces by Leonardo da Vinci, Raphael, Rembrandt and other artists who've broken through the fog of history so their names will be remembered. The vast spaces inside are hardly ever busy and Amélie occasionally spends afternoons here, her children in tow, in intimate contemplation of the art. She dreams about the day her husband's own work might be on show here.

But today, the Louvre offers no such reprieve. Her mother dabs her cheeks with her sleeve, and tries to shrug away this uncharacteristic burst of emotion.

'It's nothing, darling. I'm tired, that's all. It's non-stop with the Humberts. They never rest and expect all of us to match their pace. Your father and I are exhausted.'

Amélie feels very uneasy all of a sudden. She gets the sense that something dangerous is brewing and she doesn't know how to stop it.

'Maman, you can tell me. Please. What's going on?'

'Oh, all those rumours two summers ago came to nothing,' Catherine replies as they enter the gallery. 'Thérèse reassured me. She reminded me that it's no use paying attention to them. Their rivals are out to discredit them. It's not the first time and it won't be the last. So don't worry, darling,' she says, taking in a landscape Amélie knows her husband would find unforgivably stuffy. 'There's nothing to worry about.'

'But if it's causing you this much stress, Maman, maybe it's time to look for another role, with a different employer. You've worked for the Humberts since I was a baby.'

'You said it yourself. I've worked for them my entire life. I can hardly stop now.'

Her mother turns from the artwork and there's pain etched across her features.

'Maman? You're scaring me. Please, tell me the truth,' Amélie says.

Catherine takes a deep breath, and seems to be considering the words she will use next. 'They have a safe,' she says eventually. 'One that has always been closely guarded.'

'I don't understand.'

Catherine glances around, to check if anyone might be listening.

'Just last week, Thérèse and Frédéric were served a notice,' she whispers. 'An investor is disgruntled. And now a judge has issued an order that their safe must be opened.'

Amélie doesn't understand why this is so significant, but it's clear from her mother's tone that it's a substantial decision.

'And how does that affect you and Papa?'

'The judge has demanded to inspect the documentation which promises that Thérèse will one day inherit this great fortune from her uncle in America. There are rumours – and I really shouldn't be saying this, I feel so disloyal . . . but there are rumours it doesn't exist.'

'What doesn't? The will? The fortune?' Amélie asks.

'Any of it,' her mother replies.

'But that would mean . . . ? All the credit they've been given. They couldn't pay it back.'

'That's the point. They're calling her a fraudster, a liar, a thief. The Humberts have many creditors,' her mother continues. 'Hundreds of them all through France, people who've lent them a great deal of money. They're understandably nervous. They fear their money won't be repaid, so they're all asking for it back.

Demanding it, making threats. Of course, it couldn't all be repaid immediately, even if Thérèse is telling the truth and she is due to inherit a fortune one day. So she's doing what she can to keep them at bay. If she can reassure everyone that there's nothing to worry about, there's a good chance it will all blow over.'

Amélie thinks about the emerald, demanded with such force.

'And what if she can't?' She knows trust is fragile and fleeting, and once it is breached, the whole structure may crumble. The trust the Humberts have built an empire upon is locked in their safe. Which must now be opened.

Catherine bows her head.

'It would be a disaster. For all of us,' she admits.

'I'm sure Thérèse has everything under control,' Amélie says. But she isn't so sure.

'We'll find out tomorrow, when the safe is opened,' her mother replies, turning her attention back to the artwork. 'One way or another, all will be revealed.'

12

E lectric whispers whip through the crowd, as people jostle and
gossip while they wait for the moment for which they've
massed: the unlocking of the Humbert safe. The judge's order to
open it was reported, with some glee, in *Le Figaro*, accompanied
by lewd caricatures of Thérèse and Frédéric. But still, Amélie is
astounded that so many people have taken the time to come to
this wealthy area of Paris solely to catch a glimpse of the proceed-
ings. She hadn't expected that the road would be closed, nor that
bespectacled journalists would line the street, pens poised, impatient for a glimpse of her mother and father's employers.

Do people suppose they'll see the documents with their own
eyes? Do they imagine the turn of the key, the safe's old hinges
squeaking and straining, sunlight cast inside for the first time in
decades? She marvels at the nature of humans, so keen to be part
of a spectacle.

Amélie and her father push through the thickening throng
towards the main door, which is guarded by the prefect of police.
He holds up a hand as they approach, an ironic smile on his face
that says, Come no further. She's unsettled by the unexpected
demands of navigating this situation. And her father will need a

fresh shirt by lunchtime, if he's not to insult those in attendance at his next appointment. Henri wanted to come, too, but he offered to stay at home with Jean and Pierre, as well as Marguerite, who is still tender after her operation. Her voice has returned, and the wound is healing as well as can be expected, but she's nervous and clings to her father much of the time.

Amélie has had her doubts about Thérèse, but she knows it's no good jumping to conclusions before evidence proves things one way or another. Her father always says there's no pride to be found in being part of a braying crowd. She's willing to uphold that belief, and let the couple prove to the world that what they've always said is true. After all, her parents are decent people, with integrity, and they've pledged a good part of their lives to the couple.

Amélie's father approaches the prefect and talks to him quietly. After a moment, the man steps aside and gestures that they can pass through the heavy doorway to the mansion. Inside, they're enveloped in a hush, the thick walls insulating them from the noise outside. Amélie feels her heartbeat calm. The house on Avenue de la Grande Armée, which everyone refers to as *le chateau*, has become a familiar place to the Parayres over the years. The hallway is larger than Amélie and Henri's apartment. She and her father climb the staircase to the reception room, which has entertained politicians, priests and ministers over the years.

But Thérèse and her husband are not there.

It feels to Amélie as if it's all part of the performance. This is what Thérèse does best: this grand delivery, executed with the panache of a magician, full of hyperbole and sleight of hand. She always entertains. And her absence in this moment is the biggest spectacle of all.

'They must be running late.' Her father looks at his watch. It's five past the hour. Frédéric said to meet at ten. He gives the impression of being a man who values punctuality, but it's his wife who's dramatically insistent on being early.

There's a rise in volume from the crowd outside. This must be them.

But when the door swings open, it's not the Humberts who appear, but the Procureur de la République, dressed in his ceremonial red gown, trimmed with ermine and adorned with heavy medals. The man looks equally surprised to see them.

'And you are?' he asks. He carries a leather holdall, and places it on the floor, removing a handkerchief from his pocket and wiping his brow.

'Armand Parayre, sir. I work closely with the Humberts. This is my daughter.'

'Very well. Would you do me the trouble of calling them down for me? That sharp-tongued man outside is insisting we conclude our operations here as quickly as possible, so the crowds will have reason to disperse.'

'We're afraid they're not here, sir,' her father replies.

The procureur taps his watch. 'Monsieur Humbert assured me there'd be no delay.'

'I've no doubt they'll arrive,' Armand replies respectfully. 'Any moment now.'

The man looks at him with curiosity, as if he were dealing with an imbecile.

'You can be certain of that, can you? You are willing to vouch for these people?'

'I'd pledge my life on their honour,' Armand replies.

Amélie looks towards the door, willing the couple to step through it. They'll be pushing through the crowds, Thérèse's impatience flaring, her face shining at the drama of it, Frédéric bristling at all the noise.

'There are hundreds of people out there,' the procureur says, 'and there'll be more with every passing minute.'

There's another great swell of noise, and the grand portal lurches open.

Amélie finds she's holding her breath, but it's her mother who appears.

'And may I ask who you are?' the procureur says.

'Madame Parayre. I run the Humbert household.'

Her mother looks around at the stern faces. 'Did I miss it?'

Amélie's father clears his throat, and the sound seems to echo.

'The Humberts are not here,' the procureur says. 'They're nowhere to be found.'

'Thérèse wouldn't miss this,' Catherine says. 'She told me as much this morning.'

'You saw her?'

'I dropped off some money she'd requested,' she explains.

'And?' the procureur demands.

'And . . . I had some errands to run, as did she. She told me she'd meet me here.'

'There was nothing out of the ordinary?'

Catherine processes her memories of the morning's encounter. 'She took the money – it was a large amount, but I didn't think too much of it. She was well dressed, wearing a large hat and most of her jewels, but there's nothing untoward about that. Frédéric was in the car already, and Thérèse got in while I was there. They said they'd see me in an hour, then drove away. I had no doubt they'd be here.' Her mother shifts under the watch of the procureur's gaze. 'They wouldn't abscond. That's not their style.'

Amélie feels sick. Why does all of this feel like a trap?

'Do you have a key for the safe?' the procureur asks.

'I certainly don't,' Catherine says. 'Thérèse guards the key closely; it's upon her own body at all times. But I can take you to it.'

The four of them pass the great studio, stuffed with furnishings upholstered in silk, statues in bronze and marble and Renaissance carvings. They pass the billiard room, where much of Parisian social life takes place. Three successive presidents of the republic and at least five prime ministers have been personal friends of Madame Humbert.

Catherine leads the group to the third floor, an area of the mansion that's forbidden to everyday guests. Amélie's mother is granted access once a week to clean and polish the safe, but has only once seen inside it, when an important creditor demanded reassurance and was mollified by a momentary glimpse of the interior, full of thick bundles and sealed envelopes.

Amélie's mother unlocks the door to the room and, with reverence, approaches the safe.

'What is it we hope to find inside?' Amélie asks, trying to mask her nerves.

'Inside will be everything or nothing. Everything Thérèse has, everything we believe, is built on the fact that the safe carries what she says it does. The will. Her inheritance.'

They each stare at the cold metal box unwilling to reveal its secrets.

⌣

Over the next hours, not a thread of the Humberts can be found. The procureur sends for a locksmith, the best in Paris – a man who can work fast and under pressure. Amélie's father wants to leave to look for his employers himself, but the procureur forbids him.

'If any of you step outside this door, you'll be arrested,' the procureur says.

'I must send word to my husband,' Amélie says, writing down their address.

'There's been a mistake,' her mother repeats.

Her father is staring – a stern, calculating look in his eyes.

The locksmith arrives. The safe can't be cracked in the confined attic space, so it's moved to the street. The crowds must be pushed back and cordoned off, away from the action.

Then the locksmith gets to work, sparks flying as he hammers and drills through metal.

Henri arrives, perturbed when he sees what's under way. The children are safe with Anette, he reassures her. 'But the bonds,' he says, after she explains the situation. 'Thérèse would never . . . Her father-in-law was the Minister of Justice – that would mean . . .'

Amélie knows what he's thinking. Her mind has conjured those same thoughts. Has she deceived them all?

The locksmith downs his tools, removes his glasses and wipes an arm across his forehead. After a second's rest, he turns to the procureur with a nod. The safe is ready to open. Its door is ceremoniously removed, and everyone sways closer, louder.

The procureur places his pale hands inside.

He brings out a wad of paper.

Amélie hears her father say, his words bright with relief: 'The documents were there all along!'

But when the procureur releases the edge, it unfolds to reveal a broadsheet newspaper, the kind that was in circulation twenty years ago.

The procureur puts his hand inside once more, patting around, careful not to miss the dustiest corner. He then pulls out two small objects. 'There seems to be . . .' he announces, puzzled. 'An old coin, from Italy perhaps, and . . .' He inspects it closely. 'A trouser button?'

Does the will not exist? Or have they fled with it? Either way, it makes them look guilty.

The crowd erupts in jeers and threats.

'It's the swindle of the century,' someone shouts, and the phrase is repeated.

The procureur is furious. 'For the very last time, we've fallen for the Humberts' lies. I hereby issue a warrant for their arrest, effective immediately.'

The guillotine has fallen. Amélie looks at her parents and husband, each one weighing the cost of their proximity to this unfolding scandal. They understand instinctively that without the presence of the guilty party, there's only one place blame will fall: at their door.

13

Paris, 1902

The following months take a huge toll on Amélie and her family. They've tried to continue as normal – Henri pushing on with his commissions, even if he's permanently distracted, Amélie finally opening the door to her cherished boutique, but with none of the celebration or satisfaction she'd once imagined. Still, it's solid, decent work that keeps her mind occupied and brings in just enough to help support them. It hasn't been the best timing to start a new business, but Amélie had to do something for herself. She's thirty years old, has two sons under the age of three, and there's also little Marguerite. To make matters worse, she suffers from crippling pain each month, which confines her to her bed for days at a time. It started after the birth of Pierre, although she blames the stress of the Humberts for exacerbating it.

Despite everyone's best efforts, the Humberts cannot be found. A deluge of tip-offs turns up little more than was discovered in the safe – a fistful of nothing. The Humberts' empire implodes. Investors large and small declare bankruptcy. Pensioners who've poured their life savings into Thérèse's ventures see their investments wiped out. Some of them, tragically, take their own lives. The ripples are felt up the political ladder, and resignations are tendered.

Public anger mounts, and without anyone to direct it towards, another target is found: Armand Parayre – the man who has been intimately involved in their business and life. Armand and Catherine leave Paris and head to stay with Berthe.

Anonymous letters arrive, *PARAYRE* scratched with malicious intent.

In the days before the end of the year, a firm knock lands on their door and interrupts breakfast. Armand stands, honey dripping off his knife, and opens it warily. There, he finds a dozen officers, their boots gleaming – the one at the front bearing a warrant for his arrest. Amélie's father is in handcuffs before Catherine and Berthe can put their cutlery down. Requests for an explanation, for leniency, are kicked between the pebbles. The women are powerless as Armand is led away, Catherine running after her husband with his shoes.

∽

Amélie receives the news from her sister immediately after the arrest – her father has been cuffed and is on his way by train to Paris for indefinite detention. She wants Henri to hold her, tell her everything will be all right, but he looks at her blankly. They are both astounded that Armand, a man who has always fought to expose lies and hypocrisy, a staunch advocate for truth, has been stripped of his liberty in an act that they know will crush his soul.

Amélie arrives at the station early, but the area is packed with people jostling to get a glimpse of her father. The place is horrible, with its grimy engines and the breath of angry humans. Then Amélie sees his familiar face; she takes in the missing jacket, how the cuffs of his shirt are unbuttoned. There's a defiant slant to his jaw, but still, she can hardly believe this diminished man is her father.

'Papa!' Amélie calls, but her words are drowned out by the braying crowd.

It takes her an hour to get to the police station after he's taken away in a van. When she arrives, she explains that she's Armand Parayre's daughter.

'Monsieur Armand is being processed, ahead of his trial.'

'Trial?' Amélie gawps.

The officer behind the desk can't be older than she is, but he asserts his authority like a baton. 'Your father is complicit in the greatest scandal in the history of France.'

Is it possible her father knew what was happening, that he was complicit in the Humberts' deception? No. She can't believe that for a moment.

'But you can't hold him without charge?' she says.

'Your father is charged with fraud and forgery,' he continues. 'Monsieur Armand faces a decade in prison if the court finds him guilty.'

Amélie is astonished. She could be forty before her father enters the world again. He wouldn't see his grandchildren grow up. How on earth would her mother cope?

'But he's innocent! He's as much a victim of the Humberts as anyone else.'

'Your father says the very same. He's refusing to eat until he's released.'

Her father, in a cell, on hunger strike! Once again, it feels as if everything is crashing down around them.

⤶

Day after day, her father refuses food. Amélie and Henri don't want to become further embroiled in this hurricane scandal. But they cannot watch Armand have the key thrown away without a fight.

'I'm loath to step back into the law again,' her husband admits. 'But it is what I trained for, before my head was turned by art. What better opportunity to put those wasted years to good use?'

He takes out his old textbooks, pores over them. He advises Amélie on what to say to the press, drafts letters that will form the basis of Armand's defence in court. He's looking for details that will crack the case, that can unilaterally prove that Amélie's father is innocent. It's not easy, but Henri never falters. Amélie, who has for so long offered Henri her support, now receives it.

Within three weeks, Armand is released from prison, all charges dropped.

Henri's confidence and expertise surely expedited matters. Amélie wonders if perhaps her husband had the makings of a great lawyer, after all.

14

Paris, 1905

Amélie, from her position on a chair in front of the canvas, marvels as colours are applied. She wears a wide-brimmed felt hat – her own ambitious design, one so large that it partly obscures her view. Her dress is dark and dour and her skin has taken on a greyish tint over the winter. She watches as her husband daubs his brush into a bright-pink paint on his palette rather than a pale wash to reflect her skin tone. It will certainly confront the viewer.

In the years since the Humbert disaster, the dust has settled and the shame of that period has transformed into a steady kind of silence. Henri's career has advanced at a reasonable pace. He earns an income, has reliable contacts, and a few commissions have started to land at his door, which has taken off some of the financial pressure. The scandal is rarely mentioned, not even within the privacy of their own home. One night, in a bar, a man threw a punch at Henri. Her husband ducked easily, got his coat and promptly left, backed by his friends André, Maurice and Raoul. But as the door swung behind him, it wasn't scathing words about the nature of his artworks that he heard shouted in his direction – which he'd come to expect – but that the man's parents had lost money in the Humbert affair and were suffering in their old age. Henri still worries that his name will be forever associated with it and tarnished.

One good development has been that last year Henri had his first major solo exhibition at a gallery owned by Ambroise Vollard. Amélie can't be sure, but she wonders if the invitation was offered to dampen the impact of the scandal on Henri and present him with something to get his teeth stuck into. Whatever the reason, she was grateful. Henri selected his best works from their honeymoon, and the positive reaction from people whose opinions he admires has given him the confidence to continue. As an artist, he's still subdued, but the fact he's picking up a trajectory that began a few years ago fills her with hope. He's ready to return to the south, he says, this time to a new place on the coast – Collioure, near Spain. He'll invite his friend André, with whom he shares a deepening vision.

In front of her, now, Henri spreads the paint over the canvas, his eyes flicking from the work to her, little jolts as he takes what he needs from the physicality of her. She's not sure what it is he's seeing, but the intensity is consuming. She has become used to modelling for her husband in this way, but the experience is always a challenge – discomforting, transformative. A theft of sorts. He captures a strength in her that she wants to see preserved. It succeeds in reminding her that, after all, she's a woman in charge of her own destiny.

Henri picks up a new tube of paint, examines the colour description, discards it and chooses another from his box. He gives a firm squeeze and fresh colour is ejected on to the palette: smooth and vibrant. Amélie is startled. She knows her husband is loath to use conventional colours, and she has seen him take pleasure from choosing more unusual ones in the past, but usually only small amounts, distributed with gentle brushstrokes. Now he covers the canvas with long streaks of heavy green – a colour she's not wearing, but which is full of vitality. The paint is still wet on the canvas when one of the studio assistants knocks on the door. The space belongs to a friend of Henri's and he can only use it occasionally. Her husband is ready for a dedicated space of his own, after painting at home for so long. Amélie is determined to find a way to make that happen soon.

'You have a visitor, monsieur,' the young woman says.

Amélie's husband drags his eyes away from his work.

'Monsieur Desvallières,' she adds, looking at the canvas.

Henri nods and, while she fetches the visitor, he wipes his hands on a rag and says that Amélie must not move a muscle. 'I presumed George had forgotten.'

'Do I know him?' Amélie asks, resisting the temptation to adjust the angle of her hat.

'I'm sure you've met? We studied together at des Beaux-Arts. I admire his art, even if it is too absorbed by religious sentiment for my liking. Don't tell him I said that,' he adds. 'You'll remember, he helped set up the Salon d'Automne, to exhibit works rejected by the formal Salon. He'll be here to offer me work hanging pictures. I'm too exhausted by the politics of it to get involved.'

Footsteps can be heard approaching and the door creaks open. George – a thin-faced man with a generous moustache, a red cravat tied in a flourish around his neck – steps into the room, and holds his hand out to Henri. He's about to leap into all the usual greetings, when his eyes fall on the work before him. Amélie watches as he looks from the woman in the painting, to her, searching to match the reality to the image.

'Henri,' he says. 'What is this?'

'It's a painting of my wife,' he replies. 'You've met Madame Matisse?'

'It's . . .' George pauses, trying to pluck the right words from the air around him.

'It's not yet finished,' Henri replies. 'Amélie is a generous model. Still, it could take me another three months.'

'You have to submit it to the Salon d'Automne.'

Henri looks at his friend. 'Come now, don't tease me, George,' he scoffs.

'But those colours, that face. This portrait demands to be seen.'

Amélie feels a flicker of alarm.

'You know they won't take it.' Henri addresses his guest. 'Even the Salon d'Automne. I'm under no illusions. My style is too much, even for their liberal taste . . .'

'It's exactly what we're looking for. Something to shake all those bourgeois minds from their dull pretensions. Something to set them chattering. I'm head of the hanging committee this year. I have full power to include whatever I like, wherever I like. Your work will be the star of the show – I'll see to it.'

There's a moment's silence as the words sink in.

Amélie can only wonder what her husband is thinking.

'The only thing that will be hanging is my head, in shame, if I listen to you,' Henri says. 'And it won't be finished in time. Not this year, anyway.'

'Henri, it's my turn to beg you not to tease me. You can't have invited me, welcomed me into your studio, and not expect me to twist your arm.' The two men eye each other. 'I won't lie and pretend I haven't heard what they're saying about you across Paris. I wanted to see your work for myself. The reality is beyond anything I imagined.'

'I can hardly open myself to further ridicule . . .'

'There'll be no mockery. This is a serious show, by serious artists. There's none of the stuffiness of the official Salon. The quality is far better than the Salon des Indépendants.' Amélie knows that one only has to pay a fee to exhibit there. Henri says any fool can do that. 'Your peers admire you,' George continues. 'We understand what it is you're striving for.'

Henri picks up his paintbrush again and looks at the artwork carefully.

'I'd like to be able to say that I wouldn't be offended if you said no. But you know me; I shan't pretend otherwise.'

Henri turns to George with a smile.

'I know you mean well, my friend. But my gut tells me this would be a terrible idea. And as you're speaking frankly, I will too.' He takes a breath. 'You may be willing to offer your support. For that, I'm grateful. But the public hasn't caught up with my vision yet. And the press seem intent on hounding me out of Paris. What's worse, the collectors just aren't interested in what I'm offering, so there's not even the promise of payment at the end of it. I believe I need more time, then we'll see where things stand.'

Amélie watches as George's face falls.

'As you wish,' he says simply. 'But you know there will be a space for you, on the walls of the Salon, if you change your mind. And if you do, I can promise you won't regret it.'

15

Paris, 1905

The opening night is a grand affair. In its third year, the Salon d'Automne is notorious in the Parisian art world, and rumours spread with the intensity of wildfire about the nature of the works inside. George hadn't backed down, promising that Henri's work would be handled sensitively, that it would be the art around which everything else was pinned. There would be grumbles of discontent, the curator admitted – there always were with any art that pushed at the boundaries and broke with the past. But, at least, in this space, surrounded by the offerings of other like-minded artists, Henri would have a chance of being understood and appreciated. All the works are for sale and George has set the price tag for *Woman with a Hat* at five hundred francs, which would be an avalanche of cash, almost beyond imagining.

Amélie and her husband walk into the space at the Grand Palais des Champs-Élysées with a light step. The Salon is at a prestigious location in the 8th arrondissement, and the kinds of people who have come for the opening night are those with money and connections. Guests mill around the rooms, long-stemmed glasses in their hands, bubbles on their lips, eyes not on the works but each other. There's light chatter, and some bursts of laughter, as people catch up and exchange gossip and opinions. Still, Amélie can tell that this exhibition is a melting pot of artistic experimentation and innovation, and she's determined to enjoy herself.

Henri mingles, unrecognized, among the public. He has a tight band of friends, other artists whose opinions he holds dear, and she knows he doesn't want to draw attention to himself with any kind of fanfare. He wants to see the artwork, his painting of his wife in her oversized hat, on display for the first time, as if he were a gallery-goer who knows nothing about art.

Amélie's eyes search the walls for her husband's portrait of her.

She brushes up against a man wearing a grey pinstriped suit, who carries a notebook. Henri whispers urgently that the man is Louis Vauxcelles, an eminent art critic. Her husband follows in the journalist's wake, watching at a distance as he takes in the classical sculptures and oil paintings, fine watercolours and pencil works. He jots down notes, long loose marks that are indecipherable to anyone but the author; as he moves around the gallery, he taps the end of his fountain pen against his elbow in a kind of iambic pentameter.

Amélie and Henri haven't yet seen his artwork in the gallery. They know he's been grouped with a handful of artists who share the same values and a similar aesthetic. There's André Derain, Jean Puy, Raoul Dufy and Maurice de Vlaminck. These men are younger than Henri, more comfortable taking risks. They've less to lose. He has a wife and three children to feed, and she wonders if they secretly find him risible, this thirty-five-year-old man with a widening middle and thinning hair, thrusting into unknown territory as if he still has time to spare.

They turn the corner into a side room and, at once, Amélie is centre stage, demanding to be looked at. The real Amélie stops, heart hammering, breath caught; but nobody pays the flesh-and-blood woman the slightest attention. They are all circling the portrait, the woman there looking upon them with disdain, her lips downturned, her body angled sharply from the chair, wearing that grandiose hat. She steps closer, nervously.

In the middle of the room is a singular statue – the pale marble sculpted to reveal taut muscles, tender flesh, the eyes downcast, as if the conjured form is affronted by this raw assault of pigment. The journalist has also stopped. He stands by the statue – a work by Albert Marque, in Renaissance style – taking notes, his eyes flicking towards the woman in the hat, returning again and again to the portrait of Amélie, the lime green and brick red of her skin, the cobalt blue of her hair, the bold lilac that has been worked into the shadows on her face. A group gathers around the painting, their hands raised, eyes alight with mirth. One man touches a fingernail to the oil paint, to see if it can be flaked off.

Amélie takes another step closer, and sees that the journalist's earlier loose script has been transformed into urgent, thick capitals in his notebook. *GARISH. WILD. SAVAGE.*

She becomes as flat and immobile as her portrait. The journalist has moved closer to the painted face, which looks back at him, through him, unerring. Amélie notices afresh the jaunty slant of her shoulders, the way she exudes a confidence that the real version hardly feels. She realizes she will need to separate herself from this other version of who she is, or risk being consumed entirely. But as she turns to leave the room, she knocks into the plinth of the statue, and the journalist's eyes are upon her immediately. He looks from her to Henri.

'Monsieur Matisse,' he says archly, satisfaction slipping between his words, like a cat who has stumbled upon an injured bird. 'To what do I owe this pleasure?'

'Monsieur Vauxcelles,' Henri says. 'I trust you need no explanation for what you find in front of you.' Her husband is stiff with discomfort.

'Indeed, it's all perfectly clear to me,' the journalist replies, choosing his words carefully. 'Donatello among the wild beasts,' he adds with a flourish, gesturing between the stone-cold statue and the blazing burst of colours on the wall.

'I don't see what's so wild . . .' Henri replies.

'So, you deny that you're a wild beast?' the critic demands.

'*Un fauve*?' her husband replies, his eyes widening in miscomprehension. 'I couldn't be any further from such a characterization. I'm determined to be an unremarkable man. The most curious thing about me should be the art I create, nothing else.'

'If you say so, Monsieur Matisse, if you say so,' the journalist replies, a new energy to his step, his pen poised to write the words in his notebook as soon as he leaves the room.

Amélie has a terrible presentiment of what is to come in tomorrow's newspaper.

⤳

'Irredeemably ugly. That's the verdict,' Henri announces, slamming the door.

'You're exaggerating.' Amélie tries to soothe her husband. He has just come into the apartment, and these are his first words to her, before even a greeting or a kiss. She's up to her elbows in a bowl of washing-up – cutlery bent from overuse and plates crusted with food from three children, who insist on spilling and smearing what little sustenance their parents can provide into the rugs and across windows. They are the real wild beasts around here.

She passes the clean items to her husband, who throws the newspaper on to the counter and takes up a drying cloth. 'You know better than to care what other people think.'

'That idiot journalist had some good things to say about me in his article, but his inane comments about Donatello and our "wild" paintings were printed nonetheless, and now all of us are being branded as *fauves*.'

He can't even laugh about the nickname. She recalls how, just a few years ago, he'd have mustered the energy to find it amusing, but now a plate nearly slips through his hands.

He rests his elbows against the counter and leans forward.

'This is a nightmare,' he says seriously. 'It only emboldens the other critics, makes them more deranged in their criticism of me. If it's not ridiculous barbs about our use of "orgiastic colour" or condemning us for being like children with crayons, then there are comments about our art being "a pot of colours flung in the face of the public". We're using pigment like sticks of dynamite, apparently. Of course, my work hasn't sold. I doubt even a madman would be tempted now.'

Amélie washes another plate as she listens to the insults he has memorized.

'People's misconceptions, their prejudices,' he adds. 'How is one expected to make progress amid such a climate of snipery and sarcasm?'

Amélie dries her hands then places them on her husband's shoulders.

'You have to be deaf to all that,' she says, 'as well as blind. I know you can't separate yourself as a man from the artist you know you must be. You wouldn't be relevant at all if you weren't fighting against something that demands to be changed.'

'It hurts all the more that it's the picture of you they're poking holes in.'

'It's my face, but it's not my heart or soul. They still belong to you,' she says.

He looks at her with a playful smile. She never talks like this; it's the kind of soppiness they scoff at. But perhaps he needs to hear it now. He kisses her. There's still tenderness between them. They've always been pitted against the world, and the more it bashes up against them, the more they draw together and fortify.

Five days later, Henri comes home once more in a depleted mood. He has been drawn, day after day, to the exhibition, where he eavesdrops on the gallery-goers who loiter in the room of the 'wild beasts'. The room is the busiest, the most talked about, of the whole show. He should be happy, but people turn up with paint smeared on their faces, streaks of violet and turquoise and blue. He has seen others run the edge of a coin down the surface of his canvas.

Matisse sends you mad, he has read, scrawled on a wall near Montparnasse, an echo of the public service announcements that are plastered outside bars and public lavatories across the city, warning that absinthe can render a person senseless.

'A letter arrived for you,' Amélie says, pushing it across the table, the youngest boy, Pierre, on her hip. Henri rips the seal of the envelope. His mouth falls open. He continues reading for a moment.

'A damn miracle,' he stammers. 'Someone has made an offer for your portrait. They want to buy it . . .' He looks up at her. 'And they're confident or stupid enough to pay three hundred francs!'

Amélie snatches the letter. 'But that's two hundred less than the price.'

She reads as Henri sits down at the table. He leans back in his chair, his body relaxing. 'This will go some way to silencing my critics, at least,' he says.

But Amélie is thinking. 'If those collectors . . .' She scans the letter to find the name. 'The Steins. If they want to buy it, then they should pay the full price, or not at all.'

Henri pales. 'Amélie, dear, you've heard what people are saying. The fact that anyone in their right mind – and I suspect these Steins must know a thing or two – is prepared to pay a single sou for my work is staggering. They've made a generous offer. They'll know of the furore around the piece. If I try to squeeze the full price out of them . . . why, instead of adding another two hundred francs to their bid, they may very well subtract it. We could be left with nothing!'

Pierre wiggles out of his mother's grasp and goes in search of his siblings.

'You said it yourself,' Amélie continues, unperturbed. 'They'll have heard all the controversy and it hasn't deterred them. If they want the portrait – about which everyone in Paris is talking, and everyone has an opinion – then they can pay the full price. You deserve to be paid properly for your work. Write back and outline your case.'

Henri's knuckles whiten. 'It won't work . . . It's a very risky strategy,' he says.

'You may be mocked at every turn, but don't let them snuff out your self-respect.'

Henri remains silent as he lets the words settle into some kind of sense.

'For better or worse, your name is on everyone's lips,' Amélie continues. 'And my face is the most talked about in France right now. You're seen as a madman and we hardly have enough money as it is, yet we get by. Let's take the risk. Write to them and see what they say. We might just secure the future we deserve.'

16

Issy-les-Moulineaux, 1909

Amélie has to steady herself as she stands in front of the huge house, with its steps up to a private front door, shutters framing several large windows and lashings of fat yellow roses trailing up the brickwork. She feels as if she has walked into a vision. This is their home, and being in front of it represents the culmination of a chain of events she hardly dared imagine could come to pass. Now that it has, she's speechless. Amélie is thirty-seven, and finally, finally, she's upon a daisy-strewn lawn in a pretty neighbourhood, Issy-les-Moulineaux. She takes a breath. All she can hear is birds and the faint lull of young children playing a distance away. Her own have dashed ahead to fight over the attic bedroom. From now on, this is where the Matisses will call home – gone is the stinking Seine, the squalor and streets paved with other people's rubbish. Henri, for many years, promised this would be the outcome of their daring, their shared hard work. He always said they'd have a sanctuary, away from it all. He promised her peace. He promised her calm and community. He delivered.

It's not like Paris won't always be there. It's an easy train ride away, less than half an hour. Henri can have all the chorus and chaotic culture of the capital when he's teaching at the Académie

Matisse, the art school he founded last year. Stubborn once again, his desire is to create an open and experimental space where students can freely explore their creativity.

Their priorities have undoubtedly changed. She'll take soil – in which to plant her seeds and watch them grow – over society and all its trappings any day. Amélie has finally been able to admit that she has been deeply unhappy for a very long time. She can see how her health floundered after the Humbert affair. Even as the years go by, she rarely feels much energy or enthusiasm. She tries to pull herself out of it. Some days are better than others. She does her best to support the smooth running of Henri's artistic affairs, even if sometimes she presents a weaker version of the woman she used to be. It was a further blow when her mother died last summer, aged just sixty. Amélie still grapples with grief. After the Humberts, Catherine had become ill, unable to bounce back. Still, her death was a shock.

The other root cause of that dissatisfaction, Amélie knows, is having been forced to live for so long in cramped quarters in wheezing Paris – five people jostling for space, for just a little silence. It's enough to send anyone mad. It has strangled the equanimity from her – navigating around the energy of two boisterous boys, one shrewd daughter, and a husband who sulks if his creative conditions aren't precisely perfect.

Amélie has long planned for a room for herself. One with bookshelves and a personal gramophone, drawers full of her own creative projects, a private desk for letter writing. She plans to keep the door closed to any and all unwelcome interruptions.

Their change in circumstances is, of course, down to a significant change in their fortunes. After years of drought, of near poverty and penny pinching, the inflow of money, once Henri's artworks started to attract the attention of the right collectors, was a shock.

The turning point, without doubt, was the sale of *Woman with a Hat* – the portrait of Amélie in a hat of her own making. The renowned American art collectors, siblings Gertrude and Leo Stein, bought it four years ago. Their confidence in Henri's vision unleashed something unstoppable. At Amélie's insistence, they paid the full price for the artwork; it felt, at the time, like a monumental gamble, holding out for those additional two hundred francs. The money was important, but it was the message it sent that was essential. It spoke of pride and promise, and how, despite everything, the Matisses believed they deserved to be taken seriously.

The Steins reported afterwards, once their friendship with the couple grew, that they had admired Henri's strength of character for holding out. That it had changed their perception and appreciation.

Amélie had resisted saying, 'I told you so.'

Gertrude Stein and her brother Leo must be twenty years older than her husband. They're knowledgeable and cultured and not afraid, like many of their contemporaries, of art that goes against the grain. In the time since that first purchase, the Steins have become favoured buyers, introducing Henri and his work to collectors in Russia and America. Now, at nearly forty years old, Henri feels that the tide of their luck has finally turned.

The trappings of this new life are also down to the generous patronage of a man who has become a valued collector of Henri's artwork: Sergei Shchukin, a textile magnate from Moscow, one of Russia's richest men. At the turn of the century, Shchukin began to visit the salons of Paris and developed a taste for Impressionism, buying art by the old guard – Monet, Cézanne, Renoir and van Gogh. His attention then settled on the new generation, including Amélie's husband. His support has helped revolutionize the perception of Henri's work.

For the first time in their lives, the Matisses are comfortable. Henri has lived cheek-by-jowl with other poverty-stricken artists for so long that he reveals now that he's anxious about the silence that might descend upon this suburban location at night. There'll be none of the screeching from the streets below, nor the horns of passing trade boats on the river; none of the blasting of street carts and drunks, their voices ricocheting around the buildings. The only noise will be him playing his violin, a treat that has been denied him for many years in living quarters with thin walls and rotten-tempered neighbours. They can invite friends and fellow artists to visit. The location is close enough to Paris to be appealing. There's enough space for everyone to set up an easel in the garden or studio. He can, and will, paint with abandon.

It was with a sense of resignation that she closed the hat shop once and for all. Amélie was glad to see the back of it. She feels disappointed that her ambitions amounted to so little, but the money she brought in helped to buy her husband time. He says he couldn't have survived those years without her acumen. On her better days, she knows this to be true.

⤸

Once they've unpacked and settled themselves into the contours of their home, Amélie spends time assessing the garden. She wants to make her mark on it, get mud under her nails, create something she can watch unfurl and grow. She'll plant the borders leading to Henri's studio with bright flowers – bursts of red, yellow, violet that match the colours on his canvases. At Issy, life will be different, she decides. This is the fresh start she has been craving.

Henri can't contain his excitement about the work he can make here. He has the validation he has desired, and it tempts him to become even more daring. This fuels Amélie to push her own boundaries, too. She surprised herself, a couple of years ago, by agreeing to be the model for her husband's first nude oil painting, *The Blue Nude*, which was inspired by his trip to Biskra in Algeria.

She undressed and positioned herself, reclining, day after day for him, her flesh made other by his observation. It was another of his works to shock the public, almost dangerously so. People decried it as a violation of traditional standards of beauty and realism, after it was exhibited in 1907 at the Salon des Indépendants.

At the time, Amélie was frustrated, tired of such trite criticism. What was it that was so threatening about the exposure of the female form? The public hankered after it, but when they were faced with nudity, frothing madness emerged. She knew that the blues of her body were striking against the yellow and greens of the background, her breasts, thighs and calves swollen and sumptuous. She did feel self-conscious about her depiction, though, and had asked her husband not to advertise that she was the model. But privately, she was proud.

Henri sets up his studio at the bottom of the garden. The boys will no longer have to be silent while he works, tiptoeing around him, suppressing shouts and giggles. Now they may even pick up paintbrushes themselves. Marguerite, at fifteen, is shy, but strident. She takes no prisoners. That girl knows how to make herself indispensable – she's practical, no-nonsense; her head is not filled with fluff. The place she loves the most is her father's studio. Ever since she was a little girl, she hasn't ever wanted to leave his side. As Amélie has become more unwilling in recent months to pose for Henri, Marguerite has stepped in. She radiates an assertiveness on the canvas that the older woman admires – and slightly envies.

⌐

Soon after settling in, Henri invites his parents to visit. He knows the damage his artistic pursuits have done; how much shame he has brought upon the Matisse name. Henri hopes that as his future becomes secure and the responses to his art more respectable, his father will realize the sacrifices have been worth it. Is it wrong to want his parents to admire his success?

Émile and Anna arrive on Friday. Amélie and Henri pick them up at the station. The house is clean, the children in their best clothes; Henri has even trimmed his eyebrows. Her husband sent his parents first-class train tickets so they could enjoy a comfortable journey. Émile is approaching seventy, but shows no signs of slowing down. His own father lived to almost one hundred, and worked until the end. But it's a shock to see them step off the train, their shoulders hunched, their frames shrunken and hair silvery.

Amélie fusses once they're back home. She brings out drinks, plates of snacks. Émile says little but his wife makes appreciative noises as they tour the property. Henri is keen to show his father his studio, talk him through the pieces he has been working on. He hopes that by seeing the art for himself, without the middleman of malicious gossip, his father might finally understand. But Émile seems particularly unsettled. He frowns as Henri walks him around. Émile shuffles on his feet and clears his throat, but says nothing, and this evasion of opinion, this wilful silence, is more hurtful than the man's questioning miscomprehension. It feels as though, in not being acknowledged for this most fundamental part of himself, Henri is being rejected once more by the man he admires most in the world.

His mother, in comparison, asks a couple of clumsy but well-intentioned questions, and squeezes his shoulder. Still, she remains at the surface of her understanding of him, her adored eldest son, and Amélie can tell that Henri feels dejected. This is his moment to impress, to shine. She tries to distract the trio, and defuse the tension, by pointing out zinnias, marigolds, dahlias and lilies she has planted in the gardens and the border leading back to the house. They're all in full bloom, their colours dancing against the dark soil. She's proud of what she has coaxed into growth.

'Aren't those petals unusual?' Henri asks, taking his mother by the arm. 'I'd like to paint them, if Amélie will permit me to cut them down in their prime.'

Émile bends down to examine the display more closely. He rakes his fingers through the soil, rubbing to get a feel for the texture, then brings them to his nose. He slaps his hands to rid them of the residue and stands to face his son and daughter-in-law.

'You know what, the soil isn't half bad,' he says, with more enthusiasm than he has shown for anything since he arrived. 'If you want my advice, it certainly deserves a better crop than flowers. You really should plant something practical. There'd be no harm in potatoes, my son . . .

17

Issy-les-Moulineaux, 1910

It's true, Amélie feels, that time seems to speed up as you get older, as life becomes more stable. They've lived at Issy for more than a year. It's as if now that they've anchored themselves in comfort, there's less to define their day-to-day lives. And the picture at the end of it is one that's quite bland. Perhaps it's not this way for her husband. Henri has more to keep him busy. He travels often – to Algeria, Germany, Spain – in search of inspiration. Amélie used to want to be by his side. Years ago, she accompanied him to Italy. But more and more, she craves the calmness that descends when he's away – his moods pollute their shared atmosphere. Her nerves are frayed. Now she prefers to stay home, wrapping herself in solitude. But the cost is that every day feels the same. She feels the colour draining.

Her marriage to Henri has always rested upon that delicate balance of their needing one another. Before, in Paris, they were rooted together. They worked from that tightly bound centre. Now that tension has dissipated. It turns out that her husband needs her less, not more, in their new environment. So Amélie finds herself at loose ends. She is, for the first time in her life, a simple housewife. She wonders if she has compromised too much, after all.

Over the past months, Amélie has deflated, like a kite sinking in a limp breeze; some of the fight has gone out of her without the tension of the struggle to survive. She thinks of her sister, Berthe, teaching. She's living with their father, who's still adapting to life without their mother. Berthe had her own ambitions; she didn't construct them in symbiosis with a man. Amélie thinks back to the passionate young woman she herself used to be, ready to take the world by storm, and is filled with longing for her former drive.

A bored woman is a dangerous one, her mother used to say.

⁓

Her husband's Académie is booming. He has attracted aspiring artists from around the world. And while his methods might be unconventional – he eschews formal instruction in favour of hands-on experimentation – the students thrive on his feedback and encouragement.

Indeed, he has gained an enthusiastic gaggle of followers who hang on his every word. His most dedicated, his most effusive, are a pair of cultured, ambitious Russian women – Marie and Olga. They're the kind of bright, challenging young things that make Amélie feel past her best. As a woman, she has always tried to do things differently, but they are a new breed entirely. They want and demand what's being offered to men – the careers and challenges. They've discarded lives of luxury in Moscow in order to come to Paris and live hand-to-mouth, trying to earn money through art. Neither is married, nor shows any interest in children. It's as if they hold themselves apart from Amélie, treat her as if she were just a wife, a woman to be patted and indulged, before they turn to the serious business of debating colour and form. She knows the three of them spend long afternoons arguing over the future of art, fizzing with righteous indignation and polished rebuttals. Henri thrives on their energy.

It's a world to which she no longer has any access.

Both women are striking. Marie, the younger of the two, in her mid-twenties, is petite, with fine dark features. Olga is six years older, and has rich brown hair and high, rounded cheekbones, which give her face a warmth that her eyes often don't possess.

Amélie is wary of the pair; they are so hungry for artistic learning and want to mine it directly from her husband – making themselves indispensable in his Paris studio, ingratiating themselves into his conversations, posing for artworks when the opportunity arises.

Amélie wonders how her husband responds to them when she's not around. She saw first-hand, in Paris and the south – and heard the rumours about – the behaviour of other artists; what happened when their wives weren't there. Pablo Picasso, a young artist from Spain – his name comes up again and again. People say he's charismatic – perhaps that's to be expected from a man a decade younger than her husband – and the two have developed an uneasy friendship, bordering on rivalry. She has advised Henri to keep his distance.

But, with Henri, her heart always told her that she had no reason to fret. She doesn't consider him dissatisfied. Still, what man wouldn't be flattered by attention?

She once glimpsed, quite by chance, a scene at the Paris art school, where Olga had Henri by the lapels of his outer coat, pulling herself towards him with a fluttering intensity, firing yet another question at him as he tried to leave for an appointment. Henri did not lift her hands off him, but allowed himself to be held in that position, a mild look of impatience on his face, like a controlled father before a child. Eventually he touched her wrist and she released him. But since that moment, Amélie has not felt easy around Olga.

She doesn't want to believe that her husband could stray. But, like any wife whose husband is frequently in the company of emboldened young women, she's wary that his fidelity to their marriage may be tested. She'd never have contemplated such a thing before – it was unthinkable in their early days. But it would be madness to ignore the threat now.

↜

As time passes, the days weave themselves into subtle tapestries of months. Amélie is not wholly unsatisfied, but has a sense that something is permanently amiss, although she cannot put a finger upon precisely what it is. What person approaching her fortieth year of life does not take stock of the impact those many years have made upon the self? And what impact that self has, in turn, made upon the years. She knows she has forged her own path, but sometimes she wonders where it has got her. It makes her realize how small her world has become.

Henri spends more time in Paris. She's sure he'll be with those young Russian women. She tries to assess what kind of threat, precisely, Olga in particular may be. Is she dangerously obsessed with her husband? No. Amélie tries to push the thought from her mind. It's simply that Olga is an eccentric, genteel but needy woman, searching for validation in her ambitious art, for which she turns to Henri. It's the only thought that soothes Amélie.

Until she finds the note, dashed off hurriedly, written by her husband. It's then that she realizes she has blinded herself to some terrible truths. Amélie finds it while searching his studio. She tells herself she was cleaning, that she had every right to be there, but the burning sensation she experiences when she chances upon it, the swift sense of satisfaction, makes her realize she has been looking for evidence all along. And now she has it.

I can only think of it as an impulse of madness. She jolts with intrigue; the tips of her fingers burn. She pauses, before reading again. *Nothing gave me the right to do it. My suspicions were imaginary. Please, Olga, tell no one.* Amélie is breathless, her chest tight. She can't help but absorb the following lines, eating them in a hurry, enough to make herself sick. *I'll make no mention of it at home.* Everything around her seems to tumble. *Even if you forgive me, could I ever forgive myself? Can things really become so irreparable so quickly? Couldn't you allow for a moment of unreason, of irresponsibility . . . I think I was mad!* Amélie is winded by the urgency and intensity of her husband's feelings. She turns the paper over. The words are so baffling and unbridled. What on earth has passed between them?

She doesn't want to think the worst, but she's unable to drag her thoughts to certainty. She'll have to find a way to question Henri about this. She can hardly ask him outright, but if she tries to forget about those words, she will lose her mind entirely.

⌐〜

It's winter, and Henri travels to Spain. Alone. They've never been apart for Christmas before, and the loneliness tugs at Amélie. She misses her mother especially at this time of year. She had an invitation from Berthe and her father to stay with them, but she cannot face the journey, the forced merriment and memories. The children have travelled to Bohain to stay with their recently widowed grandmother. Émile Matisse died suddenly, aged just seventy, and it has come as a huge blow. Amélie made excuses that she was unwell.

It feels as if all certainty has abandoned her in recent months.

Amélie is torn apart, unsettled by her husband's affair – if she can call it that – with Olga. In the face of his denials and evaded questions, she is responding to it as if it were one. Ever since that day she found the letter, she has been consumed by rage at her husband for making promises to another woman, and desolation at the state of their marriage, which once seemed so solid, and anger at herself. Amélie is foolish for having missed the signs, for her wilful passiveness – so unlike her, but a defence that enabled her to pretend everything was more or less fine. How could she have been so stupid; why did she not ask questions, not put her foot down? She should have been more forceful in pushing him to be rid of Olga. The truth is, their marriage has been deteriorating for some time; she just hadn't noticed how much they'd grown apart as Henri's star was rising, leaving her surplus to requirements.

When she finally confronted him about Olga, gave him a chance to explain, Henri brushed her concerns aside. He insisted there was nothing to worry about, hinting that she was paranoid, that her imagination and fears had got the better of her. So when she showed him the evidence she'd found, he was speechless. He couldn't find the words to deny it, and the fear in his eyes seemed to confirm what she'd dreaded. Yet even with his own words in front of him, Henri wouldn't admit wrongdoing. He wouldn't say more, 'for Olga's sake'.

But Amélie wanted the truth. What did he mean when he wrote, *Couldn't you allow for a moment of unreason, of irresponsibility . . . I think I was mad*?

Eventually, he mustered an excuse about finding Olga in a stupor, after she had consumed opium – and implored his wife to imagine what an indelicate scene he had stumbled into. And how Olga had flown into a violent rage with him when he threatened to write to her sister. But something about the turn of phrase on the page, the intensity of his plea to be understood, made Amélie feel there was more to this interaction than Henri was telling her.

So now there's an impasse between them. He has asked her not to speak of it again. While Henri is away in Spain, he writes to Amélie every day, begging that she come to her senses, reiterating words he has used in their arguments. He's a simple man, not consumed by passions he cannot control. He's loyal. Her husband has always had such well-constructed defences, and the logic of them makes Amélie feel more alone than ever. His earnest letters arrive like fired bullets, each one inflicting more pain than the last. Each one telling only part of a story. Is he writing to Olga, too, making promises he cannot keep? She hopes that, eventually, they'll reach an equilibrium, and they'll never have to see that woman again.

It's something to hope for in the new year.

⤸

By the summer of 1911, a new calm emerges between husband and wife. Amélie doesn't have the energy to be annoyed for ever, nor to disbelieve him. The tensions are papered over. She has built the world she occupies, what choice does she have but to live in it? Still, it feels as if someone had cut at her soul with a pair of scissors, but she has to cope.

Henri persuades her to travel south, to the coast, to Collioure. The change of scenery will do her good, he promises. The heat is intense, and the pace of life will suit her. Nobody expects anything to be done in a hurry. She used to achieve so much, so fast. And now she is dulled. Henri, as always, is determined to paint for as many hours as possible. His dedication to art never falters. He extends an open invitation in August to his artist friends from Paris, who arrive sweating and hungry, keen to see the sights. Amélie mostly enjoys the company and interest they show in her and the children – the boys are nearing eleven and twelve and gaining opinions on all matters. There are trips to the beach, picnics, outings to local villages, walks along the river to skim stones. Is this what she has been missing, she wonders – the company of others who are prepared to engage with her on a human level?

She's enjoying herself, casting off some of the blackness that suffocates her.

Until one day, when there's a knock at the door. It's delicate, uncertain.

Amélie opens it. When she sees Olga, her equanimity curdles.

Henri never thought to mention that he'd invited the woman, and she knows why – she'd have told him, to his face, that it was completely unacceptable. She does not want Olga in their home, during their family holiday. This woman has wreaked enough havoc in their lives, poisoning their marriage with her entitled expectation of attention, her wilful naivety.

Amélie wants to slam the door in her face.

But Olga looks so pale and unsure of herself, a ghost of the woman Amélie had seen in Paris, that she allows her to stumble over the threshold. She leads her out to the gardens.

'*She's* here,' Amélie hisses, accosting Henri in the middle of violin practice. He pauses, the instrument resting on his collar-bone, his chin lifted from its curve. He looks utterly baffled, searches his brain for who could possibly prompt such a severe reaction from his wife, then asks, 'Olga?' He stands up, a nervous flush descending. 'I didn't invite her, I swear. Why would I when I know how much it would upset you?'

Amélie despises his interminable logic – why *would* he invite Olga, when he knows it upsets his wife? That's not for Amélie to answer. She's not meant to offer evidence or provide an excuse for his motivations, but she does want an explanation, because there's no other way this woman would be here, on their patio, sipping lemonade, if he hadn't offered their address. 'She just turned up, entirely unannounced,' Henri insists.

Amélie shakes her head, not accepting his words. 'But you're pleased she's here.'

'Not at all!'

'Why is it that she cannot keep away?'

'Olga's vulnerable. People exploit her, and it leads to this fragile state.'

'You don't have to save her,' Amélie says. 'Not at the expense of me and our marriage.'

Henri turns to pleading. 'This might be an opportunity for you to get to know each other better,' he says. 'You've shaped her into a monster in your mind, and made assumptions about the nature of our relationship, when your suspicions couldn't be further from the truth. Perhaps if she were to stay here for a few days, a week even, you'd see that she's not the threat you perceive her to be. She's a proud woman, like you.'

Amélie despises his insinuation that she is the one not in control of her emotions, that she's full of petty sentiment. All it would take is a little more respect from her husband, for him to show her the thoughtfulness that he's bestowing upon this other woman, and Amélie would have no need to cause a scene.

He misinterprets her moment's silence.

'You might enjoy her company. And realize that you have nothing to worry about.'

The fight falls from Amélie, through sheer exhaustion.

Very well, then. Against all her better judgement, Amélie will put up with Olga, and observe the way this woman interacts with her husband, see for herself what passes between the two of them. Perhaps this is her opportunity to gather the evidence to evict Olga from their lives once and for all. So why does it feel as if she's the one at risk of being cast aside?

Over the next week, Amélie observes the pair. She's alert to any hint of intimacy between them and becomes adept at listening at doors during private moments. But there's nothing that ignites her temper, and she cannot fault Henri for his earnest interactions, which border on tedium. Olga is indeed a nervous and sensitive woman. Amélie comes to believe Henri's assessment that the

Russian needs wrapping in cotton wool just to survive the onslaught of modern life. At times, she seems dazed. The intensity of Amélie's fears dissipates the more time she spends with the woman, although her discomfort remains.

Amélie asks more than once when Olga will be returning to Paris. Henri had indicated that she'd not want to stay for more than a week – that, as a Russian, she'd find the southern heat intolerable – but she still has made no indication when she might depart.

Amélie, on the other hand, has to return to Issy with her boys to get them ready for the start of term. Henri intends to remain on the coast to make the most of the cooler weather.

'And does Olga have any plans to leave?' she asks.

'She's planning to stay a little longer, to paint.'

'I see,' Amélie replies.

'I'd like it if Marguerite remained, too, to put your anxieties at rest,' he adds.

'You know how I feel,' Amélie says. She can only hope that her instincts are wrong.

In the winter, Henri travels to Moscow, to see his collector Shchukin. Her husband is admired in Russia, treated with a kind of reverence. They don't know the real Henri Matisse, sniffs Amélie. Olga, at her family's determination, has been sent to a clinic in Switzerland, to treat what may – so the rumours go – be an addiction to morphine. Henri tried to 'help' by meeting with her sisters in Russia, but it only started a chain of events that saw her carted away against her will. Olga is distraught at Henri's interference. Amélie can't comprehend why her husband is so embroiled in this woman's life. Why he risks yet another scandal with this ongoing obsession to save her.

Olga's doctor writes to Henri, keeps him updated as to her health, her mental state.

Once he has finished reading, Henri tucks the typed pages into the pocket of his blazer.

Later, when Amélie looks for it, the letter is gone.

～

A few days afterwards, Amélie receives a call from the post office. A letter has been sent from abroad, postmarked Switzerland. The return address is the Arnold Clinic. The postage is insufficient. Would a member of the household be kind enough to bring the remaining fee?

Amélie leaves immediately.

Fifteen minutes later she has the envelope in her hands, bearing her husband's name. Without hesitation, she opens it and scans the content. The doctor conveys his updates on the patient, recounting details of her treatment, and her sessions with the psychologist.

Her deep, personal, romantic feelings for you, Monsieur Matisse, only complicate matters, as you know. She recounted feeling betrayed, much like a wife by her husband, at the situation you have placed her in. This hinders her progress. I suggest you write to her, stating your position, and reassuring her of your continued commitment. With such, I believe our patient will make a prompt recovery; without it, she will continue to flounder and blame you.

Amélie's scalp tightens as she reads. All this time, Amélie has been made to feel as if she was exaggerating things, that her jealousy was baseless. She's floored by the weight of the truth that has been kept from her. Henri always said that nothing had happened between them, but Amélie knows that – whatever may have occurred – another woman has infiltrated their marriage. And everything she has given up for Henri – her own ambitions, her drive – has all been sacrificed at the altar of his art. Henri has let in water while admiring the horizon, threatening to sink them all and reprimanding Amélie for sounding the alarm. She's not sure she can forgive him, or herself, for not taking a stronger stance from the start.

Once, Amélie had been the rock on which her husband's sanity depended. Now, she's an irritant. He's the great artist, and who is she? Madame Matisse. The artist's wife. What does he want of her now? Marguerite can take over the running of the house and studio, if he has such disdain for his wife. She'll never allow herself to be pushed aside again. Amélie is seething. But she only has herself to blame. Henri warned her a long time ago that he'd always love art more than he'd ever love her.

ULTIMATUM

Nice, 1939

A lone in the bedroom, Lydia checks the contents of her brief-case. This maroon leather case has been packed, ready to leave with her at a moment's notice, for many years. Inside the case is the most precious thing she owns, a relic from her child-hood, a thing she slept with beneath her pillow as a young woman and turned to in times of loss: the gun.

She picks up the revolver and holds it to her cheek. Lydia hasn't handled the elegant Lefaucheux for a long time. A 7mm calibre, it's the type of weapon that can be slipped into a pocket, easy to conceal. Its polished ivory grip is smooth to the touch, and there's evidence of corrosion on the etched silver of the barrel. She exam-ines the chamber. There are only two bullets left.

The gun is as it has always been: her great secret, her only love, her cold inheritance.

She traces its shape the way men have run a finger along the dip of her waist, pushing intent into the dent of her spine. She feels a deep vibration within her, a warning that the trigger will soon be pulled once more. Lydia imagines it calmly, but when the time comes, she knows she'll have no control over it, as has always been the way.

The sad truth is, if she'd wanted to break this woman's

marriage, she could have done as much by now. People think it's uncontrollable lust for another that destroys a union. But any bond can be broken with a little attention, a little kindness. It's the lack of it that kills.

Amélie must once have been a beautiful woman, many years ago. Lydia has seen the portraits Henri made of his wife at the start of their marriage. *Woman with a Hat* – such radical art, and Amélie looked every inch the fierce and powerful woman. What happened in the intervening years?

Lydia thinks of that departing memory of Amélie, making her way to find her husband, her lips fluttering in annoyance. The old woman's back was hunched, the damage inflicted upon her spine pulling her into a questioning shape. Her eyes are always wary, primed for suspicion, and her hair has faded from its former richness to chestnut streaked with grey. It's like a painting that has been distorted: the model is still as she once was, that long hair piled atop her head in a wide bun, the cheekbones giving the same frame to her face. But the optics are slanted, as if seen in a broken mirror, much like the work of Pablo Picasso, whom Lydia once met at Henri's side.

Make no mistake: Lydia doesn't care for beauty, certainly doesn't chase after it as currency, though she understands the privileges it affords her, as a woman about to turn twenty-nine, with pale skin, ice-blonde hair and blue eyes. She has caught the eyes of enough men in her time, usually the wrong kind. But Lydia knows such beauty is not a thing to build a life upon; it will not last for more than a handful of years, nor would she want it to.

She's sitting alone in the dark with the cool instrument clasped to her breast, lost in a meditative daze, when she hears Monsieur Matisse calling for her. There's a shift in his tone.

Lydia returns the gun to her father's briefcase and checks the clasps are locked securely, pushing her thumbs up against them to test for weaknesses, to see if Amélie's meddling has inflicted permanent damage. Then she conceals the case once more, hidden until the time comes.

Once it is safely put away, she passes from her room, down the stairs, to the studio where Monsieur Matisse spends his days. Birds call from their cages, wings darting. The artist has his back to her as he tops up their seed. She notices the slope of his shoulders, pulling at the centre of his taupe jacket, the material tight between his shoulder blades. He feels her eyes on him and turns expectantly. Her gaze roams to the fireplace. She looks at a pair of pressed violets, long past their best, their colours faded after many years trapped behind a pane of glass.

'There you are, Lydia. It's not like you to keep me waiting,' he says gently.

There's a seriousness to his features, and Lydia knows something has changed.

'Your wife was looking for you. Did she find you?' she asks.

He nods, and gestures that she take a seat.

He inhales. Pauses. Her body tenses as she waits for him to continue, her heart pounding. She waits for the words she knows are coming.

'I'm afraid my wife has given me an ultimatum,' he says slowly.

PART TWO

LYDIA

1

Lydia jumps from step to step, dodging patches of icy snow that could pull her feet from beneath her, her satchel swinging from her shoulder. Her ruby ribbon, which her mother tied that morning to hold her blonde hair in place, has come loose and trails halfway down her back. But she has no time to retrieve it as it flutters free and curls with a flourish on a wooden plank that has been nailed in place at the bottom of the stairs leading to her home. The girl cannot wait to show her mother her report card, which her teacher placed on her desk this afternoon, resting her fingers for a short moment on Lydia's shoulder.

'A great mind. You take after your father,' she said, bending to whisper in the seven-year-old's ear. 'Top of the class,' the teacher announced, before turning to the blackboard and writing her name in the middle – *LYDIA DELECTORSKAYA* – the chalk scratching with each flick of her thin wrist, as the children in the classroom shuffled and groaned.

Lydia's socks have loosened as she ran home from school and, good news or not, she knows well enough to tug them back up to her knees before she enters the house. The streets of the town were almost empty, except for dogs licking their hind legs and old women wrapped up against the wind. Tomsk, Lydia recites inwardly, recalling her teacher's words, is one of the oldest cities in Siberia. Gold was discovered in 1830, although there's no evidence of it now. To Lydia, the town seems flat, featureless. She hopes one day to visit Petrograd. Her father has told her how colourful it is there – the capital of Russia. She has seen drawings of its bulbous buildings in his heavy, hard-spined books. There's a war happening, she knows. Fighting. She's used to that – the sight of soldiers and guns. The boys in her class pretend to have guns, and chase Lydia and the other girls around, aiming at their hearts.

Lydia rummages in her satchel for the report card, eager to see the look on her mother's face as she scans her teacher's handwriting. Her mother will smile, hug her, spin her off the ground and place the report on the mantelpiece for Father to see as soon as he returns from the hospital, bone-tired from his work as a doctor.

At the top step to her home, Lydia hesitates. The door is ajar.

Lydia swallows her confusion. This isn't right. The door is never left open, especially not in Siberia in the autumn, when the temperatures rarely nudge above freezing. She takes a step forward. There's no noise from within, no authoritative voices from the wireless or operatic music streaming from the gramophone. Her mother is not preparing dinner, and the kitchen is empty of the usual chorus – steaming pans, the scent of onions and sizzling spices reaching out to make her tummy rumble – that she finds when she arrives home at this time, after her clarinet practice on a Wednesday.

Lydia nudges the door further with her foot, steps into the hallway. And stops.

Her mother is collapsed, sprawled across a chair in the parlour, her head back, mouth open, the whites of her eyes visible. The afternoon's shopping is scattered across the floor – globes of cabbages, turnips, beetroot and carrots tumbled to the ground. Lydia dashes over, puts a hand to her mother's cheek. It's damp to the touch. Her mother lets out a mewl of recognition, her eyes struggling to focus. She reaches for the girl's hands, grips them with as much energy as she can muster, and whispers: 'Aunt Nina. Bring her to me. Hurry.'

Lydia abandons her satchel, flings the door wide open and runs back down the steps. The ribbon that fell from her hair earlier now appears like a streak of blood in the snow.

⌐

Lydia runs through the narrow side streets of Tomsk to her auntie's house, the cloak of cold wrapping tighter around her with every step. She has never seen her mother in such a state and it makes her breathless and blind. She runs head first into a soldier, his rifle swinging at his hip, the rough material of his green uniform scratching her nose and cheek. He grabs her by the shoulders, the pressure of his fingers tight around her body, then pushes her on her way. Lydia keeps running and doesn't turn back.

Her father has warned her how dangerous these men who 'guard' the streets are, how they are appearing all over Russia with guns and gritty stares, their numbers increasing since the uprising earlier in the year – a series of wild events that excited her father at first, but scared him, too. The word used then was 'revolution', and it seemed to carry much weight. It has echoed in Lydia's consciousness in the months since, and the adults still seem to shudder when it is mentioned. Things at home, in Tomsk, haven't been the same since March, when Tsar Nicholas II was forced to give up his throne. She knows well enough that the Romanov family had ruled for three hundred years and owned a great deal of Russia's land and wealth. She has heard how they were hated by the Bolsheviks, who wanted to see the wealth of Russia returned to its people. Since the uprising, though, her parents have seemed less sure of their place in the world. Certain foods have been harder to come by. She has heard them talking about money and how they can make ends meet, even though her father works as a doctor, helping sick children, in a hospital. Her parents had avoided the initial protests, when angry people demanded political reform, an end to the war and improved living conditions.

Despite her young age, her father was not afraid to talk to Lydia about sacrifice, duty and devotion to one's country. It felt as if he was drumming it into her. He talked about power, and what it meant to be power*less*. She had listened, swallowing each word into the serious chambers of her heart, so that she could remember them when she was old enough to consider his words properly. He explained that because he was a doctor, they were vulnerable. Each day since the uprising, the voices on the wireless had become more menacing and, as the revolutionary movement gained momentum, people like him had become a target of the Bolsheviks' ideology. Educated professionals found themselves caught in the crossfire between the Bolsheviks and the old regime, and many had left the country already. Lydia couldn't understand why such people wouldn't like those who were educated. And did that mean she shouldn't try so hard at school?

Her father had pursed his lips at this.

Mother had come in at that point, kissed Lydia on the crown of her head, then frowned at Father, asking him why he was filling a little girl's head with promises, politics and other nonsense.

'Our daughter needs to know,' her father replied. 'A revolution is under way. It's not over. She needs to understand the mindset of her country. The Russian Empire is in its death throes,' he said to his wife. 'There'll be anarchy, bloodshed . . .'

Lydia's mother had given him a stern look and put a finger on his lips.

Lydia turns abruptly, spinning in the street. She's lost. All the houses look the same – low wooden structures that seem as if they've come straight from her book of fairy tales. She knows wolves from the surrounding forests prowl at night. She thinks of teeth and claws.

She tries to get her bearings, searching the street signs for anything familiar.

Eventually Lydia finds her aunt's home, which she has been to many times. She slaps a palm against the door until a splinter slips under her skin. Aunt Nina is her mother's sister, with the same ice-blue eyes and pale skin. The woman answers with one hand on her chest, looking out above Lydia's head, a shovel raised defensively in the other. She looks down at her niece, sees her face stained with tears, and pulls her into a reassuring hug, before taking her hand and running back through the darkening streets, not stopping to ask questions.

They push through the main door. Vegetables are still strewn across the parlour, but Mother is not where she was, though the cushions still show the indent of her body. Lydia wants to call out, but her voice is stuck in her throat. Father emerges from the bedroom and closes the door softly behind him. He must have returned from work, found the carnage, carried Mother from the parlour and set her in their bed. He's not a tall, muscular man. His strength is in his mind, in the knowledge he holds there, his understanding of how to make people better. Lydia is sure he will use his expertise now to make Mother well again.

Lydia sees a look pass between her father and her aunt, a small shake of the head, her father's lips tight as he pushes his glasses back up his nose.

'Am I too late?' Aunt Nina says.

'There's not much time,' Father says. 'My suspicion is cholera. And the Bolsheviks are running amok in the city again. There's no escape this time.'

'I know, I just heard about it on the radio,' Aunt Nina says.

'It's a death sentence.' Father sighs. 'Another uprising. If they come to our door in the night, what chance do we stand?'

'Russia has always been dangerous,' her aunt agrees. 'Every day, I'm scared for our lives. Now this new violence.'

'It's time,' he says heavily. 'Take the train to China; there's a community of Russian refugees in Harbin. You should be safe there. Take Lydia with you, please?' he says. 'I can't leave now, not with Vera in this state. And my patients need me.'

'Of course.' Her aunt squeezes her arm. 'But I need to see my sister first.'

He nods and turns to his daughter. 'My precious girl, I want to show you something outside,' he says to Lydia. Then he turns to her aunt. 'Before you go in, please just give me a moment.'

Father returns to the bedroom, slipping through the door and closing it quickly, but not before Lydia sees the pale hand of her mother hanging from the bed. Her aunt sees it, too, and bends to her level, her eyes searching Lydia's, brushing her hair out of her eyes.

'We must be strong; we must not let our emotions get the better of us,' she says, wiping her own cheeks, her brows bent together.

Lydia nods.

A minute later, Father emerges from the bedroom. He has his thick leather jacket on, with its red fur collar. Whenever he wears it, Lydia begs to be carried, even though she's too tall, but still, she always jumps on her father's back and buries her nose into his neck, where the smell is intense – like burnt wood. This time she tells herself that she isn't a child any more and stays where she is.

One of Father's hands is in the pocket of his jacket, and there's something bulky there – he looks nervously around, clearing his throat. Lydia's aunt steps past them both and enters the room, where the candlelight is gently flickering.

Father puts a hand on Lydia's shoulder and they go outside.

Night has fallen, but a full moon bounces off the fresh snow like a ball. She looks across the fields at the back of their house, icicles hanging from the trees, her breath blooming in front of her face. Father shuffles from foot to foot, blows on his hands, his eyes refusing to settle. Lydia can see the muscles around his mouth twitching, as if he's rehearsing his words. He exhales deeply and bends down to address his daughter directly. Lydia sees tears in his eyes.

She throws her arms around her father, and he pulls her in. She must be brave, so she does not cry. When he releases her, he puts his hand into his pocket and pulls out a gun.

'This is for you,' he says, holding it tenderly.

Lydia looks at the gleaming metal, the long shaft with its dark hole.

She is very, very scared.

Father turns the gun over, so she can see both sides, then nudges the barrel, which opens with a spin. 'Five bullets,' he says. 'See?' He tips them into his palm.

Lydia narrows her eyes and nods. There are indeed five rounded gold pellets, each the size of her little finger. She doesn't understand what they have to do with her.

He pushes one into her hand.

'These are very dangerous, and very precious. Don't waste a single one.'

Lydia holds the bullet for a second, then gives it back. Her father carefully replaces each one into the chamber of the gun, then closes the barrel again with a spin.

'Each one of these bullets is a chance for your survival,' he says seriously. 'Use them wisely.'

She begins to shake from a place deep inside her small body.

He smiles with kind eyes. 'The world is ugly. This is your future. I'm sorry,' he adds. 'I never wanted to tell you this, but there are bad people out there who may want to hurt you. You must never let that happen.' She takes the gun in both hands. It's a huge, horrible thing, heavy and cruel. 'This is how you hold it,' he says. 'If you pull here, a bullet will fire out.' He pushes her finger through the trigger. 'Pull back this clasp. That's the one, but be very careful. This is something that must be treated with respect, always.'

Lydia is pointing the gun into the thicket of trees. Her knees feel molten hot and there's a vibration in her head she has never experienced before.

Then a rabbit comes into the clearing, its long ears lilac against the snow.

'Shoot,' her father whispers. She wonders if he has lost his mind. He has never asked anything like this of her before. He saves lives. He would not roll up his newspaper to use against a fly. He's gentle, a man of books and letters and languages. He's not a killer.

The rabbit's nose is twitching, its eyes like the buttons on her doll.

'Shoot,' he says again, more firmly this time. He looks so terribly sad. Lydia has never disobeyed her father before. She wants to go back to the classroom, see her name on the blackboard. 'I wouldn't ask you if it wasn't of the utmost importance,' he says gently.

She pulls the trigger. The rabbit flinches but, a second later, it hops along, unscathed. The noise reverberates around the clearing, and is taken up by the cawing crows, shocked from their night-time nests high up in the branches. A tree bears the scar of her stray bullet. That is one bullet down. She wants to fire out the other four as fast as possible, so there will be none left and she will not have to bear the weight of these treacheries on her shoulders.

Her father takes the weapon from her. She hopes this is all over. But he stretches out his arm, points quickly and fires. The rabbit falls on its side, the snow beside it bursting red.

Lydia hammers her father, on his thighs, his torso, with all her might. She burns with rage and shame and confusion. 'No!' she shouts. 'No, no, no! I hate you.'

'I understand how you feel right now, but this is how it has to be,' he says, trying to contain her. 'I hope one day you'll forgive me. My wish for you is that you have a long life, and that you find fulfilment and joy. For now, just know that this gun may be the difference between you making it alive to Harbin or not.'

The words melt in her ears, and they fail to make any sense.

He walks over to the rabbit, picks it up by its hind legs and returns to her.

'Your mother is very unwell,' he says with difficulty. 'I'll stay with her, for as long as it takes. But tonight, you, my only child, my sweet, clever daughter, must leave on a difficult journey, all the way to China. It breaks my heart that it has come to this, to see our country being ripped apart. But it's too dangerous for you to stay. A revolution is under way and there are people who have nothing left to lose. They will kill for whatever they believe in, and many innocent people will get caught in that violence. Your aunt will look after you. You'll make a new life. We'll join you as soon as your mother is better, when it's safe.'

Lydia cannot keep up with the cadence of his words. She can only grasp his message by reading the horror and hurt playing out on his face. She woke up this morning, and her life was normal, the lines straight. Now nothing will ever flow in the right direction again.

'Come now,' he says. 'Your Aunt Nina will be wondering what's kept us.' He walks towards the house and she understands that she's meant to follow. 'There's time for you to wash yourself while I do what's needed with this,' he says, indicating the rabbit. 'Pack what you need in your satchel – clothes, books, any toys you've not outgrown. And don't forget the gun. It's yours now. You must never be without it. Promise me,' he says.

Lydia will not let her emotions get the better of her. She looks at this man, who she thought she knew: who is he now? She doesn't want to hate her own father.

'The gun has three bullets left,' he adds gently. 'You must use them wisely.'

Lydia only hopes that one day she will understand the lesson he has tried to push upon her. That she'll appreciate the choices he had to make in this moment to keep her safe.

⌇

Only a few hours later, Lydia and her aunt are herded on to a huge train, the side battered as if by metal-tipped branches, mud splattered up from the wheels. The train ploughs through Siberia into China. The man who sold them their ticket had explained, in gruff tones, that it would take them at least five days to reach Harbin in the north, but the harsh weather would cause delays. The station is overflowing with people who are making the same trip, their suitcases hurriedly packed, their eyes wide, fleeing the danger wrought in their own country for the unknown territory of another. Lydia knows her geography, but had never heard of Harbin in northern China before this evening. All she knows is that there will be other Russians there, people who have the money to leave. She doesn't let go of her aunt's hand.

Lydia had hugged her father as she left her home, and felt the familiar warmth for him return. He was Father again, not a stranger with a weapon. She'd packed what she needed – a bottle of her mother's perfume, her prized collection of stamps, and one of her father's medical textbooks – into a briefcase embossed with his initials, rather than her school satchel, and his face lit up with a sad smile when he saw her carrying it. He pressed into her hands a photograph in a silver frame: Lydia between her parents, a huge frilly bow in her hair, pearls around her mother's neck. 'Your mother and I believe in your potential,' he said.

To her aunt he gave a knapsack containing the rabbit, hastily skinned, prepared and cooked, to feed them in the days to come.

'It might be the only food you have. Write to me as soon as you get there,' he added. 'I'll miss you with every breath, mouseling,' he added to his daughter.

'Goodbye, Nikolai,' her aunt replied, hugging him tightly. 'May good luck smile upon you and my sister. Pray for us to come home soon.'

Lydia and her aunt find their cabin – they are lucky to have been able to secure a shared one with bunk beds, three to each wall. Lydia climbs to the top and her aunt settles in the middle bed beneath her. A family of four – an elderly grandmother wrapped in furs, a mother with pencilled arches for eyebrows, and two sons, one about her own age, the other on the brink of adulthood – squeeze into the space after them, and bang around with bags and boxes, trying to settle down for the night. The lights are bright, emitting a low buzz – a sound that's dulled as the engine starts and the brakes release.

The speed picks up and the chugging is rhythmic, like she's inside a pumping heart.

The younger boy smiles at Lydia from his position in the top bunk opposite hers.

She frowns and turns her back to him.

Lydia stays awake all that first night, listening to the strangled snores of the elderly woman in the bottom bunk, images running through her mind – the red ribbon, the strewn vegetables, the blood in the snow. She's only seven years old, and without her parents for the first time in her life. Beneath the thin pillow rests the briefcase with the gun.

This is Lydia's inheritance – and there are three bullets left.

She wonders how and when she will use them.

2

Harbin, 1917

Aunt Nina and Lydia arrive in China after several days in the packed carriage – human body odour mingling with the smell of food and the stench from the lavatories. They are all relieved to tumble out of the vestibule, even if they are stepping into an uncertain future. Harbin is one of the final stops on the Trans-Siberian Express, a route fed by the newly constructed train line that cuts through the epic landmass like an artery. Most Russians disembark at the town; few continue further. Nobody makes such a journey or starts a new life here out of choice, and that fact is scrubbed on to the faces of everyone they see: the locals – who are aware that their traditional way of life is being superseded by Russian traditions and design – and refugees, who long for a home that's fragmenting into a disjointed memory.

Lydia and her Aunt Nina share a damp room with two other women, in a building in an undesirable part of town. The wall by Lydia's bed blooms with a dusting of black spores and long-antennaed insects disappear into the rotting woodwork. Ants mountaineer over every piece of furniture, and march back to a crack in the glass carrying dusty crumbs. Her mattress is on pallets, and she keeps her father's briefcase, her precious belongings locked inside, within arm's reach. Her throat dries and she develops a persistent cough.

There are dozens of strangers coming and going all day, most of whom speak in languages she has never heard before. Her aunt and the women are careful to lock the door to their room. Lydia has seen how the handle twists in the night, how the heft of a body seems to push up against it, testing to see how easily it will give. The door has held firm, so far.

Lydia can't help but wonder how this place, far from her family, thousands of miles from home, is meant to be safer than what they left behind in Russia. She does not feel safe. She has become a stranger in a new land, her history wiped out by relocation.

‿⟍

Lydia never leaves her aunt's side; together, they explore Harbin, looking for work. Aunt Nina leaves her name at run-down establishments – places that sell parcels of steamed white dumplings, where long-necked ducks hang in the window and unidentifiable vegetables are diced in corners. Back home, Aunt Nina spent her days in the office of a government department, assisting with administrative tasks, correspondence, record-keeping. She's a smart woman, dedicated to her job, with no husband or children to distract her, she'd say. Her husband died when she was young, after they had only been married for a few years. Lydia can't remember him. All she knows is that he was an engineer and that it was an accident that claimed his life.

There are no such opportunities here. Instead, Aunt Nina offers her services washing dishes, sweeping out at closing time, cleaning bins or toilets. It doesn't help that Aunt Nina can't speak a word of this language, and that the city is already overwhelmed with Russian émigrés. Their labour can be bought cheap, and they can't afford the luxury of worrying about respect or dignity. As they hurry through the sleet back to their accommodation, Lydia sees a Russian officer in a tattered uniform begging at the door of a theatre. It seems that nobody's luck has turned for the better away from their homeland. Aunt Nina pulls her firmly by the hand. 'You've seen enough for one day, little bee.'

Lydia craves the moment when they'll be able to return, to Tomsk, to her parents.

'They'll arrive here soon enough,' Aunt Nina reminds her. 'They'll do everything they can to be with us again. You know they miss you dearly, don't you?'

↜

Three weeks after they arrive – having crossed thousands of miles by train – a letter is passed through several hands at the hostel until it lands in her own, bearing her father's elegant handwriting. Lydia passes the envelope to her Aunt Nina, who looks at it with surprise.

Lydia holds her breath as Aunt Nina opens it, the older woman scanning the paper, a small smile on her puzzled face. Her eyes continue in this way for a few seconds, before they stop again, abruptly. The letter drops on to the bed.

'My sister, your poor mama, lovely Vera.' Her aunt's voice breaks. 'Oh, little one, I'm so sorry, but she didn't make it. Your father couldn't make her better.'

The inside of Lydia has turned to stone. She's unable to move her tongue, her fingers, even to blink. Her breath is a concrete cloud. Aunt Nina notices and moves closer.

'You do understand what I'm saying, mouseling, don't you?'

Lydia's lips move but no sounds come out.

In the corner of the window, a spider cocoons a fresh catch in its web.

'Your father's heartbroken,' Aunt Nina continues, picking up the letter, a faraway look in her eyes, her shoulders slumped. 'We all are.'

Lydia is acutely aware of the inhalations of air passing through her nostrils.

'Very good,' her aunt concedes. 'You're strong and brave. You don't get overwhelmed, like other little girls.'

She kisses her on the head, and a little warmth flows up Lydia's spine. If she doesn't look up, she can imagine it's her mother holding her, saying sweet words. If she refuses to believe it, it doesn't have to be true. Her mother is back in Russia – that is all.

Lydia coughs, that strange strangled sound she's getting used to, forcing the phlegm up her throat so that she can get the air she so desperately needs.

'And Father?' she manages to ask. 'How long till he can join us?'

'It doesn't say.'

Another month passes, and Aunt Nina makes the decision to enrol Lydia at the local lyceum, with new classrooms established for the overspill of Russian émigrés pouring into this cold corner of China. Lydia works diligently, as ever. But her teacher notes that she's serious and withdrawn, and the other girls, young Russians and Serbians, are not drawn to her. Those who attempt interaction are subtly repelled – questions linger unanswered, offers to sit together at lunchtime go unheeded, Lydia choosing instead to read alone in the playground.

The books she borrows from the library are Russian. Lydia writes her name in the ledger one week and returns the book the next, having stayed up all night to reach the final pages. She's eight years old and starting to read Chekhov, Tolstoy, Dostoevsky. She's unmoved by the romance, grand gestures and wild passions that consume the protagonists' lives. Instead, she's interested in structure, spiralling syntax and the complexities of language.

⸺

One morning, several months later, as she's entering the school gates, she notices a boy with a crown of chestnut hair, wide eyes, high cheekbones and a pale forehead. It's the younger brother from the train. He'd smiled at her that first night as they fled Tomsk. She'd ignored him, but he'd persisted, presenting her with half his pack of cards, encouraging her into a game, silently conducted across the gulf between their bunk beds. He'd shared his bagel, amused as she nibbled at it, half starved, having refused every morsel of rabbit. And later, as they disembarked in Harbin, he'd pushed a little figurine of a cat into her hand.

'You're the girl from Tomsk,' the boy says now. 'Do you like it here?'

She shrugs.

'My father says I can return home when it's safe,' she replies.

'My brother says there's no going home,' the boy announces.

His words feel like a betrayal. Long before the revolution, everyone in Harbin was aware that the Tsar had been dethroned. That's what the Bolsheviks wanted, wasn't it? So why was it taking so long for them to be allowed to return to Russia? Although she's young, Lydia has been listening in to conversations, keen to understand the events happening back in her homeland. She knows that following the revolution that saw thousands flee Russia, those who'd led the uprising had established a republic and they were transforming Russia into a socialist state – nationalizing industry, redistributing land and putting the workers in charge. Yet everyone said it *still* wasn't safe.

'Not after what happened to Tsar Nicholas and his family,' he adds. Lydia cannot bear to think about the harrowing murders of the emperor, his wife, Alexandra, and their five children, the details whispered between the women at night. Her own family hadn't necessarily supported the Tsar, but his death meant the past was over, the future a terrible unknown.

'I still have the white cat you gave me,' she says, changing the subject.

'You do?'

'The tail broke, but I glued it back on.'

'It belonged to my little sister,' he says.

His mouth twists in a way that makes Lydia think she shouldn't ask questions.

'I'm Lydia,' she decides to reveal, to crack the silence thickening between them.

'I know, I heard your aunt say it on the train.' She's surprised he remembers. 'I'm Mikhail,' he says, his hands in his pockets. 'But my friends call me Misha.'

~

Every night, Lydia dreams of Tomsk. She's always alone, the streets she grew up on empty, huge petals of snow falling around her, bullets beneath her feet amid the cobblestones. She prowls like the wolves past the school and the bakery, past the swimming pool and the park, never encountering another soul, never satisfying her hunger. Again and again, she passes her family house, the front door boarded up, the windows blackened with soot.

Occasionally, she dreams that a light is glowing in her parents' room, its warmth flooding out. The next day she suffers such sickness that she can barely leave her bed.

She fears she will never return home.

Time passes – months, then a year. She advances at school, her intellect expands. She studies at weekends, licking her thumb to turn another page, squinting, sighing. She passes exams easily.

Her father writes weekly. He tells her about the latest battles, about the White Army and the anti-Bolsheviks, the territorial losses since the end of the war. Lydia wonders if he'd look the same, were he to disembark from the train in Harbin – whether his moustache would have altered in style, or his skin taken on the wrinkles of older age. She wonders whether he'd recognize her with all the changes her growing body has undergone.

But he doesn't arrive. He's not yet able to make the journey – he's needed, desperately, at the hospital in Tomsk. He's one of the few qualified doctors left, and without him many children would die, especially with the fresh waves of epidemics sweeping Russia – typhoid, and cholera, which is what killed her mother. Why do those children get to have him, and not her? He sends his love with each letter and asks for her news. She tells him she intends to be a doctor, like him, when she grows up. She wants to help people, ease their pain, make them better. She wants to leave this world better than she has found it.

That's a noble ambition, he writes in reply. *I'm humbled you want to follow in my footsteps, and very proud of you, my daughter.*

⸎

The letters stop in February 1922, when Lydia is twelve. By this point, she has not seen her father in five years. In that time, Lydia's and Aunt Nina's fortunes have gently improved. Each day has been a negotiation for survival, a lesson in using their wits and initiative. They have just enough money. As an educated woman, Nina has been able to find shifts as a tutor, helping the children of other émigrés with Russian language, literature and history.

Aunt Nina says Lydia is not the girl she would have been if political events at home had not uprooted her life, stripping away everyone she cared about. Thank goodness she still has Nina, her lovely aunt, who has taught her to mould dignity from her

distress, and that being a woman in a modern world holds opportunities for those smart enough to spot them.

One week passes to the next, then a month, without any word
from her father. Aunt Nina writes to anyone she can think of who
might still be in Tomsk. Then, after three months, they get a letter
back, with a newspaper clipping folded inside.

*Nikolai Ivanovich Delectorski, 50, renowned paediatrician at the
medical faculty of Tomsk University, where he worked for more than
two decades, succumbed to typhus, having caught it from a patient
in his care as the epidemic ravaged the country.*

Typhus is a vector-borne disease spread by lice, fleas or mites,
Lydia knows from her textbooks. It is prevalent in unsanitary and
overcrowded conditions. It's caused by the parasitic bacterium
Rickettsia prowazekii and transmitted through infected faeces. She
has read Chekhov's story 'Excellent People', in which typhus kills a
man. She'd always imagined her father at his hospital, wearing a
starched white coat, attending sick children in a sanitized environment. She realizes how much of a fantasy that was and what a
sacrifice he'd made.

*Dr Delectorski selflessly continued at the hospital when others
refused. He remained in Soviet Russia when others fled – and he put
others, always, above himself, and sacrificed his life for the greater
good. Widower of Vera (née Pavlovna), he is survived by a
daughter.*

Survived, Lydia thinks. She must do whatever it takes to survive,
for his sake now.

Lydia places the obituary in her briefcase. She rarely opens it
these days, but inside is the cat figurine with the disjointed tail, the
perfume, the framed photograph of her parents – the pearls still
gleaming around her mother's neck – and the gun.

3

Harbin, 1928

At the age of eighteen, tall, and with fair hair that falls to her waist, Lydia is set to graduate as one of the top students at the Russian lyceum. It's strange, but her academic success brings her less satisfaction than people around her seem to expect. She has simply done what comes naturally. Misha, her only friend, squeezed through his exams and is now working as a mechanic, his hands already toughened and greasy from the labour. He has no great intelligence, he admits, and is in awe of all she has achieved.

Lydia Delectorskaya has now lived for more years in Harbin than she ever spent in Russia, yet this cold quarter of China has never come close to feeling like home. In eleven years as an émigré, she has learned many hard lessons, even though she and Nina – because of her aunt's resourcefulness – have enjoyed privileges others weren't able to access. Nina has passed on cooking skills to Lydia, making sure they always have food on the table, even if it's conjured from meagre ingredients. They rent a small apartment and don't have to share. It's clean, well organized. Nina has taught Lydia the meaning of sacrifice, initiative, hard work.

The events of the past decade could have unfolded in many

ways, especially after her father died, but Lydia understood she had a path to follow. The only ambition Lydia has ever known is to become a doctor, like her father, and improve the lives of other people. She wonders about her future, while living with the ghosts of her past. She still dreams of returning to Tomsk, to take up a position at the hospital where her father worked, even if it's politically impossible.

The Russian Empire has undergone its own transformation in the time she has been away. Under its most recent leader, Joseph Stalin, Russia has a new identity – the Soviet Union. It has become unrecognizable. The émigré community in Harbin have been warned that the country is still unstable and that, for those who left, it remains dangerous to return. The five years of civil war may be over, but those who fled are now perceived as enemies of the state and will face persecution if they go back. Lydia hardly believes it can be true. She doesn't want to fear, or pity, the place that was once her home.

Her aunt, now fifty-four – older than her mother or father ever became – is starting to slow down. Nina complains of aches and pains, as is normal at that age. Lydia asks if she can examine her, to help apply what she has learned in her textbooks, but Nina always brushes her off, and insists she has some chore or other to attend to. She doesn't want fuss, is her refrain.

The hard truth is that university, especially medical school, is a distant dream. Aunt Nina has worked hard all her life, but has nothing to show for it financially. There isn't a higher education institution in Harbin that teaches in Russian, and Lydia doesn't have the skills to take such a demanding course not in her native language. On top of that, she doesn't want to leave her aunt. She adores the woman and can't imagine being separated. They've been through everything together. Nina is the only living link Lydia has to her past and her parents.

Lydia talks about her future with her favoured teacher at the lyceum – a feline-looking man from Moscow, fond of high-waisted trousers. Lydia wants to get his advice on whether she should apply for a scholarship, and where, near Harbin, might be suitable for an educated-but-poor Russian woman with sky-high ambitions.

'You really should consider the Sorbonne School of Medicine, in Paris,' he says. 'France would be lucky to have you.'

'France?' she asks. She'd never considered leaving China for another country.

'It's only the best medical school in the world,' he says.

'But I can't imagine leaving my aunt, my life here.'

'Paris is full of culture, art, young people having fun,' her teacher says. 'It's liberal. Harbin has offered you a safe place since you left Russia, but the world is waiting.'

'You must know me better than that by now, sir,' Lydia says.

'You might surprise yourself, young Lydia.'

She frowns.

He looks at her seriously, as if he's reading her mind. 'Your aunt told me she'd encourage you to do whatever it takes, for the sake of your future, if that's what you're worried about,' he says. The elegant arches of Lydia's dark brows clench together.

When have her elders had these private conversations about her fate?

'I'd never leave her,' Lydia replies.

'Your aunt's of the opinion that your father, Dr Delectorski, would have been delighted at the prospect of you studying in Paris.'

Lydia's heart contracts. Nobody has mentioned her father directly in many years. But he exists so vibrantly in her own mind, it's as if he were still alive.

'If I go anywhere, it should be home,' Lydia insists.

'Home is a memory we all nurture,' her teacher replies. 'But what you long for is already gone. Memory is fickle. You need to find a new home elsewhere.'

Lydia feels a flare of defiance. Why does everyone let go of their past without a fight? Her fellow Russians here seem to have abandoned their history so easily. News about Russia is hard to come by, and when it arrives now, she notices that it passes through the expat community with far less urgency than before. It's depressing that nothing has improved.

Her teacher talks to her about scholarships and funds that might help her. Fees for foreign students are exorbitant, she knows, and Lydia cannot afford to harbour such illusions. The world has proved itself to be hostile, immune to her wilder hopes. There will be no favours for her. 'Such a thing isn't possible for Russians like me,' she reprimands him.

'Destiny will take you where you need to go,' her teacher replies, passing over the application forms, already bearing her name alongside his elegant signature.

⌒

It's a cold day in early spring when her aunt asks Lydia to go for a walk with her. This is not an unusual request – Nina, with her ash-grey hair and mustard cardigans, can often be seen walking with her niece. Together, they head south along the Sungari; the river seems to flow most calmly in the areas it is deepest. They typically sit on a bench and talk of not much at all – certainly not the circumstances that drew them together and have kept them wrapped around one another so tightly, only the day-to-day musings of two women who share a striking resemblance and who love each other deeply.

Today, Lydia observes her aunt closely. There's something about her demeanour that sets Lydia's nerves on edge. The young woman has been caught up in thoughts of her future; she has failed to see that Nina might be struggling to come to terms with hers, too.

'My little mouseling,' Aunt Nina says, with that typical warmth in her voice. She smiles reassuringly, looking so much like her sister, Lydia's mother. 'I need to tell you something.' They have gravitated to a familiar stop in their favourite park. Men play chess at stone tables to their right, chins tucked against necks; children pull themselves up a climbing frame, swinging from bar to bar, arms crossed as they take the old metal slide.

'My darling Lydia,' Nina continues, and takes a deep breath. 'Last year, I found a lump. In my stomach. I didn't want to worry you and I saw a doctor, who reassured me it was nothing to worry about. But a few months ago, I had more trouble. It seemed bigger, and I lost my appetite. I suppose you've noticed my meagre mouthfuls at mealtimes?' She pauses while Lydia takes in what she's saying. 'You've been through so much, and been so stoical. I'm sorry to tell you, my sweet girl, but it's a tumour. I don't have very long left to me . . .'

Lydia is breathless. There's a moment of disorientation. Everything in her mind seems to tumble. She thinks of her aunt, of everything she has sacrificed. When they left Russia, Nina was forty-three. She could have met someone, married again. But she gave everything to make sure Lydia would thrive. She has always treated Lydia like a daughter; she said the girl was everything she could have wanted in this world.

Instantly, Lydia is crying. Tears that she swallowed down, following the death of her mother and father, and now she cannot stop them rolling down her cheeks. 'Nina, no,' she says, wrapping her arms around her aunt, burying her face in her scarf. 'It can't be true. Did you get another opinion? Did you talk about treatments or surgery?'

Nina looks at her, and nods.

'I've made my peace with it,' she says. 'The only thing I fear is leaving you.'

There are tears in her aunt's eyes, too. Lydia can see her future reflected there – one in which she is utterly alone, with nothing to anchor her. It's terrifying.

'I need to know you will be strong, my little mouseling, like you've always been. I need to know that you will make good decisions, but not be afraid to take your chances. Be sensible, but not too sensible.'

The children in the playground scream in circles around them, oblivious to their pain.

'I know you'll get better, I just know it,' Lydia says.

'If I see the end of the year, I'll count myself lucky. I do, anyway, because of you.'

Nina strokes Lydia's face, brushing tears over the curve of her niece's cheek.

'I don't know what I'd do without you,' Lydia says.

'There's Misha,' Nina says delicately. 'I know he thinks the world of you.'

'Misha?' Lydia hasn't wanted to notice the way he looks at her.

'He's been in love with you since the day we left Russia. He's become a good man.'

Lydia adores Misha, but as a friend. She imagines life as his wife, as a mother to their children, their little family settled in Harbin for decades to come. It's not a bad future, but no matter how kind Lydia is certain he'd be, it's not enough. She'd feel she was compromising something of herself, her potential. To him, she'll always be the girl from Tomsk, a woman haunted by tragedy and destruction, by upheaval. Lydia wishes things were different but, against her will, that girl is gone and she needs to forge a new path.

Her aunt hands her an envelope. 'I've been putting a little aside each week, ever since you were a girl. It's not a huge amount, but it should set you up on your own,' she says.

Lydia takes the money. The selflessness of the gesture knocks the air from her lungs.

'Aunt Nina, I couldn't. Please.' Lydia is wiping away her tears again.

'But you must. Find something to believe in. I hope your life is a long one, my little Lydia. And that whatever you do, you will make me and your parents proud. I've no doubt about it. Whether you marry Misha, or find a way to go to the Sorbonne, or something else entirely, I know you'll leave your mark on the world.' The sun slants between the trees and there's a new intensity to the fall of light. Lydia does not know how she'll get through the days. 'And I know, of course, about the gun that Nikolai gave you,' Aunt Nina adds delicately. She has never mentioned it before, and Lydia wasn't aware she knew about it. 'My brother-in-law was a decent and dedicated man. I know he'll have warned you to be careful with it. But you're not a child any more. What I mean to say is, I'm sure you're aware that it's a dangerous weapon, and you should use it only when there is no other choice. I believe you're sensible enough to do that.'

Lydia hangs her head. It feels as if a shameful secret has been exposed. But her aunt smiles and runs her hands up and down Lydia's arms, to warm and reassure her.

As Nina tries to stand, Lydia can already see the evidence of illness across her aunt's features. How could she have missed it? And what else could be hiding in plain sight?

4

Paris, France, 1929

L ydia arrives in Paris alone. She's nineteen years old, once more in a foreign country, and determined to cut a shape for herself out of the fabric of France. A year has passed since that afternoon in the park, when her life shifted on its axis. Aunt Nina died four months ago. A strong woman, with a constitution of steel, she outlived even the most optimistic predictions from the doctors in Harbin. Lydia was by her side every step of the way, taking her to appointments, measuring out and administering medicines, massaging her feet when they became so swollen she could no longer walk. She'd read to her when Aunt Nina woke in the night. Towards the end, Lydia would bathe her aunt's fragile body. She'd comb her hair, and sponge water into her mouth to keep her hydrated. She held Nina's hand as she got weaker and her moments of lucidity became shorter, her mind spiralling into a kind of blessed unconsciousness over the course of those final few weeks. Nina would mumble anecdotes about her younger days alongside her sister, Vera, talking to Lydia as if she were her mother – her mind distorted by pain. Lydia found it strangely comforting, to become her long-deceased mother in those moments. She hoped it brought relief to Nina, to feel, for a few brief spells, that she was sharing a room with the sister she'd lost.

When the day came that Aunt Nina's energy dipped for the final time, Lydia closed her eyelids, sitting with her for hours as the light faded. It felt as if Nina were on a journey once more, a long train ride into the night, returning to the people who loved her eternally.

In the aftermath, Lydia's grief felt insurmountable. Everything had collapsed around her, even her belief in medicine. It hadn't come close to helping her save the people who had meant the most to her in the world, just as her father's medical knowledge hadn't been able to save her mother. For the first months, Lydia didn't leave her apartment. The rent had been paid in advance for the following three months, which bought her time. Misha would come with food and supplies, try to coax her from the darkness back into the moment. When he left, she'd stare at the gun, wondering if one bullet was all she'd ever need.

It brought Lydia no joy when Misha handed her the letter confirming that she had been accepted into the Sorbonne – her aunt and teacher had insisted that she send the application, saying there must be a way to make it possible, that she should just apply and hope for the best. But Lydia didn't believe in miracles. The money her aunt had given her would help her survive, but there was no way she could afford the exorbitant fees for the school, whatever her hopes and dreams. She was angry to be offered a place and not be in a position to accept it. How cruel that one's life is defined by money – the never-ending lack of it.

Misha, after a respectful pause, proposed marriage, as Aunt Nina had predicted. He said he adored her, that together they'd create the stability they craved. It was a kind gesture, but Lydia had to turn him down. She'd always feared that she didn't have the capacity to love, and in her darkest days after Nina's death, she doubted she'd ever have a normal relationship, or anything resembling marriage or children. She feared the bond of needing others, of making them integral to her life. Everyone she loved had been taken away, and she couldn't bear to lose anyone else who mattered, especially someone as good and gentle as Misha.

The only way out of her grief, Lydia felt, was to start afresh. She no longer wanted to remain in Harbin, with its painful memories, and Misha would find it easier to move on without her there. Despite the fact she couldn't afford to train as a doctor, Paris was the place that she couldn't shake from her mind. It was the place her aunt had envisioned for her.

～

Lydia arrives in Paris after a spine-destroying month's travel from China. She's exhausted by a journey that included long stretches of time on a steamship, and dizzying weeks on a train. But walking through the streets, she instantly feels as if she has stepped into another world. After more than a decade of living in China, Lydia is surprised by the fashions of this European capital. Women wear stylish, figure-hugging dresses, stepping confidently along the road in modest heels and carrying chic handbags, their hairstyles considerably different from those she has known in Harbin. There's evidence of modern technology and cultural life. She passes bakeries and jazz clubs, theatres showing motion pictures, hidden galleries. But there are shared signs, too, of people whose lives have been affected by the economic downturn of the past few years – drunks on street corners, the homeless.

Lydia has her aunt's savings stashed safely, but she's determined to find a way to earn a living as soon as possible.

Paris is a fast-paced melting pot of many cultures and communities. But still, Lydia is surprised to hear people speaking English, a language she learned at school in Harbin. She spots a group of young women who sound as if they may be from Russia, and she gravitates towards them, hoping they might lead her in a direction that feels familiar – a cheap part of the capital that's hospitable to foreigners, where new arrivals won't be harassed or stand out too much. The women stop at a boulangerie. Lydia approaches. They exchange a few words in Russian, and Lydia explains that she's looking for a place to stay, just for a short while, before she makes any decisions about what to do next. They give her the address of a friend who has space for a few weeks while her housemate is away in the south. They tell her the girl is hoping to break into the movie scene in Nice – to get work as an extra on set or even to land a more significant role. Directors are always on the hunt for pretty young things, apparently.

By the evening, Lydia has secured the room and paid to stay for two weeks.

She wants to explore Paris, get a taste of the city her teacher had been so enthusiastic about, the place where her aunt had projected her into a dazzling future – and see if it's the right fit.

～

Lydia makes trips to landmarks, including Notre-Dame – where she lights a candle for Aunt Nina, who's never far from her mind – and visits the Louvre. Lydia was hardly exposed to much art in Harbin, and has only seen poor reproductions of masterpieces in books, but she knows that Paris is a magnet for artists, writers and intellectuals from around the world.

In the Louvre, she takes in the *Mona Lisa* and works by van Gogh and other artists: Rembrandt, Delacroix, Cézanne. But she can't help feeling she's missing something, the language to understand it. She feels there's more beauty in biology – the nucleus of a cell – far more light to be found in the photosynthesis of a plant, more magic in the development of pigment in petals.

The place that keeps calling to her, of course, is the Sorbonne. She may not be able to afford the medical school, but she also can't stay away. It's in the 13th arrondissement, a grand building, once home to a gunpowder factory. She lingers, sees young men and a few women her age, or a year or two older, carrying armloads of books from the library. The women wear berets and rouge and silk scarves knotted at their collarbones. They sit at roadside cafés, eating macarons and madeleines, drinking coffee with frothed milk. This world is not open to her, Lydia realizes with a shock of sadness.

This city just reminds her of all the doors that are closed.

~

After two weeks, Lydia still can't shake the feeling that Paris isn't for her. Amid the grief of her aunt's passing, the city had seemed like a promise, that somehow she was fulfilling her aunt's belief in her by coming here; yet despite the beauty of its buildings and the buzz of its streets, Lydia can't find her footing. The city feels too big, too turbulent. She likes her community to be smaller, to know the people who sell her vegetables and bake the bread she eats. She's intrigued by the lure of the coastline, tempted by the promise of a bright punch of heat – something, as a Siberian, she has rarely known. The Russian girls she has met in Paris tell her the south is ripe with potential. It's always hot and money flows readily, they promise, with bar work easy to come by. There's a thriving Russian community, too.

It sounds too good to be true. But she doesn't have much to lose.

Yes, the south of France, she thinks, with its sunshine and sea. Why not? Lydia feels as if she were rolling a dice, gambling with fate.

She's a woman who knows one thing: she needs to make her own luck.

~

Just minutes after stepping down from the train in Nice, Lydia is already sweltering, the Midi sunshine working a line of sweat between her shoulder blades. The pavement seems to swell with the sun's heat – it rises from the tarmacadam to her knees in a thick, hazy layer, and slips under her skirts, moistening her thighs. She walks along the Promenade des Anglais, her grip loosening on the handles of her luggage that contains all her worldly belongings. Unexpectedly, she feels a wave of homesickness – a new experience, as she has only ever missed Tomsk before; now it's Harbin, her aunt, and the life she used to have there.

Gulls shear through the expanse of sky, and the golden light on the sea's broad horizon reminds her of the vastness of the Siberian plains. The place is frothy with crowds – bronzed women in bathing suits, wet-haired men on the grey-stone beach glinting with oil and untold desires. She thinks of her own desires; how they have been reshaped over recent months. Already, Lydia is not who she thought she was. But she's determined to give her life new meaning, to find a purpose, whatever that may look like.

She books into a cheap hotel in a less popular part of the Old Town. Her room, at the top of the building, is small but clean, the mattress firm, with one thin pillow. She stores her cases under the bed and opens the window, which has a view over the rooftops, the narrow ribbon of sea in the distance. She's tired and achy after the long journey, but still, she smiles. Somehow this place already suits her better than the frenzy of Paris.

But she isn't here to relax. The journeys from Harbin and to the south, plus the weeks in the capital, have eaten into her reserves, so the first thing Lydia must do – ideally today – is find a job; anything that pays enough to keep her afloat. It won't be easy – people like her don't have the necessary employment status in France. It's forbidden for foreign nationals to earn a salary in a traditional way, so they're often exploited and options are limited. All that will be open to her are unregulated roles for a minimal wage.

Lydia's French is poor, unsophisticated. She's hoping for work as an au pair, perhaps, or serving in a restaurant. If she can't find that, she may have to be open to bar work, cleaning, deliveries, offering her services as . . . what, exactly? She shakes the worst-case scenarios from her mind.

~

Two weeks later, Lydia is still without a job, and her funds are running dangerously low. Every day since she arrived, she has traipsed around Nice, leaving her details in places she could imagine working. But when she does get a response, she has to admit she has no experience, so none of the leads prove fruitful. She'd been told in Paris that work would be easy to come by. But all she has to show for her efforts is sore feet.

Tired and crabby, Lydia takes a seat in a bar and orders a cheap, cold drink. She's spent the last of her money paying four weeks' rent upfront on the room. Like most young women on the Riviera, she has no safety net, nothing to fall back on.

The waiter brings chilled peach juice in a tall glass and she takes a sip. The street outside is bustling and smells of hot horses and uncollected refuse. She finishes the peach juice, mopping the condensation from the glass-topped table with a paper serviette. She puts the wet tissue in the ashtray, and holds it and the glass out to a passing waiter, who is rushing to answer the phone. Her eyes follow him, and she sees the man behind the high bar, talking in accented French, his cheeks rough with frequent exposure to the sun. He's polishing glasses as he talks, the phone nestled against his shoulder. She walks up to the counter, waits for him to finish. He laughs robustly, then hangs up the phone, flips the white polishing cloth over his arm, and notices her waiting.

'Mademoiselle,' he says with a finger in the air, turning his back on her to collect the bill for her drink, but maintaining eye contact through the mirrored panels above the register.

'Do you need a waitress . . . ?' she asks in halting French when he turns.

'Ah, but of course, *vous êtes russe!*' he says. 'It was my home, too – Moscow – but I have lived in Nice for the past thirteen years. I prefer the weather here,' he says with a shrug.

Lydia's tension loosens when she hears him reply in her own language.

'I arrived two weeks ago.'

'I can tell,' he says. He grimaces an apology. 'You don't want to work in a bar,' he adds. 'Certainly not this one. The hours are unsociable. The pay's terrible. So's the clientele. The men are insatiable. Surely, you can find better work? They're always in need of extras along this strip of coast, from here to Cannes and Saint-Tropez. That would suit a girl like you, no?'

'I'll work hard, do whatever's needed,' she says.

'There's good money on those film sets, you know, for doing not very much at all. You might meet a famous director, someone to take you on one of those nice yachts you see out there . . .' He gestures to the ocean.

'I don't want complications,' she says.

He juts his jaw to the right, a show of disapproval. 'Most girls are willing to turn up their skirts, plaster on their best smile, and hitch a ride along the coast quicker than . . .'

She turns. She was stupid to think he might be offering to help.

'Wait!' he shouts after her. 'No, no, don't listen to me. I'm just jealous that no director is going to notice me and get me on the red carpet. If you're looking for work, we might have something. Nothing glamorous. Just a few hours here and there to start with – evenings and weekends. If anything changes . . . there might be more, but nobody in Nice plans more than two weeks in advance.'

Lydia signals agreement, but inside she feels a swell of relief. She'll need to find other jobs to make ends meet, but it's a start.

'Like I said,' he continues, 'the pay's not great, but you'll be able to top up nicely with tips. You'll learn which of the old men are keen to open their wallet for the price of a smile, and which won't show you a penny no matter how much leg you flash. Come back tonight at six thirty – we close at one and there's at least an hour of cleaning after that. You can have a drink from the bar as you're doing it, which helps.'

'I rarely drink,' Lydia says simply. 'But thank you, really. I'll see you this evening.'

'Then you're not really Russian!' he shouts after her, whipping the polishing cloth on the bar. 'My name's Borislav, by the way,' he says. 'But you may call me Borya.'

Lydia walks back down the promenade, hoping that she has landed on her feet, at last.

~

Borya was not joking when he said the hours were long and exhausting. After that first shift, Lydia was crippled by her swollen feet, blisters swelling and bursting against her heels. She had never stayed up so late, nor worked so hard and fast, dealing with men who wanted more than she could give from the moment they stepped through the doors. That first night, she rolled up the sleeves of her blouse, the drinks on the tray she carried sloshing up her forearms as she ricocheted from one group to the next. She wore her hair scraped back into a low bun, her face bare, no jewellery or embellishments. But each group tried to break what they assumed was the shy or frosty exterior of the 'new girl', spurred on even more when they realized it was not an act to attract more attention. She shrugged off the jeering, reported anything worse than leering to Borya, who said: 'If I had to write down every time a customer was an ass to my waitress, the world would run out of ink.' She managed to administer a few well-timed missteps on to the feet of the worst offenders, who roared in pain, as if she'd broken a bone. But within a week or two, their respect came, or they'd simply got used to seeing her.

Lydia has found more permanent accommodation, too. She now shares a spartan apartment at the top of six flights of stairs with another young woman, from Corsica. She's usually in bed late – after her shift – and is up again early, when the sun crashes insufferably through the uneven shutters. She's out of the small apartment half an hour later. She paid peanuts for a rusty second-hand bicycle and uses it to dash along the promenade, heading away from the beach crowds to secluded spots further down the coast. She never sunbathes directly, like the tourists who flock to Nice's most popular stretches, but allows herself a few hours each day to enjoy the wraparound warmth from a comfortable spot in the shade, where she attempts to read yesterday's French newspapers, rescued from the bar's bin, and watches people make the most of their leisure time.

It all comes so naturally to them, she thinks. There's a part of her that hasn't softened in this new environment, as she'd hoped she would. She has always been such a dutiful girl, a young woman dedicated to her studies. Even now, she has a routine that sets her apart from others who are experiencing freedom for the first time.

The other Russians in Nice are just as keen as she is to survive. That's what they have in common. They'll do what it takes. They make connections and alliances, create networks of support. But Lydia mostly keeps to herself. She's once again setting up life in a new country, viewed perpetually as an outsider, cut off from her mother tongue. It makes her realize how much she misses Russia, that sense of being exactly where you are meant to be, with people you love.

Borya is helping her acclimatize. He's everything Misha was

not – strong, suave, with a stoic sense of his place in the world – but he also has significant weaknesses: arrogance, a flippancy regarding the correct ways of doing things, a complete disregard for the demands of law and order. His white trousers are tight, and he likes to show off his well-honed, sun-kissed arms. He's in no way the type of man she would usually choose to spend time with, but he's her boss, and in charge of the rota. Lydia has noticed that he schedules their shifts and days off at the same time. He hasn't proposed that they spend any of their free hours together yet, but she wonders how she will respond if he does.

Would she bring him to this secluded cove? Would he invite her to swim in the sea? Or suggest she rub lotion on to his back and shoulders? She pushes the thought from her mind.

She likes to think that she is not that type of woman – the frivolous, carefree kind. But she knows she has the capacity to act in ways that confound her; to make decisions that defy sense. She thinks of everything she's carrying from her past. A history in her blood of violence and brutal death. Lydia wants to think she'd never be the kind of woman to erupt or succumb to dangerous passions – or fire the gun she keeps – but how can a person say with any certainty that things will never come to that?

5

Nice, 1931

When Lydia has been in Nice for more than eighteen months, she accepts an invitation to move in with Borya, who has insisted she has no need to pay board while she's under his roof. They've been in a flirtatious relationship for several weeks, and while nothing has been acted upon, Lydia feels certain that the possibility is brewing. She can admit that she's attracted to him. He's older, which she finds reassuring – and established in Nice.

'I'd rather pay you a fair rent,' she says. 'My aunt taught me to look after myself.'

Borya shrugs, a gesture of mild confusion. She wonders if he can understand the delicate interplay for women between staying independent and forming allegiances to survive.

Still, she accepts his logic and agrees to move in.

Borya doesn't have much to offer, other than the promise of continued work, but there's something about the directionless nature of their potential union that appeals to her. He's so unlike anyone she has known before. She has a few female friends, women she knows from the bar. She could move in with them, she supposes, but it feels like delaying the inevitable. She also knows that if she's living with a man, the expectation is that they should be married. French society upholds a no-sex-before-marriage ethos, and to be seen to be living in sin is very much frowned upon, even along the Riviera. Whatever may develop between them, she'll be cautious, she decides, take it slowly.

Lydia isn't sure she trusts Borya, but then, she doesn't trust anyone.

In the past eighteen months, her French has greatly improved. She can hold a conversation, as long as she listens carefully. Working in a bar and spending time with less salubrious characters means she has a knowledge of the rougher side of the French language.

After she moves in, Borya doesn't push things. He's a man of nocturnal habits, and always sleeps late after his shifts. On his days off, he heads into Nice at dusk, a bundle of cash in his pocket, the notes crisp, folded and secured with a clip. He wears a silver necklace, the chain chunky, and undoes all the buttons of his shirt, except for the bottom three. He invites her to come along on these excursions, but she declines.

He often returns spinning on his feet, the alcohol strong on his breath. And the clip of cash much thinner – if it exists at all – than it was before. That's his business, she decides. He's a grown man. If he needs to gamble to feel alive, who is she to challenge him? Their lives are not so entwined that she can ask anything else of him. She can leave whenever she wants.

But she does not leave. As time goes on, she lets him stroke her thighs in the late afternoon, when she returns from the beach and has washed before her next shift at the bar. She wonders what it would be like to have sex with him – it would be her first time, and she expects he has much more experience in that department.

She often hears the words of Aunt Nina in her mind: Be sensible, but not too sensible.

Lydia knows she could let loose a little more often. But she's scared of what she might find if she stops being in control, if she lets a darker version of herself emerge.

⌒

One afternoon, reading the papers on the beach, Lydia notices a classified advertisement – it's for an artist's model. No nudity, the ad states bluntly, daytime hours. Lydia has been intrigued by the art world since her brief stay in Paris. She's rarely seen anything that quite captures the cacophony of feeling hiding beneath her steely exterior, but she's drawn to creative ways of interpreting the world, how others might make her see it afresh. She wants to understand art, and how better to do so than by being part of its creation?

'That kind of gig pays nicely,' Borya tells her. 'But, please. Be very careful. I wouldn't trust an artist; they're usually more lecherous than the drunkest drunk on payday.'

She still scrapes through with other daytime jobs – has even done a spot of dancing on film sets, like other girls her age – but none of them lasts more than a few weeks or months at a time. This might be more pleasant than most of those jobs, she hopes.

But there's something else that fuels her decision. It's a further relinquishing of her good-girl persona: being daring, blurring boundaries between what is and what is not respectable. She feels it in her proximity to Borya, too. It's dangerous self-destruction; survivors' guilt – for escaping the Revolution, for living when her parents, her aunt, have not.

⌒

Lydia knocks on the door to a house on the outskirts of Nice. She notices that the yellow paint out front is peeling, and she finds it ironic that a man whose profession is to wield colour has not resolved the issue. But she understands that there's a divide between the practicalities of painting to fix an unkempt door, and the creative impulse. It comes down to the question of what makes a person an artist, she supposes, as opposed to what makes a lawyer or doctor. What are the qualities that set one apart?

After a minute, an older man, lithe like a ballet dancer, opens the door, and looks her up and down. His gaze is not rude but appraising. He's weighing up her contours, her essence, seeing if she's the right shape for him. It's a strange experience, utterly devoid of anything sexual, which is how young women are typically evaluated. The sleeves of his shirt are rolled up and the veins in his arms protrude like worms, ready for the hook. His hair is greying at the temples, and there's a line of pastel-pink sunburn across his shoulders and neck. He'll have sat in the midday sun too long, she thinks.

'Welcome. You must be today's model,' he says, opening the door wide and ushering her through. 'I'm Paul. Pleased to make your acquaintance, mademoiselle.'

She nods and enters. 'Mademoiselle Delectorskaya. Lydia,' she says.

'Russian?' he asks. 'That will surely do.'

Lydia is led through the cool corridors to a dappled courtyard thick with overhanging vines. She's shown to a chaise longue strewn with decorated cushions and blankets.

He busies himself around the space. 'You sit here, no need to speak,' he says.

So this is her first interaction with an artist, she thinks. Perhaps they're not so bad. This man is middle-aged, erudite; classical music plays from another room.

Lydia isn't quite sure what she's supposed to do, so lies back on the cushions, arranges one ankle over the other, moves her hands across her stomach. She cannot find a natural position with his eyes upon her, so she shuffles self-consciously, until she feels she can move no more. She's not comfortable, but the artist is watching her, pencil poised. She supposes he's waiting to start. She feels tension across her shoulders, a need to fidget.

But the artist, even when she is still, doesn't make any marks on his sketchbook.

For the first hour, he just sits, looking, elbows on his knees, observing the shape of her. Then, eventually, he sighs in a self-satisfied way, and takes up a sketchpad, marking the paper with haphazard lines. During this time, his eyes flicker once or twice to her. She blinks away the discomforting feeling of being surplus to requirements. It's a strange experience for Lydia – this mixture of boredom and irritation. She's the kind of woman who only finds peace when she is busy, and can't relax unless she has made herself useful. She's not the type who can stare into the distance for hours on end. She tries to distract herself by looking around the courtyard – at the potted geraniums, a fragrant fig tree; catching the puttering chug of a fat small dog sleeping in the shade. The artist stops again, puts down his pencil. He sets up a canvas on an easel, opens a box of oil paints, selects a tube, unscrews the lid.

'Where did you say you're from?' he asks, addressing her once more.

'A small town in western Siberia,' Lydia replies.

'And your age?'

'Twenty-one,' she replies.

He accepts the information with a nod.

They make small talk for an hour or two, the artist asking a question, then losing himself in his work, moving his brush from the palette to the canvas, picking up the thread of their conversation when it strikes him. She doesn't have an advanced grasp of French, so he helps with words or phrases. Paul seems gentle enough, unthreatening. She wonders if he's successful, if he has made a name for himself. Either way, Lydia is intrigued by what he's creating on the canvas. An image of her, as she has never been seen before.

Lydia finds herself relaxing, despite herself. Perhaps it's the warm air, or the music, or the sound of the artist at work, but she closes her eyes, and when she opens them again, she realizes she has been sleeping. She sits up with a jolt, and Paul looks surprised.

'I didn't want to disturb you,' he says. 'I worked for a little while, then let you rest. I made some more sketches – I hope you don't mind.' He turns his sketchbook, and she can see several images of herself in repose, the lines of her body loose and languid. 'I hope you don't think I'm overstepping in saying this, but your features and form completely changed when you were asleep. You carry a defensiveness in your body, and it lifted as soon as you closed your eyes.' Lydia feels as if a very private part of herself has been exposed to the light. She's sure nothing untoward occurred, but still, there's a vulnerability at having let her defences down so thoroughly in a stranger's presence.

'I'm so sorry,' she says. 'You must find me very unprofessional.'

'It's perfectly normal.' He smiles. 'I prefer my models to be relaxed.'

Lydia stands, straightens her blouse. She feels impolite expecting payment, especially when she has been dozing on the job, but he reaches into a drawer for an envelope and passes it to her. It's the easiest money she has ever earned. Still, something doesn't feel quite right about the exchange, as if she has compromised something of herself. But she reminds herself that modelling for an artist is not prostitution, however it may be perceived by others.

～

Lydia is so pleasantly surprised by her experience as an artist's model that she keeps an eye on the classifieds, looking for similar requests. Several weeks pass until she spots another. She calls the number and arranges a time for the sitting. The address the artist provides is further along at Le Cap. She knocks. The door opens quickly, and the man behind it looks at her, questioning. The braces are hanging off the waistband of his trousers.

'Are you not expecting me?' she asks. She has arrived on time, and is as certain as she can be that she has the right address. The man is without doubt an artist, from the paint streaks on his trousers, where a brush or his fingers have been wiped clean.

'You're late,' the artist says.

Lydia appreciates punctuality and is rarely late – so this criticism stings. Well, the man is certainly brusque, but she's used to dealing with boorish characters at the bar. She can swallow her desire to put him in his place; after all, he's paying for her time. If she has learned anything as a woman, it's that a sweet smile can usually prevent an altercation.

The artist, Édouard, ushers her into his studio. It's a small room, packed with crates and canvases. There are several easels propped against one wall, and shelves filled with books on the theory of art. There are also framed photographs in the room, including one of the man with a woman and two boys, posing at a cottage with roses around the door. She's reassured that he's a family man. Édouard may be consumed by his work, but he clearly has responsibilities, although his children must be grown now. Lydia wonders what kind of father he has been. With her own, she often felt she had to compete with his job for his attention. She can't imagine how much more challenging it must feel to be the child of an artist.

While he draws, Édouard smokes a thin cigarette and taps the ash into a nearby glass. He seems unfocused at times, but produces sketch after sketch, looking at her appreciatively.

She shifts her position to give him more range. He talks about his process.

Then he asks her to remove her blouse.

'The advert stated no nudity.' She had checked before she took the job.

'Did it?' he asks. 'Well, you're here now.'

'I wouldn't be comfortable removing my clothes,' Lydia replies.

He looks at her steadily. He leans over and opens a book, revealing a bundle of notes.

'I suppose this might tempt you,' he says.

'As it happens, no,' she says carefully.

He changes tack.

'What did you expect today?' he asks.

'That you'd draw me. With my clothes on,' she replies.

'There aren't many perks to being an artist,' he says, defensively. 'We live in virtual poverty, scorned by society. A little of this is what makes it worthwhile.'

Lydia doesn't move.

He pulls out another large note and tries again. 'Your looks are too unusual to be convincing. You should be flattered that I want more.'

Lydia is angry – one hundred francs is a lot of money, but this is an abuse of his position. She wants to admonish him, but where would that get her? She needs to be smart, keep her head and emotions in check. But inside, she's shaking.

'Put your money away,' she instructs. 'I'm not removing my clothes.'

'Fine,' he says, sliding the notes into his pocket. 'Go, if you won't give me what I need. You foreigners are usually grateful, less frigid. I hadn't expected such glacial treatment.'

Lydia has heard enough. She picks up her belongings and makes for the door. But he steps in front of her as she tries to leave, a final act of power. He smells sweet, like overripe figs. He reaches for her shoulder, his hand grazing her breast. She assesses the distance to the exit, and makes a calculation. She knows women have to make such reckonings every day of their lives. She has been relatively lucky until now – roaming hands at the bar quickly slapped away, inappropriate comments from men twice her age defeated with a few well-chosen words. Strangers have occasionally followed her through the streets, and the fear she feels in those moments is overwhelming. One wrong gamble could mean the difference between life and death, between escape and humiliation.

Lydia wonders what the best approach is now.

Édouard makes his move: a clumsy and cruel attempt, pushing the money from his pocket back towards her at the same time. Something in Lydia snaps. She unleashes a wave of words in Russian and administers a fierce slap. The sound of her flesh against his skin is unnerving, but she's gratified that he looks shocked enough to step back, nursing his cheek. She takes the opportunity to flee through his front door, out into the Midi sunshine.

Artists! She vows never to put herself in the path of one again.

6

Nice, 1932

B orya is all charisma, and it can be hard to resist, even for a
woman as immune to flattery and charm as Lydia. As a result,
they've been in an active liaison for a few months now. As his girl-
friend, Lydia is having fun, letting her defences down. Being with
Borya is her first real relationship, her first sexual experience. He's
boisterous. He thrives on being with others – the opposite to
Lydia, but she finds that his energy balances her froideur. However, she has made a promise to herself that she mustn't get
involved in his escapades. He still operates as he did before: going
out, drinking, betting. She doesn't ask questions or make demands
on his time. For months, Borya has been trying to convince Lydia
to join him at the casino he visits on the glitzy promenade. She has
made excuses time and again, but he has a knack for spiralling a
firm no into golden maybes, lacing them before her eyes into a
possible yes.

'It's a big night,' he enthuses. 'All the Riviera's biggest players will
be there,' he says. 'I need to make an impression. And there's one
way to do it, to throw everyone off their game. With you on my
arm, they'll get a sense of what I'm capable of . . .'

The implication is that Lydia is beautiful. It's something she has never thought about herself, but in France, she has the vague sense that she is attractive.

She's resistant, but wants to please him, so for tonight only, she relents. It's at times like this that Lydia thinks of Misha – her lovely, loyal friend from Tomsk – and wonders who she'd have become if she'd accepted his proposal and stayed in Harbin. That version of herself would be appalled by the way she lives here, the excess, bustle, proximity to drama.

As they approach the casino, the exterior is bathed in bright light, fat flashbulbs making her squint. She's wearing a striped dress that skims her knees and reveals her shoulders. It isn't sensual like many of the dresses worn by women here tonight, which plunge down the cleavage and up the thigh, glittering, but it is as risqué as she is willing to get. Borya appreciates the effort. He holds her arm tightly, as the bouncers look her over and respond in his direction with a satisfied smirk.

Inside, she is bombarded with the noise of winning and losing: roulette wheels, slot machines, dice rolling; cheers of rapture, the sucked intake of a near miss. She's exposed to raw human emotion, much of it masked with expensive perfume, luxurious fabrics and vibrant make-up. Lydia grips her handbag. Borya told her to bring as much as she can afford to lose, which is nothing. He flashes a gloating wad of cash, and she knows him well enough to understand that he'll use it to impress her. Borya gives her some and tells her to place a bet. She has already told him she doesn't need any shows of extravagance this evening, and he has promised to be restrained, but she expects his ego to kick in at any moment.

A croupier greets Borya by name, accompanied by a solicitous smile and an invitation to join the table in time for the next roll of the dice.

He plays a few rounds, bets small, and there's a modest win and a few losses.

'I'll be back for more later,' he replies smoothly, taking Lydia by the elbow and steering her towards the bar. He orders her a martini, a whisky on the rocks for him. He brings the drink to his lips, inhaling, before he knocks it back in one. She takes a hesitant sip of her own martini, swirling the frog-green olive stuffed with a curl of red pepper. The drink tastes like the froth of the crest of a wave, but it isn't entirely unappealing.

Borya chats with the bartender, laughs loudly, makes a few comments leaning towards the man's ear while Lydia looks around. Lining the walls, older women wearing strings of long pearls sit on tall stools, pumping the handles of machines with spinning images, feeding in coins between pulls and spins. Occasionally there's the sound of cold coins cascading into the tray, insatiable fingers reaching inside. Men in expensive suits smoke cigars, tapping ash into the potted plants, which are yellow around the edges.

Borya passes over another two drinks, then takes her hand and leads her to the roulette table. A man with a gold tooth claps him on the back, a thick medallion hanging from his neck. He's Russian, Lydia knows instantly. He whispers in Borya's ear, and she notices that her boyfriend pauses, whitens a little, before laughing it off. Borya turns to Lydia and introduces her with an oversized smile. The man places a lavish bet on black, and Borya ponders, before putting a similarly sized gamble on red. The croupier winks at her, caught in the middle, and runs the roulette wheel. Seconds build and build. She holds her breath, watching the ball bouncing between black and red and back again.

Finally it settles. Red. Borya's body doubles in length – his arms shoot up, he raises himself on to his toes and punches the air. Everyone within reach pats his back.

'You're a winner,' she says, sipping her martini. 'It's a good look on you.'

'You're my lucky charm,' he says, taking her arm and raising it in victory.

Lydia feels dangerous pride in Borya in that moment. There's something seductive in seeing people close to you succeed, in receiving the good luck they believe they deserve.

The Russian looks at Lydia through short lashes. He's sore from his loss, and turns his back on them and heads to the bar. Borya shrugs, pulling his mass of tokens towards him. Drinks are sent by regular patrons who know him and want to share the energy of his success.

'This is more than I've won in five years,' he beams. 'You'll have to come with me every time from now on.' He holds her close, and she allows herself to yield to his affection.

'If I can be your good luck, I can be your bad luck, too. Remember that,' she warns, before he gets too carried away. She orders another martini. She's having fun. Borya looks at her with eyes that are glowing with alcohol-infused love.

'Lydia,' he says, as if a thought has just struck him. 'Marry me.' He moves the hair out of her eyes. 'I adore you. You make me better in every way.'

Lydia stands very still. Marry Borya? She does love him, she supposes, sees a great deal of good in him. And they're living together, so it's certainly expected. Borya is attentive to her needs without being suffocating, and has a magnetic energy she likes being around. However, he's so little like her father – not an intellectual, not someone dedicated to doing good in the world. But she refused Misha for being too sweet and kind.

'You?' she asks, the gin and vermouth coursing through her veins.

Lydia is constantly caught between two sides of herself, neither of which promises true satisfaction. After the death of her parents and aunt, she told herself she was incapable of feeling anything for anyone. Borya has awakened something darker, hungrier, in her.

She doesn't have to hem herself in for ever; she can take life by the horns.

'Why not?' she says, kissing him energetically. 'I suppose I will marry you, Borya.'

He looks at her, spins her off her feet, overjoyed. 'She said yes!' he shouts across the casino. Lydia banishes any trepidation.

This is a gamble she has to be prepared to take.

⌣

Later, the Russian who lost his money approaches her. He's a large man, and has the air of someone who gets what he wants, not through conventional means – which could sum up so many of the people living on the Côte d'Azur. Lydia has heard of tough Russians who control sections of this coastline, using violence if they have to, though she hasn't knowingly met them yet. Lydia wonders if he'll have some word of warning for her, but instead he places a hand on her shoulder and says: 'If there's ever anything you need, or if anyone bothers you' – he says it pointedly – 'think of me. My friends and I aren't the kind of men to be messed with.' He passes her a card. 'The concierge here knows how to find me.'

Lydia pockets the card, but she'll never use it. She doesn't want to mess with the Russian mafia. They exist everywhere, but here, on this coast, they're known for robberies, trafficking, people smuggling, prostitution – none of which she has any inclination to be associated with. This is the community she'd hoped to avoid, but by working in a bar, being with Borya, and making her own choices, she has perhaps opened that door. Their lawlessness appals her, reminding her of the most dangerous elements of Russia's history.

Outside, as they're leaving – Borya in high spirits, drunk and dancing – they stumble into the perimeter of a fight that has broken out between two henchmen she'd noticed inside the casino alongside their wealthy patrons. One is struck firmly on the jaw, his head juddering back, before he regains himself to administer an opposing blow, catching his attacker in the temple. The second man drops to his knees, panting, before he jumps up to start again. Borya leaps between them, pushing them out of each other's reach. He's a lot shorter than both, and considerably lighter, despite his efforts at bulking up.

The men continue to swing at each other, with Borya caught in the middle, folding like a concertina under their combined pressure. He shouts in a snapping Russian – orders to stop, loaded insults and a plea to remain sane, all in the same breath. Lydia watches from a dozen steps back. She hates violence, hates any form of conflict. Eventually, their bosses emerge from the casino, smiling together, lighting one another's cigars, before noticing the tangled collection of people and bloodied noses. The crowd disperses. The man who took the blow to the temple and dropped to his knees is grateful for Borya's intervention. He knows that if he'd fallen to the ground, the story could have been different for him and his continued existence. But the man who took the first punch is furious at the turn of events, that he has been robbed of his rightful retaliation, as he surely sees it, and points a finger at Borya.

'You're going to need eyes in the back of your head, maggot.'

Borya takes Lydia's arm. He's as sober now as a sharpened spear and they walk along the promenade in stony silence. Lydia wonders at the altercation, wonders what Borya is caught up in, how much he isn't telling her. Her head hurts and she wonders what she has just agreed to. Will she really marry Borislav? Become Madame Omeltchenko? Perhaps, before she becomes irrevocably tied up with this man, she should find out who she's dealing with.

⸺

The next day, bearing a hangover, Lydia walks for miles, setting off in the early morning and expending her energy until she can go no further. When she stops, she finds that she hasn't the energy to turn around and walk all the way home again, so she heads to the nearest bus stop and hopes she won't have a long wait. It's a sweltering day – another in a cruel line of them. She came to Nice craving the heat, but it's at times like this that she misses the freezing temperatures of Siberia. She wonders if this is a symptom of being a refugee, of losing one's home and one's family: that you always want what's out of reach.

It's then that she notices a piece of paper pasted to the glass of the shelter, the letters written in elegant script: *Companion wanted for a woman in her sixties. Six-month position. Serious and hard-working applicants only. Immediate start. No. 1 Place Charles Félix, Nice.*

Lydia remembers caring for her Aunt Nina back in Harbin. It had always been Lydia's ambition to make others more comfortable, take away some of their pain. Despite her grief, being able to make a difference to her aunt in those final days had given her a deep sense of worth and it felt good to be doing something that mattered.

Lydia writes down the address on the back of a receipt, her eyes blurring slightly, salty from the sweat on her forehead, and tucks it in her pocket as the bus pitches around the corner. She lengthens her arm to hail the driver. He's not paying attention and speeds past, then reluctantly comes to a halt a hundred yards from the stop. The doors open and Lydia runs to board before he changes his mind and takes off without her.

⌒

The following day, Lydia decides she will go along to the address from the advertisement. The apartment building is set on the waterfront. When she arrives, she looks at the brass buzzers, and finds that the top name is Matisse. It's a strong name. She wonders if she recognizes it, but can't be sure where she's heard it before. She enters the cool foyer and tells the concierge she's looking for Number One – he directs her up the stairs. A girl with a mass of dark hair is being escorted out of the door of the apartment by a woman in her sixties as Lydia approaches.

'Thank you. I appreciate you taking a chance on me, Madame Matisse,' the girl says.

'Very good. See you on Monday, nice and early,' the older woman replies.

The young girl disappears down the stairs, her eyes lit with victory. Then Madame spots Lydia, waiting in the shadows.

'The position has been filled,' she says, 'if you're here about the job.'

'I'm too late,' Lydia replies, unable to hide her disappointment.

Madame Matisse leans against the door frame for support, her stockings slipping. Through the door, Lydia can see dozens of plants – it's like an oasis – and canvases lining the walls, along with exotic rugs. The older woman wheezes a little. She looks unwell, puffy from her chin to her collarbones, her eyes shot with red. She coughs into the crook of her arm.

'Your shawl – it's very beautiful,' Lydia says, noticing. 'The detail is very impressive.'

Madame Matisse looks at her suspiciously. 'It's full of holes! I repaired one in it this morning. But, yes, it's my own design. I have a lot of time to myself now and would rather not be idle.'

'You made it yourself? It's so lovely.'

Lydia reaches out to touch it and pricks her finger on a needle wedged in the material.

Blood rushes to the tiny wound, and Madame Matisse can't help but notice.

'Look now, you're bleeding,' she says a little impatiently. 'I'm sorry, I must have missed that earlier. My eyesight isn't what it once was. Come in – I'll fetch you a bandage.'

The woman is heavy on her feet. Even the simple act of shifting from one foot to the other seems to exhaust her. Inside the apartment, it's greener and even more vibrant than it seemed from the hallway, with plants positioned along the windowsill – one with elegant tranches cut from each plate-sized leaf, as if with scissors. Cages of birds are positioned away from the window, white-winged doves flitting for attention as the women enter their line of vision.

'Don't mind them, and all their squawking,' Madame Matisse says, releasing herself into a wicker chair. 'Oh yes, your bandage,' she adds, as if she'd quite forgotten. 'Would you mind – there's a roll in the kitchen, the drawer on the left of the stove. You'll see it.' The woman indicates a set of doors on the other side of the room.

Madame Matisse wheezes again. It sounds like she has an infection.

Lydia steps into the next room, opens the drawer, searches for the bandages. She cuts a piece and applies it to the pinprick on her finger. Through another open door, she sees a bespectacled man, of a similar age, his hair grey and feathery around the edges, his wide stomach pushing against his house gown. He's reading, his head at an angle, his lips moving in their own kind of rhythm. She fills a glass at the tap, and takes it back to the woman.

Madame Matisse thanks her. 'That's very considerate, young lady. If it doesn't work out with the other girl, I'll let you know.' She points to a pad and a pen by the telephone.

Lydia writes down her name and contact details clearly, hopefully.

Then Lydia lets herself out, the sounds of the birds rustling eagerly behind her.

7

Nice, 1932

A week later, in the afternoon, Borya presents Lydia with a message when she returns from running errands. 'Oh, you mustn't hate me, but someone called the phone at the bar a few days ago. A woman,' he says, as if trying to recall the conversation. 'She asked for you and said it was important.' Lydia's fiancé returned late last night and has been sleeping for most of the day. 'I forgot yesterday, I'm sorry. You know me. But she was insistent that you call.'

'Who was it?' Lydia asks, instantly alert. She has a few casual friends, mostly young women she has met at the bar or in the few precarious temporary jobs she has had, working as a dancer or an extra – roles she occupies for days, weeks or months, but which never bring in enough money or security. They are the kinds of friendships that blossom through proximity and shared frustration, but soon fall away when people move on.

'She didn't say. She was a little rude. She asked me if you were still available . . .'

Madame Matisse. Lydia remembers how brusque, how plain-speaking the woman had been the day they met. It could easily be interpreted as rude over the telephone.

'What did you say?' Lydia feels a deep anxiety that she may have missed her chance.

'That you weren't around, that you were busy, but that you'd call her back.'

'Did you take her number?' Perhaps there might still be time, if she moved quickly?

'I did, I did . . .' Borya looks around and seems unperturbed when it can't be found. Lydia had put the companion job to the back of her mind, thinking there was little chance it would work out – but now there's a possibility, she realizes how desperately she wants it. To have some purpose. To feel needed. The role feels like a calling in some way, the only thing that seems worthwhile in a world that can be so cruel and catastrophic. And she can't deny that such a role would also be the kind that would make her father proud.

'You've got plenty of work at the moment, so you mustn't be angry if it's too late,' Borya adds. He can be careless and contra-dictory, wanting her to find a job she loves, where she feels valued – even he says he doesn't want her to work in the bar for ever – but then failing to pass on this important message. Lydia wonders if he feels more comfortable when she's on the same level as him, nothing changing, content to let life just roll along.

Whatever his motivation, Lydia hasn't a moment to spare. She dresses smartly, knotting her hair and tying a silk scarf around her neck, before hurrying to the apartment on the promenade. On the way, she buys fresh flowers for Madame; when she was there last, she'd noticed a desiccated vase of once-vibrant tulips, their petals browned around the edges. The first thing Lydia intends to do if she gets the job is swill away the stagnant water, wash and polish the vase, and fill it with fresh stems. Lydia chooses a posy of col-ourful anemones. She hopes Madame will appreciate a little initiative – doing away with those stale items that bring down the energy of a household, although it also crosses her mind that

Madame Matisse may be the kind of woman who doesn't appreciate change.

Lydia arrives at the apartment and greets the doorman. He's smartly dressed with a twinkle in his eye. 'I'm here for Madame Matisse, in Apartment One,' she says.

'The new girl,' he replies, as he dips his hat and raises his eyebrows in a gesture of kind complicity. 'Not the artist's type,' he adds, after she has passed him and is halfway up the stairs. 'He usually prefers the southerners, girls with curves, dark hair and big brown eyes, like the one who came earlier this week.' He smiles in a conspiratorial way. 'Perhaps that's why Madame has done away with her – too close for comfort!'

The concierge is clearly a man with too much time on his hands, and not enough people with whom to share the insights he gleans from his role. But an artist? Lydia hesitates. The information is useful, even if crudely shared. She racks her brain for evidence that would support the statement. She hadn't spotted anything that made her think the man she saw last time was an artist, but it's not impossible. She considers whether this Monsieur Matisse won't be another menace, a man with wandering hands, even at his age. He looked respectable, but she knows looks can deceive.

Perhaps that is why Madame is so strange and brusque? Lydia wonders whether to turn around. She still has time to walk away. Madame Matisse could easily find another girl, if she hasn't done so already. Lydia is suspicious of art, of the way it seems to inoculate those who create it against operating within the same framework, the same unspoken laws, as the rest of society. She feels that artists have privileges that are not afforded to others. How is that fair?

Lydia wonders what she'll be getting herself into if she steps forward with the flowers. But the thought of continuing on as she is at this moment – at the bar, with Borya, living aimlessly in Nice with nothing to pull her in any direction – makes the decision for her.

She lifts the knocker.

This time, it's not Madame Matisse who comes to the door, but a younger woman, a decade or so older than Lydia, with dark hair, suspicious eyes set wide apart, and a dark velvet ribbon around her neck. Lydia holds out the anemones and the woman accepts them cautiously, bustling into the kitchen that Lydia had entered a week before to fetch the bandage.

She attends to the flowers, without even looking up.

'Madame Matisse asked me to contact her . . . about the job,' Lydia says.

The woman fills a jam jar with water. 'Ah! You're the replacement!' she says. 'Papa couldn't abide the last girl. She barely knew her left from her right, let alone could be trusted on a work of this scale and importance.' She places the jar of flowers on the dusty windowsill where the decaying tulips had been. Then she turns to assess Lydia. 'We can expect more from you, I suppose?'

'I thought . . .'

'Come with me,' the woman interrupts. As an émigré, Lydia is used to being talked over, used to people not bothering to enquire about her name, or giving her time to ask questions.

The woman leads the way. At the end of the corridor is a spacious room, the ceiling high, windows large, light flooding into the corner. The place is crammed with books, easels, cushions and rugs of every colour, together with a stack of tablecloths, brightly patterned, folded into neat squares. It's clearly a studio. There's work propped against the white walls; cartons of pencils; piles of paper, some bearing loose lines; those huge potted plants, the leaves laden with dust and debris. She spots a violin.

In the middle of it all, almost exempt from notice, is a man, the one she glimpsed days before, now wearing a brown tailored suit. He looks, for all intents and purposes, like a lawyer on his way to the courthouse. She'd never have guessed this person was a practising artist. His wire-rimmed spectacles sit on his neat nose, his hands rest against his belly, and his face is ruddy but taut. He's holding a coffee cup, a little finger raised absent-mindedly. He turns at the sound of the women entering, irritation softening when he sees his daughter.

'Ah, *ma fleur*, Marguerite! My afternoon coffee has gone cold – would you mind topping it up?' he asks, stretching his face into a sweet smile.

Marguerite takes the cup from him tenderly and turns to leave. 'Oh, this is . . .' she says as an afterthought. 'Your new assistant.'

'Yes, yes, very good,' the artist replies, already returning to his newspaper.

Lydia takes one last look around the room and is ushered out.

Back in the kitchen, Marguerite takes a sip from the remains of the cafetière, wrinkles her nose, empties it into the sink, and begins grinding more coffee beans. The rich smell reaches Lydia's nose. She likes to be helpful, but feels unsure how to make herself useful right now.

'Papa takes his coffee black, with just a little sugar,' Marguerite says. She shows Lydia a teaspoon, the front dipped with golden granules. 'Any more is bad for his heart.'

'I'm here to help Madame Matisse. Your mother, she said . . .'

Marguerite interrupts, a hand in the air. 'Amélie is very dear to me – she's like a mother, better than my own for certain – but she is not my mother,' she says.

'I thought . . .'

'It's an honest mistake. Many assume the same, but you are wrong.'

Lydia pauses. 'Well . . . Madame Matisse led me to believe that I'd be helping her . . .'

'Oh, Amélie will need plenty of help, but Papa is the priority,' Marguerite says. She turns on the gas. 'He's been commissioned by a wealthy, tasteless American, Mr Albert Barnes,' she says, affecting the accent, 'who has demanded a large mural – three panels, depicting dancers – for his very expensive, very large, very important gallery.' Marguerite sighs, clearly closely wrapped up in her father's work. 'The deadline was six months ago. The only problem was that, just as Papa was preparing to pack the finished work, after a year of his exceptional efforts, he realized that he'd been working to the wrong dimensions. Don't ask me how *that* happened.' The sides of her mouth tighten. 'You'll work alongside Lisette and a few other girls for the coming months. Papa needs the utmost dedication and attention to detail. No time wasters. But first! My father must have his coffee.' She turns off the gas. 'When he needs you, he'll ring the bell. I advise you to keep your mouth shut when you're with him. He does not like idle talk. His only priority is the work. He has sacrificed everything for it, so don't take it personally. You are little more than a pair of hands. Think of yourself in that way and life will be easier for you.'

Lydia moves to the percolator, which has begun to hiss loudly. She feels a similar need to release some pressure. What will her responsibilities here be – to look after Madame Matisse, or to assist her husband? Lydia has avoided artists ever since her bad experience, but perhaps this environment will be different? At least it doesn't sound as if she will be asked to sit for him, or be expected to remove her clothes. She'll be an assistant, not a model.

Lydia is aware she's an outsider to the world of art – she doesn't understand it and is suspicious of its language and intention. Is the aim of art to make the viewer more comfortable, more sure of his or her place in the world? Or less? Lydia swallows her anxiety.

She wants to help – that's her ambition. As a companion or in the studio, it doesn't matter. As long as she's respected and can work with dignity, Lydia won't rock the boat.

After a frank conversation with Amélie Matisse, it seems that, whatever Marguerite has said, officially Lydia will be employed on a six-month contract to look after the older woman. She'll be her assistant and nurse, attending to her every need. During the initial two-week trial, Lydia is aware she can be dismissed at a moment's notice – foreigners are utterly disposable. One wrong glance, or if she inadvertently does the smallest thing in the wrong way, and she knows she'll be fired. But she's confident that this is a role she'll succeed at – operating quietly, creating calm, working in the background. She has a special kind of intuition for what someone in pain might want and need, which she learned caring for her aunt.

Madame Matisse is very different from Aunt Nina, however. Amélie has already lived with her pain and discomfort for many years and is impatient with those who are around to help her, especially if they talk over her, act as if she were not in her right mind, or take liberties. She resents that she cannot do things for herself; things that she once took for granted. Amélie clearly doesn't want to feel indebted to anyone, unlike Aunt Nina, whose illness was relatively short and swift and who was grateful for every inch of Lydia's love and support.

Amélie is practically bedridden for most of the week, but she sequesters her energy so that she may have a day or two up, and marginally active, around the house. She never ventures outside. Marguerite, on her visits from Paris, has implied that Madame has not left the house for more than fifteen years, information which comes as a surprise to Lydia. She thinks about Amélie's pale skin, untouched by the southern sunlight for so long; she imagines her lying in her bedroom, a shawl around her shoulders, the shutters drawn, a stack of books on the table, alongside embroidery, yarn and needles.

Fifteen years is an interminable stretch to be in one room, one apartment – a prison sentence. Lydia is not privy to Madame

Matisse's afflictions – it could be a bad back or chronic stomach issues that keep her from her feet for the vast majority of her day. Lydia wonders if, with a little attention and support, she could be coaxed back into a new dance with the outside world? Could she help Amélie forge a more fulfilling future?

Lydia is aware that she's also expected to work alongside Madame Matisse's husband on the mural for the American collector, Albert Barnes. In the afternoons, while Amélie is resting, Lydia helps Monsieur Matisse draw out the precise measurements of the arches on large pieces of paper that are pinned to the walls, ready to receive his new sketches. *The Dance* is a work in progress – the previous version, made to the wrong dimensions, has been set aside and the work begun afresh, with a new twelve-month deadline, six of which have already passed. It's an unconventional piece for the artist, commissioned to fill three arched spaces above the French windows in Albert's gallery. She has heard Monsieur speak of figures in states of movement, exuberant poses – to make the space feel dynamic, alive.

Lydia's job is to arrange sheets cut from a stack of painted paper, then trim and pin his billowing dancers in place for the artist to move a little here and there, until they're in the right position. She has never done work like this before, and didn't know that it could be classified as 'art'. For her, art is painting – landscape, still lifes, portraits. She now recognizes that it's a limited view of the world, and art in general.

Often, Lydia will leave in the afternoon, all the figures pinned to the walls, only to return the following day and find them released, draped over rattan chairs and bannisters, or folded over the potted plants as if they've moved of their own accord in the night. Then she must start the task all over again, Monsieur directing her, Lydia joining the troupe of dancing figures, as malleable and free of thought as they are.

Lydia works alongside Lisette, a young woman who was the

model for the commission. Matisse, she confides, is very strict about her appearance – monitoring her diet so her weight does not increase, allowing her only one hour on the beach, very early in the day, so she doesn't burn. For other commissions before this one, he even chose her clothes and applied her make-up, the girl says. Lydia enjoys the company of Lisette. She's French and left home at an early age. She is confident but contained, a perfect mix.

Lydia is energized by this work – combining the conventional and the emotional. She enjoys learning how the memory of something can be transformed into creative output – it's not just about painting what's in front of you, but about capturing how it feels to be alive in that moment. With her academic background, geared towards science, the world has made sense to her in more structured ways. It's enlightening to understand the passion of artists, what inspires and motivates them, how they transfer that emotion through colour and form. It must take great courage . . .

While Monsieur Matisse is working, Lydia does her best to make herself invisible. She is indeed little more than a pair of hands to the older artist, who she discovers is sixty-three – and who suffers from asthma, insomnia, nervous tension and headaches. He's also busy correcting the last-minute proofs of a book of poetry he has illustrated, and it drives him to exhaustion. All that shifting of infinitesimal lines. He complains often of how badly he sleeps.

But it's not Lydia's place to engage with Monsieur, regarding his ailments, his work, or anything else. She's reluctant to say a single word to him, to make eye contact or stray into his field of vision. It's not just the warning from his daughter, but also the fact that while she can chat freely to the clients in the bar, order a meal or make everyday conversation in the street, when it comes to more complex ideas, she still struggles to express herself thoroughly in French. It's strange to be immersed in another language, and to feel its words and phrases, its grammar and idiosyncrasies shape themselves around one's tongue. Even after nearly three years of being in the country, words still swim away from her, and she imagines large blank patches in her mind.

Lydia does miss much of her old life, the small, everyday things that she took for granted in Harbin: spending time with Misha, getting groceries with Aunt Nina, walking along the river. But still, she remains in France. She doesn't know where else she would go, where else she'd be wanted.

8

Nice, 1933

M adame Matisse, Lydia notices, has a small reserve of patience for her husband, and it wears thinner almost every day. Each afternoon, around five o'clock, Monsieur visits her room for an hour – to sit and discuss the progress he's making, catch up on news of their adult children and relatives, and talk about the way the world turns. Lydia has overheard details of their family life. She knows that their older son, Jean – who lives with his wife, Louise, and their two children in Antibes – is set slightly apart from the family and writes less frequently to his father. What she has gleaned is that he's unsettled, trying his luck as an artist and sculptor, attempting to step out of the shadow of his father, which seems impossible. By contrast, the younger son, Pierre, writes often. He's also in his thirties, living in New York and – much to his father's chagrin – well established as an art dealer, and already attracting an esteemed clientele. Joan Miró has recently joined his gallery. He's had a second child, a son, with his American wife, Teeny, having fled a disastrously short marriage to a fiery Corsican when he was just twenty-two. Finally, there's Marguerite, who is very much part of both their lives and visits often. She's currently living in Paris with her high-spirited and erudite husband, the critic Georges Duthuit. The pair have been married for a decade, and can be Henri's fiercest critics – it was Georges who told his father-in-law a few years ago that his work was going nowhere, which perhaps is what makes Marguerite bolder than her brothers in response to her father's work. Lydia intuits that there may be some difficulties in Marguerite's marriage – growing tensions as Georges spends more time in London – but little is said in front of her.

As the weeks and months progress, Lydia often hears the Matisses sniping at each other as Madame works her needle through her latest embroidered cushion cover. It's the normal back-and-forth of two people married for a great number of years – decades of the same conversations, the same irritations, fired like clay.

While the couple are together, Lydia and Lisette have an opportunity to talk. Lydia receives an education from her friendship with the French woman. Lisette talks about how Madame Matisse would pose for Monsieur, that it was her face, painted in greens and pinks, that earned him infamy as part of *les fauves* – but that she hasn't posed for him in almost two decades. The story goes that Madame endured so many sittings for one painting that the couple almost came to blows. When she saw the result, she cried. Amélie never posed again.

'Madame can hold him to ransom with silences that stretch for days,' Lisette adds. 'Monsieur is no better. His moods blacken the entire household if his art doesn't go to plan.'

Lydia likes Lisette – the way she sees the world with a cheerful cynicism, not expecting too much of anyone, but with a quiet contentment when she's allowed to do things her own way. She occasionally shows her annoyance, only to Lydia, when Amélie comes into the studio – bossing her husband around, delaying his progress. Lydia wonders whether there's any flirtation between Lisette and the artist. She hasn't witnessed anything, but then she's not around all the time. And dynamics can emerge where they're least expected.

⟿

Today, Lydia enters Madame's room bearing refreshments – sweet biscuits she learned to make with Aunt Nina. She tidies the room, making Madame comfortable. Amélie, as usual, is confined to her bed, her ankles showing signs of swelling, while Monsieur sits combing crumbs from his beard, rosy with his own ailments. As Lydia leaves, there's a spatter of harsh words about 'the commission', as it's called by Madame Matisse, and the time it's taking up in her husband's life.

'It's certainly not my fault you got the dimensions wrong,' Amélie says.

Her words pinch, she can tell. Monsieur Matisse is twenty-one months into a project that should have taken a year. It has exhausted all his creative reserves and the end is still not in sight.

He sighs, says nothing, but this only seems to aggravate her. 'I only want what's best for you, Henri, and all this tension is not good for your health, or mine. The sooner that commission is complete, the better. Then we can both get on with our lives.'

⟿

Some four months after she started work as Madame Matisse's companion, Lydia arrives on the first day of the week, a little earlier than normal. She goes, as usual, to Madame's room, bearing a tray heavy with fresh orange juice, strawberry jam and glazed almond croissants. Lydia turns the handle, the tray balanced on her hip. She enters the room and finds the window open wide, the curtains billowing out like an exhalation. But aside from the movement of air, the bedroom is empty – the bed made, sheets tucked tight around the mattress, pillows plump. Lydia looks around cautiously, as if infirm Madame Matisse might spring out of the wardrobe. But the silence confirms her absence. Lydia leaves, juice spilling over the edge of the glass as she hurries back to the kitchen. She dries her hands on her apron and approaches the studio.

Lydia knocks gently. The artist is sitting by the window, his hands on his knees, his back straight, his eyes closed.

'Excuse me, Monsieur?' He looks up at her.

There's a letter on a pile of books next to him. He folds it up as she enters.

'Madame's not in her room,' Lydia says.

'My wife left at the weekend. To stay with her sister for a little while. We had a disagreement, and she couldn't tolerate it here a moment longer. Berthe will make her see sense, I'm sure.'

'And when will Madame be back?' she asks. On the one hand, Lydia is surprised that Amélie has made it out of the apartment for what appears to be the first time in more than a decade, that she seems to have travelled on her own. But on the other, it confirms a thought Lydia has carried with her for the past few months: that Madame Matisse is not as frail as everyone has come to believe. She has a core of steel.

Amélie should never be underestimated.

'She didn't say,' he replies. 'She left in quite a hurry, so I suppose I'll have to go and see her to find out. Another thing to slow my progress.'

Lydia must be sensible in how she proceeds. She's employed to look after Madame, after all. It would seem impertinent if she stayed to help the artist with his work now.

'Would it make sense for me to join her? Your wife must need my assistance, no?'

She thinks of Borya, and flushes with guilt that she'd be happy to be away from him.

'You're quite right: you should be with her,' he says, the thought landing on him. 'My wife will need all the help she can get. Lisette can stay with me. We'll have to make do without you for a little while.'

⌣

Lydia arrives at Berthe's apartment bearing a letter from Monsieur Matisse. Amélie blooms with indignation as she reads it. 'I told him, I will not set foot in that apartment until the commission is finished,' she flares. 'I've put my life on hold for him long enough.'

Amélie seems revived in her new environment. She still spends most of her day indoors, but appears to draw on the energy that courses through her veins every time her husband's name comes up in conversation.

Lydia makes herself quietly indispensable, anticipating the needs of Madame before she has the opportunity to bridle. She enjoys the company of Berthe, who's had a very successful career as a teacher. She occupies a prestigious role as headmistress at a school for girls and has no plans for retirement. This dedication to service, to helping others, resonates with Lydia, and the two women spend long evenings in deep discussion.

After a few days, Henri arrives bearing gifts – a basket of brightly coloured candied fruit, a box of elegant fondants, a pencil drawing depicting a bearded man looking miserable – hoping to coax his wife back to their shared home.

Lydia and Berthe share another simple supper while, in the room next door, the raised voices of Amélie and her husband can be heard through the walls. Lydia listens carefully, while pretending not to pay much attention. It seems that Amélie has put her own ambitions to one side for her husband, to the extent that she feels she has nothing left. Even her children hardly appreciate her. She says she's tired of coming so far down the pecking order. She is sick of her husband's moods, the way they must all suffer when his creativity falters or a commission demands too much.

Henri's reply is muffled.

Lydia takes a mouthful of her food. She wonders what precisely she will regret when she's the same age as Amélie. Will she believe she made a mistake saying no to Misha? Will she look back on her time with Borya and decide it was all a youthful error? She wonders about her parents, and the decisions they took that led to their premature demise. Did they wish they'd left Russia sooner, when the violence first started? Could it all have been different?

Thinking about Borya makes Lydia sad. They are due to be married in two weeks at a registry office in Nice. There will be just a few guests – Lisette has agreed to be a witness – and a small celebration at the bar afterwards. But Lydia has become so dedicated to this job, day in, day out, and now travelling outside Nice to be with Madame Matisse, that he's starting to resent it. He's increasingly aloof, drifting in and out of the apartment, never bothering to leave a note as to his whereabouts, nor any indication of when he'll be back. Most of the time, they pass as ships in the night, Borya returning drunk and dazed, slipping between the still-warm sheets just as she – clean and well rested – is up and ready to start the day. Sometimes, when she gets home, there's no evidence of him having been there at all.

Lydia thinks of marriage, of how it will be with Borya, and whether they can make it a success. She has always believed that marriage should be the union of two people who respect each other – that it's about compromise and commitment. She reflects now on what hopes Amélie might have had at the start of her marriage, whether she would have done things differently if she'd known that she would feel this way later in life. She thinks of her own parents, married for fifteen years, in what appeared to her, as a child, to be a very functional and loving relationship. Would they, too, have been bickering by now?

There's a loud smash – glass against the thick-plastered walls – and Lydia jumps out of the hard seat to intervene. Berthe places a hand on her arm and shakes her head.

'Leave them to it,' she says. 'They need this argument, to let out everything they keep inside. It's like burning a forest to the ground and allowing new life to spring through.'

⌒

Amélie reluctantly returns to Place Charles Félix. She's ready, or she wouldn't be here, but she does her best to cloak her acquiescence in shady reproaches and a grim expression. Marguerite had much to do with the reconciliation, Lydia gathers – writing to Amélie as well as her father, extolling the virtues of marriage and pointing out that at times it's indeed necessary to employ stubbornness as a technique to survive the toughest periods of uncertainty. But who would either of them be today without the other, she asked.

Henri treats his wife tenderly from the moment she is through the door. Her pains are still bothering her, but the apartment has been set up to accommodate her more comfortably: the gramophone has been moved from the studio into her room, the bed positioned so she has a better view through the window. Monsieur now pushes even harder to get the second version of *The Dance* resolved as quickly as possible. That's the promise he has made to his wife.

Lydia works as hard as possible, too, staying late, pushing her energy into supporting him so that he might succeed. Her absence is noticed at home, by Borya, but this feels more important. And she tells herself it's only for a short period of time, before this role comes to an end.

As the contract draws to a close, Lydia experiences a pang that her time with the Matisse family is almost over. She has spent nearly six months in their home, and has found a sense of purpose unlike anything she has known before, other than when she was a young student, dreaming of being a doctor. Her understanding of their world has deepened – she has a better appreciation of what it's possible to achieve, through art that challenges perceptions, and has found solace in the creative environment. She has also grown rather fond of Madame Matisse, and perhaps understands her in ways that nobody has attempted for many years. They've formed an alliance, the two of them balanced against the needs of Lisette and Henri.

Lydia wonders if they might keep her on after the contract ends. There has been no mention of such a thing yet. And even if they did, she hardly knows if she could accept once she's a married woman. Borya, surely, would be against it.

⌣

It's a few months later when Lydia and Borya run into Lisette one evening in the queue for the picture house. She looks different now – her skin is golden, her hair short and stylish, her lips painted a coral shade that the movie stars have made popular. Lydia hasn't seen Lisette since the day of her simple and low-key wedding to Borya, not long after the completion of Henri's commission. Lisette had acted as a witness that day and they'd shared drinks afterwards on the seafront. From the moment Lydia and Borya were pronounced man and wife, she'd tried to shake the sense that their union was a disaster. She'd long had her doubts, but she'd put them down to nerves. But ever since their wedding, Borya has been gambling more and seems to be on a losing streak. She can feel his desperation grow. Secretly she fears that he may have become involved with the Russian mafia, which would be fatal.

Other things have changed in Lydia's life since she became Madame Omeltchenko. She's twenty-three and wears a band on her wedding finger, and perhaps she imagines it, but she seems to receive a degree more respect from women at the shops and market. Lydia wonders what Aunt Nina would say to this development. Whether she'd applaud the union – which gives her more stability – or view it as a waste of Lydia's ambitions.

Sadly, Lydia also no longer works for the Matisses. With *The Dance* finally complete, Monsieur held a private viewing, to which she was invited, before shipping the artwork off to America. The couple no longer needed both Lydia and Lisette, and so Lydia is back working at the bar. Borya is victorious. Initially, he'd been enthusiastic about her job in the Matisse household, but over time he'd become suspicious. Now, his uncontrolled jealousy means he's frequently scathing about 'the old man', and the way the job monopolized her time and her capacity to consider anyone else – even though her main priority was Madame Matisse. He accuses Lydia of having got above herself, of mixing too much with the boring and bloated bourgeoisie. Lydia thinks he's just jealous, his masculine ego threatened.

She knows Monsieur Matisse set sail for America in May, to personally deliver *The Dance* to Barnes and see it set up the way he always envisioned.

'You've not heard?' Lisette says now, placing her hand on Lydia's arm. Borya is impatient, that roll of his eyes saying this delay is too much to ask of him on his night off.

'No?' Lydia asks, alert to whatever gossip her friend has to impart.

'They say it was a heart attack,' Lisette reveals. 'In America . . . While Matisse was installing the artwork. Barnes was too much of a brute, and it all proved too stressful for Henri.'

'But he survived, didn't he?'

It seems, to Lydia, that everything hinges on this moment.

'Only just, after turning blue,' Lisette reveals breathlessly. People push past them into the movie theatre, the two women blocking the entrance, Lydia rooted to the spot. 'He had to be revived with whisky,' Lisette continues. 'They're taking no chances. Doctors told him he must have complete rest. For the next few months! You know as well as I do how well he'll be able to stick to that.'

Borya is pushing ahead through the crowds, not waiting for her.

'And Madame Matisse?' Lydia asks, the woman's unhappy face flashing through her mind.

'She fired me not long after Henri left. Said she could cope well enough on her own. She never did like me.' Lisette shrugs. 'She'll find a new girl who'll be able to tolerate her for a few months at best. Then who'll care about her? She'll be left with nobody at all.'

Lydia is fascinated, but can't ignore Borya for a moment longer. She will pay for devoting this much of their shared time to the topic of the Matisses. She kisses Lisette on both cheeks and dashes into the theatre, just as the curtains part and the light falls to darkness.

9

Nice, 1933

Lydia cannot stop thinking about the Matisses, especially Henri, who pushed himself to the brink in order to deliver his vision. She wonders how poor Madame Matisse must be feeling, too, with her husband suffering a heart attack so far from home. She decides to visit. First, she spends an hour with Madame Matisse and they catch up on life in general. She tells her about her wedding, which sounds very modest in comparison to the grand society affair Amélie had in Paris when she married Henri. Amélie is subdued about marriage and tells Lydia to make sure she never abandons her own dreams in favour of a man's. After a while, Amélie loses her energy, and suggests Lydia step in to see Henri, who's back home and attempting to rest.

'Ah, Lydia, the only nurse I've ever known that my wife can tolerate for more than a month,' he says as she approaches his bed. She has brought his favourite candied plums and is pleased to be able to pass them on to him directly.

'How are you feeling now, Monsieur?'

'No need to fuss, I've had enough of that.'

He talks to her candidly for an hour. They've never exchanged more than a few sentences before now. It seems the heart attack, and the ensuing vulnerability, has made him more open with her. Or perhaps he's just lonely and out of sorts. He's clearly more comfortable talking about the injustices inflicted upon him artistically than his own health, she notices. Lydia hears about the disaster in America with *The Dance II*, how it has been locked away in Mr Barnes's home, how Monsieur doubts it will ever be seen again.

'Whenever I pick up a paintbrush these days, I feel as if I'm drowning,' he says, gesturing to the blank canvas set up in a corner of the room. It has long been untouched.

'Inspiration can't escape you for long,' Lydia replies.

He changes the subject and quizzes her about the state of politics in Russia, and how she feels about Stalin's purges. Lydia reveals that she has wed since she last saw him, and he's surprised, as she has been so private, but he's pleased for her. He says marriage is a great galvanizing force, and adds that he wouldn't be the man nor artist he is today if a woman like Amélie hadn't gambled everything on his future.

'What are your grand ambitions?' he asks after a moment.

'Well . . . There's one goal I have in mind,' she says, aware that she has never spoken the small dream out loud before. 'A tearoom. A place for locals and expats to gather, people relaxing side by side, experiencing a kind of sanctuary, even if only for a short while. Something that isn't encouraging people to get drunk and lose control. It's silly, I know . . .'

'But why not? You don't want to be dealing with the likes of us all your life.'

It's not studying in Paris, Lydia thinks. It's not being a doctor like her father, but at least it's the kind of dream that she can hold on to, perhaps with Borya by her side.

Before Lydia leaves, Henri disappears, then returns, leaning heavily on a walking stick. He takes her by the elbow. 'I'm unlikely to see you again,' he says. 'But I must show my appreciation. You were the professional at all times, you cared for my wife, you lightened my load, and you did it all with grace. A conscientious girl is hard to come by, and I know myself – I remember it only too keenly – how damn hard it is to live from hand to mouth, wondering where the next payment will come from. For that reason, I'd like to give you this.' He holds out an envelope with her name written on it.

'I can't,' she insists. 'I . . .'

'Before you protest!' he interrupts her. 'This is a gift to help you on your way. I wouldn't have completed that commission without you. And that would have cost me my marriage. Don't think I didn't notice you arriving early, staying long after you were obliged to. You gave everything. It helped me greatly at a time when nobody else believed in me.'

'It was no trouble,' Lydia insists. 'You've already paid me for my time.'

He pushes the envelope into her hands.

'I completely understand,' he continues. 'If you won't accept it as a gift, accept it as a loan towards your tearoom. You can repay me when you turn a profit.'

Lydia looks around uncomfortably. To refuse would seem churlish. 'Thank you, then,' she says awkwardly. 'A loan. I promise I'll pay you the money back as soon as possible.'

'This can be something of a fresh start for you,' Henri says. 'You're young; you have the world at your feet. I hope you make the most of your potential.'

⌒

When Lydia gets home, Borya isn't around, but still, she shuts the door behind her carefully, before slipping the weighty envelope from her pocket.

She opens it and squints as she counts the bills, then counts them again.

'This can't be right!' she mutters. There is far, far too much money here. She steadies herself against the wall. It's practically a year's salary. She wonders if Henri has taken leave of his senses – does he know how much he has given away? Her aunt always taught her to stand on her own feet, without charity or feeling indebted to anyone. She hugely appreciates that Monsieur Matisse noticed how hard she worked, but this doesn't seem appropriate.

It's almost as if he pities her or sees her dreams as youthful desperation. It's too much. Lydia cannot accept. She'd run back to his apartment this minute, if it weren't so late. She'll return in the morning. She thinks about telling Borya when he gets home, but decides against it. Her husband will tell her to keep it, to buy herself something frivolous. He's always encouraging her to do reckless things. That was part of the appeal at the start, but now it's beginning to cause friction in their marriage. It can no longer be denied that Borya is as far away from Lydia's own father as it's possible to be. He's moody, prone to depression and drinking to excess. Of course, she knew all this before she married him, but she'd thought he might stabilize under her steady influence.

She should have known it would pose a problem before long.

She leaves Borya a note, inviting him to be home for dinner the following night. She'll cook and buy wine and try to have a serious talk with him. And before that, first thing in the morning, Lydia will post the money through the Matisse letter box, with a note telling Monsieur she is very grateful, but really, she must deserve what she receives. Afterwards, she has a couple of interviews lined up, and she's hopeful one will work out. But for now, she is exhausted; all the tension of the last few months has caught up with her – her eyes sting, the lids heavy. She slips off her clothes and, for once, leaves them in a pile on the floor.

She wants to make it work with Borya, for however long such a thing is possible. She can hardly claim to be happy, she thinks, as her mind loosens itself from the demands of daily order and logic, but she's searching for stability, for some kind of meaning. She doesn't want to just fritter her life away, dulling her mind with absinthe and sleeping all day to ward off the hangover. She wants to be part of something that matters – and she got close to that, for the first time in her life, in that studio with Henri Matisse.

Lydia's mind quickly unfurls, and she's asleep, and dreaming, within seconds.

The night passes as one solid block and Lydia does not stir. When she awakes, the light breaking through the shutters, she's instantly alert. She feels absolved of the grief she usually carries, the survivor's guilt with which she typically exists. She stretches her arms above her head, twisting her body in the sheets, her back popping. She turns her face, remembers the money, then she reaches for the envelope in her handbag.

It's gone. It was there last night; she couldn't possibly have imagined it.

Lydia leaps out of bed, her hands on the dresser, irrationally pulling at drawers and peering down the back to see if the envelope has somehow fallen between the wood and the wall. It's then that she notices that her clothes, which had been discarded in a pile on the floor, have been moved to a chair, folded, her gloves and watch set neatly on top. The hairs stand up on the back of her neck.

'What time is it?' she asks out loud, demanding an answer from thin air.

She grabs the watch. It has not been wound, so it still says ten thirty from the night before. Then she notices the second hand ticking. But it's not possible? It can't be ten thirty in the morning! That would mean she has slept for more than twelve hours, that she's already late for her first interview, that she cannot return the money to Monsieur Matisse first thing, as planned. The money – a fresh wave of anguish surges through her. She rummages desperately through her things, her mind racing to make sense of what's happened. She cannot remember the last time she did not wake up naturally by half past six in the morning, and to have lost so many hours feels like she has been robbed in the night. Robbed! She *has* been robbed. Her head pounds, her heart a hammer, her mouth sour. Where *is* the money?

Borya, she knows at once, his name bitter in her mouth.

He must have come back in the early hours. She was so exhausted, in such a deep sleep, that she didn't even hear him. Did he pick up her clothes, fold them into a pile on the chair? Did he approach the bed, intending to kiss her, slip between the sheets, pull her body to his? Or did he instead rummage in her handbag – perhaps this is something he does regularly – and notice the envelope? Did curiosity get the better of him? Lydia's eyes are wide as she imagines the scene playing out in her mind. Borya, with his hair slicked back, his shirtsleeves rolled up, his cheeks rough with stubble. Borya would have taken the envelope in his hands, lifted the flap, his dilated pupils coming sharply into focus as he took in the thickness of the wad of notes inside.

Lydia pounds her fists on the wooden floorboards. She feels sick. She has always tried to deny to herself that Borya might be capable of betraying her like this – but who else could have taken it? She screams into a pillow. There is no chance it could have played out in any other way – the very act is written deep into the cellular level of Borya's nature. It's impossible that he could have seen the money, smelled it, felt the grain on his fingertips, the red-hot desire at the back of his throat, and not taken the lot. It would have been like asking a parched man not to drink from a glass of ice-cold water after a prolonged spell in the desert. To think he could have behaved in any other way is to show a profound misunderstanding of human nature – or, at least, Borya's nature. So the blame falls to her, for having trusted him, for not having been more careful with the envelope before she fell asleep.

All the money will be long gone by now, frittered away in one of the twenty-four-hour casinos that line the coast.

And with this sickening realization, she vows revenge.

⌇

At midnight, Lydia hears a bang and a crash, as the weight of an inebriated body stumbles along the corridor to their apartment. She'd almost let herself believe that Borya wouldn't return at all. That his sense of shame would be too strong, that he wouldn't be able to face her and make excuses for stealing her money. But he has nowhere else to go. Once the adrenaline rush of his windfall has worn thin, he'll be jittery, unstable on his feet, unfocused.

Her worst fear is that it's all gone, every penny. That's how Borya operates: once he starts, he cannot stop. He keeps telling himself he will win big, more money than he started with, and that it will all have been worth it. But his luck rarely rewards him for long.

After a prolonged period in which she can hear him fumbling for his keys on the other side of the door, she stands and goes into the darkened kitchen, the gun weighty in her right hand.

Finally, Borya stumbles through the door, slamming it behind him. Perhaps he'd assumed she'd have left by now, that she'd have packed her bags and walked out of his life. But here she is, in the shadows. She can smell the alcohol coming off him before he's even entered the kitchen. He paws for the light switch, misses it, and his hand slides down the wall. He hiccups, then shuffles one foot in front of the other, making his way in the dark.

Lydia holds her breath. She despises him in this moment. She wants to scare him with the gun. She doesn't intend to use it, but she does want the satisfaction of an explanation, to see the look on his face when he has to own up to what he's done. Borya peers into a cupboard and, when he finds a glass, lurches towards the sink to fill it with water, drinking it down in one long gulp.

She waits for him to turn around. When he does, she's pointing the gun at his chest.

He freezes, his hands in the air on reflex. He's a man who has clearly had a gun pointed at him more than once.

'Thief,' she whispers, as his eyes feed the information they are receiving to his sluggish brain, and his rictus smile turns into puzzled relief.

'Oh, it's only you!' he erupts, laughing. 'You got me.' He mimes clutching his chest, as if a bullet has penetrated his heart, then turns back towards the sink.

'I'm not joking around, Borya,' she warns. 'What did you do with my money?'

Borya faces her and rolls his eyes. 'It's all here; I was just looking after it,' he says, exasperated. He pats the breast pocket of his jacket, then reaches in and pulls the envelope from inside, holding it aloft with childish glee. Lydia can see that her name is smudged across the front, the letters dissolved. She wonders desperately how much is left.

Her gun hovers in Borya's direction, and he trains his eyes on it, before blinking slowly. He opens the envelope and theatrically tips it up, like he's trying to shake a pebble from his shoe, then pulls an exaggerated look of horror when nothing falls out. 'Someone must have pickpocketed me,' he says, and she's shocked at how easily he tries to deceive her.

Lydia cocks the gun. Borya stands a little taller. She wants to scare him.

'I'm sorry, I didn't know it was yours,' he says, and grimaces at the ghost of her name on the envelope, clearly visible to them both.

'Liar,' she says. 'You knew it was mine and you stole it anyway.'

Abruptly, he begins to cry, tears spilling down his cheeks. His face is wet in seconds, and he sobs as if he were a little boy about to be spanked and sent to bed without dinner.

'I didn't mean to,' he bawls. 'I couldn't help it.'

This, perhaps, is the closest she will get to the truth. She sighs.

He sees a softening in her and pounces on it.

'You're my wife. I was only borrowing it. I planned to give you it back, and more. I thought I could win, that I'd double our money, even triple it!' he boasts. 'Then we'd have some security in our lives and we wouldn't have to scratch around like pigs in a farmyard. I thought you'd be proud of me.'

Lydia lowers the gun, almost winded by his words, and he takes a step towards her. She lifts the gun again quickly, but her resolve is broken, and he can see it.

'I never seem to make you proud,' he adds. 'You're always so proud of your father, and that damn old man Matisse. I wanted to show you that I have value, too.'

She's shaking and, even blind drunk, Borya notices. He's four or five steps away, still out of arm's reach, but that could change in a second, and they both know it. 'Lydia, I love you,' he pleads. 'I was only trying to do my best.'

She bites her lip and tries to control her breathing.

'It's only money, at the end of the day,' he adds. 'There's no real harm done.'

'It wasn't yours to gamble away,' she says, her voice deep with emotion. He cocks his head. 'It wasn't mine, either,' she adds.

'Where did it come from?' he asks. It seems to be the first time he has thought to ask.

'The money belongs to Monsieur Matisse.'

'Oh, him! Well, that changes everything,' he seethes. 'I see how it is,' he says, his rage building. 'I'm sure the old man took a liking to you, took a little of what he fancied. Is this how he repaid you? You liked it, didn't you? Not the first time, no?'

Everything in front of Lydia's eyes turns red in a single flash, like spilled pigment across the insides of her eyelids. Her finger burns against the trigger, and nothing she can do in that moment can prevent the signal speeding along her synapses, from her brain to the index finger of her right hand. She can feel the pull in her wrist as her finger moves, and she knows what's coming – the shocking burst of noise as the bullet is dislodged, the jolt of her arm, and the strong smell of gunpowder that will linger in the air afterwards.

An image of the long-eared rabbit, its feet burrowed in the snow of her home town, reels before her eyes. She sees it, and an image of her mother, the candle flickering as her life ebbed away; and her father's face as she walked away from her home for the very last time, looking so stoic and strong at the window; and now Monsieur, the kindness in his eyes as he handed over the money, with his best wishes for her future – it's a look that reminds her so much of her own father that it crunches the air from her lungs.

Then Borya's hands are upon her, around her neck, over her mouth, and she can't breathe.

She fires as the room fades to black. There's silence.

10

Nice, 1933

The bullet Lydia fired is lodged in the ceiling. She had aimed at Borya, but, in their scuffle, he'd grabbed for the gun, and when it went off it was wide of its mark. She has worked so hard her whole life to be controlled, not to betray any emotion, to keep her grief tightly wrapped inside her. She'd never known what it meant to really snap until that moment. It was a terrifying experience, the way the urge overtook her. She can hardly believe it could happen to her, but the evidence is all around. In the seconds afterwards, Lydia and Borya lie crumpled on the floor of the kitchen, shocked, listening to the sound of the tap dripping into the sink, waiting for the wave of emotion to dissipate like a retreating tide. Borya is unblinking, still subdued by his thirty-six hours of distortion and sleeplessness. Lydia is terrified of what she has become in that moment of madness.

Fast-paced footsteps can be heard in the apartment above: their neighbours, disturbed by the gunshot. Lydia wonders if the gendarmerie are being called, and how they'll explain themselves if the authorities turn up at their door in the middle of the night.

Lydia could have killed Borya. She's pleased, in this aftermath, that she didn't. She's able to tell herself that she acted out of self-defence, that she was pushed to violence by Borya's reckless behaviour. But she also felt a strange and raw thing while she was brandishing the weapon – an engulfing sense of power, a desperate thirst to inflict revenge. She had badly wanted to hurt Borya. Her rage had found a home. Not just rage for the theft of the money, but for everything – the fact she's an orphan, the loss of her homeland, the long stretch of cold, numbing her emotions, that she had lived through in Harbin. The loss of her dreams. The lack of dignity she endures every day, in Nice, trying to make money to survive.

The bell to their apartment sounds, breaking the silence.

Borya and Lydia look at each other. The gendarmerie will be outside the building.

'Go,' he says. 'I'll deal with it.'

Lydia finds her feet and dashes from the room. She stows the still-warm gun in the briefcase, grabs another case and fills it with whatever she can find. She vows never to be caught unawares like this again. She'll always keep a bag packed, for whatever emergency or unseen circumstance might arise.

Borya has left the apartment to open the door downstairs, leading on to the street, to the police. She's grateful for this gesture from him. Lydia slips out, unseen, behind him, and watches as two officers accompany Borya inside the building. She walks lightly down the stairs, checking that there aren't more police waiting on the street. She does not know what reason Borya might give to explain the situation. That's up to him. But, needless to say, their marriage is over.

For now, Lydia has only one priority. To live by the values instilled in her by her parents, by Aunt Nina. To start anew and support herself. And she vows to find a way, any way at all, to repay the money to Monsieur Matisse, with as little delay as possible.

↬

The moon outside is fat like a swollen fist. How is Lydia going to conjure up so much money – especially as she has nowhere to live? She can hardly go back to working in the bar. She walks through the backstreets, carrying her cases with her head dipped, in the direction of the port. It's the first place she thinks of to wait out the remaining hours of darkness – she'll be reassured by the sight of boats loading up before dawn, men anticipating their haul, and she wants to be surrounded by that busyness, that purposeful activity. She's puffy-eyed, dazed and disorientated, running on adrenaline. She'll crash soon enough.

Lydia passes people spilling out of late-night bars as she walks towards the seafront, and sees ahead the casino with its sound of fortunes being lost and won inside. She curses under her breath – it is Matisse's money that has been lost, that will flow into the pockets of other punters in the hours to come, or be added to the casino's considerable takings. She imagines the trajectory of those notes, passing from the hand of one gambler to the next, to someone more dangerous, perhaps; making their way along the coast, from one desperate story to another. She thinks about the mafia man she met with Borya, and his offer of help.

As she passes the entrance, a woman in very high heels, her lips painted an electric red, approaches waving a piece of paper.

'Coo-coo,' she trills. 'Can we tempt you to take part?'

'Whatever it is, no,' Lydia replies promptly.

The woman pushes a leaflet into her hand. The words swim – *DANCEATHON* – and a figure is clear – *PRIZE 1,000F*. It's a fortune. Enough to get on her feet and pay Monsieur back.

'Few people make it past twelve hours, even fewer to twenty. I've never heard of anyone actually making it all the way,' the woman replies. 'But you might just be our lucky winner.'

Lydia puts down her cases. 'What time does it start?'

'Ten o'clock tomorrow night. The dance marathon is the

knockout event of the year for us. It'll be packed, and spaces for dancers are limited, so get there early if you want to try your luck.'

Lydia can't imagine herself on a stage, in the middle of the casino, dancing non-stop for everyone to see. She has occasionally earned money as a dancer in the past, working on film sets, or in some of the music establishments along the coast, but never for more than a few hours. The lack of sleep isn't too impossible to imagine. But what would she eat? And drink? And she supposes going to the toilet isn't an option. She shudders at the very thought of it, imagining how delirious and inhuman she'd feel by the end. How the body would overcome the brain, hijacking any hope of victory.

The woman sees that the suggestion has taken seed. But Lydia continues walking. 'Oh, and my advice? Wear something alluring,' the woman calls after her.

⌒

The idea is outlandish, yet here she is, returning to the casino at nine o'clock that evening. The place is already bustling with bright young women, glittering in sequinned dresses, their hair curled as if they were movie stars. They're the main attraction; they must put on a show. Anyone could be in the audience tonight – famous movie directors, handsome actors, rich bachelors and men with muscle. It's clear that, for them, the opportunity is about more than the prize money. Lydia would rather not be here at all, but she has next to nothing to lose.

She has put on a simple black dress, buttoned at the back, her hair tied up, a red scarf around her neck. She has worn heels – as stated in the entry requirements – but has opted for those that have the lowest elevation so they might be comfortable for the coming hours. She read the small print carefully before setting off. She has to be the last woman standing. In the event of two women making it the full twenty-four hours, the contest will continue until one or other of them runs out of steam. The rules also state that any form of dancing or movement is permitted, only that the contestant should not stop, or at any point fall, which would result in immediate disqualification. There must be no touching of other contestants, or interference from anyone in the crowd.

Lydia is determined. She wouldn't be here if she hadn't thought it possible, and she's resolute when she sets her mind to something; she knows her steely Siberian strength of will can get her across the finish line. Plus, there's her experience in hospitality, working long hours on her feet, the resilience that involves. The majority of the women here aren't in it for the long haul, that much is clear. For at least three quarters of those present, it's more about being *seen*, and she doubts many of them will last beyond four hours. But she also senses a harder core of jaw-set women, backs straight, eyes scanning the competition rather than the gathering crowds. She feels herself being weighed up, and refuses to let her eyes betray emotion.

It's ten minutes before ten p.m., and there are tinkles of laughter all around her in the dressing room as the posse of women inspect their reflections in the mirrors surrounded by fizzing light bulbs. Some are very young, others seem to be in their thirties. They put finishing touches to their make-up and hair. One woman is massaging oil into the back of her neck, like a fighter about to enter the ring. Another is sitting in a corner, her ankles crossed, her eyes closed. Lydia has no prematch nerves or rituals. She wriggles her toes, checking the space at the end of her shoes. The women are not allowed to take anything on to the stage with them, no handbag or accessories, but Lydia has stashed some sticking plasters inside her brassiere in case of blisters.

Twenty-four hours is a very, very long time, Lydia considers. She has never been awake for such a prolonged stretch in her life.

Of course, she's young, has energy in reserve. Still, she has imbibed three strong espressos in the time between waking – Lisette, luckily, has kindly taken her in – and arriving at the casino, conscious that any more liquid could be problematic as the evening progresses. The injection of caffeine will work its magic, for a while at least. She straightens the scarf, takes a breath.

A bell rings, and the women gather as one, ready to be ushered on to the circular stage. A man with a microphone is speaking, whipping the crowd into applause and exaggerated whoops as the women file into view. Lydia hangs back. She catches the eye of a dark-haired woman wearing gaudy cocktail earrings. The woman smiles, a large open grin that's as genuine as it is disarming. Lydia is taken aback, and missteps on to the stage, regaining her footing as the man with the microphone draws attention to her with a sweep of his hand. The crowd titters, and Lydia feels her cheeks burning. Out there, with hundreds of pairs of eyes trained on her, she realizes she has made a terrible mistake.

But still, Lydia begins dancing, moving from one foot to the other, swaying in time to the music of the live band and the other women around her. The stage is so crowded that there's very little space to navigate, but she moves, rubbing shoulders and thighs with women who are vying for a front-row spot. She can see the punters closest to the stage with stark clarity, the whites of their eyes, and even the cufflinks as one man raises a hand to get one of her fellow dancers' attention. But those three or four rows back disperse into blackness, thanks to the brightness of the lights trained directly on the dancers. The heat of the other women makes her sweat and, once again, she wonders how she will manage to survive. But Lydia's nerves are fortified. She thinks of the gun, those fired bullets. There are only two left now.

By midnight, two dozen women have peeled away, some of them taking a bow at the front of the stage to enthusiastic bursts of applause, their eyes still bright, their smiles still genuine. They sashay to the bar and men crowd around them, with offers to buy drinks – a click of fingers to summon the waiters, who arrive bearing bowls of nuts and olives. Lydia is not hungry, but her throat is dry. She swallows and tries to count the number of women moving around her. Three or four dozen remain. Only another twenty-two hours to go.

By four in the morning, another swathe of women has left the stage. Lydia's body is full of aches and pains. Her feet are hot and her limbs feel numb, but, for the time being, this is no worse than the bar work she used to do. Many times, she'd start at two p.m. and work until the early hours – more than twelve hours on her feet, so this is nothing new. She dances fluidly, her body moving in its instinctual rhythm. It's the boredom that gets to her more than anything. The mindless repetition. She has no floor to mop, no regulars to sweep from their position slumped at a table, no Borya to chat to, propped against the bar as he tots up the evening's takings. At the memory of him, Lydia's resolve hardens.

The live band signed off at three a.m., and generic music is piped through the speakers. The musicians won't be back until the lunchtime shift tomorrow. Now is the dead zone, when only the hard-core casino punters remain. This, Lydia calculates, is the hardest stretch, and women around her drop like flies.

She remembers dancing classes at school in Tomsk, when she was a little child. Her father swirling her around playfully afterwards. She'd had lessons in Harbin, too, when she was tall and thin, awkward with the new height of her body. She'd danced with Misha, and the memory of that brings tears to her eyes. How she misses him now.

⌐

The daytime tourist crowd starts to appear from around eleven in the morning. The women on stage are a novelty by this point – thirteen hours into their endeavour – sloppy on their feet and goggle-eyed. Audience numbers will swell throughout the day, the later stages of the danceathon attracting those who are keen to view desperation up close, to examine the condition like a biologist would a Petri dish. Lydia is aware she's debasing herself. But this is the only way she can stay true to her values – standing on her own, being resourceful, not relying on others for her survival. She counts to a thousand, then starts again, trying her best to remain alert. She thinks of Borya's betrayal and feels her resolve spike.

By midday, there are twelve women left on the stage. Each carries a look that is more crazed than content. The dark-haired woman has lost one of her earrings. Lydia saw it being kicked over the edge of the stage, but no one has thought to retrieve it. Some of the punters clap half-heartedly from the sidelines, drifting from the croupier table to the slot machines. Lydia wants to shut them up. Her nerves, after the past few days, are shot – and the taste of violence she experienced threatens to rear its ugly head again.

By three o'clock in the afternoon, there are five women left. Lydia, the woman with one earring, and three others, one of whom Lydia had dismissed at the start as one of the beauty queens she thought would have given up by midnight. Despite her white dress showing off toned arms and a pair of perfectly tanned thighs, it's clear that she's not here to find a husband, after all. Lydia thinks about what it will mean to crash out at any point in the next seven hours. She's already broken, but she will be all the more so if she leaves the stage under any circumstance that doesn't involve the winning sum.

By five o'clock, Lydia's head is pounding, her vision blurring. She's hallucinating about objects on to which she could retire – a leather armchair, comfy and welcoming; a bed with fresh sheets; a sunlounger, on which to doze for the rest of the day. She's so close to dropping to her knees, the pull of gravity as strong as she has ever felt it, and there's nothing she wants to do more than press her cheek to the scuffed dance floor.

Around six o'clock, she notices a woman edging to the lip of the stage and looking on with worried eyes. Lydia makes eye contact. She recognizes her face from the Matisse studio. It certainly isn't Marguerite, but it could be one of the few other girls, mostly young French students, who came and went during the months she worked there. Lydia kept much to herself, so cannot recall her name, but yes, she knows in her delirium that she has been recognized. To someone in the crowd, she has a name, and that feels excruciating.

There are now four of them left, and Lydia has no choice but to continue. The clock moves in slow sequence to seven p.m., and she moves from her right foot to the left, swaying her hips with as much energy as she can muster. Nobody is expecting anything more energetic at this stage – in fact, they're here to see the sloping shoulders and slack jaws. With just three hours to go, Lydia's dark-haired rival still looks disarmingly alert, her back straight as a plumb line, her eyes retaining a sparkle. Lydia knows this woman is the biggest threat to her walking away with the money she so desperately needs. The woman in the white dress is fading, her eyes rolling back in her head, her neck loose like a piece of old rope. Lydia wants so desperately to be out of this space, to enter the world once more, but the world does not belong to her, a poor immigrant with no family; a woman who does not count.

~

With less than an hour to go, there are just two of them left. Then Lydia sees the student again. She pushes to the front of the stage, a determined look on her face as she elbows her way past the well-heeled clientele. This time, a man in a brown suit, his spectacles slipping down his nose, is beside her. Monsieur Matisse looks at Lydia with what seems like horror and a touch of bemused admiration.

Her heart skips a beat, and she slips and almost lands on her knees, but stabilizes herself under the watch of the glamorous one-earringed woman. Lydia has never felt shame like this. It takes everything she has not to fling herself from the stage. But she has come this far. The only thing she can hold on to is the thought that in less than an hour, she can place her prize money directly into Monsieur's hands.

The other woman shows no sign of slowing down, and Lydia feels something slipping through her fingers. Her energy is faltering – this isn't going to go her way, and she knows it. Monsieur Matisse is trying to say something to her, but his words are lost. He beckons her, but she cannot bear to look. The student swaps to the other side of the stage, and shouts something directly to Lydia. The band is playing again, a lively number.

'Monsieur Matisse says stop!' she instructs.

'You don't understand,' Lydia wheezes.

'The money,' she says. 'Your husband, he came to the studio looking for you, and Matisse got the whole sorry story out of him.'

Lydia almost turns inside out with horror. Her knees vibrate with a new weakness.

She turns to Monsieur with puzzled eyes.

He's waiting for her to look at him.

'Lydia, listen to me,' he shouts. 'This is insanity, but I understand why this is so important to you. I understand.' He raises his hand as if to calm the situation.

The weight of her body is becoming insurmountable.

'You needn't do this, not on my behalf,' he shouts over the music.

Lydia hardly knows if she has heard him correctly.

'Come back to work for us,' Monsieur Matisse shouts as the

band's song comes to a halt. Everyone turns to look. Lydia stops. The compère is on her immediately.

'You! Mademoiselle! If you stop for more than five seconds, you are disqualified,' he warns. Lydia knows the rule well; she has been testing it to its limit all day.

The music begins again, and every pair of eyes in the house is upon her.

'Five,' the compère says, looking her hard in the eye. 'Four . . .'

He expects her to start moving her feet, but she can't; she no longer wants to.

The beautiful woman, her one earring swinging in place, moves in closer to check if Lydia needs assistance. She'll win outright if Lydia forfeits, but there's no gloating from her.

'Three,' the compère continues, raising his arm. The stage lights are blinding.

Lydia stands stock still.

'Two.'

It is ten minutes to ten. She's so very close.

Henri Matisse looks at her, the promise of his words painted across his face.

All the lights seem to sparkle around her, the tears in her eyes refracting them.

'One,' the compère shouts, about to bring his arm down like a guillotine.

11

Nice, 1933

Lydia returns to the Matisses' home. There's no mention of the disastrous danceathon, and she's grateful. The memory of those hours has pinned her tongue in her mouth, where the taste of shame lingers like bitter soil. After that fateful night in the casino, Monsieur Matisse reassured her once more that while he was sorry, for her sake, that the money had been gambled away, he in no way held her responsible for Borya's actions. Lydia had been overwhelmed at the end of the danceathon. She'd forfeited her place. But in an act of extreme compassion, the final woman left on stage had come to her rescue, dropping to her knees at the same time as Lydia. They'd been declared joint winners, and split the prize money.

One of the first things Lydia does is cut her ties: she submits the paperwork to annul her marriage. She hopes never to hear from Borya again. He doesn't protest. He knows the trust is irredeemably broken. He has told her he will leave Nice, move along the coast, try his luck elsewhere.

For the first few weeks, Lydia picks up where she left off. She tends closely to Madame – who complains constantly of aches and pains – while her husband fades once more into the background.

Lydia sometimes hears Henri playing the violin, but mostly he's working. He pays little more attention to her than he did before.

Over this time, new assistants, models, muses and young artists looking for help arrive in the household – Annelies, Jacqueline, fellow Russians Hélène and Natasha. Some stay a few days, while others remain longer, before their situation changes and they move on.

Lydia's priority is Amélie, with whom she is gently encouraging. Each day, she persuades her to rouse herself from the bed, stand on her own feet and, when she's up to it, spend time out of doors. Madame Matisse leans on Lydia's arm as they do a short circuit of the port; later, she returns to bed, wincing as she lowers herself back on to the pillows. Lydia reads to her, Russian classics translated into French, and it helps with the development of her own French language skills, as she already knows the stories inside out.

Lydia goes out of her way to make herself unchallenging, smiling away barbed comments or digs. She has seen enough not to be offended by the vagaries of an old woman who is bored and in pain, as well as permanently frustrated with her husband who, she believes, still doesn't give her enough attention. Amélie spends the majority of her hours reading, typing, embroidering items for her grandchildren – she enjoys making stiff little jumpers for Claude, Marguerite's son, who's becoming a smart, sweet-natured toddler. Marguerite visits from Paris every few weeks and is satisfied that things are working with Lydia, that her parents have found a girl they can trust, who doesn't seem intent on inserting herself into family matters. They don't interact much. Lydia continues to find Marguerite overbearing, dismissive. From small hints, Lydia picks up that the tensions in her marriage to Georges remain.

Marguerite always disappears for hours at a time into her father's studio. It's clear that they have a very close relationship. And Marguerite treats Amélie with warmth and touching impatience. Seeing this family in motion, and destined always to be on the outskirts, tugs at something in Lydia. She wonders about her mother, how she might be now if she'd lived, and what their relationship would be like. Would Lydia brush her off mid-sentence, tenderly chastise her for being slower today than yesterday, or dismiss her contributions? And how she wishes for an hour with her father, to argue about the big issues of the day, or complain about some smaller aspect of her life.

Lydia wonders if Marguerite knows just how lucky she is.

$\backsim$

After several months, a firmer schedule emerges. Lydia continues to work hard to make Amélie comfortable, reading to her or massaging the older woman's hands. Marguerite sends a large batch of papers from Paris. She has got too much on her plate at the moment, Amélie tells Lydia, with a frown that suggests something more serious is afoot, so Marguerite is relinquishing, for now, responsibility for her father's correspondence.

'The trouble is,' Amélie says, 'I can't make head nor tail of it all. It's like a foreign language these days. When I was younger, I used to take such matters in my stride. It's all there, by the bureau.' Lydia looks at the stack, which is almost as tall as the water jug. 'Would you mind?' Amélie continues. 'You'll be better able to sort through them.'

This is the kind of task Lydia enjoys, bestowing order where there was none before. She spends the next few days organizing the papers into a system – she places all the letters together, from dealers and gallerists with requests for commissions and in-person visits; she sorts the invoices by order of which need to be paid the most urgently, and files those already paid in a newly purchased folder. She separates out articles which have been clipped from international newspapers, many of which will need to be translated into French.

Lydia updates Madame each evening and, when finished, she takes the separate files into her mistress's bedroom, indicating which matters need urgent attention – letters that demand a reply, bills that remain unpaid, or requests that are in danger of expiring. Lydia has also been tasked with overseeing the donation of a painting that has hung on the wall of Henri's studio the whole time she has known him – a painting by Paul Cézanne of three bathers. Henri and Amélie want to donate it to the Petit Palais, which houses the Musée des Beaux-Arts de la Ville de Paris, with the request that it be hung with care in a prominent place. Why do they want to donate the artwork now? Lydia has no idea. All she knows is that the work meant a great deal to Henri at the start of his career, when nobody else believed in him.

Amélie places the files to one side, satisfied. 'You're meticulous, as I expected.'

'Will that be it?' Lydia asks, pleased to have completed the request. She wants to make sure Amélie is content. Despite her brusque manner, she likes the woman.

'That will be all for now. I'll talk to Henri and bring these matters to his attention.'

The next day, the papers on Madame Matisse's bedside have not moved. Lydia expects her mistress will be talking to her husband at the next available opportunity, when he makes his afternoon visit. She's not in a position to go around Madame. She knows well enough the unspoken dynamics of a marriage to understand that such a thing would not be appreciated. But she also knows that there are opportunities within those files that Monsieur will not want to pass him by, as well as payments he's owed and articles singing his praises that he should know about.

Two days later, the files at Madame Matisse's bedside remain untouched. Lydia bristles with impatience. Another thick envelope has arrived from Paris, bearing Marguerite's handwriting. It presumably contains further documents that need attention. It sits alongside the organized files that are gathering dust. For now, there's nothing more Lydia can do.

A week later, she can bear it no longer. 'Can I take these off your hands?' she asks Madame Matisse as she clears away the breakfast tray. She picks up the envelope from Paris, wondering at the possibilities it might contain. 'I can sort these, as I did with the first batch,' she offers. Amélie glances at the documents as if she has never seen them before. 'I'll discuss anything pressing with Monsieur, if that's convenient?' she adds. Amélie looks uncertain. She wants to remain at the helm of this family, as she has been for decades, but her resolve seems to have abandoned her. Lydia does not blame her. The older woman is in a great deal of pain and needs tending to daily, her capacity for action depleted after so many years of ill health. Not for the first time, Lydia feels caught in a delicate balancing act between Amélie and her husband. It's a fine tightrope to walk.

'Do with them as you will,' Amélie says. 'I've hardly seen Henri enough to talk to him about such things. When he comes by in the afternoon, he has no interest in dealing with missives and moaning from the rest of the world. He needs to concentrate, to get his work done. That's paramount. The last thing he needs is endless distractions and the begging requests of strangers. You might congratulate yourself on having put these things into a neat order,' she says firmly. 'But let me tell you, if I were to pester him about such things day in, day out, he'd never have become the artist he is today.' She looks to see if her words have landed. 'So, by all means, take these off my hands, talk to him, push them under his nose.' She passes Lydia the remaining folders. 'But he won't thank you for it.'

⌐⁀

One day, around mid-morning, Amélie excuses herself to go to the bathroom. Lydia offers assistance, but is batted away, so she takes a moment to sit on a chair placed by the window. She wants to look out, so sits sideways – the seat squeaking as she sinks into it – and twists her body so that she can extend her folded arms across the back and rest her head, just for a moment. She sighs deeply, a calm falling upon her in this position. She looks out of the window at the azure sky, closes her eyes.

There's the sound of a mop hitting the side of the stairs in the internal corridor on the other side of the wall, an echo of footsteps from the streets below. It's then that she hears the door handle creak. It will be Amélie. She'll not like a fuss to be made or for Lydia to jump up and help her, so the young woman allows herself another moment. But the steps that emerge into the room are not as flat-footed as Amélie's. They are solid and sure. Lydia opens her eyes in a flash. Monsieur is looking at her. She jolts at being found not working.

'Wait!' the artist interjects in a serious voice. 'Please,' he says. 'Don't move!'

Lydia doesn't know if she's in trouble or not, but upon instruction she holds her pose.

Henri takes a sheet of paper from the table and a pencil from his pocket, and begins to sketch. He draws quickly, his eyes flicking between her and the page.

Something about the exchange feels impertinent, like she's overstepping a boundary. It feels intimate, and urgent, and Lydia does not want Amélie to catch them at it.

The sketch takes a minute or two, and is over before she can decide against it.

'Here, did you enjoy that?' Henri asks, showing her the sketch.

It's as if the artist has seen her for the very first time.

Henri Matisse has drawn Lydia twice before. First, when she initially started working for the family, as little more than an afterthought. The result was rather dour and dreary and she looked every inch the woman employed to serve in his household. The second time, he needed a model with long hair – nothing more – and again the result disclosed very little about her personality or inclinations. Although perhaps it was she who hadn't revealed a hint of her true self at that stage. He knows her better now – they have conversed more openly about his art and the world; and she has shared stories about her early life in Siberia.

Lydia isn't sure why he has avoided using her as a model – she can only presume it's because he has plenty of other young women willing to do the work. To have inspired him in this moment feels unsettling, but the result is surprising. Lydia looks relaxed, for a start, her eyes soft, her pose indicative of someone daydreaming. He has captured that soft, faraway longing in her – a side that so few people have seen.

'It's . . . very well executed,' she ventures.

'That's hardly an adequate response!' he says.

Lydia looks at the portrait of herself afresh. She looks melancholy, a little lost.

'Is that how I seem to you?' she asks.

'I suppose it must be,' he replies.

Amélie returns. Henri doesn't think to conceal the sketch.

'What's this?' his wife asks, handling the portrait.

Lydia excuses herself, to make herself busy elsewhere.

Still, she pauses to listen to their conversation behind the closed door.

'I caught her just now, in your room, having a moment's rest,' Henri replies.

'Whatever would you draw her for?' she asks.

'Look at the way she was resting her head against her arms – she was daydreaming.'

'Well, it's done now, I suppose,' Amélie concludes.

'I may come to use her as my model again,' he admits. 'I've felt blocked for such a long time. But something about Lydia seems to have ignited something. An old fire that I've been missing. It's like I've been waiting for a signal, and here it is.'

'Whatever do you mean?' Amélie retorts.

'It may be that I can face picking up my painting brush again,' he says. 'For the first time in a long while, I feel inspired. You know how rare that is. Lydia may be my muse.'

Muse? Lydia recoils. The word is one-dimensional, so extractive. She feels a shudder of foreboding. She turns on her heel and leaves before she can hear his wife's response.

12

Nice, 1933

A few days later, Lydia carries armfuls of clothes into Amélie's bedroom. She lays the dresses on the bed – ones Monsieur has collected over the years from his travels in Morocco, Seville, Algeria, France, Tahiti. He buys them for his models to pose in, dresses he knows will look good in his artworks. The materials are beautiful, some of the fabrics slipping between her fingers and others rough to the touch. The colours are rich, the patterns intense, some in styles Lydia has never seen before. Monsieur has insisted that he draw her every day since he caught her daydreaming. And now he has prepared his paints. Lydia isn't quite sure how she feels about this new direction in her job. She isn't exactly keen on posing, but it's not demanding and she can hardly deny the opportunity to her boss when he feels fired up to paint again for the first time in years. She's touched that he has seen something in her, and that it has inspired him. Especially as he has never talked this way about her before. But undeniably, it will add a new pressure to her workload and take her away from Amélie, whose needs are unpredictable. She's a woman who doesn't like to be kept waiting – even if she's very happy to keep others waiting – and Lydia quite admires such contradiction. It's not often women wield the power to behave badly.

'What choice will you make?' Amélie asks, as Lydia picks through the pile. The artist's wife seems to want to keep Lydia close, and keep an eye on what passes between her and her husband. Lydia doesn't mind. She can see that Amélie doesn't want to discourage her husband's creative outburst and probably hopes that, ultimately, he'll get his fill of Lydia as a model, and move on to another obsession.

When it comes to the dresses, Lydia has never seen so many in one place before.

'How am I meant to decide?' she asks, touching one bright garment, then another. She picks up a bright one, holds it against herself, puts it down again.

'Don't make it difficult for yourself,' Amélie says. 'Whatever you make a decision about in life – whether it's what to wear or who to marry or anything in between – the choice ends up being the only one you could have made. So there's no reason to fret, or to consider alternatives. Just go with the instinct that fuels your heart, that's what I always say.'

Lydia flinches at the reference to choices; all of hers seem to have been disastrous. She's still tender about what happened with Borya and feels sick that she ever thought that marrying him might be a good idea.

'Did you hear what I said?' Amélie pushes, shifting her feet under the eiderdown.

Lydia picks up the dress that first captured her eye. It's rose with flecks of gold and thick printed flowers in turquoise and red. The pattern, the craftsmanship, is exquisite. She holds it to her body. It feels right. She raises her eyes to the image of herself in the mirror.

'Then this is the one,' she says.

'Well, don't be shy,' Amélie instructs. 'Try it on.'

Lydia turns her back and begins unbuttoning her blouse.

'And I've got some tips about how to model for him. It's been a long time since I last posed for Henri. I was a younger woman then, but some things you never forget. How to relax, ways to gain a little confidence,' she says. 'He sits very close when he's working, and it can be unnerving. I can tell you where to look, when he's looking at you. There's much you can glean from me, to make your path a little smoother. If you'll listen, that is . . .'

$\backsim$

Lydia puts on the dress and the weight of the fabric pulls across her narrow shoulder blades, displaying her body in a new way. She is not inclined to admire herself, but the dress itself is a work of art. Amélie nods approval, before picking up her embroidery, grumbling about her companion being purloined for the rest of the day. 'I'll make do, I suppose . . .'

Monsieur Matisse, too, is impressed, when Lydia walks into his studio.

'Look at the golden mass of your hair, alongside those bold colours,' he says.

Lydia offers a short smile and tucks her hair behind her ears.

She takes a seat upon a bloom of cushions, a drape hung behind her. It's a scene that Henri had prepared the day before, and he's like a puppeteer, delighted to see his creation coming to life. He's a decent man, she reflects, and has a similar energy to her father – dedicated, single-minded, but kind and generous, too.

He works for a while, getting used to the feel of paint brushing across the surface of canvas. Lydia is surprised to have been a catalyst, but wants to give it her all. She has sat for artists before, watched them work. She has also seen art in the Louvre, and spoken to other women who've modelled, including those who've posed for Monsieur. At the end of the day, this will be known as a painting by Henri Matisse, not a portrait of a woman by the name of Lydia Delectorskaya. Most people will look at it and hardly see a real woman there at all.

Throughout the whole process, Lydia stays silent and lets the artist work around her. She has always borne Marguerite's first words in mind: that she must be silent in Henri's presence, not disturb the flow of his thoughts. For her, it's strange not being expected to move while someone else is exerting so much energy and attention and, as always, she finds it hard to relax. She remembers her early experiences of being sketched and painted by other artists, and how outside of herself she'd felt at those times. But now it's different: she knows Henri; she has learned to trust him and feels that their relationship is more authentic.

After a while, Monsieur begins to reassess his work. He continues painting, running the brush into his palette of oil paints and applying more colour to the canvas, but before long, he's muttering that he can't get the pattern of the dress right. He tries for a while longer, then abruptly puts down his brush. It slips from the easel's ledge.

'It's ruined,' he says. 'It's not working. It's not you,' he adds. 'I'll start again.'

He frowns at the image before him and walks across the room to fetch a cloth and a small bottle, which he uncorks. Lydia can instantly smell turpentine. Henri uses it to wipe the canvas, moving the cloth across the surface as if he were cleaning a window. Lydia moves her limbs, feeling the blood flowing back to her stagnant muscles.

'Right,' he declares when he's finished and the canvas is blank again. 'Now I can begin once more, and make my mistakes all over again.'

Lydia resumes her pose, the material of the dress pooling against the brightly patterned cushions. Henri works for another hour, a frown pulling at the corners of his lips. His brush swirls in the red pigment, then the pink. He cleans the tip with a rag, dips the brush in yellow.

'It's still not working,' Henri announces eventually. 'The patterns – they're not in harmony. They don't even clash with grace. I need something new . . .' He looks around.

'I won't be offended if you'd rather use another model,' Lydia says.

Monsieur's brows knot in the centre. He starts to speak, then stops himself.

'Might it be possible,' he begins again. 'The dress . . .'

'I could choose another, a little plainer?' Lydia answers.

The artist looks at her, weighs something, then makes up his mind.

'The painting would be better without it, if you're comfortable?'

A silence falls between them. An artist once before expected Lydia to remove her clothes, and she walked out, leaving him with nothing but a well-positioned slap. Now this one is asking the same of her – but politely, at least.

How does Lydia feel about taking her clothes off? Uncomfortable, uncertain. It will change something in this household, of that she's positive. She examines Monsieur's request for undertones of any sexual urge, but can find none. He's more than sixty years old, forty years her senior. He has always been cordial with her, respectful. She has observed nothing lecherous in his behaviour. He does not create discomfort in the way he moves around her, or, as far as she's aware, with any of the other women who've worked for the household. She has never heard any untoward rumours about Henri or his behaviour. People describe him as dedicated, demanding – grumpy and exacting, at worst, but never inappropriate.

Lydia has known many men, of all ages, who have behaved in unpleasant ways – placing a thumb against the bolts of her spine, fingers on the exposed flesh of her wrist, or the palm of a hand on the flat of her thigh. Monsieur Matisse has never laid a finger on her. She could be mistaken, of course. Men – especially those with talent and power – are skilled at hiding the worst of their impulses, only to reveal them when one least expects it.

As for her own impulses, Lydia rarely has reason to assess what it is she desires. She certainly received an education in the bedroom with Borya, but it isn't one she's keen to repeat. He was inconsistent in his lovemaking, sometimes dedicated and tender, other times rough and cruel. Every now and again, he wouldn't be able to perform and would sleep off the effects of alcohol, waking up irrationally angry with her. Lydia enjoys being intimate with another, but she's not sure she needs it or would use it as currency, the way others do. Wherever her own passions take her, she's determined not to be caught out again. But this is about trust. Lydia is not sure if she'll come to regret turning hers over to Henri.

She blushes, in the realization that she will agree to his request.

He notices and turns his eyes away, nodding gently.

Over the coming days, Lydia finds herself relaxing without her clothes in front of Monsieur Matisse. There's a new-found awareness of her body, as seen through the eyes of an interested observer. She wonders about her flaws – the knot of a broken rib, damaged when she was a child and fell off a horse while riding in Tomsk with her parents; the constellation of pale freckles under her breast – and how she measures up to the models who have come before her. Are they all the same to Monsieur Matisse, these female physical forms – all curves and contours, deserving of his curiosity?

Lydia has never been able to work out if she's plain or something of a beauty. She has always assumed her looks are rather neutral – nothing out of the ordinary for a woman of her age and background. They are, she believes, the least interesting thing about her, and she has never carved additional glamour out of what she already possesses. Women treat her with indifference. But many men have treated her as if she were worthy of attention.

As he works, Monsieur's shoulders lose the tension they always carry when his art isn't going well. The lines on his forehead soften. He bears the look of a schoolmaster, peering over the frame of his glasses at a new cohort to whom he must impart wisdom and discipline. There's nothing sexual in his gaze.

To fill the silence, and because of the new intimacy that has opened up between them, Lydia gently recounts stories of her childhood. It's a way for her to make herself more real in his eyes, more authentic, so she's not just his assistant, or his wife's companion, or a body to be painted. She rarely speaks of Russia these days – she doesn't want to share the horrors of her country – but Henri listens contentedly as she paints a picture of the frozen landscape of her early years, her school days before the Revolution, her father, who was a respected man in his community, and how she and Aunt Nina fled in 1917. Her words act like a balm.

'You have a touch of the doctor's assistant about you,' Henri says eventually. 'You know what is needed, and when. It's not always the most obvious remedy.'

∽

The portrait of Lydia, *Pink Nude*, has taken shape. It's eye-catching, provocative – her naked body poised on a background of chequered blue-and-white cloth. She likes the way it challenges the viewer to reconsider female beauty. Henri is galvanized by the success of this oil painting, and appreciates her involvement, the calm way she conducted herself, how she helped nurture the development of the work. 'It seems that I have found an ally in you, he says, with particular reference to the way she has documented his work on film, keeping a record of his studies of her – the ways in which he started afresh, time and time again.

By the start of the new year, as well as the finished *Pink Nude*, Henri has established an impressive collection of pen-and-ink drawings – all of Lydia. In almost all, she lies naked on a floral bedspread, cushions positioned around her body. These sketches aren't unlike his other works in recent years – the lines and style are undeniably his – but there's something new, electric, to them. Henri feels it, too. He's energized, drawn to continue using her as his model.

A couple of months ago, Lydia had identified among his files a request from Leicester Galleries in London: *Does Monsieur Matisse have any artworks that could form a suitable exhibition?* The invitation, it seems, has gone unanswered, and, in the meantime, the gallery has written a second time, enquiring more urgently if there are any of his creations that could be put on display. Lydia drops the note into his studio, just as Madame Dorothy Bussy, the elegant and opinionated English wife of his painter friend Simon, arrives. Henri reads it and, as Lydia tidies the kitchen, she overhears him discussing which pieces he could exhibit, soliciting Madame Bussy's opinion, which he clearly respects.

'These could make a striking impression,' Lydia hears him say. It'll be the drawings of her that he's referring to. She knows he's proud of them, the direction his work is now taking.

'I respect you dearly, my old friend,' Madame Bussy says, 'but you're mistaken.'

'How so?' Henri asks.

'I shouldn't have to spell it out,' the woman replies.

'Oh, I don't care what people say. It's nothing that hasn't been levelled at me before.'

'I'm thinking of your dear wife, Amélie,' she says.

Lydia knows exactly what's coming. She knew it would come to this: divided loyalties, Lydia pulled between husband and wife, rumours and gossip disrupting the balance . . .

'What about my wife?' Henri says, seriously. 'Say it plainly, if you must.'

'These works are captivating, that cannot be denied. Nor can one deny' – she takes a breath, grappling for the right words – 'their erotic intention.'

'I don't like what you're suggesting.'

'*I'm* not saying anything,' Madame Bussy replies. 'It's just, you can appreciate how these might be interpreted, by people who don't know any better. A collection of drawings of a young model in your care, living in your home? Naked, cavorting.'

'Stop!' Henri interjects.

'Of course,' Madame Bussy says, retreating. 'You won't hear another peep out of me.'

～

Marguerite arrives from Paris. Henri asks her opinion on the drawings of Lydia. Surely his daughter won't feel there's anything amiss and will be able to see the works for their artistic merit rather than whatever 'erotic intentions' are supposedly captured there.

Marguerite, Lydia has discovered, is a shrewd operator. She's succinct in her opinions, to the point. She'd never allow herself to sugar-coat any of her verdicts on her father's work. In a world where so many people's opinions can disrupt the process and play havoc with his mindset, she has to be the voice of reason, she has said. She offers crystalline judgements that Henri knows he can trust. Lydia admires Marguerite's forthright nature. Under different circumstances, perhaps they could have been friends. But the truth is, there's tension in all their interactions. Marguerite can't trust anyone who's involved in the lives of her parents, especially around her father. She's protective, territorial. Lydia knows Marguerite won't like this other new development in the household – that she's helping with Henri's correspondence, in order to support Amélie, along with posing for her father. It won't matter that Lydia is involved in both these things for self-less reasons.

Marguerite looks through the series of sketches of Lydia which Henri has earmarked for the exhibition. She recognizes their energy, their urgency. 'But I'm just not sure viewers will connect with these images,' she concludes delicately. She doesn't mention her reservations specifically, but it's clear that she has the same hesitation as Madame Bussy.

Henri listens to his daughter's concerns, all the while plucking fluff off the forearms of his suit. He admires Marguerite and trusts her opinion above all others, but Lydia can tell that he has been hurt by the distance she has placed between them over the past year. The marriage between Marguerite and Georges that had been faltering for so long has finally foundered, and Henri resents the accusations that were levelled in his direction; namely, that the marriage had failed because he had put too much pressure on Marguerite, as a child and as a young woman. *You expected too much of me, and it wasn't fair. What chance did I have as a wife, with a father like you to live up to?* she'd written.

Now he nods as he takes in Marguerite's words. But later that day, he says he will go ahead with the London exhibition, and will display the pen-and-ink sketches. He does not refer to them as 'the sketches of Lydia', as everyone else seems to do. Instead, he adds that they are the pieces he's most energized by, and he knows his public; they'll be energized by them, too. Marguerite tries to interject, but he holds up his hand. It's among the few times he has defied her opinion, her advice, and she's clearly bemused.

Neither Amélie nor Marguerite can change Henri's mind. He has made his decision and is going to stick with it. Lydia is unnerved by the turn of events. There have been rumours of an affair between Henri and his assistant, Lydia knows, swirling around Paris and London. She fears that the whispers will have made their steady way to Marguerite's ears, and been passed on, in an act of solidarity, to Amélie. Lydia has always been so careful. Yes, there's emotion and intimacy between Lydia and Henri. She'd hoped it might be invisible to others, but clearly it's not.

She doesn't have an opinion on whether the drawings of her should form part of an exhibition or not, but she's upset by what's unfolding. It feels as if battle lines have been drawn, with his wife and daughter on one side, Lydia and Henri on the other. She isn't sure how this has happened, but she's nervous about where it might lead.

ULTIMATUM

Nice, 1939

Lydia is numb. There's a taste in her mouth, cold and metallic, like a mouthful of snow that has melted to acid. She feels sick and sad. She has been cast out and it feels like the end, not just of her job, but her life. She doesn't know how long she has been here. Her suitcase is pushed carelessly under the bed in this temporary room that she has rented at short notice, the few items that she owns stuffed inside. It's very little in the grand scheme of things: some items she has carried with her from her childhood, reminders of her parents, her time in Harbin and with Aunt Nina, the briefcase and the gun; not much to show for almost thirty years of life. She knows Henri hesitated, that he fought for her. But it's not enough to sustain her through the pain. There's a burning feeling around her neck, as if an old rope has been tightened around it.

She rereads the note Henri slipped into her pocket before she left. He'd had to choose. It had to be his wife. He knows he cannot be forgiven, especially after everything Lydia has done for him. He appreciates her attention and, dare he say, the deep value of their partnership. She doesn't know if she has the energy to sustain his absence for the rest of her days. The pain of being cut off from his world. It's hard to describe what has passed between the two of them – it sparks with rebellious energy; it is indefinable. Nothing untoward has happened – they can't be accused of that. Henri's morals are set in that regard, and Lydia has her own self-respect to uphold. But over these past few years, with increasing frequency, there have been times when Lydia has felt as if she were his true wife, the woman wedded to his soul, who understands him as no other can, who can elevate him to the greatest heights of his potential. In this regard, she has, in her wildest moments, considered herself to be the true Madame Matisse.

An incendiary idea, she knows.

Lydia picks up a pen and finds a fresh sheet of paper. She composes herself and begins to write. But she's surprised by what's unfolding in her: it's not to Monsieur Matisse that her words are directed, but Berthe, Amélie's sister, who has always been kind.

Dear Berthe, she writes. She keeps it brief, but explains her position, how she has been removed from the household at Amélie's request, and how she cannot see a future for herself. *I'm emotional, but I hope you won't read regret in my words. I only want to be understood by you. And not judged for my actions, for what I am about to do. Forgive me.*

Lydia seals the envelope, and inscribes Berthe's address on the front.

There's a half-empty bottle of vodka on the desk, and she takes another drink.

It comes down to one thing, really: Lydia cannot imagine any meaning in her life from now on.

She dresses and resolves to get to the post office before the last collection of the day. This is a communication that she wants to arrive promptly. She puts the letter in her briefcase and leaves. For where she's now heading, she will need the gun.

She walks through the narrow streets of the old town to the port, barely glancing at the sideshow of life all around her. At

255

the post office, she hands the letter over to the teller with a moment's hesitation. A part of her has been sealed inside that envelope.

After, Lydia takes a different route, climbing up Mont Boron – the vantage point overlooking the sea. She feels heavy, as if her lungs were laced with lead. The vodka weighs in her pocket. At the top, she opens the briefcase. Inside is the closest thing she has to an inheritance, the only thing that feels like family. She picks up the gun and experiences the cold shock of it. She holds it to her lips, remembering that day in Tomsk, and the rabbit, and the shot she fired at Borya, the anger that had overtaken her, and which still burns inside her.

She wants the revenge this weapon offers.

Lydia takes another swig of vodka. Then another. She tips her neck back and her tongue reaches for a final drip of alcohol, but there's nothing left. She throws the bottle over the cliff edge and hears it break on the rocks below. Lydia curses in her native language, then repeats the words, louder this time, through clenched teeth. She leans closer to the edge of the cliff and clutches her head. She always knew she was unhinged; that's why she worked so hard at keeping things in order, withholding her emotions, containing herself.

Sounds from the bustling promenade below reach her ears through her fingers.

One thing remains firm, solid: it has an elongated snout, glinting scales, one unblinking eye. Like all the little girls from the fairy tales her mother once read to her, Lydia is unable to heed the warning, to see the danger. She reaches a shaky hand to the weapon. All it would take is for the safety catch to unlatch and for the trigger to pull and it would all be over. Her mind dances around, the phrase tight in its grasp, examining it from different angles. *All* and *over* bounce back and forth. Lydia steadies her breathing. She runs the metal flank underneath her nose, as if savouring a cigar, then kisses it gently. She directs the gun at her chest. Her heart pounds.

Lydia squeezes her eyes shut as a wave of nausea passes through her body. She so wants all of this to be over. And it can be, so easily. Without her place in the Matisse household, she has no direction, nothing left. The future she fears – alone and untethered – no longer has to be a reality. She can write her own fate. To fire a gun, at herself, against herself, seems like an act of tenderness, as if she were her own mother offering herself ultimate protection, a promise of return. Lydia so wants to be held, to return home, to be free from suffering. She nurses the gun. All she has to do is exert a little pressure, here . . .

She swallows, and her throat is dry. She feels weak and sick and tired. She does not want this, she does not want any of this, and it is all rising in her, and she cannot keep it at bay any longer, and the gun, the gun, the gun . . .

Her finger finds the trigger.

PART THREE

MARGUERITE

1

Nice, 1939

It's the middle of the night when the stark ring of the telephone by Marguerite's bed cuts into her dream. She isn't used to much disturbance. Since her husband Georges left six years ago, after ten years of marriage, she has slept alone. Her little boy, Claude, at nearly eight years old, is at boarding school in central France, so she's a woman used to freedom – and blessed silence. For a moment or two, Marguerite stares into the darkness, dazed by the insistent noise.

She comes to her senses, picks up the receiver.

There's quiet on the other end, interrupted by broken breathing.

'Papa?' she asks, her stomach clenching. She turns on the bedside light and checks her wristwatch, set to one side before she went to sleep. It rests next to the ribbon she wears to cover the deep scar on her throat, which is still visible after all these years. 'It's almost two in the morning. Whatever in the world could be so important?'

She hears him struggling to articulate his words.

Possibilities run through her mind, all wild and terrible.

'I didn't want to worry you, but it's Lydia . . . well, your mother, too. I don't know where to start. It all sounds so improbable. But Amélie left me,' he says.

Instantly, Marguerite feels her body relax. 'Papa, you scared me,' she admonishes him. A call in the middle of the night, just to say they've had a disagreement! 'Maman has done this before and she'll do it again. Give her some time. She'll be back.' Marguerite loves Amélie dearly, but she has a tendency to react to every slight, creating drama for the whole family. 'It'll blow over soon enough. Why don't we talk about it in the morning?'

'It's different this time,' he insists, ignoring her request. 'She gave me an ultimatum. She said it was her or Lydia.' He breathes. 'Of course I chose her. And Lydia left.'

'Then Maman should be happy,' Marguerite says. 'She finally got what she wanted.'

Lydia's leaving isn't a negative outcome, not in Marguerite's opinion. Girls like her come and go. Her father behaves as if Lydia is instrumental to his success as an artist, as well as his health and happiness, which is nonsense as far as his daughter is concerned. That woman has long abused her father's generous spirit. Well, Marguerite's glad she's finally out of the picture. Amélie has been complaining for what feels like years of her frustrations, her suspicions, the way she feels undervalued, over-looked. Marguerite has given her all the advice under the sun – from ignoring it, to talking to Lydia directly, to challenging her father.

Now Amélie has played the definitive card of a marriage: an ultimatum. Marguerite isn't surprised it has come to this. At least things in that household can return to normal. And Marguerite can get back to uninterrupted sleep.

'But your mother *isn't* happy, not at all. I've only made things worse,' he insists. 'Even though I chose Amélie – I said, quite clearly, that I wanted her over Lydia – she walked out anyway. And she's never coming back. Not this time. And, well, you see, then there's Lydia . . . ' He swallows. 'I've just received the most terrible news. Lydia shot herself.'

Marguerite pulls the phone closer to her ear.

'Papa,' she says. 'What did you just say?'

'It's because of me . . . because I told her to leave.'

'My God, no?' She inhales. Marguerite can hardly believe the words her father is saying. She has never been close to Lydia, but she's horrified the woman felt desperate enough to do something as reckless as this. She fleetingly wonders if her father is in his right mind. A lifelong insomniac, he needs people in the night. He hates being alone in the darkness. It's when he's most vulnerable. Marguerite imagines him steadying himself against the edge of his bed, gulping from a glass of water, nightmares chasing his waking moments. Lydia, she knows, has often been there to settle him, to read from the newspaper or offer medicine. He'll be uneasy with-out her. That's what this is about. Perhaps this idea of Lydia having shot herself is a nocturnal fabrication, a bad dream, born of his deepest, darkest insecurities.

'Are you absolutely sure, Papa? You're telling me Lydia wanted to end things?' Marguerite can hear the doubt in her voice – either he's mistaken, or he's telling the truth, but both outcomes are ter-rifying. She tries to hold on to the thought that none of this is real.

Her father chokes on his affirmation.

'Is she . . . still alive?' she continues, her brain struggling to pro-cess the information.

In reply, Marguerite is horrified to hear that her father is crying.

Quickly, the sound takes her back to the moment when a doctor took a scalpel to her throat as a child. Her father had to hold her down on the kitchen table. The last thing she remembers were the tears welling in his eyes, as she felt his weight push down on her shoulders. She'd thought his anguish meant she was about to die.

'Lydia is alive, just about, thank God,' he says eventually.

Marguerite feels a burst of relief. She feels guilty at the fleeting thought that her family didn't need a suicide, nor the ensuing scandal, on their hands.

'She's in hospital right now,' her father continues, his voice small. 'Your Aunt Berthe is with her. I don't understand the details, but Berthe called to tell me Lydia shot herself in the chest. The bullet lodged in her breastbone. Somehow she survived.'

'Aunt Berthe?' Marguerite's mind spins further. What is Amélie's sister doing at Lydia's side? Amélie will *not* like that. Marguerite lights a cigarette, smokes fretfully, hoping it will restore a sense of order. 'Do the doctors believe she'll make a full recovery?'

'I'm keeping her in my prayers. All accounts, so far, seem fairly positive. But it could too easily have been a very different outcome.' She can hear him tapping his fingers against a hard surface, a sign, she knows, that he's trying to control his emotion. 'I'll visit her at the earliest opportunity, try to talk some sense into her. I must apologize.' He breathes deeply, before his mind picks up a different thread. 'Marguerite, your mother really isn't coming back this time and . . . I plan to ask Lydia to return, if she'll have me,' he says quietly, as if he were in a confessional. 'I don't deserve it, after the way I behaved, the way I discarded her. How will she trust me again? But Lydia means the world to me. I need her by my side.'

'Papa!' Marguerite says quite firmly. 'Is that really a good idea? You know better than anyone what people will say.' Someone has got to think about his reputation. In his right mind, her father would be thinking the same way. In the past, there've been rumours about him and Lydia, born from the intensity of the artworks he makes of her, the nudity, the shared trips. He has admitted he finds such talk distressing, always protesting the innocence of their relationship. 'It would be madness, would it not, to invite her back into your home now?'

'If people talk, well, let them!' he snaps. 'She's my assistant, that's all.'

Marguerite is taken aback. She'd mostly dismissed Amélie's fears over the years. Yes, her father might be taken in by a pretty face, and might rely on Lydia for inspiration and help in the studio, but there was no real sign there was something untoward in their closeness. A little jealousy, at such close quarters, and with the stakes so high, was only natural. But now she sees their relationship through unsettled eyes. Was it that Marguerite didn't want to look at the truth head-on? Why else did this woman try to take her own life when she was forced to leave her father's side? And why is her father so very heartbroken at the news? Could he really be carrying on with a woman more than a decade younger than herself? It seems impossible, but, at this unholy hour, Marguerite doesn't know what to believe.

'Papa, tell me the truth now. What is the nature of your relationship with Lydia?'

She holds her breath, waiting for his answer. It feels like a bomb, set to explode.

'We love each other dearly,' Henri says eventually, stating the words with great care.

Did her father just say *love*? The word takes Marguerite's breath away.

'There's nothing wrong with that,' he affirms. 'Two people who respect each other, who want the best for the other person. Why must that arouse such suspicion and distortion?'

'But is there anything more I should know about?'

'Why does everyone presume that love must be sexual? Or that I'm taking advantage of her?' he demands. '"Old man Matisse and his beautiful young assistant,"' he mocks. 'I thought you'd understand that love can blossom in the purest way, beyond desire.'

He sounds cagey and defensive. Is he evading the question, or is it truly that he and Lydia have a companionship that transcends sex? She cannot believe that she's even formulating these thoughts about her own father.

'Please don't be foolish,' she warns him. 'Understand how it seems.'

'You're always accusing me of being foolish! I'm not past my best yet, you know. Lydia understands that; she doesn't make me feel that I'm incompetent or careless or cruel.'

This is worse than Marguerite could have imagined. Her father is truly under the Russian woman's spell. And she's succeeded in driving a wedge between him and his family.

'This is out of control,' Marguerite says. 'I'll get the first train south in the morning.'

'Don't,' he insists. 'Come in a week or two. I plan to see Lydia tomorrow; I'm going to ask her to come back, and I don't want anyone here who'll try to talk me out of it.'

'Papa! You must see there will come a time when she is asking too much of you,' she says. 'Lydia is still a young woman; she might want children one day, or a life away from you – then what will you do? And what do we know about her, really? I'm only think-ing of you, your reputation. Think of the future, your legacy. You owe us that.'

'This family has suffered plenty of scandal already, thanks to the Humberts,' he says. 'We rallied then and we survived. But my legacy is out of my hands.'

Marguerite's thoughts turn anxiously to the woman who brought her up. 'And what about Amélie? Where even is she?'

'I've no idea,' he admits. 'She swore she was leaving Nice, men-tioned Paris, but heaven knows how she'd get that far alone. I expect you'll hear from her soon enough.'

'Aren't you going to fight for her?' Marguerite pushes.

'I still love your mother. Amid all the mess of her reckless ulti-matum, I chose her, my wife of forty-one years, the woman I've long been loyal to, and she left me anyway! She couldn't tolerate me a moment longer.' He sounds perplexed. 'What woman, at the age of sixty-seven, walks out on her husband? After everything, all the hardships we endured, all we created together? But I can't say I'm surprised. That woman has never failed to surprise me!' Henri takes a deep breath. 'And here I am, an old man nearing the end of my life, left with nobody at all.'

'You still have me, Papa,' Marguerite says. Why does she suddenly feel second best?

'*Ma fleur,*' he soon says, seeming calmer. 'Promise me you won't turn away.'

Marguerite feels a flicker of that former closeness they used to share.

'I promise, Papa,' she says. 'Now get some rest. We'll tackle this together.'

But in truth, she wonders if something irrevocable has happened. How will she navigate the next stage of her relationship with her father, with Amélie gone and Lydia so terribly wounded? She has no idea. Amid the shadows and silence that fall around her as she puts down the telephone and turns off the light, she fears the worst is yet to come.

2

Paris, 1939

There's no chance of Marguerite returning to sleep. After she ends the call with her father, her heart races for the remaining hours until dawn. The ashtray by her bed overflows.

Ever since she was a small girl, Marguerite has always been the peacekeeper, the person who deflects calamity. She remembers holding her breath while her mother, Camille, and her father argued. She'd get to the point where she felt dizzy and dazed, jagged images flickering in front of her eyes, the breath caught in her throat. She'd felt as if she deserved the pain, as if her parents had fallen out of step with one another because of her. As she grew older, she learned to bite her tongue as a way to control the bad things happening around her. Then her vocal cords were damaged by the tracheotomy and she almost gave up speaking altogether. By the time she was a young woman, Marguerite was self-contained and serious, and struggled to make friends. She grew in confidence thanks to Amélie's care, but was always more comfortable around adults, spending as much time as possible in her father's studio, posing for him or his friends. It made her feel essential. She enjoyed being indispensable to his art and seeing herself conjured on the canvas. In his world, she did have a voice.

Despite Marguerite's abiding love for her father, today her loyalties are with Amélie, the woman who raised her, who sacrificed everything for her husband's success and the unity of the family. Amélie's grit has become hers. Marguerite may seem sensitive, but she has a core of steel. Yet look how Amélie has been repaid. Yes, her father chose his wife after her ultimatum, but he clearly needs Lydia in a way that defies logic, not to mention the laws of marriage. And that, Marguerite understands all too poignantly – after she left her own husband following his affair with that wide-eyed British trollop, Lady Georgia Sitwell – is too much of a betrayal for any wife to bear. There comes a point when, as a spurned woman, one's sense of self-preservation overtakes the fear of leaving, the fear of change, the fear of being alone for ever.

Just as she thinks she might sleep after all, there's a knock at the door. It's the doorman with a message. *Café de Flore, midday. Amélie Parayre.*

It must be serious if she's signing off with her maiden name. Of course Marguerite will be there. To support Amélie, to see if she can offer a little sense around what has come to pass. Seeing her father will have to wait. As he said, he'll be with Lydia. But what promises will pass between them, she wonders? She mustn't leave it too long.

It's unthinkable that Amélie is in Paris alone, that she has made it this far, and is navigating her way around the city. She has been persistently ill for decades, bed-bound. Is that something else that Marguerite has misunderstood: the nature of her adopted mother's pain, the way it has curtailed her? Did it have another root cause altogether?

Marguerite feels apprehension as she prepares to leave her apartment on rue de Miromesnil, in the elegant 8th arrondissement, her hands shaking as she smokes another cigarette. What else might be revealed today? She dreads to imagine.

Outside, Marguerite discovers it's one of those blue-sky, early

September days – the light is never sweeter in a city often sullied by pollution from factories and endless industry. Although it's quite far to the café, she needs time to think, to mull over the events that have occurred, so she decides a walk will do her good. She has been working hard recently on designs for a fashion show in London, which is the best way she has found to channel her own creative spirit; before that, she dabbled in art but felt too constrained. Her style, unsurprisingly, closely resembled her father's – and that wouldn't do. So she destroyed her work.

She hurries along, her low heels clicking against the pavement.

Her mind is occupied, but, not far from the café, she notices a commotion.

People are gathered around a vendor selling the day's newspapers.

'Germany invades Poland!' he shouts. 'A date for the history books! First of September 1939!'

Marguerite stops dead in her tracks. No! It cannot be – just twenty-five years after the last world war broke out, wreaking havoc. And now they're back on the brink again.

People hurry to buy copies of the paper.

Marguerite feels a sickening lump form in her stomach. Everyone knew it could happen, but after the Munich Agreement last year – which was signed by France, Germany, Italy and Britain in the hope of avoiding a full-scale European war – many had allowed themselves to dream that the worst had been averted. She buys a newspaper and scans the print. France and Britain, in an effort to uphold international agreements, have pledged to defend Poland, as a way to maintain peace and security in Europe. Their aim is to counter the growing violence and expansionism of Nazi Germany.

That means France is poised to join the war.

Marguerite was nineteen when the first war broke out. Her

brothers were conscripted as soon as they turned eighteen. Thankfully her father, at forty-four, was deemed too old. She remembers her darkest fears, how the world seemed to have been ripped at its seams.

If the worst does come to pass, and France joins the war, it's only a matter of time before Hitler invades Paris. What will become of them? What will become of the country she loves?

Marguerite's nerves are shredded. But when she spots Amélie across the street, seated at an outside table, the moment their eyes meet feels like a point of safety. Marguerite hurries to Café de Flore, her footsteps heavier than before. Amélie's walking stick is propped against her chair. In this moment, her maman looks old, but not infirm, the way she did in Nice. In fact, Marguerite would even say she seems revived – there seems to be something of her former spirit coursing through her veins. Amélie is wearing a red jacket, and the colour evokes passion and purpose, new-found energy. Perhaps she shouldn't admit it, but Marguerite feels proud of her mother in this moment – at the age of sixty-seven, Amélie has shown she won't be diminished. She has left the man who was making her ill and unhappy – even if that man is Marguerite's beloved father.

Marguerite embraces her. There are tears in Amélie's eyes, and the look confirms everything her father said on the phone – she has no intention of going back.

There's so much to say. Amélie talks instantly and openly about the frustrations she felt in Nice, how Lydia took control of everything, spreading her reach like poison ivy, until Amélie could not tolerate it a moment longer. That ultimatum had been brewing for years.

'But why now, why this moment?' Marguerite asks, curiosity getting the better of her. She thinks back to the uncertainty she battled with when leaving Georges, the doubts that plagued her, the worries she had for Claude and how the separation would affect their young son. She wonders how Amélie could be so sure that this was the right path to take.

'I found something shocking in Lydia's room,' Amélie admits. 'Perhaps I shouldn't have gone looking, but I just knew she was hiding something.'

'Tell me, Maman!' Marguerite instructs, her nerves spiking once again.

'A gun,' Amélie says sharply, her eyes cold. 'That woman brought a dangerous weapon into my home. I had no doubt she was capable of using it. I felt I didn't have a choice. It was her or me. I wasn't prepared to stay under the same roof a moment longer.'

Marguerite realizes that her mother feared the weapon would be pointed in her direction. Instead, Lydia had turned it on herself. 'Maman, have you not heard? Lydia shot herself. She must have used the gun you found. It's a miracle she survived.'

Amélie's eyes widen. 'I knew it! I knew she was dangerous. Of course, Henri wouldn't listen. But I never imagined she'd do anything like that. Well, I'm glad she didn't succeed.' Amélie reflects for a moment, possibly remembering the gun's troubling glint. 'What an awful mess! What on earth possessed her? Good Lord, it wasn't because of Henri, was it? I knew there was more beneath the surface than either of them would admit.'

'I think your suspicions may have been right all along,' Marguerite says gently.

'I'd hoped I was mistaken, but this confirms everything,' Amélie says.

They're lost in their thoughts for a moment or two.

'I have to ask,' Marguerite says. 'Why did you leave anyway, when Papa chose you?'

'When I gave your father my ultimatum, I saw how much conflict it caused. I think I finally understood that he loves Lydia, in the purest sense. I may never know for certain if it was more than that,' she says. 'But it was clear how tormented he was at the thought of being parted from her. What he feels for me is duty, loyalty. But I knew right then that there was no longer an ounce of love left between us.'

Amélie lifts the coffee cup to her lips, appearing to savour the taste.

'Is there nothing I could say to change your mind?' Marguerite asks. 'I know Papa loves you dearly. He's heartbroken you've left. I also know how difficult he is to live with, how single-minded and selfish he can be. It's also selfish of me, to want you to stay together for the sake of the family, when it's been making you ill.'

Amélie looks at her evenly. Even without words it's clear she won't change her mind.

'Well, at least you'll live with me here in Paris, won't you?' Marguerite says. 'I have the space, after all.'

'Thank you. Until I find my own place,' Amélie says. 'I won't stay in Paris for ever.'

'Do you think, one day, you might regret it all – leaving Papa?' Marguerite pushes.

'I won't say I'm not nervous,' Amélie admits, watching the newspaper vendor pass on the other side of the road, all his papers sold, his promise of impending war spreading through the streets of Paris. 'But I haven't ever really had the chance to know who I am away from him. For so long, I've not had any purpose. You're still young enough, you hardly know how that feels . . . But at my age, it'll be a long, slow process, working out who I am.'

Marguerite sighs. Her maman has no idea how bereft she often feels, too.

'I plan to file for divorce,' Amélie continues, pausing to acknowledge the pain this will cause. 'I want what I'm owed, what I deserve, which is half of everything. If I don't, it'll only go to that scheming witch. I was the one who helped make him who he is today!'

Marguerite can't help but admire her dignity.

'This doesn't change anything between us, does it?' Marguerite asks. She feels like a little girl again, hiding behind Amélie's skirts in the Jardin du Luxembourg as Amélie and Camille debated in the pouring rain where she'd live. They'd both wanted her, and Camille had fought hard to hold on to her. But that day, young as she was, and as much as she loved her mother, Marguerite prayed she'd be taken in by Amélie. She longed to be part of a family, to live with her father. Marguerite has never regretted becoming Amélie's daughter.

'No, my sweet little daisy,' the older woman says, using her old nickname and taking Marguerite's face in both hands, kissing her on each cheek. 'It most certainly doesn't.'

3

Paris, 1939

B ack at her apartment, Marguerite immediately lifts the phone
to call her brothers. She's certain the news will have filtered
through to each of them already, but there are things only she can say
to them, and that only they can say to her, in this moment of crisis.
They may not always have seen eye to eye, but the siblings share a
deep connection, forged in childhood, when they learned to suppress
their propensity for noise and movement, and developed a deferen-
tial appreciation of art, the creative process and their father's need for
space and silence. Marguerite is close to them both, but contact is
infrequent, as can often be the way when adults become increasingly
consumed by the demands and dramas of their own lives.

It is Jean's number she dials first. He's the older of the two
brothers, and has become a rather stubborn man now he's reached
his forties – struggling, like the rest of them, to define precisely
who he is from under the weight of the Matisse name. He tried his
hand at a creative life – painting, sculpture – but what is there to
say that hasn't been said already, and by his father, no less? His
wife, Louise, answers. She shouts for her husband, and there are
urgent whispers at the end of the line, a hand held over the receiver
to muffle meaning.

Jean sounds wary. 'I've already heard the news,' he sighs. 'Give Maman time; she'll be back,' he adds. 'You know as well as I do, they can't live without each other.'

'You didn't see her,' Marguerite tells him. 'It's different this time.'

'Oh, she'll come to her senses,' he says. 'This will blow over.'

'Jean, their marriage is finished. Papa is hardly in his right mind. He needs us now.'

'He has Lydia.'

'Isn't that the problem?'

'So you believe Maman? You think there's no smoke without fire?'

'I think our father is under that woman's spell.'

Jean exhales. She hears more whispering.

'She had a gun, Jean, and she wasn't afraid to use it. It's a miracle she didn't kill herself, or anyone else. This is a scandal that we don't want on our hands. Our father claims to be in love with her, and has left Maman to fend for herself . . . You can imagine how I feel. We don't want this to go down in the history books, in the official accounts of who our father is.'

'Love!' he scoffs. 'But it will hardly come to that. We can keep the details quiet. That woman is his hired help, nothing more. The only story that'll be told about our father is about his art. Not the private affairs and melodramas of the women in the background.'

'I wish I had your certainty,' she says. 'But we need to be there now, with him, to manage things, to make sure Papa doesn't do anything he'll come to regret.'

'Oh, shush! Maman will find she can't live without him . . .'

Marguerite thinks of Amélie earlier that day, dressed in warrior red, that old determination in her eyes. 'She has every intention of being her own woman, Jean. You should have seen her. She is furious.'

'Maman always loved a fight. But you know she'll back down eventually.'

Her brother can't see her, but Marguerite is shaking her head. 'And you heard about Germany, I suppose? Are you telling me they'll back down, too, no need for me to worry?'

'That's different. You should leave Paris, while you still can.'

'Nice won't be any safer, not when Mussolini decides to cross the border.'

'The least you can do is send Claude to safety. You know Pierre would take him.'

'I am not sending my son to America!'

'But it's safe there. For now. I fought, don't forget. I've seen the horrors of war.'

Jean always has to know best, about everything. He always has to tell her how things are. She's certain that stubbornness is one of the curses of this damn family.

But still. Marguerite feels the tremors of the world shifting beneath her. Must everything change so fast, and all the certainties she held dear be stripped away?

'Meet me in Nice later next week,' Jean says. 'Sooner rather than later. I've no doubt we'll be dragged into Hitler's war before long. Then all hell will break loose – and nobody will give a damn about the torrid affairs of foolish old Henri Matisse.'

꙳

When Marguerite arrives, she's frazzled – her anger fired up over the long journey. Jean's prophecy proved right, and France did indeed declare war on Germany, just two days after Hitler invaded Poland. Upon hearing the news, Marguerite had felt an unexpected flicker of relief that France, finally, had taken a stand against Nazi aggression. But still, she fears the worst. Everyone is reeling – faced with the potential of air raids and enemy attacks – and while it's currently business as usual, many Parisians are leaving the capital, which has made her journey south more complicated. She was delayed by several hours as the train trundled through the countryside, and it's dark by the time she reaches her father's apartment. She has no idea what to expect. Will she have to face Lydia, confront the woman who has torn her family apart?

It's Jean who opens the door. He looks harried and tense.

Her brother closes the door quickly behind her and pulls her to one side in the corridor. Briefly, Marguerite spots Lydia, her back turned, chopping vegetables in the kitchen.

'She's here,' he hisses.

'I can see that,' Marguerite replies, her cheeks flushing. Lydia can't have been out of hospital more than a few days, and already she's back, making herself indispensable.

'Papa is acting as if it's the most normal thing in the world. And Lydia is obliging.'

'How dare she?' Marguerite whispers. 'This is Maman's domain. That woman has some nerve, acting as if she has the right to be here.'

Jean opens the door to the living room, and their father is in his usual seat, surrounded by his beloved birds, which coo and caw as the siblings approach. Henri looks hollowed out, the skin hanging bleakly under his eyes, the hair at his temples a fiercer shade of grey.

'Tell me,' he says urgently, upon seeing his daughter. 'What did your mother say? What's your impression? Will she return?'

'Papa . . .' She bends down to hug him, considering her words. 'I don't see how you can think that's a possibility, with Lydia back here under your roof.'

'But this has been Lydia's home for almost a decade,' he says in an urgent whisper.

'That really shouldn't be your concern.'

'She can hardly go elsewhere,' he insists. 'Not with Hitler on the warpath.'

'You can't have it both ways, I'm afraid. I thought you'd have realized that by now.'

Marguerite wants to strangle the obstinacy out of him. She decides to be frank in the conversation that follows. Lydia could be listening at the door, for all she cares, but she has no intention of tiptoeing around that woman, of giving her an inch more power in this house than she has already cleaved for herself. Marguerite's loyalties must never be in doubt. Her father needs a dose of the cold, hard truth, however fragile he may be.

Jean shifts around as she speaks of her meeting with Amélie. He's tetchy, unsettled. Her brother looks pale, she notices – his clothes looser, his hair thinning. The stress of the situation must be getting to him, too.

After their conversation, Marguerite follows Jean into their father's studio, ostensibly to look at his recent artworks. They are mostly of Lydia. Marguerite feels nauseous.

Before entering the kitchen, she listens for sounds of Lydia on the other side of the door, but is met with silence. Lydia must have slipped away, taken to her attic room for the rest of the evening. Still, Marguerite enters cautiously. The table has been laid, cutlery polished, candles lit, wine glasses turned expectantly, linen bearing no evidence of stains. The bread is sliced, greens prepared ready for steaming, and a stew has clearly been bubbling for hours. Fresh flowers brighten the room with their effortless charm.

Marguerite brings a spoonful of the stew to her mouth. It's over-seasoned. She pours water instead of wine and removes the butter from the table. Lydia should be more considerate of the risks to Henri's health. She's indulging him. He's always complaining of indigestion and other ailments. Marguerite serves the food reluctantly. If she'd been able to arrive earlier, she'd rather have prepared the meal herself. She doesn't have much of an appetite, anyway.

The ghost of Lydia is here in every outline.

And Marguerite knows a confrontation will soon be inevitable.

⌒

Later, Marguerite and her brother speak candidly deep into the night. Once upon a time, a family gathering would have included bursts of laughter, boisterous exclamations, teasing and tale-telling. But now, their intense conversation revolves around blame. They look back to their childhood, for signs that might have foretold the present chaos. Both agree, in different ways, that the blame lies at their father's door, for not appreciating Amélie more. For pushing her away with his obsessions.

With the flicker of movement, they're aware that Lydia is at the door to the kitchen, holding an empty glass. Her footsteps are light and they didn't hear her approach. Marguerite wonders if she has heard all the torturous things they've said about her, their suspicions about her intentions towards their father, the way he bends to please her. Also, their surprise at her brutal act of violence. How close did she really come to killing herself? Was it a cry for help to get his attention, or did she really mean to end it all?

As soon as he notices her, Jean gets up and says goodnight, telling Marguerite he hopes he'll manage a few hours' sleep. Marguerite squeezes his hand. He passes Lydia without acknowledging her. She keeps her head down, but doesn't move out of his way.

Lydia goes to the kitchen tap and fills her glass. She turns and looks at Marguerite. It's the first time they've made proper eye contact since she arrived. Lydia's cheeks are sharp and the skin of her chest is visible through her open nightshirt. Marguerite's eyes are drawn to the spot instinctively, the same way she has noticed other people's hungry gaze roaming over the scar tissue on her throat when the ribbon slips. The skin on Lydia's chest is angry, bruised and red around an epicentre of stitches. The wound is far from healed. Marguerite has the urge to touch it, gently. In it, she recognizes something of herself and her own vulnerability, their shared proximity to death. The sight of it moves her. Suddenly, and despite herself, she feels emotion for everything Lydia has been through, too – the turmoil hidden under her icy exterior.

'Why did you do it?' Marguerite asks softly, trying to hide the tightness in her voice. It's not meant as a challenge or a criticism, but a question born of genuine curiosity.

'It's late,' Lydia says, sharpened. 'I must be awake early to tend to Monsieur.'

She turns quickly and leaves the kitchen, taking her glass of water with her.

'Are you in love with my father?' Marguerite continues in a whisper as she departs.

But all that is left is the flourish of Lydia's shadow.

4

Paris, 1940

Marguerite looks at herself in the mirror, turning her head to left and right, observing her odd reflection, with her newly issued gas mask in place. She looks ridiculous. This thing is abominable, with its pronounced snout, and eyes as wide and convex as a bluebottle's. She rips it off and stuffs it in her handbag. She may hate this contraption – it's not exactly the height of fashion – but she doesn't intend to set foot outside the apartment without it. Ever since war was declared in September, France has been fortifying her defences, preparing for a bigger conflict. This strategy, with very little military action on the Western Front, means every woman and man is perpetually braced, and the strain is starting to show. As well as having to carry these gas masks, air-raid drills are being conducted, with information distributed on how civilians should seek shelter and protect themselves during bombing raids. A fat lot of good that will do! Marguerite imagines bellowing bombs, burning buildings, molten shrapnel. Thoughts of sending Claude to America linger at the back of her mind. Not yet, though. He's safe at his school. The headmistress there, an American, Maria Jolas – Marguerite's close friend since the days of her marriage to Georges – has made a personal commitment to look after him.

Christmas passed in a joyless blur. Her father's birthday – on the final day of the year – fared the same, with little celebration. He wanted no fuss, feels he deserves little by way of happiness. Marguerite and Claude spent time with Amélie. They've come to an agreement never to speak of Henri, which is strange for his daughter. But Amélie still believes he has been unfaithful, and if she gets started on the topic, it unleashes fresh fury and ruins the occasion.

Amélie has decided that their legal separation should be made final on 10 January – their wedding date, forty-two years after they made their vows of eternity to one another – which suggests the woman is trying to inflict a particular cruelty, or neatness, to their end.

So, a few days ago, her father made the journey to Paris. Marguerite didn't dare ask if Lydia was accompanying him, but she has assumed as much. Of course, she has no intention of seeing her or acknowledging her presence.

Yesterday, he and Amélie had an appointment – made through lawyers – at a café at the Gare de Lyon, to finalize details of their legal separation. Marguerite joined them to discuss how best to divide the money and artworks, and the split was equitable. It's not exactly a divorce – Amélie has been persuaded against such a thing for the sake of the family name – but otherwise, it's as close as can be. She knows Amélie intended the meeting to be the very last time she ever saw her husband.

Her father, on the other hand, seemed quite bereft.

'Your mother didn't look at me once,' he says now, as the two of them walk past the Louvre – she notices her father's eyes linger on the building where most of his youthful dreams were forged – and through the Place du Palais Royal, a tranquil square lined with leafy trees. 'I can't bear that she despises me so thoroughly. It seems that she is hell-bent on revenge. She thinks Lydia is a thief, trying to steal what is rightfully hers.'

Her father stops abruptly. She has been keeping pace with him and, when she notices him looking at the ground, she takes his elbow.

'Papa, are you quite all right?' she asks, nervous suspicion cracking her words. He seems bloated and tired, as if misery has sucked something essential from him. He has been complaining about a pain in his stomach. She's sure it's an ulcer, exacerbated by stress.

'Look, there!' he says, pointing down. Marguerite feels agitation, but looks nonetheless.

A flash of purple at the edge of the pavement catches her eye.

'A violet?' she says, bending down to see it more closely.

'Don't pick it!' he instructs. 'Please. I'd rather leave it to grow this time.'

‿

Today, Marguerite is accompanying her father to the Banque de France, one of France's oldest financial institutions, in the 1st arrondissement. Among her father's great anxieties – and the source of sleepless nights – is the state of his artworks being safeguarded at the bank. Now he wants to see them again, he says, before Hitler's cronies maraud into the capital and loot the lot.

Once inside the vault, they're faced with crates, all of which must be unpacked. They spend a few moments in silence, her father lost in reflection, before she opens one. He joins her and pulls out a large canvas. It's as she remembered, the colours pristine. They talk of the circumstances in which it was created at his studio in Issy, her father throwing out memories – recalling the creative battles he fought to bring it into the world, making it sound as if it were a child he'd birthed, rather than a painting. As he talks, Marguerite searches another crate, examining pieces, looking for signs of deterioration, checking them against a ledger she has prepared in advance. Each artwork has a story to tell, one so closely bound up in her childhood and family life, her own existence, that it feels like meeting her ancestors.

After a couple of hours of working steadily, Marguerite eases a heavy canvas from the back. It's large, but she almost missed it. She opens the protective cover, not sure what she'll find. What she sees almost winds her. The canvas shows the figure of a young girl reclining on a rattan chair, her breasts bared, her body lengthened, floating against a vibrant pink background dotted with daisies. She knows instantly that this artwork is *Large Nude* from 1911, a painting not seen for decades and only glimpsed later in another artwork, *The Red Studio*, which was commissioned by her father's Russian collector, Sergei Shchukin.

It was Shchukin's patronage that had allowed her father to build his dream studio in Issy, and to move the family into the comfort of the very spacious house. But Sergei didn't want *The Red Studio* by the time it was finished, so both paintings were hidden away.

She'd forgotten them – but here's *Large Nude*, like a body exhumed.

The naked model is Marguerite, aged sixteen.

Marguerite takes a moment to examine the captured version of herself. The image of her girlish body sets her heart racing and she can't help but flinch at the memory of posing naked for the first time at such a young age. She feels conflicted. Looking back, she can't remember feeling particularly nervous or self-conscious; it was just something she did. But at the age of forty-five, she feels a pang of shame: a girl on the brink of womanhood, exposed for the world to see, to be sold to the highest bidder in the name of art, encouraged by her father.

Her father's back is turned to her. She touches him on the shoulder.

'Papa,' she says. 'Look what I found.'

His eyes search the pigment, and he seems satisfied with the distemper and the depiction of the female form. It's the artistic processes that are top of his mind, but for Marguerite, she can still feel the way the sea breeze from the open window played across her skin that summer in Collioure – alone with her father and the bohemian young Russian woman, Olga, who played so fast and loose with the rules.

'I remember what a professional you were, posing in this way,' he says.

'Does it not seem strange to you now?'

'The work demanded a nude,' he says simply. 'You always wanted to pose and we were comfortable together. Amélie would have known about it, I'm sure. I wrote to her about all of my artistic developments that summer, and she didn't have any concerns. Olga was there. It wouldn't have been right to ask her, given your mother's fears.'

Marguerite rubs the side of the canvas. 'Hardly anyone even knows this painting exists. I'm not sure anyone would suspect the model is me. Only the daisies give it away.'

Henri looks at it fretfully. 'Do you realize I've made more por-traits of you than the rest of the family combined? You've brought so much to my art, so much of yourself. None of it would have been the same without you.' He looks again for a long time. 'But you know, I can't help but feel this is a painting best forgotten. I think it should be destroyed,' he says decisively.

Marguerite has never known her father, who has given every-thing to his art, make this decision about a finished piece, especially a work he admires. 'Are you sure that's necessary?'

She looks once more at the confident pigment on the canvas, fluid brushstrokes of pink and orange, her arm at an angle, raised to her head; daisies in the background. It seems a shame to get rid of work that was made in good faith, in hope, in love.

'Wait until I'm gone,' he replies. 'But I do want you to see that it's taken care of.'

It's hard for Marguerite to consider such a day. But he's only being pragmatic. She understands his motivations, and mostly agrees. 'If that's what you want, Papa,' she says.

She'll do it. When the day comes.

For now, that version of her will remain inside the vault, wrapped in shadows.

5

Paris, 1940

Georges Duthuit has hardly changed. How annoying, that the years have been kind to him: her former husband is still a handsome man, although Marguerite's determined to turn a blind eye. His dark hair hasn't faded in the years since she last laid eyes on him; the line of his jaw is no less compelling. She glances at his hands. No. She mustn't go down a path of reminiscence and regret. She left him for very good reason. Her husband had been carrying on with that British woman, Lady Georgia Sitwell, wife of Sir Sacheverell Sitwell, for a considerable time. His affair was common knowledge, with no reproach, among London's upper echelons; those literary snobs in England, including the Bloomsbury set, had never liked Marguerite, or her father, whom they considered a grand bore. But by the time the news reached her, it was still as unexpected and annihilating as a crashing meteor.

Before that moment, she'd put their marital strain down to having a baby, but the truth was that her relationship with Georges had been fracturing long before the birth of Claude. Marguerite hardly knew how to be a wife, how to dedicate herself to a man, after such religious devotion to the needs of her father. He'd demanded everything of her; her every waking thought was consumed by how to serve him and his ambition. It had left her with nothing to fuel other relationships, and the cracks had started to show.

. In the aftermath of their break-up, it was Marguerite who laid down the rules and avoided all contact. She refused to see Georges, or accept any correspondence. It was the only way she thought she could enforce the bitter break, one that had caused her so much pain and humiliation. So her invitation for them to see one another today must have bewildered him.

As an art critic and curator, Georges had harboured an interest in Henri Matisse long before he met Marguerite and married her in 1923. During their ten-year marriage, Georges curated several exhibitions of his father-in-law's artworks, helping to champion him, introducing him to a wider audience and establishing his reputation as a leading figure in modern art. He'd written a great deal about Henri, contributing to a deeper understanding of the artist's techniques, themes and innovations. At the time of their separation, Georges was working on a book – a comprehensive study of her father's art.

Of course, this had all been derailed by the discovery of the affair and Marguerite's subsequent heartbreak. Henri, protective of his daughter, had banned Georges from ever writing about him again, much to their shared regret.

But today there's a decision that has to be made together, and it cannot be avoided any longer. Germany invaded France in May, with a Blitzkrieg – a fierce and lightning-fast attack by Hitler's army that took everyone by surprise. The French and other Allied forces were caught off guard. In the subsequent confusion, and with defences across northern and western France breached, the German forces advanced, bypassing resistance and capturing key strategic points. By June, Paris had fallen. Marguerite watched, sullen and stony, as German soldiers marched through the streets of the city she loved. She'd never experienced rage like it, and every day since then, she's vowed that she will fight for France's freedom, that she will do whatever it takes to defy the enemy and all they stand for.

In the months since the invasion, Marguerite has known a different Paris. The Germans have imposed curfews, rationing and blackout measures, and have taken control of food supplies and the transport network. She carries that ugly gas mask religiously and has every expectation she'll need to use it. So today she's meeting Georges to discuss the most painful question: whether or not to send Claude to America. There's nothing she wants less in the world than to be so fully separated from her darling boy, but she knows – just as Camille knew almost half a century ago – that it's for the best. She must take every step to ensure her son is safe from danger, and that he has the best possible chances for the future. It's a sudden feeling that has fallen upon her. This proximity, this understanding, this urge to sacrifice one's own interests. Marguerite has never felt so close to that woman who walked out on her.

The conversation with Georges borders on fraught. They meet at his gallery. She wanted an excuse to see what he's doing professionally. Rumours, passed on by others in her circle, only take her so far. And she's intrigued to see in which direction his artistic interest has taken him. He talks about Picasso – the Spanish artist, her father's rival – how his art never shies away from the crushing reality of struggle and strife.

'You're aware of *Guernica*?' he asks slyly. 'The way Picasso bears witness . . .'

Georges cannot resist this dig at her father, implying, not unjustly – but still, it raises her hackles – that the work Henri has created during this period of war fundamentally fails to engage with it politically; how drawing women in repose is hardly an adequate response to the horrors of fascist tyranny. But the conversation quickly turns from art to the personal.

'And how's your mother, the formidable Madame Matisse?' he asks politely. Of course, Georges has heard the news that she walked out on her husband. The scandalous gossip will certainly have whipped around his artistic sphere like wildfire. He's probably fishing for any titbits he can share. He'd wanted to contact Marguerite at the time, he confides, but he wasn't sure his words of concern or condolence would have been appreciated. She wants to say that Amélie is indeed formidable, that she is rejuvenated, that she is living with Marguerite, and may be an irritable old woman at times, but at least it is on her own terms – but she holds her tongue.

'How is Henri taking the new direction, without the stabilizing force of a good woman to guide him?' Georges continues, trying to present a dispassionate interest.

Marguerite is loath to reveal anything, in case the details are relayed in an article or essay in the months to come, so she turns the conversation back to business, to Claude and his future.

Pierre has a gallery in New York, she tells him. His oldest son is a similar age to Claude. Our boy will always be French, in heart and soul, she says; a little time in America won't change that. Though she cannot help but wonder. We are our environments, she knows all too well, and we become different versions of ourselves depending on who we surround ourselves with. When thoughts and ambitions collide, heartbeats can't help but take on a new cadence.

He'll be among family, she concludes. Family is the most important thing.

So it is agreed. Claude will be sent to his uncle in America at the earliest opportunity. In Hitler's France, none of them are safe.

Then her thought is this: who is Marguerite now? She's no longer a wife, and, before long, will no longer be an active mother. Her relationship with her father has ruptured in recent months – and although it is not altogether broken, it's not what it once was.

Who must she become? Madame Matisse – this grown woman who goes by her maiden name. Perhaps it is time that she really gave herself to everything she believes in.

6

Lyon, 1941

The doctor places the stethoscope upon her father's bare chest. Marguerite sees him flinch. Henri's cheeks, once characteristically rosy, are ashen, and a yellow tint has seeped into the whites of his eyes. Henri has resisted this appointment for many months, despite the increasing frequency with which he complained of stomach cramps and a feeling of nausea. He wouldn't admit it, but she knew he was eating less. Lydia, too, had noticed the loss of appetite and reported it in a formally worded letter expressing her concerns.

Marguerite had been putting it all down to stress. Who wouldn't be thrown off course by the fall of Paris and the final splintering of a marriage? Marguerite knows from experience, when she left her husband, Georges, that there were months when she couldn't face the sight or smell of food. Her frame drastically diminished and she kept herself going with chains of cigarettes and endless coffee, which set her heart racing and led to sleepless nights.

But recently, she hasn't been able to shake the feeling that something more sinister lies behind her father's prolonged sickness. She's brought it up with him, more than once, but he is becoming recalcitrant in his advancing years, especially without Amélie to administer the harder truths.

In the months since war broke out, Marguerite has worried endlessly about her father in Nice, positioned as it is along the Mediterranean coast, so close to the Italian border. In June last year, Nice and its regions were occupied by Italian forces, following the armistice between France and Italy. Italy, governed by the dictator Mussolini, is now implementing terrifying legislation that targets Jewish people, political activists and foreigners, all of whom are at risk of arrest, deportation and persecution. Lydia's position as a Russian in occupied France is increasingly vulnerable. Marguerite may not like the woman, may wish she'd never laid eyes on her, but she'll fight tooth and nail for a free France and the rights of every person in it.

It's helpful that Marguerite moves in certain circles. She recently met Paco, an influential man who will be able to introduce her to the right people, so that she can find ways of offering her support to the emerging cells of resistance – courageous people who are undertaking brave acts of sabotage, espionage and underground activism. Marguerite can hardly risk imprisonment, not with her father so unwell and her maman in need of her, but she is determined to get involved where she can, by gathering intelligence, disseminating anti-German propaganda or providing assistance to those affected by the occupation.

Amid all this turmoil, her father's health concerns have become urgent. Marguerite has suffered at the hands of plenty of inept doctors over the years. Her father's doctor in Nice – who'd insisted there was barely anything wrong, simply a problematic ulcer – hadn't filled her with reassurance, so she'd found the name of the most discerning doctor still practising in France – not an easy task since the invasion. Wartime has made accessing quality medical care more challenging. Hospitals are under strain, with shortages of supplies and an influx of wounded soldiers. If he needs surgery,

Marguerite is also worried about the availability of skilled surgeons, medical resources and post-operative care for her father. But Dr Wertheimer, in Lyon, is the one person she trusts with her father's life. And his expertise couldn't come soon enough.

It was no easy task even to get her father from Nice to Lyon. The Germans are making everything difficult and movement between cities requires authorization and permits, with checkpoints in place to prevent unauthorized travel and enforce curfews. Marguerite is loath to admit it, but she was lucky Lydia was around to oversee the journey and accompany Henri. Travelling through occupied territory required caution, discretion and the ability to navigate danger – all of which Lydia could handle. Her father would never have made it alone. For Marguerite, it was an ordeal to travel from Paris: the networks were severely disrupted, with railways and roads damaged by bombing raids, sabotage and military operations. It has taken days, and used up the last of her quite formidable reserves.

Now, father and daughter are before Dr Wertheimer; her father unceremoniously laid out on a table in an examination bay that offers some privacy, the curtain opened on one side so Marguerite may offer a reassuring hand. The doctor treats her father's body like a puzzle to be solved – prodding him in the gut, pondering strange protrusions, puncturing a vein with a needle, drawing blood for analysis, and testing all manner of bodily functions. He shines a torch into his eyes, bounces a rubber hammer upon his knee and elbow, makes blood pressure calculations. The stethoscope is the final clue to the riddle. Marguerite can tell her father's patience is wearing thin.

The doctor makes a note, then flicks through a fat file that comprises a lifetime – seventy-one years – of her father's medical records. He glances at Marguerite, before his eyes settle on her father's pallid face. 'There's no easy way to say this, Monsieur Matisse.' Marguerite feels her father's fingers tense in her own. 'But I'm afraid your condition is rather serious. I certainly don't mean to worry you, but I do have a responsibility to impress upon you that time is of the essence. All our tests indicate that you are significantly unwell.'

'It's just a harmless ulcer,' Henri says. 'I've lived with it most of my life.'

'It is, in fact, a far more serious blockage in your digestive tract,' the doctor replies. 'Most people suffering from your symptoms would have been here twelve months ago. You must be a very stoical man, Monsieur Matisse, but I'm afraid we need to operate, urgently.'

Marguerite knew her father was stubborn. And this proves it!

'And what is the cause?' she asks, determined to be thorough.

'It's hard to say. Prolonged stress may have exacerbated an existing hernia, perhaps. It may have been perfectly harmless for many years and given you scant trouble, Monsieur Matisse, but these things can flare up, as you're now aware.'

'The same hernia that stopped me from lifting sacks of seed for my father, all those years ago,' her father considers. 'That hernia set me on the path to becoming an artist.'

'Now's not a time for nostalgia, Papa. It sounds like this damn thing could kill you.'

'Indeed,' the doctor says, diplomatically. 'We'll schedule an appointment as soon as possible. In the meantime, I tactfully suggest you get your affairs in order.'

⌇

Days later, Marguerite watches as her father is wheeled away to be prepared for surgery. There's a sheen of sweat across his forehead and a glint of fear in his eyes. She'll be informed when he is safely out of surgery, and she has reassured him that all will be well. Still, shards of worry pierce her. He'd pressed a bundle of letters into her hand that morning – one for Amélie, if she'd deign to read it; one for Jean, who, unbeknownst to Henri, has secretly joined the more militant side of the Résistance in Antibes; and one for Pierre in America, with a line written on the front, begging the German censors who now control the French postal system not to delay or redact a final letter from a father to his son.

And one for Lydia.

Marguerite had turned the letter over, looking for any hint of the words enclosed. They could tell her everything she needs to know, she realized. She considered slipping it into the bin. But her own nerves about her father's operation, and her sense that she might be jinxing the outcome if she didn't follow his wishes, prevented any such action. She vowed to deal with it later. She only hopes Lydia won't turn up, unwarranted, any time soon.

Marguerite spends the rest of the day waiting for news. She paces along the corridors of the hospital, passing janitors and doctors, and relatives looking for reprieve. She reads yesterday's papers, soaking up the latest developments in the war. It's mostly German propaganda these days, but some real news still filters through. The Germans have been conducting bombing raids on British cities, which will have been devastating for morale.

Days ago, the United States joined the war. Even though she welcomes its involvement in the fight against Nazi aggression, and knows that it will provide much-needed resources, military aid and support to the Allied cause, she can't help but worry about what this could mean for the escalation of the conflict.

Today, she reads – thinking of Lydia – that there has been movement on the Eastern Front, with German forces continuing their advance into the Soviet Union. The Soviet Union is on the side of the French, and Marguerite feels compassion for the soldiers and civilians caught in the battle. She wonders if Lydia still has family in Russia. Strange, that she has hardly thought to ask about her background.

Hours later, and there's still no update on her father's progress. Marguerite is anxiously aware of the fragility of life and the unpredictability of the future. She's dehydrated, uncomfortable and hungry, and she needs a change of clothes. She'd rather not set foot outside the hospital until she has seen her father, until she knows he has made it, but when she checks with a nurse, she tells her he's still in surgery and it will be a few hours before she can see him.

Quickly, Marguerite returns to the pension where she has been renting a cheap room. She showers, changes, eats what she can, then hurries back to the hospital. She approaches the nurses' station with caution.

'I'm here for an update on Monsieur Matisse,' she says.

The nurse checks the ledger.

'Ah yes, he's out of surgery now,' she replies. 'Madame Matisse is with him at the moment. She's been with him since he woke up.'

Marguerite sees an image of Amélie rushing to Henri's side.

But just as quickly, the image evaporates.

It won't be Amélie holding her father's hand.

'But I've been waiting all day. I'm his daughter!' Marguerite comes close to crying. She has never felt so outraged, so exposed, sidelined from her father's life when he needs her the most. Marguerite endeavours to stay calm. The nurse is not the person who deserves the brunt of her wrath. The nurse takes her to her father's private room, where he's recovering. Inside, Lydia is reading to him, the woman's treacherous mouth moving with treacherous words. She looks up as Marguerite enters.

'We tried to contact you as soon as he came round,' Lydia says calmly.

Lies, all lies! Marguerite has been deliberately shut out, at her father's darkest hour, by this terrible woman. She is about to cause a scene, but then her eyes fall on her father, who looks so shrunken and sallow-eyed that she drops to her knees by his bedside. His hands are cool to the touch, and she realizes just how close he must have come to slipping away for good.

This is an argument that will have to wait. Marguerite vows to take it up with Lydia privately.

The doctor enters, with his smart suit and unruly hair. Lydia steps away from the bed and stands by the window, casting herself into silhouette, as if cut out from the blue sky behind her. Marguerite can't stand the sight of her. She shouldn't be here at all. But each of them waits expectantly, braced for the doctor's professional verdict.

'I'm afraid I have difficult news,' he says. 'During surgery, we found evidence of cancer,' he announces as dispassionately as possible. 'We believe we caught it early enough, but, as a result, we've had to remove a large part of your intestine, Monsieur Matisse.'

Her father is so bandaged and drugged that it isn't clear whether he has heard or understood the doctor's words.

'We're confident of a recovery, but you must take things very slowly. Gone are the days of endless stress and strain. It might be time to retire, monsieur,' he says gently.

Her father is hardly conscious, but Marguerite notices him catch Lydia's eye, his brows raised, as if to say, 'Just try to stop me.' She knows he believes he has more work to do.

But he's no fool, either. Marguerite can see that facing his own mortality has shaken him. He'll have to reassess his life. And finally answer the question: is art really worth dying for?

7

Antibes, 1943

Jean shows Marguerite the plans. The rolls of paper have been spread out across the kitchen table, which has been cleared of the evening's dinner. She examines the blueprints of the bridge, follows the line of his finger. He's showing her the weak spot. 'Hit it here' – jabbing his index finger to the page – 'and the whole thing will collapse.' His voice betrays no emotion.

'The dynamite is hidden in a barrel in the basement,' he adds.

Her nephew is sleeping down the hall, Jean's wife dozing on the settee in the next room.

Marguerite licks her lips, trying to match his quiet bravado.

Her brother, over the past year, has become deeply embroiled in the extremist side of the Résistance movement, and it has changed him. His anger, his ruthlessness, shines through in every word, every glance. He is already high up in the chain, and frequently liaises with British intelligence about where the next targets should be. Marguerite supports him every step of the way. She wants the enemy gone. She wants to see them suffer. They have stomped evil into the soil of the country she loves. She has said she'd put her life on the line to see freedom restored, so why does she still feel scared of committing to more? For a long time, she put this hesitancy down to the responsibility she bears – as Claude's mother, as her father's daughter. People needed her. But not any longer. She has to banish her reticence, and the only way is at Jean's side, as he lights the match that will ignite the dynamite that will blow up a bridge, thwarting the enemy from advancing any further.

It's true that there's someone else she's thinking of, too: Paco. He's a respected man, older than her by fifteen years, and more established in the movement. Jean also admires him. He's a man of intellect and brute resolve. Marguerite has been spending more time with him, and she likes his company. She has a nervous feeling that he enjoys hers, too. After more than a decade on her own – and a lifetime of catering to her father's needs – can Marguerite accept the attentions of another, especially now, at a time when there's so much to fight for?

Jean has been pushing Marguerite to do more than be part of the news distribution network. As a respectable woman, she has the ability to move discreetly within occupied Paris, and can easily gather intelligence on German military movements and troop deployments, as well as being able to type up and distribute underground newspapers, pamphlets and other anti-German propaganda. At times, she has felt as if she were leading a kind of double life. Her public, civilian identity – the artist's daughter, known, but always in his shadow – in contrast to her clandestine one as a member of the Résistance, where she has purpose but operates under a pseudonym.

Jean agrees it's important work, but he feels she is wasting herself, that she could be doing so much more, something vital, to help stop the Germans in their tracks. But she's part of a tight-knit, trusted group, and it won't be easy to replace her, she tells him. Everyone she knows in Paris is already in the Résistance, and already has their role. She'd be letting the side down if she were to take up other work elsewhere.

Jean looks at her from the side of his eye. She hates it when he does that. It's a habit she recognizes from their youth, and it always precedes an obnoxious statement she won't like. 'Who else might you know who is able to type and doesn't have much else to do?'

An image of Amélie sitting in a chair with her knitting needles springs to her mind.

'Jean, no! She's seventy-one years old! She has arthritis. Her eyesight is terrible. We can't drag Maman into this. Be reasonable, please. And besides, she'd say no.'

'Is that so?' he asks, infuriatingly.

Marguerite pauses. As is often the case with Jean, she feels she's walking into a trap.

'What have you said to her?' she asks. 'And how?'

This isn't a conversation to have openly by telephone or write in a letter.

'Let's just say, you'll be needing more typewriter ribbons from now on.'

'Jean, that is not fair! You're putting our mother in great danger.'

'So what! Everyone has a part to play. We can't just care about our own comfort and let everyone else suffer. Despite her complaints, Maman has had a good life. It's time she gave something back.'

Marguerite lets out a puff of surprise. There's something about the relationship between boys and their mothers – especially cherished oldest sons. They get away with murder, and delight in saying the most bombastic things. Yet there's hardly a ripple of discontent in the waters of their mother's love.

'This is madness,' she says.

'She'll be fine,' Jean replies. 'And it's what she wants. She's bored. She needs something to put a bit of fight into her again, not just the kind that's been aimed at Papa all these years. Besides, nobody will give her a second glance. That's the point. And if she were ever caught – which she won't be – she could plead ignorance. She's good at keeping secrets, and operating with stealth.' He raises his brows. 'And it will free you up to do something that will really take them by surprise. You're well spoken, well dressed,' he says, almost with a sneer. 'The Germans would never imagine a woman like you could be carrying a case of explosives.'

Marguerite thinks of her father, surrounded by birds and colourful artworks. Since the surgery, he has kept talking about his second chance, how much he wants to achieve. He told the doctors, before the operation, that he wanted three more years. In the months since, with his recovery, his focus has changed and he hasn't stopped working – much to her annoyance – but he's adapting to a new style: work that's increasingly simple, with bold colours and a sense of lyrical abstraction. She hopes Lydia isn't allowing him to get ahead of himself, filling his head with plans that he won't have the energy to execute.

Marguerite has never shied away from telling her father the truth. And she wouldn't deliberately drag him into the ugly underbelly of this blasted war; she wants to get him as far away from it as possible. Last month, he was offered a visa to Brazil. As the bombardment in France intensified, with Nice in the firing line and bombs falling on the Promenade des Anglais, she begged him to take it, even though he was still recovering. But would he? Absolutely not. He told her that he wouldn't abandon France in her hour of need.

But Marguerite suspected the truth was that he wouldn't leave Lydia. As a Russian in exile, she doesn't have the paperwork to exist in France without harassment, let alone what's needed to leave. So they will face whatever comes, together.

Lydia has been making plans to move them out of Nice, further into the hills, out of harm's way. Marguerite can only hope that her father will come to his senses before it's his funeral they're arranging and his fought-for second chance amounts to nothing.

Two years on from the surgery, he is still in a great deal of pain, and he hasn't walked since the operation. He needs a wheelchair to move around and wears a girdle, which provides stability and support for his abdomen as he heals. But, of course, he's still trying to be the artist he has always been, drawing on large sheets of paper pinned to the wall, with charcoal attached to a piece of bamboo. That can only have been with Lydia's assistance. She should know better, discourage him from anything strenuous, Marguerite thinks, and that includes making new work.

His stubbornness will be the death of him, the death of them all.

'Now, look, it's late,' Jean says, getting back to business. 'Are you in, or out?'

He's willing to risk everything in this fight. Is she?

Marguerite feels danger all around her. But to do nothing is no choice at all. Perhaps that's how her father feels.

'Fine, I'll do it,' she relents, pushing her brother as if they were teenagers. 'I really don't care what happens to me, but please, keep our parents safe. And I know you won't need convincing, but Papa mustn't hear a word of this.'

Marguerite's first mission for the militant resistance cell will take her from Paris to Rennes, carrying something far more dangerous than words: a case of dynamite. She will have to make this trip once a month for as long as it takes. It's a journey that will last the best part of a week to get there and back, and for two or three of those days, as she travels west, her every move will be under scrutiny. One wrong move risks death at the hands of the soldiers who patrol every inch of the network. One wrong word could have fatal consequences, not just for her but the entire cell. In June, one of the most prominent figures in the Résistance – Jean Moulin – was betrayed by a fellow member and arrested by the Gestapo in Lyon. He was tortured brutally in an attempt to extract precious information about the network and its activities, but he remained steadfast and refused to divulge a thing. However, Paco has just received the news, passed through the highest channels, that Moulin recently died in Gestapo custody. His murder has come as a massive blow to all of them.

Marguerite cannot trust anyone. Except Paco, who she's with for this initial test. He wants to be by her side so she doesn't lose her nerve, so she can learn. She intends to make the best impression, to show she has mettle. And because she can't resist the urge to impress him.

Just hours ago, Marguerite left Maman at her Paris apartment, set up with everything she will need to fulfil her part in the Résistance, which is to type up bulletins. Marguerite can hardly believe Amélie wants to take on this new role of activist, but the older woman's enthusiasm could hardly be contained.

'Do you know how long it has been,' she asked, 'since I've done something I can be proud of? Something that will make people look at me and say, "Bravo, Amélie!" I've been listening to people say it to your father for decades. Never once has it been directed at me.'

Well, Marguerite could hardly argue with that.

Amélie was rusty for that first day of typing, her fingers unwilling to navigate the stiff keys, but she quickly found a fluency and was able to work at a speed that almost matched what Marguerite could muster. Marguerite was impressed by her maman, by the inner reserve of radical energy that pushed her outside herself. Marguerite had, of course, explained the dangers, and done everything she could to mitigate the chances of her being caught – including taking the bell off the typewriter, so there wasn't an almighty *ding* every time she came to the end of a line.

Amélie certainly knows to take precautions, not to answer the door to anyone, to claim ignorance and ineptitude if anyone asks difficult questions. It's a role she was made for.

At the station, Marguerite stays as close to Paco as possible. It's pandemonium. The air-raid sirens have been blaring for hours and, while there haven't been any blanket bombings in Paris yet, people are scared, so more are fleeing the capital, heading to wherever might offer some degree of safety. The couple, having made every effort to be inconspicuous, blend into the crowd, and any anxiety Marguerite feels is easily matched on the faces of everyone around them.

On the train, there's no sitting room, and they stand for several hours by a window that won't close, the accelerated air rushing in and bestowing on her a piercing earache. The France Marguerite sees from the window is torn and edged with death. Tractors are abandoned in the middle of half-ploughed fields. Crops succumb in an overripe harvest, and crows scavenge. The train stops at every provincial station, lolling for long minutes on the tracks. In Le Mans, everyone is evacuated. The engine has overheated and there won't be a new driver until the next day, so Marguerite and Paco must spend the night.

They try to find a pension. The town bristles with animosity: the footfall of troops rings loud and people shrink as the enemy passes, fearful of receiving the butt of a gun in their face. A man, dressed in rags, stands over an open drain and shouts profanities into the blackened pipes, his arms outstretched. Two of his fingers are missing. Thank God, she thinks, that the future is invisible to us, for we'd so often not be able to bear the path we have to walk if we could see what was on the horizon.

Everywhere is full for the night, so they must push on. Along the way, they see soldiers marching before they stop abruptly. One bangs on the door of a small shop. A moment later, they ram the door and swarm inside. Paco pulls Marguerite into an obscured spot on a side street. Shouts ring out inside the raided building. There's a woman wailing, the cry of a baby. A second later, a family are pushed from the building, tripping as they go.

Marguerite's heart constricts. She wants to fight, but Paco holds her back.

'But they'll be murdered,' she says. 'The baby, too.' She is full of burning rage.

The family are herded into the back of an army vehicle that has pulled up beside the building. The engine erupts with a juddering roar and pulls away.

'This is who we're fighting for,' Paco says, taking Marguerite's arm, pulling her back on to the road. 'I'll send a message to the cell. We'll lay down our lives if necessary, but we have to be smart about it. Now, hurry – let's go,' he says, almost running, 'or we'll be next.'

8

Rennes, 1944

'Madame Matisse, you're under arrest.'

Marguerite is stopped on the street before she can step through the door. She has been operating her double life for more than a year now, and has never allowed herself to become complacent, but still, the shock hits her like a ton of bricks. She doesn't say a word as two men in enemy uniform place their hands over her mouth. She knows instantly what's happening. She's anticipated this for so long, but hoped her fears would not materialize. She feels herself go limp – the only form of resistance she can muster in these circumstances.

The men drag her around the corner to a waiting vehicle. She's cuffed and pushed inside, falling heavily to the floor. The door slams. Marguerite struggles to straighten herself, the muscles in her spine tight and unyielding as she pulls herself into a sitting position, her arms angled behind her. She might have broken something in the fall. She closes her eyes, and feels the reverberations of the vehicle as it launches into gear. They haven't told her what she's being arrested for, but Marguerite has her suspicions. There's been a leak in the Résistance; someone has blown their cover. She has no idea where she's being taken, but has a terrifying image of how things could play out once she gets there.

She takes a scared breath, in through her nose. Her botched airways always constrict at times like this, and she longs to loosen the ribbon, to scratch the itch that's gathering along the line of her scar. She puts her head on her knees, and endeavours to control her breathing. Brutal images flash through her mind and she tries to shake them away.

She believes in France. There's nothing she regrets. But the thought of her father gives her pause. She prays Amélie is safe. She tries not to panic, but she feels it growing.

Perhaps she has underestimated what this might mean for those she loves . . .

⤷

In the holding cell, Marguerite is handcuffed to a long chain dangling from the ceiling. Her feet touch the ground, but only just, so she can't sit, and all the weight of her body pulls on her arms. The ground crunches underfoot, covered with sawdust, the hard shells of cockroaches and human hair, much of it her own, as the guards have cropped it closely. She's exhausted. A soldier has taken the belt from his waist and whips it across her back, the buckle bashing into the hard bones of her spine. The pain is excruciating. Marguerite has not opened her mouth once to speak to these bastards, and she has no intention of offering them a single word.

One day, she comes to, and realizes that she has been here for weeks, months even. She has no idea what day it is, and can't remember when she last saw natural light. What these persecutors don't know is that she has all the light she needs inside herself. She can hardly formulate words, but torture hasn't yet drained her capacity to envision beauty. She gathers strength from the memory of the colours in her father's paintings – the luminosity of his pinks, his turquoises, his butter yellows. Henri was always able to trap the glorious brightness of a day on his canvas, as if he were painting with sunshine itself. She dreams of stepping into one of his artworks now, to be sitting on a chair by an open window in the south of France.

Another lash lands upon her, and she retches with the pain.

⌒

Marguerite is herded out of the building for the first time in a long while. She sniffs the air – it's woody and damp – and notices the angle of the shadows on the ground. The seasons have changed, not once, but twice, in the time she has been incarcerated. Her father may have died, for all she knows; she can only pray that Amélie has been able to flee Paris, and that her brother Jean has not suffered the same fate. She thanks God that Claude has left France. She knows what delight these bastards would have taken in finding him, torturing him, too.

Marguerite has no idea where she's being taken now. Only that her clothes hang off her body and her eyes burn in the weak morning light. Her skin feels as thin as paper.

She'd heard whispers that the prisoners would be transported but, as with everything in this place, she'd no idea if that would include her, or when it might happen.

It appears that today is the day.

Marguerite looks closely at the soldiers' faces, but they are as cold and closed as ever.

Do these men have emotions, families, people they care for, who they wouldn't want to see tortured, as she has been? She's sure they must be loved by someone. The monster before her is a man on whose lap a baby might be bounced, or on whose cheek a wife will plant a kiss. He'll congratulate himself, no doubt, on how hard he works, the sacrifices he must make for his country. She imagines him sleeping soundly at night, sure of himself and his right to operate in the world. He represents everything she hates, everything she has tried to fight, but, at the end of the day, his power exceeds hers, and it's possible she'll die by his hands.

Will he face the consequences?

She wants to live for that reason: to make men such as him pay.

⌒

'Where are you taking us?' a fellow prisoner demands. He's immediately struck on the back, between his shoulder blades, and he stumbles on to the rough ground in front of him.

All the prisoners hold their breath.

A guard laughs and kicks dirt into the man's face. Marguerite feels her blood burning.

She's loaded into the back of a vehicle with three dozen others – mostly men, along with a couple of women. Seeing them – dirty-faced, their clothes ripped, limping – she gets a painful glimpse of how she herself must appear. She can only imagine that her eyes are as hollow, the bones at the base of her neck as sharp, her hair as matted to the scalp. She holds her stomach against the pain that is roiling there. Her body has never felt as if it were truly her own: as a child, it was always a source of pain, and getting air into her lungs was a battle. In the years since, she has continually been betrayed: when her windpipe had to be forcibly opened, then during childbirth, when she had to fight her own flesh. She found her body uncomfortable, unfathomable, her scars a reminder of that fine line between life and death. But strangely, she has never felt more connected to the needs of her body than she has been during her confinement and torture. It speaks to her, in a language she now understands. She feels tender towards it.

Inside the vehicle, the prisoners glance sideways at each other, their eyes darting. Marguerite catches the eye of another woman, younger than herself. A small smile, a reflexive gesture she knew from the time before, slips to her lips. It is returned, briefly.

～

The engine of the lorry vibrates steadily for an hour or more, then finally comes to a standstill. Marguerite attunes her ears to the sounds outside, listening for any hint of what's to come. She can hear the repetitive noise of metal against something hard – a shovel, perhaps, being rammed into rocky ground. She hears birdsong, before the noise starts up again, drowning out the tune.

A soldier opens the door, and fresh air floods in. It knocks them all sideways.

People stumble out, shielding their eyes.

Marguerite follows. They are standing by railway tracks, about to be transferred into an empty carriage. Hundreds of people from other vehicles are making the same transfer.

'Where are we going?' a man with a wild ginger beard asks.

The soldier raises his gun, and the man shrinks away.

'On holiday,' he says, using the butt of the gun to push Marguerite forward, in through the open door of the carriage. Inside, people are mute with fear. Marguerite feels it herself, that constriction. Night is falling, and none of them have any way of knowing how long they'll be on this journey, or what state they will be in when they arrive. The woman who caught Marguerite's eye earlier is in the same carriage, and she wipes a torn sleeve against her nose, her eyes tightly closed.

Marguerite watches her lips move and realizes that she's praying.

Marguerite closes her eyes, and now she, too, prays.

～

The train has been in motion for a long time when it comes to a halt, the brakes applied abruptly, the screeching of wheels as high-pitched and stabbing as the notes she played on her father's cherished violin as a child. Marguerite lurches forward, cracking her jaw against the person in front of her, while the person behind falls on top of her, twisting her arm at an awkward angle. There's a sickening moment of silence. She pulls herself upright and sees that her hand is crushed, two of her fingers splayed. She holds them against her chest.

They listen for gunshots. One man stands and tries the sliding door to their carriage. It has come loose from its external lock. He pulls again, his weakened arms futile against the weight of it. Marguerite can tell by the anguish that crosses his face that he was once a man who prided himself on his strength. He pulls once more, but the door does not give more than an inch or two. Another man jumps up to help him, then a third; even the woman who'd been praying at the start of the journey leaps up to lend a hand. The door gives a little more, and Marguerite can see the moon through the gap. It's as bright as a flashlight, and she's transfixed, caught in its beams for the first time in many, many months.

'Now!' the man with the ginger beard shouts, and they all pull at once, including Marguerite with her throbbing fingers, widening the gap between freedom and captivity.

The door finally gives and they slide it fully open. The people behind her surge forward, and Marguerite tumbles from the carriage into the mud. She knows instantly that she's at risk of being trampled, and so she rolls and shuffles with what little strength she has, under the carriage, her body on the tracks. She has no idea if the train will start up again as suddenly as it stopped, or if the German soldiers will have been alerted by the noise of them pulling at the door. She steadies her breathing, her nose to the underside of the train. To the left, she sees pairs of feet in quick succession as people jump from the train. All are barefoot.

Marguerite hears a door slam further up the tracks. Her heart jumps to her mouth. The sound of a gun being fired. She knows she has to get out of here. Fast.

She pulls herself out from under the train on the opposite side to where people are now running off into a ploughed field, heading who knows where. This could be madness, heading away from the crowd. Or it could save her life. All her senses are on fire; her heart is racing. On her haunches, she takes a moment to assess the landscape, and sees the tops of trees in the distance. Will there be enough cover to hide there, amid the undergrowth? There's only one way to find out. A dog barks somewhere near by, and she has no doubt it's getting closer.

Marguerite's body feels lumpen and uncoordinated, but it's filled with adrenaline, so she bolts, like a rabbit from a trap, wild-eyed in an attempt to survive. She runs through fields – the light from the moon, or an enemy's torch, chasing her every step. The ground is uneven and she stumbles, crashing into a ploughed furrow, the mud rising on either side. Her threadbare clothes are ripped, and there's a throbbing in her shin that she doesn't want to think about right now. All she has to do, all she has to concentrate on in this moment is getting across this open space as fast as she can, without being seen by those who would kill her in a heart-beat. Marguerite clambers back on to her feet and runs, as low to the ground as possible.

She's running towards the thickening of trees and anticipates the hotness of a bullet travelling into her skin. She keeps going, panting, determined not to pause. It's not that she wants to live so desperately – intellectually, she knows the cruelty of life and has mentally made her peace with the end of it one day – but right now, it's her whole body that wants to live: every cell, every neuron, every fibre is pushing her on.

Marguerite hears the dogs and feels the spotlight on her back. She is terrified. She runs, and the woods are so close, and there's a pain in the back of her head where she knows a bullet will strike. Just as she is approaching the final stretch before the woods, she feels something grip her foot. She stumbles, fighting off whatever has pulled her to the ground. She comes face to face with the woman from the train, who clamps a hand over her mouth and puts a finger to her own lips at the same time.

'The woods will be the first place they search,' she says. 'Get in here.'

There's an overturned water trough, made of rusted iron, the size of a coffin.

They slip their bodies underneath. There are plenty of holes, giving them a view in both directions. 'I saw you coming, fleeing like a hare,' the woman says. 'You're lucky they didn't set the dogs on you with all that noise.' She rubs a handful of mud on Marguerite's face. It smells of cow shit. 'That will throw the dogs off our scent. This isn't perfect,' the woman continues in a whisper, 'but it's safer than being in the open. A better place would be up a tree. Now we're together, we can help each other up. I wouldn't make it on my own.'

Marguerite is fizzing; she's still on high alert and her body keeps pushing her to run. But she decides to take her chances here. Underneath the water trough, which had tumbled into a ditch, they at least have a chance of not being seen during the initial search. But they'll have to move on shortly, and get out of this area entirely before dawn. Marguerite has no idea where they are, let alone where she'll go. How far is it to the nearest town? Will she be able to trust anyone? When will she next be able to put food in her stomach, let alone rest in a bed, or speak with her father? Her father. Is he still alive? He'll be crushed with worry about her, and she's sickened with that knowledge. How to let him know, from her mind to his, that she's not dead, that she's fighting to be free?

Hours later, it's still dark, but the moon has moved across the sky.

Together, they crawl from the ditch, pulling their bodies through the mud and clumps of stinging nettles towards the edge of the forest. Once there, they stand up cautiously, backs erect against the trunks of trees, hiding, slipping from one to another as they head deeper into the forest. After a while, the woman from the train stops, and puts her hand to her ear, listening closely. Persuaded that they're not being followed, she offers a foothold so that Marguerite can climb into the lower branches of a tree. She's stinking and scratched, but manages, with a further push from below, to clamber up. Once she has got her footing, she reaches to help her companion, and notices again her own damaged hand. The bones in her smallest fingers feel limp and the flesh around them is swollen, but still she offers it and ignores the pain. Slowly they make their way further up until they've climbed as high as they can. Then they sit in the branches like birds, picking mud from their elbows. Marguerite scratches the stings along her forearms. The woman from the train pulls a fistful of dock leaves from the front of her top. 'Rub these where it hurts,' she says.

Marguerite takes one and it's instantly cooling. Once she has tended to the bumps on her arms, she uses the leaves like a flannel, wiping them across her face and forehead.

'I do hope you've enjoyed your spa treatment today, madame,' the woman whispers, keeping her voice from carrying, her lip curling in amusement.

Marguerite starts to laugh, a bursting noise that she does her best to choke back. It could be mistaken for an owl, calling in the darkness.

∽

In the forest all around them, there's the rustling of creatures, all their senses alert in the dark. Marguerite is not sure she'll ever feel safe again. In the distance, there are cries and gunshots, and Marguerite doesn't need to imagine the worst, for it has already happened and continues to happen all around her.

Marguerite reaches over to the woman from the train and removes a spider that is weaving a web between the tendrils of her hair and the bark of the tree. The spider curls into a ball on contact. Marguerite has the absurd desire to put it in a jar, carry it with her, this talisman of life, of determination. But she has to leave it here, in its natural habitat.

She has no destination, other than a place of safety. Other than her father.

Just then, the barking she has heard at intervals during the night grows louder. Marguerite flinches, and the other woman almost loses her balance. The pair look at each other, their eyes flashing with fear and unspoken questions: should they stay and take their chances, or run, run for their lives, and see where it gets them? Marguerite's instinct is to stay up in the branches. There's every chance they won't be spotted, and that the dogs won't catch their scent. But if a dog does lead a soldier to them, it will be a certain death.

'We must run!' the woman whispers, and begins to slip back down the tree towards the ground. Without thinking, Marguerite follows. She hits the ground, stumbles, then sets off, her limbs aching as they fire into action.

But the woman from the train has not moved from the spot where she fell. Marguerite returns to her. She's gripping her ankle, her mouth twisted in pain.

'Go! Now!' she instructs, turning her head as the sound of barking increases.

Fear courses through Marguerite's body. It's like nothing she has ever experienced before: a bomb detonating in her brain. She's utterly frozen.

'I'll catch up. I just need a moment,' the woman says. When

Marguerite fails to move she hisses at her: 'If you don't go now, we'll both die.'

Marguerite can see the woman's lips moving, but cannot hear her next words. She cannot hear the dogs getting closer, or the shouts, in German, from approaching soldiers. The world continues to contract to a tiny point – this woman's face, her bright eyes.

'They will kill you!' the woman insists.

Marguerite throws her arms around her. The warmth is seductive, and she wants to stay there, knows she'll die there, and it would be enough. In her mind is an image of them, found together, entwined like this. 'Go, for my sake,' the woman urges.

At the instruction, Marguerite's body begins to move. She separates from the woman and races off through the forest, the ground slippery, sweat streaming down her mud-caked face. It's a cold, damp dawn and the mist is thick around her. She glances back, and already the woman is obscured. There's only one direction: forward. She puts one foot in front of the other.

Marguerite runs and runs, as fast as she can. A gunshot.

One. Two, three.

She keeps running.

She cannot stop.

EPILOGUE

MARGUERITE

Nice, 1954

Marguerite wonders if this might be the last time she'll arrive at this station on the Riviera carrying such a feeling of homecoming in her heart. The place where one's parent lives will always be more of a pull than anywhere else. Just hours ago, she received one of the most upsetting messages of her life, from Lydia Delectorskaya, a woman she has studiously had little contact with for the best part of a decade. The message said her father has suffered a stroke, that he's stopped working. He is dying.

Marguerite left Paris immediately. She can only pray that Lydia is mistaken, but that woman has an unnatural instinct for the state of her father's health; she knows every inch of him, can read him clearly. He's eighty-four. If she says it is time, Marguerite listens.

In the fifteen years since Henri and Amélie separated, Lydia has adopted the role of companion – to all intents and purposes, as close and loyal and dedicated to Marguerite's father as a wife. The attachment they have formed is intense, and the extent to which they orbit one another has been, for his daughter, embarrassing. But it cannot be denied that, against all the odds, Lydia has created an environment in which her father thrives. It pains Marguerite to acknowledge it, but he has made the best art of his life, facilitated by his cherished assistant. What daughter wants to admit that about the woman people assumed was her her father's mistress? Lydia has made it possible, giving him the greatest gift of all: the ability to keep working. She has been ruthless in that regard.

Marguerite certainly doubted her father as he got older, especially after his surgery. She begged him to take a step back from art. She's glad he ignored her every word. He had so much more within him – and it would have been a travesty, everyone agrees, for that to have gone uncreated, unseen. His cut-outs are unlike anything anyone has ever imagined – each made by a man who was bed-bound, unable to move freely, who, even in the final stage, couldn't say no to art.

Her father called it his second life, and Marguerite knows how that feels, to be gifted more time than one felt one was destined to be dealt. She had that feeling when she returned to her father after her escape from the Nazis. She'd been arrested in Rennes, held captive and tortured for a year, then managed to flee – she later came to learn – from a train that was taking political prisoners to Ravensbrück, a German camp where it's certain she'd have perished.

Her freedom came just days after the liberation of France, about which she'd had no idea. Her father told Marguerite that he was so bereft that when bombs fell on Vence that August he'd sat in the garden and hadn't flinched as shells exploded around him. Lydia had shouted at him to take cover in the basement, but he wouldn't be moved. With his daughter imprisoned, he'd lost his will to live. When the liberation of France was finally complete, at a time when he'd still had no word of her, he'd been unable to celebrate. People flooded the streets, singing. His shutters remained closed.

Upon their reunion, it was as if gold had been poured into the contours of her life. She doesn't think she will ever forget the brimming crush of joy of that first embrace with her father, who'd been out of his mind with worry for the twelve months she'd been missing after her arrest.

The shock had been that Marguerite discovered on her return that Amélie, too, devastatingly, had been arrested. The seventy-one-year-old had been rounded up hours after Marguerite's own arrest. Once Marguerite was in the custody of the Gestapo, they'd taken the clothes off her back. A German woman had worn them to impersonate her, entering the apartment she shared with her mother. They'd caught Amélie in the act, typing bulletins on an old typewriter. She was sentenced to six months in prison.

Selfless, courageous Amélie, who, even in her seventies, believed in a better world. It causes Marguerite anguish to know that she and her brother were the reason that Amélie spent time in a prison cell, just like her own father, Armand, all those years ago.

After her release, Amélie moved to Aix-en-Provence. She has friends, spends time in her garden, sees her grandchildren. Amélie has gripes and disappointments – her sister, Berthe, died of cancer at the end of the war. But her disappointments can't be ascribed to a man any more.

In the days following their reunion, Marguerite's father drew her. It had been a long time since he'd last done that, but it was their way of pulling their souls back together. In his sketches, she exuded a radiance, a new resilience. She told him things in those sessions that she vowed never to repeat again. About how she'd been shackled by her wrists to a table, beaten with a steel flail by a man who removed his shirt to more successfully work up a sweat, until her eardrum burst; that she'd been plunged head first into buckets of ice water, held by the neck until she couldn't hold her breath for a second longer; deprived of food, of water, left to rot in isolation, her mind spilling away from itself like lava flow.

But somehow she'd survived.

Sometimes, even ten years later, Marguerite feels as if she is lost in those woods, like she left something of herself there. She knew she had to live. From the day she returned to Paris and found the

Germans gone, the war behind them, the only choice she had was to put it behind her, too. Just like her father, she felt as if she'd been given her own second chance. And she refused to waste it.

It's dark by the time she arrives at the Regina. The first days of November have pulled the spirits of All Hallows Eve into this month of frost and fires, and she's worried about what she might find once she steps inside his apartment. Lydia lets her in. It has been many years since they last spent time together. They have succeeded in avoiding each other during Marguerite's visits, choreographing their hours with Henri. Lydia is in her forties now and has aged in a surprising way – the lines of her body more pronounced, that icy youthfulness softening into something that offers comfort, that promises care. Her hair has dulled to a darker shade, which suits her; her eyes are still gleaming and sharp, missing nothing at all.

Lydia wears a clean apron, as if she were indeed a trusted assistant, paid to care. Marguerite once again experiences her feelings of confusion about this woman's role in her father's life. But her father is the priority, not a decades-long rivalry.

'He's waiting for you,' Lydia says generously.

Marguerite follows her into a dimly lit room. When she gets to him, he's on the edge of consciousness. Her father is clinging to life with a ferocious energy, cutting death into fragments, scattering pieces of it across the walls with his sharpened scissors. He is propped up in bed, looking painfully fragile.

Marguerite is shocked but tries to hide it; to show any fear would be the cruellest way to greet him. He'd know it was the end.

'Papa,' she coos. He's eighty-four years old and has enjoyed far more life than he once bargained for. He manages a weak smile when he sees her and tries to grasp her hand. There's no strength left in him, and she drops her lips to his forehead, kissing him ever so gently, for fear of hurting him. His breath is rasping, unsettled. Marguerite sits, pulling the chair close to him. She notices a new sketch of Lydia next to his bed, presumably made just hours before; he has captured her fresh from a bath, her hair wrapped in a towel, a faint smile upon her lips. Marguerite tries to swallow her annoyance that if the worst were to happen, the last drawing her genius father ever created would be of Lydia. He hasn't drawn Marguerite since she escaped the Nazis a decade ago. Marguerite was once ethereal – with her long dark hair, translucent skin and that intriguing black ribbon. Now, at almost sixty, grey-haired and wider than she used to be, she's still captivating, but toughened by life's harrowing experiences.

Marguerite also notices candied fruit and a note sent by Monique, the young woman who used to be a night nurse for her father, and would sit for him, too, inspiring him deeply, before she changed her path and found God. A decade ago, she took the veil to become a nun – Marguerite still hasn't got used to calling her Sister Jacques-Marie. Her mind jumps to the chapel in Vence, designed by her father, inspired by Sister Jacques-Marie – it had been completed just last year. It was the pinnacle of her father's career, all that holy light . . .

Lydia tops up Marguerite's empty glass from a pitcher, nothing spilling on to the polished nightstand. She knows to be mindful of leaving a stain.

Her father drifts off into sleep, and Marguerite, tired from her journey, dozes too.

～

'What time is it?' Marguerite demands, opening her eyes warily as Lydia eases her father into a more comfortable position.

'After midnight,' Lydia responds quietly. 'You should rest; I'll watch over him for a while, if you like. The doctor was here earlier and will return in the morning. There's time.'

'I'm not leaving his side,' Marguerite replies. She hasn't the energy to decipher whether Lydia is genuinely trying to be considerate, or is pushing her to the sidelines, as is her way. There's a pattern to their interactions, an undertone of hostility that's hard to shake, even in crisis. Marguerite straightens her father's nightshirt, to show that she, too, is capable of care.

She strokes his hollow cheek, overgrown with bristles, to avoid the emotions she knows are coming. In the morning, she'll give him the dignity of a shave.

Lydia treads carefully around the bed, checking to see that Henri is asleep and unable to hear them. 'I've known your father since 1932,' she says. 'Back when I was twenty-two years old. That's more than half my life,' she adds. 'Before his surgery for cancer all those years ago, I promised I'd be with him until his final breath, and that's a promise I intend to keep. After that . . .' Lydia says, looking into the flame of a candle burning in the corner. 'After that, I don't know what I'll do. But I've kept a packed case under the bed in my room for many years, ready to leave at any moment. I'll go immediately. Your family won't need to worry about hearing from me again. I know what's expected.'

'You'll be paid until the end of the month regardless, if that's what concerns you,' Marguerite says. She knows she's being cruel, but there's something about seeing her father so vulnerable, clinging on to life, that means she cannot think straight. Her pain is suffocating, and she's incapable of not spreading it. She rests across her father's barrelled chest, her forehead pressed to his heart, claiming both of his hands in her own.

Lydia chuckles softly. She presses her fingers into Marguerite's shoulders, in an act of reassurance, trying to massage away a little of the tension. The relief is immediate.

'Let's find an equilibrium, shall we?' Lydia says. 'We can stay calm, for his sake.'

Marguerite nods. She knows it's what's needed.

Lydia disappears and returns a few minutes later with two cups of steaming coffee. They sit on opposite sides of the bed, sipping in silence. Waiting. Listening to Henri's breath, that steady rhythm, that sign of life they both desperately cleave to.

⧉

In the darkest, quietest, most sacred hours of the night, it happens. The colours mute, the breathing stops, and the flame flickers gently in the breeze. The ensuing silence is overwhelming.

Marguerite closes her eyes against the reality of it, squeezing away the truth she knows she'll soon have to acknowledge. She hears the almost imperceptible sounds of Lydia swallowing her own grief.

After a moment, the women look at one another, across his body, eyes overflowing. Each of them understands what the other has lost, as nobody else in the world can.

But with her father's death, the nucleus of what has kept these women united unfurls. They're nothing further to each other without him – all their tensions, all rivalries dissipated.

Henri's world has come to its end. And they both must start afresh.

Marguerite thinks of Amélie, how she'll react to the news. As the true Madame Matisse, she'll be expected to attend the funeral – she's his widow, after all. They've lived apart for fifteen years, with no contact except for lawyers, but they are still married.

'You know, my mother . . . you won't be welcome at the funeral,' she says to Lydia delicately.

Marguerite is conflicted. She knows how complicated love can be.

'I'd never dream of it,' Lydia replies. She has gathered herself. 'But you must permit me this.'

Lydia strokes the soft hairs at Henri's temple, releases the button of his calico nightshirt where it rubs against his neck. She presses her lips to his cheek, with great tenderness, great familiarity. It's a brazen act, especially in front of his daughter. But with that, Lydia closes her eyes, seeming to fix this moment in her mind.

'Goodbye, Marguerite,' she says. 'It's been the greatest privilege of my life to know your father, to be by his side.'

Without seeking permission, she picks up Henri's striped shirt, which is draped across the back of his chair. She inhales the scent of the fabric and takes it, too. She walks out of the room.

Now, finally, Lydia Delectorskaya will leave for ever: the family can exile her upon his death as they failed to do in life. Marguerite hears her go to her room and pull out a suitcase. She imagines her placing the final few items inside: her dresses, undergarments, hairpins, lipstick, novels and notebooks. Marguerite wonders where she'll go. She'd like to say it's not her problem, she doesn't care. But what Lydia has achieved with her father this past decade has been nothing short of a miracle. And for that, she must be grateful.

She believes in the love between them, whatever its nature, whatever its motivation.

'Goodbye, Lydia Delectorskaya,' Marguerite says, going to the door to see her off.

She can't help but hope that her name will be forgotten, that any association between Lydia and her family will be erased. But whether she likes it or not, she understands that the legacy of Lydia will live on, threaded into the very essence of her father's greatest art.

AMÉLIE

Nice, 1954

T he coffin, covered in masses of daisies, is eased from the rear of the hearse. Heads bow. Her suited sons, Jean and Pierre – ageing men themselves – are waiting, and take the weight of it upon their shoulders, alongside their own grown sons. The frost on the ground crunches beneath their feet as the cortège makes its way through the grounds of the Monastère de Cimiez and its ancient cemetery in the hills above Nice – offering up views of ochre-roofed buildings, grand hotels and ornamental church towers. Beneath, the ocean glitters, even on this biting November day. The mass, held in the monastery itself, is over; the mayor of Nice spoke to the mourners of Henri Matisse's great contribution – to the city, to France. He said Henri will always be an honorary son of the Riviera, even though he was born in the north.

The archbishop leads the way to the final resting spot, his long robes dragging along the gravel path, his footsteps dignified and deliberate. Around eighty tight-lipped mourners weave their way after him, through closely packed mausoleums and grand tombs, past religious statues and weeping angels. At the front of the procession, bearers carry huge sprays of lilies. Finally, they all gather in a secluded spot surrounded by olive and pine trees. A breeze, like a deep exhalation, sends a chill down Amélie's spine, despite the fur coat in which she's wrapped. Her gloves, lined with more fur, also do little to protect her arthritic joints. She's seated next to Marguerite, a short distance from the open grave into which her husband's coffin will soon be lowered. Her face is obscured by a black veil, like the good widow she must be today. But in truth, despite her defiance, she is bitten by grief.

Once the final prayer is complete, her sons join her, flanking her on each side. Marguerite stands closest, by the head of the grave, as if in conversation with her father. She's lost in sadness, too, swollen against the unforgiving beat of it. Amélie looks on. It has been fifteen years since she last laid eyes on Henri at the train station in Paris. Does she regret her decision to leave him, to never see him again? This is hardly the day for such thoughts. Still, the question nudges again and again at the corner of her mind as her husband is lowered into the ground. She remembers leaving him that day, after they'd met to discuss the terms of their separation.

She'd wondered if it had all been a terrible mistake.

Yet it was something she felt she had to do, to discover who she was and what she was capable of without him. She'd been brave enough to make her own decision. And once she'd burned the house down metaphorically, she found she had no desire to return. In the end, their divorce never came to pass, but their separation had been permanent.

Amélie hasn't thought about Lydia for a long time. But she feels her presence here. She looks at the women to see if she can discern her arch features. She hasn't been invited, but that doesn't mean she won't show up, wiping away tears that aren't hers to shed.

Over the years, she's wondered afresh about Henri's relationship with Lydia. She'll never be certain if there was something romantic between them, but she still suspects as much.

He may have said Amélie's name when she gave him that ultimatum, but he'd chosen Lydia long before. And in the years since, they never left each other's side, making each other greater than the sum of their parts in the process, weaving an undeniable magic.

What is that, if not the definition of love?

In the years since she last saw her husband, Amélie has surprised and revived *herself*; she has pledged herself to causes she believes in, not just one man's cause, one man's vocation. She is proud to have been part of the Résistance, even if it resulted in months in prison. She survived it, as she has survived everything else. She has seen her family grow, dissipate and regroup, has kept in contact with those living in America.

She has made a home for herself in Aix-en-Provence, a house surrounded by bougainvillaea and jasmine, and has kept herself busy helping Marguerite with the details of her father's estate, tracking down missing artworks, confirming authenticity. As his widow, she will inherit it all. She'll do justice to their shared youth, their efforts as a young couple.

She looks around, her eyes following the movements of a black bird that is foraging in the grass. Her shivers return.

Amélie knows that when her time comes, she'll lie beside him in this plot.

It's what is right, what is expected of her as Madame Matisse.

What has it cost her to be that woman, she wonders? What has she earned in return?

There are so many things she would have done differently.

Amélie thinks of Henri as a young man, his wide face, warm eyes, that red beard; Henri hiding bottles of wine under the table when they met at that wedding in Paris more than half a century ago. She thinks of their honeymoon in London, the dimly lit galleries, and the way another man's paint strokes had conjured storms; she dips into a memory of their long afternoons by the sea in Corsica, the turquoise waves crashing at her feet as he sketched her. She wasn't yet pregnant, not that she knew of, and it was just the two of them, as exposed to each other as the elements, as hopeful for the future as it was possible to be.

Amélie doesn't approve of nostalgia, but she can't seem to shake it off today.

The question returns to her, dissatisfied with her answer.

She had to leave him. She asks herself again if that was a decision that she regrets.

The coffin is laid in the ground, and it'll soon be time to step away from what divided them and find her way back to peace. But the little bird is back, a seed in its beak.

Amélie senses some kind of message from Henri. We made something, at least. We may have lost ourselves to each other along the way, but I hope you'll agree that what we planted together, the seed we tended, grew into a mysterious and marvellous bloom.

LYDIA

At ten in the morning, Lydia lifts the receiver, dialling the number without hesitation. A sing-song voice answers, one she recognizes instantly. This woman, the proprietor, has been serving Lydia food almost every weekday for the past decade.

'Good morning,' Lydia says. She is practised at feigning a little jollity.

Her apartment is tidy, a fresh bouquet of bright anemones on the table by the window, the colours particularly intense in the hot wash of midday sunlight.

'And what a beautiful day it is, Madame Lydia,' the proprietor replies.

Lydia quietly agrees. It's the sixteenth day of March, and spring promises to win the fight. But what good is sunshine without those we have loved?

She was by Henri's side for twenty-two years. Longer than most marriages. Lydia Delectorskaya, now eighty-seven, has already surpassed him in years. It's a biting ache that he died more than four decades ago. Since that day, she has worked on keeping him alive for the future – helping with exhibitions, books, arranging the fragments that she had of him into

333

something like a legacy. And what a legacy that has become. She knows he'd be proud.

It was not asked of her; in fact, his family have mostly fought her involvement. But it's the only thing she can do.

In their time together, Henri gifted her a large number of artworks. Lydia has the receipts, bearing his name and signature, and a description of each work; notes upon which she insisted, so nobody – not Marguerite nor Madame Matisse – could ever accuse her of taking them without his blessing. Henri had wanted her to have these, perhaps three dozen works, to show his appreciation for their friendship, for the way she had helped bridge the gap between his soaring mind and his failing limbs. He said he couldn't have found the strength to create until the end without her. It is for inspiring that sentiment in him, and for being part of the rupture with his wife, that she will never be forgiven.

But who needs forgiveness, when you have gained the world?

She could have bought a castle in the Loire Valley if she'd sold just one of the paintings, but instead she donated them to Russia, to a museum in Moscow, where they'll remain on display for the people. It's the closest she can get to home, after the authorities refused, for the final time, her request to return there permanently. She'd always dreamed she'd return one day. But it isn't to be.

She regularly thinks of Tomsk, her parents and Aunt Nina. But it's almost a lifetime since she last thought of Misha. Here he is in her thoughts today. And Borya, even after all the anguish he caused. She sees the flash of his smile, his easy charm. She marvels that nobody has had the capacity to seduce her that way in the years since. She has not heard from either of them since she walked out of their lives, determined to take control of her future.

Her life in France hasn't been boring – she has travelled, met people, enjoyed simple pleasures. The years since she fired the gun, aimed at her own heart, when Henri told her to leave, have not been wasted. She has been grateful for every fresh morning, even if it's true that she never married again, never had children, never found more purpose than she'd known with Henri. It's fair to say that she loved him as deeply as is possible.

Henri Matisse's name will be immortalized in France's – perhaps even the world's – great historical record, but Lydia's will hardly feature. All of his family will be included alongside him – Amélie, his wife of over five decades; Marguerite, his darling daughter; his sons, Jean and Pierre, always trying to prove themselves. And it's better that way. For who was she to the great artist? An assistant, that is all. Lydia has always held her anonymity close.

But whenever she needs him, she knows where to turn.

There's a pile of freshly laundered clothes, stacked by colour, the darkest at the bottom, lightest on top. She has decided to wear the shirt that once belonged to him.

'And can you tell me . . . the lunchtime special today, what is it?' she asks.

'*Oeufs en cocotte*, with herbs and *pain Provençal*,' the woman replies breezily.

'That will suit me perfectly,' Lydia says. 'Would you mind – I'm feeling rather beside myself today. Could someone bring it up to my apartment at midday? I'll be ready, as always.'

She thinks of her legacy, failure, her father and the gun. What does it mean that every bullet she has ever fired has missed its target? Can you be fulfilled without getting what you want – can you live a life on your terms, with so many chances squandered?

Perhaps it is our misses that make us, after all?

It's true that Lydia's strength is dwindling. Not only on the physical side, but she fears she lacks the mental strength to face each day. She cannot bear the weight of living.

She has left a note on the table explaining her actions, with numbers of who to call – and instructions not to enter the bedroom – alongside the money for lunch, plus a generous tip.

'Of course, Madame Lydia. I'll see to it. We'll send a boy up. I'm sure you'll find the food particularly delicious today. Good day to you, my dear.'

'Thank you, for your kindness,' Lydia says, ending the conversation, the words coming out unbidden. There are few people she talks to these days. 'It won't be forgotten.'

Then Lydia sets to the final task of her life. The dragon-glint of the revolver takes her breath away, as always, but it's also reassuring. This final touch of her father, her home. She thinks of all the stories concealed within its chambers.

There's just one bullet left . . .

Acknowledgements

I was lucky to live in the South of France when I was a student. I read English and French at the University of Leeds, and my third year was spent as a primary-school teaching assistant in Manosque, Provence, where I discovered the work of its most famous inhabitant, the writer Jean Genet. It was a beautiful place to live and learn. Still, I envied my fellow students who'd been placed in Paris or Montpellier, with their nightlife and culture. But I was determined to make the most of my time there, even though I felt isolated, lonely and cut off from friends and family. Looking back now, I can see it was 'character forming'. Being alone meant I invested in my love of art and literature, and I decided to take my first steps towards becoming a writer. At weekends, I'd make trips along the coast – to Marseilles, St Tropez, Antibes and Nice. I visited the studio of Cézanne in Aix-en-Provence. I understood how Henri Matisse fell in love with the South of France, and how the light impacted his art.

When I got home to the UK, I quickly bought a large black-and-white framed poster of a photograph of Matisse, taken at his home in Vence by Henri Cartier-Bresson in 1944. I've had it on the wall of every home I've lived in since then. I'm looking at it now, in my writing room in Folkestone, Kent. In it, the elderly artist holds a white bird tightly in his left hand, whilst he sketches it with his right. Sunlight floods through the window. A trio of birds perch upon a cage in the foreground, conspicuously free of the bars which should constrain them.

As with my debut novel, *The Flames*, about the muses who posed for the scandalous young artist Egon Schiele in Vienna at the turn of the twentieth century – and the postcard of Adele Harms I'd had taped to my wall, and looked at, without knowing her name or questioning her relationship to the artist – it's only once I started my research into Matisse, and the relationships that shaped his art, that I could appreciate the Cartier-Bresson photograph properly. Was Lydia Delectorskaya in the room, tucked out of sight of the lens, as these two men fulfilled their purpose? I looked closely at the artist's hands – he's not wearing his wedding ring, despite being still married to Amélie. And this would have been the period when his adored daughter, Marguerite, was missing, captured by the Gestapo, her fate unknown.

There's so much to be gained from scratching beneath the surface.

Everyone I meet knows the Matisse name – most have prints of his work at home or would certainly recognize them. But very few know anything about the ultimatum at the heart of his marriage, or the relationship dynamics that propelled him into being one of the most significant and memorable artists of the twentieth century. I admire the fact that Matisse started art so 'late', that his success didn't come easily, and that even by the age of forty his name didn't carry much weight. He took huge gambles, as did the women who supported him, and it shaped them all.

I wrote this book during the pandemic, whilst going through challenges and changes in my own circumstances, and being able to escape into the glitz and glamour of Paris and the Côte d'Azur was a balsam. After lockdown, I travelled to France, and am indebted to all the experts and scholars I spoke to about Matisse there. Thank you, James, for being the most dynamic person to embark on these adventures with, and for your belief in me.

I'm particularly indebted to the incomparably brilliant biographer Hilary Spurling, whose extensive works on Matisse (*The Unknown Matisse* and *Matisse: The Master*) provide the most comprehensive insights imaginable into the life of the artist. I'm in awe of what Spurling has achieved, and the detail with which she champions Matisse has shaped his legacy. Her dedication to him is a work of art in itself, and I'm only sorry we didn't get to talk.

I also read perceptive art books, travel guides and biographies by other writers, including John Russell, Laura McPhee and Jack D. Flam, and fiction by Michèle Roberts, A. S. Byatt and Alastair Sooke. I've enjoyed conversations with those who reached out to talk about Matisse, including Adam Kemp and William Archer, who are passionate about the artist and his story.

I'm thankful for the support of my parents, as well as the enthusiasm of family and friends who spurred me on whilst I wrote my second novel – you know who you are. Especially those I got to know on the Thames foreshore and in my new hometown of Folkestone, who have welcomed me into their communities. You buoyed me when I experienced the setbacks that can plague writers as they navigate the tricky terrain of Book Two. Your kindness is golden. I'm also so pleased to have recently joined the excellent team at Creative Folkestone and to have a job that includes curating the annual book festival – what a dream role for an author.

I'm particularly grateful to my editor, Kirsty Dunseath, who is always so warm and insightful with edits. Everyone at Doubleday is a pleasure to work with, from the fantastic copyeditors and proofreaders to the impressive marketing and publicity people, the dedicated team who secure foreign rights deals, and everyone in between. Your hard work is much appreciated! Once again, my admiration to Andrew Davis, who designed the beautiful hardback cover of the UK edition. And a big thank-you to my fantastic agent, Juliet Mushens, and the team at Mushens Entertainment. It's an honour to be part of what you have created.

Finally, to the passionate booksellers and bloggers and people (you!) who have read this book – a gigantic burst of appreciation. I hope your flowers grow and you take the time to enjoy the bloom.

Sophie Haydock is an author, editor and journalist (*Sunday Times*, *Financial Times*, *Guardian*) based in Folkestone, Kent. She also curates the Folkestone Book Festival. Her debut novel, *The Flames*, was longlisted for the Historical Writers' Association Debut Crown Award and won the 2024 Premio Letterario Edoardo Kihlgren Opera Prima in Milan.

Sophie has worked for the *Sunday Times* Short Story Award, and was associate director of the Word Factory. She has been a judge for various short story competitions, including the Bath Short Story Award and the Society of Authors ALCS Tom-Gallon Trust Award.

Her Instagram account @egonschieleswomen has a community of over 112,000 followers.

For more information, visit: sophie-haydock.com